THE BONDS THAT TIE

Unbroken Bonds

Also by J Bree

The Bonds That Tie Series

Broken Bonds
Savage Bonds
Blood Bonds
Forced Bonds
Tragic Bonds
Unbroken Bonds

The Mortal Fates Series

Novellas
The Scepter
The Sword
The Helm

The Trilogy
The Crown of Oaths and Curses
The Throne of Blood and Honor

THE BONDS THAT TIE

Unbroken Bonds

J BREE

Unbroken Bonds
The Bonds that Tie #6
Copyright © 2021 J Bree

Cover & Interior Illustration by Emilie Snaith
Cover Typography by Bellaluna Cover Designs
Edited by Telisha Merrill Mortensen
Proofread by Samantha Whitney
Interior Formatting by Wild Elegance Formatting

Unbroken Bonds/J Bree – 2nd ed.
ISBN-13 - 978-1-923072-05-3

BREE

THE GODS HAVE WOKEN

THE ETERNAL LIVES WITHIN OLEANDER FALLOWS.

THE CRUX LIVES WITHIN NORTH DRAVEN.

THE CORVUS LIVES WITHIN NOX DRAVEN.

THE SOOTHSAYER LIVES WITHIN GRYPHON SHORE.

THE DRACONIS LIVES WITHIN GABRIEL ARDERN.

THE CLEAVER LIVES WITHIN ATLAS BASSINGER.

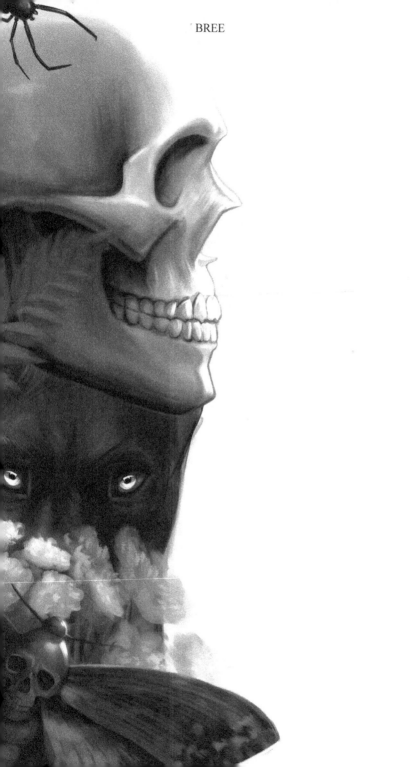

Prologue

GRYPHON'S BOND

I wake.

A new body, a new era, the same threats to my Bonded as there always are; but this time, it's different.

This time, we're all here.

I watch as one by one, the god-bonds awaken, the vessels falling unconscious under our enemy's attack. Eyes rolling back into their heads until they turn black, the voids wiping out the human life until we're all standing around our Bonded as a living, breathing shield, filled with the souls of the dead, a gift of power from our Bonded. There's *nothing* that can kill us now.

United at last.

I look over to my Bonded and the girl that it lives

within, perfection incarnate, and every fiber of my being is filled with need. A need to have them, protect them, covet them, break them apart and build them back up in the way that only I can because we were made for each other. They are mine as surely as I am theirs, as surely as the world spinning endlessly in the vastness of the expanding universe.

Danger has come for us once more, but it always does. The world doesn't want to see greatness like us happy. It wants to break us, hurt us, kill us, and bury us miles apart, just to extend our earthly torture forevermore.

I've lost my Bonded too many times.

Never again.

Protect the Gifted. The girl loves them, and they have been loyal to us always.

I glance over my shoulder to find a handful of Gifted there, blood running out of their noses as they bear the brunt of the god-bond's attack and their bodies slowly shut down. I feel something extra in the girl there, the small Flame with a strong Gift, and though it frustrates me, I leave it alone for now.

It's a problem that can wait.

Pushing my way into the other Gifted's brains and building up their defenses is easier and as thoughtless as breathing, putting in walls of impenetrable protection against the assault of our enemy who stands before us wearing the body of an older woman.

She'd deceived us all for too long, a god-bond predator hiding amongst the human sheep.

"Don't touch the Death Dealers," she says to the two men behind her as they step towards us. I'm sure they're strong for their kind, but they are nothing but men; flesh and blood and bond... not the gods that we are.

My Bonded smiles, cocking her head at our god-bond enemy. "That's cute... thinking that will save you."

Her hand rises and that unnatural shine takes over her skin, the inky black that is vibrant in a way that defies nature because she is Death incarnate, the true god of souls who can choose who lives and dies. She is as powerful and ruthless as the sun itself, burning away all lesser beings as though they are nothing but kindling for her flame.

Mine.

"You're too new. Your Bonds have barely woken up. You might be stronger than me someday, but I intend on disposing of you all long before that time comes."

The Cleaver raises his hands and his Gift pushes out of him in a violent burst, decimating everything around him in a single stroke. It doesn't touch the god-bond before us, but the two Gifted men she had brought with her are torn to pieces. We watch with the type of apathy that only the Eternal can have as the chunks litter the ground, the blood soaking into the scorched dirt around us. There's already bodies everywhere, the worst carnage of war laid out at our feet.

The Gifted at our side begin to stir with a groan. The Transporter looks to his Bonded the moment his eyes open, then to me as he waits for orders. The shock on his face at the sight of my void eyes has him faltering for a second, but his mouth sets into a firm line as he projects words to me, something he's done with my vessel a million times before.

What is the plan here? We need to get our Bonded to safety.

Our Bonded.

My eyes flick down to the little Flame at his side, dirt and ash covering her body from all of the destruction she'd wrought on our behalf. She's important to my Bonded's vessel. She's important to us all.

Important enough to save and not just from the god-bond before us all.

Take them to safety. All of the Gifted we care for. We will take care of this. Keep the Flame separated for now, the god-bond is taking refuge there again.

He doesn't answer me or nod, no visible signs of his agreement that might alert our enemy to what he's about to do. I fix my eyes back on the woman ahead of us as her lip curls in our direction. She surveys the fresh coat of blood and gore covering her surroundings.

"The Cleaver always did have such *disgusting* ways," she sneers, her face a lot more animated than ours.

She's been awake a lot longer than us.

While learning to blend in with the humans around her, it's clear that she's killed the vessel and is in full control. She slipped through our fingers with ease, because there was no battle going on beneath her flesh, no secondary being to flag with our sweeps of the area.

There's a pop sound as the Transporter leaves us all behind, taking the vulnerable Gifted with him, and my Bonded shifts a little closer to the Death Dealer at her side, murmuring quietly to him as the shadows creep up his arm. The dog-like forms at their feet all stare forward without blinking, watching the threat before us with an unerring vision. They're all still standing a little to the side where the Shield had cut her off from us all. I can see my vessel's memory of the moment, the panic he'd felt and the instant relief as the Corvus had shifted through his shadows to get to her.

My vessel didn't know he could do that.

It's a standoff, all of us waiting to see who will truly make the first move. Whatever those Gifted could do, the god-bond was expecting a lot from them, and she definitely hadn't taken the Cleaver into account. No, she'd waited on the sidelines and watched my Bonded funnel us energy and hoped that would weaken her enough to kill her, at the very least.

She has drastically underestimated the strength of my Bonded and those devoted to her.

She purses her lips at us all as though she's disappointed with the way her Gift is merely bouncing off of us before she lifts a hand, her palm turning black as she calls on her power. The shadows all move at once, darting towards her like storm clouds rolling in, but she Transports out before they can tear out her throat.

As she disappears into nothingness, she leaves behind her parting words, a warning to us all.

"Until we meet again. Next time, I won't come alone. Next time, I'll wipe you from the face of the earth."

1

OLI

I wake up as my feet hit the ground at the Sanctuary, my stomach churning horribly as my head spins. Bile burns a path up my throat, and I choke as I fight to keep it down.

Why does it always have to feel this way?

I wait for Gryphon to ease the discomfort, but when his hand doesn't come up to cup my neck, I'm forced to slap a hand over my mouth instead.

A strong arm bands around my waist, hauling me back onto a broad chest as North snaps, "Are you going to give Gryphon back so that he can help her or not?"

I don't understand what he means by that, and I'm too busy gagging to figure it out. Then Gryphon's palm finally slides around my throat and his Gift flows into my body, flooding me and chasing the sickness away. It's only once my head clears that I realize the room around us is silent, the kind of silence where a million things are floating around us unsaid, and that Gryphon's hand isn't cupping the side of my neck like it usually is.

He's gripping my throat the same way that he would when we're alone, when he's whispering filthy demands and observations into my ear as his hips drive his cock into my body.

I glance up to find his bond staring back at me.

Blank face, black void eyes, I'm meeting the god within him properly for the first time. I'm suddenly very aware of all of the eyes on us both.

Kieran has brought us back to one of the training rooms underneath the Tac Training Center, smart decision, as always, and he's already backed right away from this clusterfuck of a situation. He's hovering by the door, close enough to help out the moment we need him, but he's also perfectly aware that if our bonds are out, he's more of a hindrance than a help.

I'm the only one who can really deal with them.

A quick glance is all it takes to know that none of my other Bonded are happy about his hands on me like this. Not the bond, because they might trust Gryphon to the ends of the earth, but they don't trust the god that had lived hidden beneath his skin.

We all remember the warnings that Jericho had said.

The bonds kill their vessels.

Gryphon's bond stares at me, unblinking as he reads me like a book. "I would never harm you. I couldn't even if I wanted to. You're *mine*. Nothing changes that."

I'm not sure if he can just tell what I'm thinking by the look on my face or if he's able to get past my defenses, but I nod slowly anyway, a slow sigh eking out from between my lips. His fingers flex around my throat, tightening just a little, and there's murmurs of displeasure around us from the rest of our Bonded Group.

I should really focus on getting him to let go.

"No. You should tell them all to leave us alone. It's been a very long time since I was with you last, Bonded."

Oh, God.

Definitely reading my mind then.

A shadow twines itself around his wrist faster than my eyes can track, sliding along his palm and then wrenching his hand away from me. Gryphon's lip curls as his bond snarls, but the shadows wrap around his body to keep him away from me.

"You're effectively a stranger to us all right now, so you'll be staying there until we know we can trust you," North says, stepping between us and acting like a protective wall. I slip a hand onto his back, as much an anchor to myself in this moment as a reassurance to him.

I feel off-kilter at the turn the day has taken.

Kieran steps forward, approaching Gryphon's bond the same way that you'd expect a man to approach a barrel full of pissed-off rattlesnakes.

As though he's about to die for the audacity of breathing.

North shoots him a look, but Kieran ignores him entirely, speaking to Gryphon's bond in a formal way that speaks both of respect and the fear that's very obviously pumping through him right now.

"I've got Sage in one of the cells downstairs with the rest of our Bonded Group watching her. What exactly is in her head right now, and how do I get it out?"

In her head?

My eyes flash back to Gryphon and I snap, "What the hell is that supposed to mean? Why didn't you say something sooner? What if she's hurt right now or it's doing damage?"

The bond, who hasn't looked away from me yet, stays unresponsive to my words as his void eyes drink me in. I feel just a little bit uneasy at it, something I'd never felt around my Bonds or the bonds that live within them.

I don't understand why.

"The god-bond is in her mind again. It's been there before, therefore it's an easy path for it to take to speak with us."

The god-bond.

The one that had infiltrated her mind and used her body to kill our Shield, Dara, letting the Resistance into the Sanctuary and framing my best friend for a murder she would never commit. A violent sort of rage takes fire in my stomach, and I find myself moving before I'm really thinking about it, pushing my way past my Bonded and stalking down the rabbit warren hallways of the training center, all the way until I hit the elevator.

I can hear everybody bickering and arguing behind me, but I can't stop myself from jabbing at the elevator button, cursing under my breath as the doors open. I glance behind myself to find Gryphon's god-bond hovering behind me.

It's strange that even without seeing his eyes, I can tell that it's not my Gryphon. *My* Gryphon would have his arms crossed over his chest and a scowl fixed on his face as he assessed the situation, running through the possible outcomes over and over again until he had concocted a plan with the best-case scenario. His god-bond just stands and stares, so inhuman and expressionless as it takes everything in. Still, my heart tugs towards them both.

They both belong to me.

"Oli, what exactly are you going to do when you get down there? It's not like you can fight the god-bond if it's wearing Sage's body like some sort of fucked-up puppet," Gabe says as he steps alongside me, slipping his hand into mine and threading our fingers together.

Kieran shoots him a dark look for talking about his Bonded like that, but I only shrug. "If I can rip people's souls out, don't you think it's possible that I can also force the god-bond out? Especially if it's inside of someone it doesn't belong to? It's worth a try, and I'm sure my bond would enjoy *eating* something like that."

Atlas chuckles darkly from behind me, his eyes still on Gryphon's god-bond as though he's expecting it to attempt to touch me again. North, protective and furious at all of this, as always, and Nox are half a step away from us all, talking quietly between themselves as their eyes drift slowly between Gryphon and I.

I can't focus on that right now as the elevator dings and the doors open wide.

I can't think about anything except Sage.

When we get to the cell that Sage is being kept in, I find the rest of her Bonded Group huddled around the giant glass wall. Felix, looking harried and a little worn around the edges, is watching her every move as he ignores the other two bickering viciously behind him.

Riley still looks as though he is recovering from the years he had spent being manipulated and assaulted by Giovanna, a Resistance spy sent in to manipulate their Bonded Group. His eyes are sunken into his head and his skin is still stretched a little too tight over his bones, making him look as though he is halfway to the grave already instead of just attempting to rest and get his brain back together. Last I'd spoken to Sage about it, he was still getting frequent nosebleeds. Even with all of Felix's hard work, it was a slow and steady journey to get him back to where he needs to be.

The third man standing there is Sage's fourth and final Bond, a man I haven't formally met yet.

After North and Gryphon had finally decided to contact him and bring him to the Sanctuary, all the background checks and monitoring they had done coming up with not even the slightest taint of Resistance, Wick had been put into isolation until Gryphon had finished off the vetting process. Sage had been thrilled to meet him before we'd left, having instantly felt the same connection to him as she'd felt with the others. I'm glad that this one Bond had been a little less complicated for her. I know the path with the other three was... less than smooth.

He turns to look at us all as we make our way over and snaps, "How long are you going to keep her in there? She hasn't done anything wrong."

I don't bother introducing or explaining myself to him, it's easier to let North deal with that side of things. Instead, I give Felix a tight smile as he moves out of the way to let me face Sage through the glass. He trusts me. He knows what lengths I have always gone to for my friend.

Plus, he knows that at the very least, he's going to get an explanation.

Sage is sitting on the bed with a frown and her arms crossed, but she doesn't look scared or worried, just pissed off.

She's covered in soot and ash and splatters of blood up her legs from where she had fought alongside us at the Wastelands only a few hours ago. Her hair is a mess, and a smile tugs at the corner of my lips at the sight of her sitting there at the center of everyone's attention, looking like she's about to set someone's ass on fire for this.

It's a relief she's not going to let this push her back into that panic spiral she was in last time.

Sage meets my eye and gives me a wry smile back, though it's more exhausted than anything else. "It's back, isn't it? The thing that was in my head."

I nod, pressing my hand against the glass and looking her over again as though I'll be able to see it there under her skin somehow. "Can you feel it? Can you feel anything?"

She sighs and slumps back onto the bed, propped up on her hands and head rolling back on her shoulders as she looks at the ceiling in defeat. "No, I can't feel anything. It's only because I got put back in here that I guessed it had to be that. Did I do anything? I can't remember anything, and I don't think there are any gaps in my memory, but—"

I cut her off before she spirals too far down that path,

"No, Gryphon's bond just saw it in your head… that it's waiting in there. He thinks it wants to speak to us, and that's why it didn't fully take over. It seems to know more about it than we do."

"If it knows more, then why isn't it saying something?" Felix murmurs to me quietly, and I side-eye him just a little.

"It's only just woken up, and we're still trying to get the introductions out of the way. I don't think it is purposefully trying to deceive us."

"What do you mean 'woken up'?" Riley asks, pressing one of his hands against his forehead and the other against the glass. He looks at Sage with a mixture of sadness and longing that I'm sure is never going to change, at least, not without some deep therapy and a lot of reassurance from Sage that I'm not sure she is ready to give him yet.

Giovanna did a lot more damage to the two of them than anyone is ready to unpack.

Kieran steps up beside me and we share a look, then he glances over his shoulder at his team leader and close friend. "Take a look for yourself. If you can't see that there's been a big change in Shore, then I'm not confident in taking you on missions with us in the future."

Even an outsider can see that there's something else going on here.

Whether the god-bond realizes we are talking about him or if it's just decided that enough is enough, it steps forward, pressing against my back and immediately setting the rest of the room off with that behavior.

A wisp of smoke curls up my leg and wedges its way between us, but I reach a hand out. "I'm fine. It's fine. I think he's been asleep and separated from his bond for a little too long to wake up with the ability to read the room."

Atlas wedges himself between Felix and me once more with a respectful nod to the doctor-in-training and a wary eye at Gryphon's bond.

I have very little patience for the posturing that's happening.

I feel as though it's all at Sage's expense, like we're wasting precious time here while there's a ticking time bomb in her head.

"Can you get it out of her? Can you get it out and *keep* it out?"

The bond takes a breath, then his head tilts to one side again as he stares Sage down through the glass.

I'm glad she's still staring at the ceiling because even I can recognize that bearing the full weight of the god-bond's attention can be, at the very least, unsettling.

"It came here to speak to us. I can get it out once we've heard what it has to say, otherwise it will just find another path to us... perhaps one more dangerous."

Kieran's jaw clenches but he holds his tongue, though Wick isn't so good at restraining himself. "You're happy for it to just use her like that? Would you be so happy if it was your Bonded?"

The god-bond turns to stare at him and to his credit, he only cringes a little. "There is no one strong enough to do that to my Bonded now that we're all together."

"Which is exactly why I knew I needed to come and see you all now, as disgusting and distasteful as groveling might be. I guess we'll all have to cower at your feet now that you've won."

We all turn to Sage, her voice, but not her words, ringing through the air between us as we take in the void eyes and the god-bond in control of her body.

You would think after seeing all of my Bonded taken over by the beings that live within them that seeing Sage this way wouldn't come to such a shock, but the gods within my Bonded still feel familiar to me. They still feel like they *belong* to me, like I've known them forever. They are as magnetic and alluring as the men they live within.

The god-bond speaking through Sage makes my skin crawl.

My hackles rise, and every fiber of my being wants to reach inside her and yank it out.

It does not belong there, and I'm repulsed by its

presence.

The way it smirks at us all is horrifying. It's an expression I would never see on Sage's face, one that makes her look like a completely different person. I can't contain the shudder that runs through me no matter how hard I try. I really shouldn't be giving it any extra ammo against us, but that's my best friend.

I'm only relieved that Sawyer isn't in the room. The heart attack that he would be having at the sight of his sister right now would be at a whole new level.

"Whatever you're here to say, just say it and leave. We're not interested in making nice with Resistance scum, not now and not ever, no matter the color of your eyes."

The smirk stays put and it stares back at North in that unblinking way they all have. "I'm not discussing anything with the vessels, so run along now and give me the gods so the adults can speak."

Whoever the hell this is, they've been awake long enough to develop a human sense of humor, one that is quickly going to get under North's skin.

He stares it down for a second before an answering smirk stretches over his own lips. "You don't get to make demands here. You either state your case and leave, or we get you out of her head and then hunt you down."

I don't know where we would even start to look for it, but whether or not North is bluffing, I can't tell.

Sage's eyes flick over each and every one of us, ignoring the humans without god-bonds as though they aren't even in the room, before they fixate on Gryphon. "So, which one are you, then? I never can tell when you're fresh like this."

I feel the power build and push out of Gryphon's body before Sage is clutching at her head with a groan.

I have to remind myself that it's not her, that she can't feel or process any of this right now. This will just be a blank moment for her, but it's still not pleasant to see. Kieran makes an unhappy noise under his breath, Felix winces and glances away, and the other two start bickering about it, but neither of them are dumb enough to attempt to stop Gryphon's bond.

I'm not even sure I could.

"Soothsayer. It's been an age, or maybe even three, since I last saw you. I was kind of hoping I wouldn't run into you in this lifetime. I'd rather deal with the shadow boys than *you*."

A very inappropriate giggle tries to burst out of my lips at the very idea of someone calling North and Nox 'shadow boys'. I know that if I look at either one of them right now, I will lose the fight and dissolve into a fit of laughter.

Maybe my brain was scrambled by the fight with Davies?

I shouldn't think about that right now, not unless I want to lose my shit in a completely different way.

I'm distracted from my own spiral of doom by Nox stepping forward, his eyes shifting to black as his bond takes over and his voice echoes through our mind connection to everyone.

My bond agreed to share the helm to get it talking and this shitshow over with.

He always did have the best relationship with his bond. I can feel Gabe and North's approval through the mind connection, and while I'm sure Atlas also thinks this is a great idea, he's not exactly going to say it, thanks to their animosity.

"I don't even have to guess or hear your voice to know which one you are. You two always did come in pairs, as much tied to each other as you are to the Eternal. What stroke of insane luck did you all have to arrive together? Or was it some sort of black magic you've found and won't share? How does it feel to be the luckiest sons of bitches to ever cycle?"

I have no idea what any of that means, but Nox's bond clearly does.

It cocks its head in that same way they all have. "Patience and unerring devotion is all it took. The rest of you have spent too long fighting amongst yourselves and not enough time looking for what you really need. The

Eternal is mine. I return for my Bonded."

A shiver runs up my spine at the sound of his voice and the very public declaration of love that might be coming from Nox's bond, but it's still about me, here in front of everyone, in his voice.

I'm careful not to turn to look at him, because I'll probably make a fool of myself if I do.

The god-bond inside of Sage throws her head back and laughs. "You say that like I want to fight with the rest of them! You already know I have no choice. None of us do! They always come calling."

Nox's bond shakes his head. "What do you want? Why bother coming here, because all you have done is paint a target on yourself. We're all together now, protected, and growing stronger by the minute. You think we're just going to sit here and wait for your next move? We're going *hunting*. We're not going to stop until every last one of you are thrown back into the cycle and we're left alone here to finally live out a lifetime together."

My heart clenches in my chest and, finally, I look back to meet North's eyes. He's already watching me, and when our eyes meet, I want to cry at the longing there. It's all him, the desperation he's felt his whole life to find me and protect me, to have me for himself.

He doesn't need his god-bond to feel that way.

Sage's head cocks to the side once again, a mirror of

Nox's, but this time, the expression on her face is more human than I have seen any of the god-bonds act. It's scared of whatever others are out there, and I think it might just be telling the truth here.

"I'm not on their side. I know you don't want to believe that because I helped some of them get in here, but I was trying to keep them away from my bond."

Gryphon's arms slip around my waist. "It didn't work though, did it? You endangered the rest of us for no reason, and now you've come crawling back here for our help."

"Are you happy to hear that it didn't work and they killed my Bonded? Do you get some form of sick enjoyment out of that?"

Its eyes flick back to Nox as she continues, "No, you don't. You just hate that I'm still here even without it. You think that your form of devotion is the only one. I've lost this cycle, but I need to do what I can for the next one. I'm not just going to throw away a chance at finding some allies."

Nox's bond turns to look at Gryphon, then its eyes flick down to me, devotion and obsession in them as it traces my face. "We don't need allies. We need you all dead."

I feel as though if I leave it up to the bonds, we're going to be stuck here forever talking about who is the strongest and what nefarious plans they all have for each other. And no matter how possessed and unrecognizable

Sage might look at the moment, I can't stop thinking about my best friend and her body being used right now.

I reach out to my own bond where it's slumbering somewhere around my spleen, but it merely yawns and stretches before rolling over and going back to sleep. Fighting in the Wasteland has worn it out enough that without direct danger to our Bonded Group, it's just not interested in coming to the party.

I cast another fleeting look in North's direction, only to remember that the last thing he would be willing to do would be to let his bond out to finish this off, so instead, I focus back on Nox.

I haven't spent a huge amount of time with his bond, or any of the bonds really, but I have a level of comfort and familiarity with it that I just don't have with Gryphon's yet.

I want this to be over, I send through our mind connection to it, and though Nox hears it, he knows it isn't for him and leaves the two of us to speak.

The bond doesn't look at me, but I feel its presence in my mind straight away.

Do you want me to end it?

I scowl and answer quickly, *I don't want you to hurt Sage... but I want that bond out of her, and I want it never to get back in again. Can the Soothsayer really do that?*

With you, he can do anything. Now that we're all

together, I don't doubt his limitlessness at all.

I tilt my head back until I'm staring at Gryphon's bond, upside down and a little confusing, but I can tell he likes that I haven't tried to step away from him, that I have just allowed him to be close to me for now.

I'm tired, and this all feels like it's for nothing. I'd rather be done with it and go back to the house together. If you can get it out of her head, do it now, please. For me. Just don't hurt her.

Sage's mouth opens again, ready for the next litany of insults and sharp barbs, but Gryphon's eyes flash again, that same eerie, unnatural, blackness that they get when the god-bonds call on their power, and Sage collapses back to the bed, a groan ripping out of her chest that definitely sounds like one of her own.

Gryphon's bond looks down at me with that same expressionless face. "I closed her mind to the god-bond. It cannot use her again, Bonded."

2

Felix goes inside the cell to check Sage over, but the god-bond didn't do any damage to her that he can find. North agrees to let her go home for the night under her Bonded's watchful eyes. Kieran hovers over her like the god-bond is going to physically fall out of her and he'll have something tangible to fight, something to murder with his bare hands. Felix is also staring at her like she might drop dead at any second, so really, they're just as bad as each other.

Wick doesn't say a word.

Neither does Riley.

As I watch them all leave, I feel a little puddle of dread start up in my stomach about that whole situation. It sort of feels like I'm leaving Sage in a den of wolves, snarling at each other's throats and just waiting for the chance to rip them out.

There's also other things for me to worry about here.

North is still covered from head to toe in grime and gore from the battlefield, the war we'd fought and won today, but I don't hesitate as I lean forward and wrap my arms around his waist and soak in a little of his strength for a moment.

I'm exhausted.

The type of exhaustion that I haven't felt in a long time. The type where I could pass out for three days just to recover. I haven't felt this way in months, not since I'd stopped fighting my bond and accepted what I could do with my Gift to help my Bonded Group and our community. I knew that the fighting had worn me down, my body becoming a conduit of power as I pulled souls and churned them through to my Bonded, but I wasn't expecting it to affect me like this.

Usually, I feel stronger.

"It's the god-bond's pain. She weakened the vessel before the bond took over," Gryphon's bond says, and I feel North tense against me.

Nox steps a little closer to Gryphon, his own eyes black, but the look on his face makes it clear that he's the one in charge, merely calling on his Gift right now because of the tension in the room. Atlas and Gabe are both hovering close to North and I, their own eyes clear and concerned without a single trace of the gods within them.

We probably couldn't handle any extra power in this room right now.

"Calling me a *vessel* isn't the best idea right now, buddy," I mumble back, but he hears me well enough.

"You are the vessel. Whether the other vessels like it or not, that is what you are."

"Gryphon might be my closest friend, but I'll kill you both without question if you keep talking to her like that. You're a threat to her right now, and I know Gryphon would agree with me," Nox says, the shadows creeping up his arm ominously.

I don't like any of them talking like that.

He looks around the room with the unerring look that we are now accustomed to seeing from the bonds, unblinking and emotionless. Nox watches him closely, wary and ready to spring into action if the bond does decide to hurt me to get to the bond inside of me.

That's not really my concern here.

I'm worried because the gods within us all had released the rest of us, taking refuge in the back of our minds the moment that we'd returned to the Sanctuary. Except Gryphon's had stayed in control. It could be something as simple as Gryphon allowing his bond to experience the new world it's been born into or maybe the fight had weakened him like it had me. Maybe he's not strong enough yet to wrestle the bond back into the recesses of his mind. Either way, we really shouldn't take any chances, especially not now that we know there are more of them out there.

With one last squeeze, I let my arms drop away from North's waist, and I step around him to stand at his side to look Gryphon's bond over once more. Atlas and Gabe both watch me without a word, but Nox steps a little closer to flank my other side. His shadows swarm around our feet, shifting and writhing unhappily at the danger in the room, especially while it wears the face of one of our Bonded Group.

Procel steps out of the dark cloud and drops down to sit on my feet, his unblinking void eyes fixed on Gryphon's bond. Azrael hasn't left my side since the fighting had first started at the Wasteland, but he shifts a little to let his brother join him in guarding me.

It feels as though they're both spoiling for a fight.

Don't provoke him, I send to Nox through our mind connection, hesitating for a second before sending it through to all of them except for Gryphon, *I don't think he means any harm. I think it's the same as when Gabe's dragon came out to play. He's just… introducing himself.*

Gryphon's void eyes flick to Gabe and then back to me, proving once and for all that it doesn't matter whether or not I'm trying to block him from the conversation, my mind is an open book to him in this state.

They all see it as well, but when Atlas replies to me, he keeps it within the mind connection. I think it's more out of habit than secrecy anyway.

If he calls you a vessel one more time, starts Atlas as though he's beyond over this shit, but North just flicks his hand at him dismissively.

I'm more worried that he won't give Gryphon back. I'm more concerned that he is planning on keeping control and getting rid of his own vessel. He's already said that he is as devoted to Oli as the rest of them are. I think the god-bonds are most dangerous to whoever they live within.

My heart clenches painfully in my chest. I take a step forward without meaning to, everyone in the room protesting in their own way, but Nox's hand locks around my wrist as he holds me back from going any further. I can't stop myself though. I can't just stand by and watch Gryphon's bond get rid of him any more than I could let Nox sacrifice himself for North.

"My bond already told me that I'm the perfect vessel for it, and it won't hurt me. If you do anything to Gryphon, I will reject you until my last breath. I don't care how much it hurts me, I won't accept you. I will have you both or I won't have you at all… Do you understand that? Look at me and know that I'm telling you the truth, Soothsayer."

Even as its head cocks to the side a little, he knows I'm telling the truth. He knows that I'm as devoted to my Bonded as he is to me.

He stares me down for a moment before he finally speaks again, his monotone voice sending chills down my spine. "That is the difference between this time and last. This time, we're going to survive this. All of us. I'm not going to kill the vessel. I'm going to use it to keep you forever."

Getting Gryphon's bond back to the mansion should be as easy as calling Kieran here to Transport him but, because for some reason, the universe hates me, it's not.

After getting Sage safely back to their house, a situation in one of the other Wastelands had arisen, and Kieran was pulled away to evacuate the TacTeam personnel. As much as North would love to call him back here, he would *never* risk any of the other community members, not unless it were actually an emergency. So instead, we're forced to make a game plan.

It's not exactly going to be easy to smuggle him out of the building without anyone catching a glimpse of his void eyes and unnaturally expressionless face.

There's too much potential for panic around here

already.

Instead, we call Sawyer to bring us down some bandages and wrap those around over his brow like a large headband, not quite covering his eyes but obscuring them enough that anyone who thinks they might see inky blackness could be convinced otherwise. Okay, so it might take every last inch of North's charm and maybe a little of Nox's intimidation techniques to really make it work, but we're willing to do whatever it takes here to get Gryphon home.

I mean, what could go wrong?

"A variety of things, Bonded. Don't tempt fate," North drawls at me when I'm stupid enough to say it within his earshot.

I keep one eye on Gryphon's bond and the other eye on Atlas, who is still staring at it like he's planning on doing something drastic to get it to give Gryphon back. It would be a very sweet moment except that I know it has exactly nothing to do with the budding friendships that are finally forming between him and the rest of the Bonded Group and everything to do with the potential here for me to get hurt.

Okay, it's still kind of sweet.

North also shoots Atlas a look as I answer him. "If anyone tries to ask questions, we both know you'll be able to spin a story here. That's kind of what you do, right?"

I'm mostly giving him shit just to get a smile out of him or Nox, and the smirk that the younger Draven brother sends me has my heart skipping a beat in my chest. Being in on his twisted and dark jokes is my new favorite position to be in. It's a good distraction from the twisting pile of nerves that my stomach is in at the mere thought of Gryphon's father, the General, finding out about this before we've even had the chance to speak with Gryphon himself.

That situation is pretty far up the 'no, thank you' list.

We convince the god-bond to play along with us, but only if I agree to stay at his side the entire time. Gabe is happy enough to trust my decision, thank god, because Atlas and North both hate that. Nox agrees to stay with the two of us as a buffer and, begrudgingly because he hates this idea all the way to hell, Atlas does as well. He's poised to dive in front of me the moment things might take a turn for the worse.

I do my best to direct him out of the building and into one of the ATVs while North does exactly what I'd teased him about and runs interference like his life depends on it.

Being a pariah in the community really does have its advantages. No one attempts to get close to us, not even Gryphon's own TacTeam operatives who look stricken at the sight of the bandage across his eyes.

It's a tense fifteen minutes getting Gryphon into the

ATV and back to the house, but we make it without anyone noticing.

Or Atlas killing the god-bond.

There is a deep sense of relief that settles over my soul as I step into our house once again. I don't want to think about it too much, but there was a moment while we were fighting that it had crossed my mind that maybe we weren't ever going to get back here. A moment when the Resistance had just kept coming, more and more bodies piling up around us, where it had felt inevitable that we would be stuck fighting for our lives and our community forever. A moment where I had thought that maybe I wouldn't ever be kicking my shoes off in this front foyer again, lining them up carefully alongside my Bonded's and smelling the fresh paint of the building around us as Gabe slowly finishes it off.

I don't want to admit this to any of them, though.

The problem is that my Bonded Group doesn't need to be able to read my mind in the way that Gryphon's god-bond can to know what I'm thinking.

Gabe slings an arm around my shoulders, pulling my body in close to his as he presses a kiss to the top of my head.

"I'm just as happy to be home as you are," he murmurs quietly, and I clear my throat a little as I nod back.

Relief.

That's all I'm feeling right now.

The surprise of Senator Oldham's void eyes and Gryphon's god-bond waking up has distracted me a little from what we'd actually done in the Wasteland, of how many people I had torn the souls out of, taking their power and funneling it through to my Bonded. It's only now that the job is over, that I'm stuck facing the consequences of what my Gift has done.

Physically, I'm tired, having given most of the power away. But mentally, I now have to compartmentalize everything that I'd done back there so that I don't spiral into a pit of self-loathing.

It's a well-worn path and so easy for me to do.

I squeeze Gabe for a second longer before I duck into Atlas' arms for a quick hug there as well, wanting to check in with each of them in at least a small way before I lose myself. They all seem to know that without much said, thank God.

As I step into the kitchen area, I find the small piles of clutter still where we'd left them, as though life here had simply been put on pause while we were camping out in Alaska and fighting for our lives. As much of a neat freak as North is, his own bedroom and wardrobes both at the Draven manor and here in the Sanctuary immaculately kept, there's no stopping the small piles of *life* that accumulate. It's proof that there's six people living in this house, all of them with their own varying degrees of cleanliness and clutter.

I can't help but sigh once more as I stare out at it all, just a small happy sound at the space that we've all built together. North carefully steps in front of me, framing my face with both of his hands as he pulls me in for a gentle but firm kiss, pressing our foreheads together as he pulls away.

He murmurs quietly to me, "Go take a shower, Bonded, and get yourself cleaned up. Take a breath, get yourself feeling human once more. Then we'll deal with this."

He doesn't say what exactly *this* is, but both of us turn our heads to stare at Gryphon's bond regardless. It's standing by the table staring right back at us both, its eyes cold and calculating as it watches our every move.

I feel the same draw to it that I've always felt to my Bonds, but this time, my head can't let go of the fact that it might be plotting the death of my Bonded.

I love the god-bond. My bond also loves it.

But I love Gryphon more.

North kisses me one last time before he pulls away again. "Shower, Bonded. If it hasn't made a move yet, I'm sure it'll wait until we're all clean."

I take two steps towards my bedroom only for Gryphon's god-bond to take a step towards me, as though there's an invisible thread connecting us, and he can't be more than a step away from me at any time. He's only halted by Nox planting himself between the two of us, his shadows still playing happily at his feet in a show of relaxation that doesn't quite meet their maker's stern facade.

"She's going to go get cleaned up, and you're going to wait here," he says firmly. When the god-bond's eyes shift away from me to stare him down, North flicks a hand subtly in my direction to get me moving. He steps up to his brother's side as they both prepare to face the god-bond and find me a little alone time.

I love them both now more than ever.

I scurry away without another word, trusting them both to deal with this situation for me. I glance over my shoulder one last time at the god-bond wearing my Bonded's face so blankly and try not to puke at the clenching in my gut at the sight of him.

No one attempts to follow me.

I don't know if North knows in that way of his that I really do need a minute to myself or if he just needs the others out there as backup, but as I slip into the bathroom and peel away the filthy Tac gear from my body, I'm relieved.

While I wait for the hot water to kick in, I take stock of myself in the mirror for a moment, getting an eyeful of the mess I'm in after the ferocity of the fighting. North fussing over me wasn't anything out of the norm, especially after that shield had come up around me and Davies to keep him from me, but looking at myself now, I'm surprised at his restraint.

Underneath the filth of the fight, my hair is so white that it's almost transparent, what little color had been in it has leached completely away. I doubt it could get any lighter than this, though I suppose I felt that way the last time I had used my Gift. It still found a way to get lighter. My eyes look sunken in my skull. My skin is dry and dull and bruised, and every bit of the exhaustion that I'm feeling is etched into the lines and bruises on my skin.

I let my eyes drift down slowly and find an array of scratches and small marks littering my arms and legs, along with the bruising from Davies' attack. My Bonded might all look perfect, thanks to the power boost I had given them, but I already know a trip to see Felix is in my future. There's no way any of them will stand for me healing the slow and *normal* way once they get a look at the small smattering of damage I've taken.

The real damage is to my mind, but they'll all know that as well, I suppose.

I rub my hands over my arms as I stare off into space, forgetting entirely that the water is probably piping hot by now, and a chill settles into my bones at the sight of the aftermath of using my Gift. It's nothing that I wasn't already expecting, but it still bothers me. There's no denying how many people I killed today.

It's written all over me.

Finally, I duck underneath the hot spray and let it fall over my head, soaking through and washing away some of the disgust I feel at myself. I have to scrub viciously to clean my hair; the blood and dirt is a nightmare to wash out. By the time the water falling from me finally starts to clear, I hear the door open.

I don't need to turn to know that the god-bond has come looking for me.

I open my mouth to tell it... something, I don't really know what, when North's voice filters through our mind connection to me.

The gods have agreed to tell us what we need to know. All of them.

Gryphon's bond refuses to speak unless he is seated right next to me, so I find myself wedged between it and Atlas, his arm around my shoulders as he tucks me in close to his side. I'm still not afraid of the bond doing anything to me, but I already know that this is more about satisfying Atlas' need for my protection than anything else.

North sits across from us all with a file in front of him that's full of Nox's research notes, everything we have so far on the god-bonds throughout history. Nox sits on the other side of Gryphon with a stern face and watchful eyes as he takes in the god-bond wearing his best friend. His shadows are still out and snuffling around on the floor at our feet, pretending that they're docile and playful creatures and not the nightmare monsters they truly can be should anything happen to Nox or I.

Perfect little puppies.

Gabe is sitting on the other side of Atlas, nursing a small glass with an antacid in it. His face is still looking a little green as he sips away at the mixture. When I give him a questioning look, he grimaces at me.

"The dragon ate too many of the Resistance, and *apparently,* that doesn't agree with my stomach."

Atlas scoffs and laughs at him, barely reacting when I dig my elbow into his stomach uselessly. He does duck down to press a kiss to my hair, almost as though he's repentant.

A total lie.

North's eyes flick around at each of the Bonded Group until they land on me, sticking for a moment on the color of my hair and the bruise around my eye before he says, "I've already called Felix, and he will be down to see us once the TacTeam members who were injured are in stable condition. He's been delayed with the influx from the second Wasteland clean-out."

I shrug and wiggle into Atlas' side a little further, taking comfort in the warm weight of his arm around me. "I'm not worried about it. It doesn't hurt or anything, and I think we all have bigger issues to deal with."

North's mouth turns down a little further, but he gives me a curt nod. I already know that he is the fixer of our Bonded Group, the one who has to make everything as perfect as it can be. So his attitude is merely because there is a problem he can't immediately fix, the unpleasantness of it doubling since it's his beloved Bonded with the issue.

Sometimes, I think I don't deserve this man and his love.

I try to shake the feeling out of myself, the tendrils of self-loathing that sometimes come after I've used my Gift like this, but they have their claws dug in tightly under my skin.

The god-bond next to me cocks his head again. He looks curiously like a feline every time he does it, but when he reaches out his hand towards my face, everyone at the table reacts at the same time.

"No."

"Don't touch her."

"If you even attempt anything on her right now—"

I hear them all, but my bond moves my body regardless, leaning my face in until his palm rests over my bruised cheek. His Gift flows through me, chasing away the throbbing pain that was there before, and I think that's the end of it, his pain-numbing ability a familiar thing to me by now.

Then North's eyes widen across the table from me.

"Since when have you had the ability to heal?" he says. "Or is this something that has come with the god-bond waking up?"

I feel the god-bond stroke his thumb over my cheekbone, the first true sign of affection between the two of us, and I don't need my own bond kicking in to nuzzle further into it.

I don't think it's going to kill Gryphon.

It might be naive of me to say, but I don't think that any of them are displeased with the vessels they have woken up inside of this time around; not even North's bond, no matter how much they have argued.

It could have easily killed him long before I came into the picture.

"There is nothing in the mind that I cannot manipulate."

Atlas' arm tenses around me and he snaps, "Get out of her head."

The god-bond only stares him down, apathetic to the worries of the 'vessel' in front of it. "Healing her was as simple as convincing her mind unconsciously to do so. She was never in any danger."

But it's not as easy as that.

It never is.

Nox stares at him for a moment longer, his eyes narrowing as he examines him. I raise an eyebrow at him, questioning what exactly it is that he's seeing here that the rest of us are missing, but he shakes his head at me.

Whatever it is, he doesn't want to share it with the rest of them.

North clears his throat to get the god-bond's attention once more, before gesturing a hand at him. "We're all here. We're all willing to listen to what you have to say, and, no matter our concerns, we're willing to let you sit next to your Bonded... For now."

The god-bond lets his hand fall away from my face, only to cover my thigh instead, his fingers flexing as he gives it a squeeze. I'm not sure if this is supposed to be a power play or the beginning of a seduction, but my bond is immediately interested in playing along.

I have to shut it down pretty damn quickly.

North watches its every move, but no one attempts to stop it from touching me. Once I'm sure I have control of myself, I let my hand cover it. My own bond hums with contentment in my chest at the connection, even though I won't let it take things any further right now. It's in a blissfully happy state with how everything is going at the moment, and I take that as a good sign.

"We've been here since the beginning. Since sentient

life has walked on this earth, there have been others living amongst the Gifted."

I glance over at Nox. This lines up with what his research has been saying, but he doesn't react to anything that the god-bond is saying. He just watches it with clear eyes as he soaks in every little word, hunting for clues, as he always has.

"The first time I awoke, I did not get to meet my Bonded. I knew something was missing and that there was more to my existence than the desolate life I led. Then the second time... you were there."

He turns to look at me, and for the first time, I see some expression in his face.

Hunger.

The type that has butterflies rioting in my stomach, the type that says that this man would consume me in the most satisfying and delightful ways if only I would let him, audience be damned.

My cheeks flush, and I clear my throat under the heat of his gaze.

"Each time I woke, there were more and more Bonded, until we knew that time was repeating itself, that the six of us were supposed to walk together. But the timelines never quite lined up. The closest we got was four of us at the same time, the last two missing out by a decade. The Draconis takes longer than anyone else to re-cycle and awaken. It has always been this way."

The Draconis, the Soothsayer, they have names for themselves, but they're nothing like the ones we have for each other now.

I turn to look at Gabe for a moment, but he's grimacing as he finishes off the last of the antacid, still looking green around the edges.

"What do you want? From us, I mean?" I say, the words tumbling out of me before I really think them through.

I clear my throat again and try to be clearer. "What is it that you keep coming back for? Or do you have no control over this 'rebirth cycle' you're on?"

He leans forward in his chair, the hand on my thigh tightening a little more as it answers me slowly. "We return for the Eternal. We return because it calls out to us. The thought of a lonely existence for my Bonded is unthinkable. While the Eternal returns, so shall we."

The Eternal.

I meet North's eyes for a moment, watching his flare with interest before I shut my own and check in with my bond.

Is that your name? The Eternal?

What use is a name to a god? But yes, it is what they have called me.

I always hate when it talks in riddles like this, but the fact that it's answering me at all gives me hope.

Why do you keep returning if you've lived hundreds of lives with each of them? Why continue to come back here?

I can feel the itch of irritation on my skin, the emotion not my own, and I'm expecting a full-blown bond tantrum from it. Instead, it floods my mind and takes over my body before I have the chance to fight back.

There's smoke everywhere.

The area around us is burning, a wall of flames devouring the well-established tree as though it's nothing more than scrub. The ground underneath our feet is blackened by the ash. Even through the makeshift leather shoes on my feet, I can feel how hot the ground is, as though scorched from the sun itself.

Every fiber of my being is exhausted.

There are no more souls left to take, none but our own. And no matter how hard the Corvus pushes me to take his life force into myself to repair the damage done to my body, I will not do it.

I couldn't hurt him any more than I could hurt the rest of them.

The devastation of the battle between us and the other god-bonds is severe. Piles of bodies around us in various stages of damage and decay, hundreds more have been consumed by the shadows with little to show that those Gifted had ever existed in the first place.

Still, it's not enough.

My energy is waning, and once again, we're going to be separated from each other in death, as we always are. I look down at my vessel, and I find that I've already taken significant damage. The Corvus and the Crux are both unable to heal me the way I can heal them. The only one of my Bonded who has that ability isn't with us this time. Even if there were a Healer I found tolerable nearby, I doubt they would be strong enough to fix the mess my stomach is in.

I can see the strain around the Corvus' eyes as he looks me over as well. I can see the rampant need in him to fix me and wipe away the damage, but I have already started to accept that this lifetime of ours is over. Just another chapter in a book that doesn't seem to have a happy ending... or even just an ending in sight.

I don't know what it is that we had done in a previous life to be cursed in this way, to wake up and find one another, over and over again, but never truly finding happiness. To be hunted by those who should be nothing more than ants beneath our feet. If only we could all wake up together. If only we could complete our Bonds and find peace together.

Instead, we are cursed with nothing but destruction,

death, and decay, heartache and loneliness, over the span of a millennia.

This memory hurts my bond.

It tiptoes around it in my mind, fussing with it like a festering and weeping wound, one of a hundred other deaths they had endured at the hands of our enemies because we are separated and weakened without each other.

Without a complete Bonded Group.

The Crux returns to us, blood covering his hands and his face in the shadows as the darkness from the tree coverage bends towards him. The face he wears is different, but the soul inside is still true, still perfect and mine, no matter which vessel he wears. Even though it's nothing more than a memory, I cringe away from it inside, as loyal to my Bonded as my bond is to the other god-bonds. I suppose that's why we work together so well.

My bond agrees.

Even in the memory, I can feel that the strength of my spirit is the strongest my bond has ever felt. I had always believed that my power came from my bond, but being here in this vessel, I can see that's not true. This vessel is different. It's weaker, the limits to what it can take are much lower than mine. I can see clearly that they're not a good fit.

Even without the bond, my Gift is more than the other Gifted could ever hope to have.

"We're not all going to get out of here alive. If you need to take our souls to live, do it. We will return to you again in another cycle," the Corvus says, but I shake my head.

"There is no use being here unless we're together. There is no me without you."

He drops down onto his haunches, the shadows that wrap around his legs are obedient to their master as he shakes his head at me. "I can't watch you die again, Eternal. Don't make me watch it all over again."

The cycling is slowly starting to chip away at us.

This reincarnation of the Corvus is more open with his pain than any others have been before because the vessel might be new, but the soul is tired. The soul has been on a long journey to get to this point, and it's starting to take its toll.

"We can make it," the Crux says, looking behind us to the mountain opposite the fire, where the sun is slowly starting to set an orange glow on a blackened sky as the rays of light fight to shine through.

"If we leave now, we can make it."

The Soothsayer didn't wake up with this cycle, still decades away from his next turn on this earth, but I don't need him here to know that the Crux is lying. He's trying to give his brother something to distract him before our deaths together, something small to get him through the pain of the night, because it's always this way.

It's always standing together and watching the destruction around us as we go forth to our death.

We have a hard choice ahead of us now. Whether we choose to take matters into our own hands here and now, to leave behind these vessels and begin the cycle again on our own terms, or if we continue to fight until our bodies give out. We've made the decision many times before, never truly happy either way.

I do want to fight. I want to leave the small, sheltered area that we're in at the moment and run until I find that god-bond that haunts us. I want to tear it apart with my bare hands, to show it the same callous treatment that it has shown me and mine. But no matter how many times I've killed it, it continues to wake. It wakes and hunts us down.

I'm tired.

More tired than I ever wanted to admit to my Bonded. So tired that I hope I don't wake with the next cycle or maybe ever again. Maybe I need to give up, to know that the small pockets of joy that I have found with my Bonded are all we'll ever get, to go to my final resting place at peace, to know that at least I got to meet each of them.

If only for a few moments in a thousand lifetimes, I got to know those who complete my soul.

"Don't think like that, Eternal," the Crux says, holding out a hand and pressing it to my cheek.

He's having to take care of both of us now, something that doesn't sit quite right with me, but I lean into his hand anyway. It feels strange to do, like the hand isn't familiar to me, but at the same time, it feels like home, because the god beneath the skin remains the same.

"You two should go. Leave here quietly together. I will stay for a little longer, finish what we started and hope that our enemy sleeps through the next cycle."

He always would give every last piece of himself until there was nothing left, but the Corvus and I would never let him leave alone, not if we had a choice in the matter. Instead, we brush ourselves off, standing together. I try not to wince at the state of my vessel as the blood continues to drip down to the scorched earth beneath our feet.

"We will finish this together," I say. "We will go to sleep together."

3

NORTH

Watching Oli shut down as she speaks to her bond still sends the same ripples of unease and frustration through my gut as it always has, but I try to distract myself by speaking with my own bond instead.

My least favorite thing to do.

But my feelings don't matter right now, because as much as I have always fought with the thing that lives inside of me, I will do whatever it takes for my Bonded to be safe. Knowing that there are gods living in each of us means that it's time to get over my own feelings and start working with it to get through this, especially if there is a precedent of us losing this battle.

I'm *never* going to lose Oleander again.

Do you call her the Eternal as well?

It answers me quickly enough, clearly listening in on this conversation, though it hadn't made itself known to me. *My bonded is Eternal, always.*

And what do they call you? You must all have names if you've been around that many times.

The Crux. My brother's name is the Corvus. There's also the Soothsayer, the Cleaver, and the Draconis. They have all woken, finally.

The Soothsayer.

That's what Oli had called Gryphon's bond.

How are we going to keep them alive? What is your plan for the Eternal and my Bonded that it lives within?

I'm not sure what sort of a response I'm expecting from it, but I'm happy with what I get. Beyond happiness, the relief it fills me with is enough that maybe, just very maybe, I might start speaking to the god a little more often.

They are both mine, as they are yours. There is no distinction. When our enemy comes, as they always do, we will defeat them all. We are unmatched now.

I open my eyes and glance across at Nox to find him already staring at me. I give him a simple nod before he turns back to Gryphon's bond.

The Soothsayer.

I have to bite the inside of my cheek to stop myself from smirking, already knowing that my Bonded is going to have a lot to say about the names of the gods, but I also find myself happy with the one chosen for her bond.

The Eternal.

Without question, she is eternally and completely mine. The center of our Bonded Group, eternally the one thing that we can all agree on and come together for, all of us working together to keep her safe.

That's the difference, my bond says. *That's how we are going to make it through this time, all of us together.*

"What's going on?" Gabe mumbles into the silence of the room, and I answer back without any attempts at secrecy.

They have no place here.

"My bond's name is the Crux, yours is the Draconis. Atlas is the Cleaver, and Nox is the Corvus."

I'm expecting some sort of reaction from them, especially my brother, but Nox merely shrugs back. "The Corvus makes sense. They both link back to the Draven name. What if all of the reincarnations of the gods with shadows are born to our family bloodline? Father had them too."

I groan and rub a hand over my face. "Don't you think we would've heard more about all of this if that were true? That maybe we wouldn't have had to look so hard to find the gods?"

"Did you, though? I mean, I know a lot of the books are

rare and out of print, but it sounds like these things were hiding in plain sight... If they were ever hiding at all," Gabe says, still looking incredibly green around the edges, and Atlas gives him a pat on the back with a sympathetic grimace.

The budding friendship they'd shakily started has turned into one of deep respect, and seeing the lengths that the dragon had gone to to keep the masses of Resistance soldiers away from Oleander was inspiring, to say the least. Atlas himself had mastered the Cleaver's powers in such a short amount of time, thanks to the urgency of the fighting.

All in all, we'd walked away from everything relatively unscathed, only the now-healed bruises and scratches on my Bonded to show for it. Fighting in the Wasteland had taken too long and we'd come too close to losing her. The moment the shield had snapped into place around Oleander, separating her from the entire Bonded Group, I thought we'd lost her. It had only gotten worse when Nox's shadows had filled the space, obscuring her from our view as she'd fought her torturer off.

I don't know what I would've done if my brother hadn't made it in there to get to her.

"Do we need to be worried about that?" Atlas murmurs, running a gentle hand down Oli's cheek, but Nox only shrugs.

"She's always had a close relationship with her bond,

even when she was scared of what it could do. Whatever it's showing her right now, it's important for her to see."

Any distraction to keep her from thinking about what had happened on the battlefield at the Wasteland is a win in my opinion. When we'd returned to the Sanctuary, it was only the distraction of Gryphon's bond that had kept her from falling apart.

The moment we had returned here, I could see the cracks beginning to show on her carefully pasted-together facade. No matter how righteous she may feel in her work now that she is doing so to defend her Bonded Group and the community itself, it still takes a toll on her that no one understands as well as I do.

Her kill count in the Wasteland was only rivaled by my own and Nox's, the sweeping clouds of our Gifts flooding over the soldiers and tearing them apart in the most vicious and violent ways. There isn't an inch of remorse in me, but still, the cost of that power is heavy on my shoulders. It's part of being a human with a soul, I think. Knowing that the weight of that choice is yours alone to carry.

I might believe in my abilities to tell right from wrong, but there's no denying that to the Resistance and families of the East Coast, I'm the villain for what I can do, a role I'll gladly play again and again for our safety and freedom.

"Are we going to remember the past lives as well? Am I ever going to remember what it was like to be a dragon back then?" Gabe asks, and when I look up, he's staring at the Soothsayer.

It stares back at him with its blank and soulless eyes as though it has no intention of answering him, but Gabe stares back at it with that open and easy way of his. Whether or not it's that that breaks the god-bond down, he does eventually answer. "If the Draconis chooses to share it with you, then yes, but it has always only ever communicated with the Eternal. It's only ever wanted her."

Gabe nods for a second and then shrugs. "It communicated well enough with us both when she jumped into my dreams, so I'm not worried. I don't have to remember the past lives to know that everything is okay."

I hope it's really that easy.

I shut my eyes again, rubbing a hand over them more out of irritation than anything else, and my bond speaks once again.

I will show you. I will show you what happens if we fail.

I'm surrounded by a sea of cobblestones and bodies. Underneath my feet, there are rustic wooden slats with nails sticking out everywhere, as though the platform had been thrown together in a rush with whatever materials were on hand. The buildings around me look like quaint village houses rather than any of the modern architecture that I am accustomed to, straw rooftops and roughly hewn stone walls everywhere. It's as though I've been thrown hundreds of years into the past in the blink of an eye.

I guess I have been, in a way.

I don't know where I am or what time it is, but I glance over and find my brother standing with me.

That one thing has stayed true, no matter what.

He doesn't look like Nox, of course. His face is so different, but I get the same feeling from him as I do from Nox. It's the protective urge to kill anyone who might want to harm him and a sense of familial connection, the need to make it out of this situation alive for him as much as for myself and my Bonded.

For him to find happiness and contentment.

I feel all of that for myself as well, for all of us to make it through this hellish experience that I've found out we're stuck in, both back at the Sanctuary and here in this memory.

The cheering and shouting around us is my first clue that that isn't going to happen.

I look down at my hands, but they are bound together in front of me with iron chains. The skin all the way up to my elbows is black, the same blackness that it changes to when I call on my shadows, but they're nowhere to be seen. I haven't run out of power for my Gift. I can still feel it there, but there's a block inside of me, something stopping me from accessing it, even though I can feel the shadows pounding beneath my skin to come out, to devour, to kill and to protect, to stop this from happening.

I glance around, but my Bonded isn't here with us. It's just me and the Corvus standing on a platform in the middle of a rudimentary village, facing a crowd of Gifted and non-Gifted staring up at us as though we are monsters.

It's not something that I'm unaccustomed to. I've spent my whole life bearing the Draven name and the legacy that comes with it, but the fear in these people's eyes is so stark, the hatred all-consuming, that there's no doubt about why we're up here.

A man steps forward onto the platform with us and addresses the crowd in a booming voice. I don't recognize the words that he's speaking, a language ancient and long-since dead, but I still know what he's saying.

He's sentencing us to death for the crimes of our shadows.

I can feel my bond's indignation at this, but at the same time, it's resigned to this fate. It doesn't want to put up a fight. It doesn't want to find a way to survive here. It just wants all of this over with already.

As I look out over the rooftops of the small houses, my eye catches on the blood covering the stones out further past the crowd. With a sense of dread in my gut, I follow that blood, follow it all the way down until I find the large and scaled body of the dragon.

If the sheer amount of blood covering the streets wasn't enough to convince me that it's dead, the spear skewering the large animal's body straight through the chest and digging around as though they were attempting to spill its guts out would be a sure indicator.

I can't look away from it.

The more I stare at it, the more horrifying the vision becomes. One of the wings has been partially cut away, the other in shreds from where arrows have gone through the thin membrane. Its jaws are wide open, and I can see where teeth have already been removed, as souvenirs, I'm sure.

Its eyes have rolled back in its head, but the blood that has oozed out of the socket is black, as though the voids themselves have spilled down and onto its cheeks.

We're powerful in these forms, but without the Bonded Group together and the power of the Eternal pumping through all of us, we're not invincible.

If there are other gods here who have woken earlier, then we just don't stand a chance.

We never hunt them like they hunt us. We hunt for our Bonded, and for each other, so that we might live in this existence without the crushing loneliness we face when we cycle all by ourselves. I don't know what has happened to the other gods to make it so that all they care about is destruction. What twisted and dark things must have occurred in their cycling for them to care about nothing but blood and death and destruction. However, that is the reality we face until the Bonded Group is completed.

We will know no peace until the Eternal has all five of the gods who belong to it by its side. We will live this hollow and painful existence again and again until the end of time unless we do.

Finally, I look down at my hands again to find that in the center of one of my palms is a lock of hair tied in a ribbon. It's white, the same unnatural color of Oleander's hair due to her Gift and the power it takes for her to Soul Rend. I know without having to speak to my bond that this version of her, from this time, is already dead.

My bond won't fight back because it doesn't want to exist without her.

The Corvus' dead, void eyes next to me say the exact same thing.

It might pain me to know that his death is imminent, but I wouldn't wish another day on this earth without her or him any more than I would myself.

Without her, we are nothing.

4

OLI

I wake up from my bond's painful walk down memory lane sitting at the table alone.

The Soothsayer is standing over by the window, three steps away from me, as he looks out over the small valley of the Sanctuary. He doesn't blink or move, and I stare at him for a minute just to be sure he's still breathing. I wouldn't want him to forget that Gryphon's body, you know, requires oxygen and just decide to stop doing that.

North and Nox are murmuring together over a pile of paperwork spread out over the breakfast bar, a glass of whiskey in front of North but, surprisingly, nothing for Nox. Atlas and Gabe are nowhere to be seen.

I take a second to be sure I'm fully in control of my

body again before I get up.

The Soothsayer follows me immediately.

North watches it with a scowl, but Nox just slips away from their conversation to follow us both down the hallway to my bedroom, as though I'm a magnet drawing them all along with me without question. I hear North collecting up his paperwork and then footsteps as he follows us as well.

I find Gabe already asleep in my bed, snoring gently as he lies on his stomach, one arm tucked under his head, wearing nothing but a pair of boxer shorts. Atlas is in my shower, the water running and the door half open.

He's still the only one without a functioning bathroom, but when Gabe had tried to apologize for taking so long getting it working for him, he had merely shrugged and pointed out that he was happier sleeping in my room and using my shower every night than going back to his spare room, as he calls it.

North had seemed happy with him getting along so well until he called it that. Then he scowled in his direction because he thinks that it's disrespectful of him to take up so much space in my room. It doesn't bother me though, for the most part.

I would rather have them all here with me.

I know that's never really going to happen, not permanently, because of Nox's firm boundaries around his bedroom and having his own space, but I'm willing to take as much of the rest of them as they're willing to give.

It doesn't surprise me that Nox and North had immediately pulled out Nox's research and tried to start planning. All of this is terrifying in a way that I'm really not processing properly yet.

We're not just being hunted by the Resistance, we're being hunted by other gods.

The abilities they may have, the ties they could have with one another even if they aren't Bonded, all of it will have to be factored into our next moves. The toll of fighting isn't just our own; the battle always spills out onto the other Gifted and non-Gifted as well. All of them have been collateral in a war they had no idea was being waged over a hundred lifetimes.

Now that our bonds have warned us of the danger that's coming, it's exhausting to think about, to even consider what we might all be facing now. Bigger, badder, *stronger*—

"There is no one stronger than us." Gryphon's voice startles me out of my thoughts, and I jump a mile in the air.

I had forgotten he was following me and that he's, once again, got front row seats to every little thought in my brain.

When I come to a stop in front of Gabe's sleeping form, the Soothsayer comes to stand with me, pressing himself into my side so that the heat of his body scorches mine.

I have to clear my throat to find my voice again. "If you say so, but all I know is that the god-bond who was there managed to shut us all down with the pain it wields."

His large hand comes towards me, slowly enough that I can move out of the way if I want to, but when I don't, he presses his palm into one of my cheeks, a happy rumbling noise coming out of his chest that is so unlike Gryphon.

I want to giggle at the sound of it.

"That attack woke me up. The god-bond is complete now, and you will never feel that pain again. I will be sure of that. We all will."

I nod, too tired to question it anymore, and nuzzle my cheek further into his palm. I'm not sure if it wants this sort of affection or whether it's just tolerating the human interaction because I crave it so much, but I appreciate it either way.

He slips his other hand to frame my face completely, murmuring to me quietly, "I waited for you. We all waited for this lifetime, for these vessels... and for you. You are as vital to me as the bond within you. Without question, I see that clearly now."

I feel as though I was waiting for the god-bonds too.

As though I was holding my breath all of this time, and it's only now I've finally let it go that I've noticed. My bond is settled and calm in my stomach for the first time, truly resting in complete contentment, and a frenetic energy that I didn't know was there has finally eased away.

I'm at peace.

I glance back up to the Soothsayer's eyes and find that hunger back in his gaze. Only now, we're in my bedroom, and there's nothing really stopping us from doing something about it. No tales of death and destruction that need to be shared, no gods of pain staring us down, no obligations to get in the way, only a Bonded Group full of overprotective, jumpy men who might want to rip the Soothsayer apart for looking at me as though he wants to tear me open in the most pleasurable of ways.

The bathroom door opening wide breaks me from my train of thought and reminds me that my entire Bonded Group is here in my bedroom with me right now, and though we've definitely had, ahem, group intimacy, it definitely hasn't started like this.

I still feel awkward as fuck about it.

I pull away from the Soothsayer to lean down and brush Gabe's hair away from his face as a distraction, pressing a kiss to his lips, but it doesn't wake him up. He doesn't react to it at all other than to sigh. I know the feeling, having taken a power nap like this a dozen times before, and I just tuck the blankets up around him a little closer.

I don't like the way he's looking at you, Sweetness.

I don't look up or react to Atlas' words. There's no point in starting a fight. *He's fine. He can also hear you in here as well. He's just being polite in not pointing it out.*

North steps around the Soothsayer, pointedly keeping his eyes on me and not the surly god-bond, and I smile at him softly, the type I reserve just for my Bonded. He smiles back before looking me over from head to toe, assessing me for any damage that might be left behind, but, thanks to the Soothsayer, I'm completely healed now.

A shiver of anticipation runs down my spine.

"I don't care what the god-bond wants, Bonded. What do *you* want? If you're tired, you should get some rest. Everything else can, and will, wait."

I open my mouth but nothing comes out, my eyes darting around at each of them. I don't want to start a fight with them. I'm definitely too tired for that, but am I too tired to give the god-bond what he wants?

No.

I need the connection as much as it does, and my bond is very interested in the dark hunger in its void eyes.

It just feels impossible to speak with them all staring at me like that.

"You have a meeting in the morning. Go get some sleep, brother."

Relief floods me at Nox's words, the tension in my body leaving me in a rush. When North sees it, he turns and nods at him, and then leans down to kiss me as he heads back towards the door. The reassurance that his brother is here with me, for however long he deems necessary, is enough for him.

It's not enough for Atlas, though.

Nox stares him down for a minute before he says, "You too, Bassinger. I'll call you both if we need something."

That's Draven code for 'if shit hits the fan in here', because I doubt there's much that Nox couldn't handle for himself.

North shoots a look at Atlas and pushes the door open, gesturing for him to leave. I'm waiting for the argument to start up, and a full tense minute of silence passes before, finally, Atlas ducks down to kiss me as well. Without another word, he leaves. North just shoots me a look, one full of fiery promise and possession, before he leaves as well.

Nox pulls his jacket off as shadows fall away from his body, Mephis and Procel forming at his feet, and he takes a seat on the small, plush chair in the corner. He settles himself there without a word, as calm and self-assured in this moment and what's about to happen as ever, but my heart starts thudding hard in my chest the more I look at him.

He's here to keep me safe.

The same way Gryphon had when we'd Bonded, back when Nox had no desire to be in the same room as me, let alone have sex with me. He's here to make sure that this god-bond really is going to pleasure me and treat me with the same respect that any of them would.

He's going to watch it all.

My eyes flick down at Gabe again, checking that he really is asleep. There's nothing for me to worry about, he's out cold. My only real concern about him waking up is that he's always been my most cautious Bonded about sex, the one who draws the line at what my bond does when she takes control. I wasn't lying when I said I don't have it in me to fight them on this. I let out a sigh and roll my shoulders back, confident that nothing is going to go wrong here. The moment I look back up to the Soothsayer, he stalks back to me.

He's done waiting.

It's a good thing I'm done fighting this as well.

With a single hand wrapped around my thigh, the god-bond lifts me up and crushes me into his chest with the other, his lips crushing down onto mine in a biting claim of a kiss. There's a stark difference between the man and the bond. The ways they move are nothing more than an echo of each other. I find myself desperate to know how far those differences go.

Will they fuck differently too?

Will he eat me out like Gryphon does, as though he's a starved man who needs the taste of me to survive?

"Yes, to all of it. I will give you everything you want

and need, Bonded," he murmurs into my ear, barely louder than the sound of my heart thumping in my chest as he walks us around to the other side of my monstrously huge bed.

A shiver runs down my spine at the feel of his breath against my neck. It's a simple seduction that I'm not sure he even realizes he's doing, but it has me wiggling in his arms all the same. I want to feel that breath lower, over my chest and my nipples, the planes of my belly, between my thighs. Fuck, I want to feel it on every inch of my skin as he explores and claims this version of me.

I want to be his favorite vessel.

I want him to love me like he loves my bond. I want him to be desperate for us both, to hunger for *my* attention as much as the god's within me.

I want everything.

The god-bond spreads me out onto the bed carefully, tugging at my clothes in a rough demand until I'm naked for him, his eyes roaming over me as though he's committing every little freckle and dimple to memory. I don't feel shy about it either. I stretch out and arch my back a little, smiling at the way his eyes glue themselves to the swell of my breasts as I move.

He undresses in a frenzy of tearing fabrics and buttons popping away from their stitching, as though the very idea of unzipping and carefully disrobing is an insult to both of us and our Bond.

It's nothing I haven't seen a hundred times before and touched and tasted and worshiped in my own way, but it's still a sight to see.

Gryphon always has been too perfect for words.

The Soothsayer leans down to kiss me again, one hand on the bed and the other coming up to wrap around my throat again, almost as if he's afraid I'm going to try to run away from him.

I couldn't even if I tried.

He moves his weight onto his knees and then his fingers dip into my pussy as he bites at my lip, impatient and greedy to fill me up, to claim me, to own my pleasure and feed it to me at his leisure. I moan, and he breaks away, biting and sucking his way down my neck to my chest with his own noises of pleasure at the softness of my skin.

There's a rustling sound from the corner, and I remember that we're not alone, my eyes snapping open and finding my Bonded in the darkened room.

Nox's eyes smolder back at me from the corner, and I turn my face more towards him, my lips parting on a low moan as the god-bond's fingers tighten around my throat. He watches it all, his eyes dark as he takes it all in. I'm laid out here on display for his viewing pleasure except... I want more. I want them both. *Fuck*, I want them and their bonds and mine. I want it all.

The god-bond's fingers tighten even more, flexing until I'm gasping for breath as my pussy clenches around his fingers as he pumps them in and out, hooking them to graze over that spot inside of me that makes me want to scream.

I don't even have the chance to wish for more before his fingers are slipping out of me, my legs spread apart by his thighs as he pushes the thick length of his cock inside of me. He anchors himself on the hand around my throat, his fingers flexing in time with the pumping of his hips until I'm a shaking mess.

Every inch of his body is commanding me, owning me, using me for his pleasure even as he gives me even more of that same intoxicating pleasure.

I need more.

"Not the vessel."

It's Gryphon's voice, but still, they're not his words. I could argue with him if I could speak, but I'm still fighting for air in the best way, choking on my own bliss as he finally eases up just a little and the rush of oxygen hits me. The only way to describe the feeling is euphoria, ecstasy. I come so hard my vision whites out as my juices run down my legs.

"I'm here for her, not to follow your orders. If she wants me, then you'll just have to deal with it. She calls the shots here, not you," Nox drawls, and it's a tempting offer.

Tempting to ever think I'm calling the shots between us.

That's just never been our dynamic, never been the way that we've fit together at all. He's been in charge, the one pushing at me and pulling away, always pulling away. In the descent from the tallest heights that my orgasm had taken me, I feel tears prick at the edges of my eyes.

The god-bond sees it all.

Not just the tears, no. He sees everything inside of my head clearly. I might as well be an open book written just for him, every thought and feeling and even slightest whim is there for him to see.

He does a lot with that information.

The moment my legs stop shaking, he pulls away from me, ignoring the whimper that tumbles out of my lips as he grabs my ankles to drag me to the edge of the bed, dropping to his knees and tugging my legs open until my pussy is spread wide underneath his intense gaze. There's no questioning if he likes what he sees. His eyes drink me in as though to him, I'm the last glass of water in the desert.

Desperate and gluttonous.

His lips devour me, his hands wrapping around my hips as he pulls me closer, closer, never close enough to sate his hunger. He drives me over the edge with that single-minded determination he shares with his vessel, with my Gryphon, and my chest aches at his absence.

I want the god-bond, but I *need* my Bonded.

As soon as I've thought that, the god-bond changes his tactics, shifting from the ravenous edging to pushing me over the edge again and again until I can't think straight. Every little thought I have is used against me in the most torturous ways. The god-bond sees every part of my pleasure and manipulates it, pushes it, stretches it out until I'm sobbing out my orgasms, my head thrashing against my pillows until I'm a complete wreck.

Only once I've completely lost all control of my legs does he come up for air, moving me around as though I weigh nothing until he's holding me in his lap, his hands tight on my hips as he slowly impales me on his cock. I wrap my arms around his neck and hold on tight as he fucks me, his void eyes unblinking as he watches the perfect agony on my face. When I finally can use my legs again, shifting so I can ride his dick properly instead of being moved at his whim, he lies back to properly enjoy the view.

His eyes stay glued to where we're joined, the wet sounds of my pussy bouncing around the room obscenely as I soak his thighs with my cum.

I still want more.

If anything, fucking the god-bond has only given me more energy. Somehow, he's tapped into a reserve I didn't know I had, and with a smile down at him, my hips still sliding up and down his cock, I look over to where Nox is watching us.

His eyes have shifted to black.

He's still in control. I can see it clearly, but his bond is there at the surface as well. Nox always did work well with the extra being inside of him, and even now, he's willing to play nicely.

I want them all.

The god-bond moves me onto his chest, pulling me down into a mirror image of how I was when Nox and I Bonded, and I hear the rustling of clothes behind me.

A triumphant grin breaks over my cheeks.

Two fingers slicked up with lube press against my ass, hesitating for just a moment before they plunge into me, curling gently as he opens me up. I wiggle back against the feeling of them both in me at the same time, at Gryphon's cock splitting me wide open as Nox's fingers prep my ass for him as well.

I could have them together.

The very idea of it has my pussy clenching, my thighs shaking as I try not to collapse onto the god-bond completely. I haven't tried that yet, not since Nox and his bond had shared me in a night full of shadows and whispers and possessive demands.

His free hand runs up my side, moving me and shifting me in little ways until he can line up and push into me, slowly at first as a low moan bursts out of my lips, moving gently until he's sure I can take it, before he sets a brutal pace. Though he's never said it, I think watching the other Bonded fuck me is a big turn on for Nox, and he doesn't need much else to get him on edge.

The Soothsayer's hands tighten on my hips, holding me still as he fucks me, his cock dragging in and out of my pussy in tandem with Nox's cock in my ass so that there's always someone buried in me. I feel so full I could scream, so full I might tear open at the seams, but my bond *writhes* in my chest. It gloats and pushes at my skin as though it wants to come out and swallow them both whole. When the Soothsayer's hips begin to falter, its jaw clenching where it's watching from underneath us as it reaches its own climax, my bond pushes out and into it, sealing them together in its own demand for attention.

It wants a million impossible things but, fuck, I think the god-bonds might just give it everything it wants and more. Anything. Everything, the ultimate act of true devotion.

Nox's fingers wrap around my wrist firmly, pulling my arm back and holding me against his chest tightly. I feel so full that I can't speak, can't think, can't breathe, and he murmurs into my ear, "Do you want all of your Bonds? Do you want every hole filled up? Every last one of us fucking you until we've had our fill of this sweet, poison pussy?"

My mind shatters the moment he says the word 'poison', the tone of it a taunting endearment and a testament to how much has changed between us. A low moan ekes out from between my lips, Nox's hips still pumping in and out of my body at that same brutal pace as he follows me over the edge.

The Soothsayer watches us both, unblinking void eyes unnaturally bright in the darkness of the room.

Nox's head drops to my shoulder, his hair falling over my cheek as he breathes me in, and when I open my eyes to look back down, I finally see Gryphon's green eyes staring back at me.

The god-bond is satisfied.

I wake up as a pile of sore muscles and aching bones. My head is full of air, and it takes me a minute to remember where the hell I am.

Nox is nowhere to be seen, but Gabe is still snoring on the far side of the bed, just as worn out from his shifting as I had been from the power exchange, and, surprisingly, Gryphon is also in the bed with us. He's usually the first one up and out of the door in the morning.

His arm is flung over his eyes, and his breathing is even as he sleeps, his heart beating steadily in his chest under my ear. I lie there for a moment, listening with my face tilted towards his to watch him, enjoying the quiet of the room.

When his arm finally moves and his eyes open, I sigh in relief at the clear, green hue of them.

"Did you miss me, Bonded?" he murmurs quietly, and I nod my head as I lean forward and kiss him slowly, relieved that his hands feel like his own as he pulls me into his chest a little more securely.

As much as I love his bond and the way it had worshiped me last night, I love this man more. Is it weird to pick favorites?

"As long as I'm your favorite, no," Gryphon mumbles again under his breath, pulling me back into a kiss as his hands frame my face gently.

I press my forehead against his, enjoying this quiet little moment for just the two of us in the dark, and the tension in my body eases away.

"You scared me for a minute there. North thought the god-bond might try to take over the vessel," I say before coming to an abrupt halt, my words drying up because the thought of that ever happening fills me with an indescribable pain.

Gryphon only nods, brushing his thumbs over my cheeks once more. "I don't like the feeling of the god taking over. I know now why North fought it so much. It was like I could see everything, but I was powerless to do anything about it when it grabbed your throat to ease the sickness away. For a second, I thought I was trapped in a nightmare." He swallows and pulls back enough to rub a hand over his eyes, stress practically leaking out of his body at the memory.

I find myself fussing over him the way he's fussed over me a hundred times before, hurrying to reassure him that everything is going to be okay. "It loves me, Gryphon. I know it does. I think it respects every last one of us... They all do. Whatever it is about *this* timeline and *these* vessels, it's as if we were meant to be."

He shakes his head as if he's clearing it and then presses another kiss to my forehead with the type of devotion a man shows the center of his world. "I don't know how they keep coming back. I can't imagine losing you in one lifetime, Bonded, let alone over and over again. It sounds like a form of torture. No wonder they're all a bit... psycho."

I giggle and tuck myself back into his side, threading my fingers through his as I enjoy lying back in the bed with him. We're always the first to rise, and even when I was forced to rest by North after my time in the Resistance camps, Gryphon had still gone to the Tac Training Center early, so I enjoy the novel experience of just lying here together for however long it might last.

Eventually, Gryphon fusses around in the bed until he finds his phone, checking the messages there and grumbling under his breath about something that Kieran had sent him. "Are you going to see Sage today?"

I nod and murmur back to him quietly as I glance over at Gabe, watching the rise and fall of his chest, just a little bit concerned at how deeply he's still sleeping. "I promised her I would. Kieran and North agreed that she could be let out of the cells as long as one of her Bonded was with her at all times. Felix insisted on taking a few days off to stay with her just in case there's any physical effects of what the Soothsayer did to get the other one out of her head."

Gryphon blows out a long breath, frustration etched into the lines of his face. "I'm not a hundred percent sure, obviously, but I was aware of what it was doing to her. If I had to make a guess, I'd say that she really is going to be fine. Actually, I'd say she's going to be protected from anything like that happening again, not just from that god-bond, but any other being that might try to manipulate her."

I let out a deep sigh, relief coursing through me and unloading a heap of pressure that I have been carrying for the longest time. There had always been a fear in me that whatever had happened to Sage when she had been possessed might happen again. Gryphon's god-bond, the Soothsayer, has given me a priceless gift by protecting her in such a way.

"Do you think that it could do that for the rest of us too? If he can keep Sage's mind safe like that, could he protect the rest of us as well?"

Gryphon's head pushes back into his pillow as he considers my words, his hair falling over his forehead where it's come loose from the leather hair tie he keeps it back in. "I don't think the rest of the Bonded Group needs it. I think that I might be the only one capable of getting into their heads in the first place. I've only ever done that with their permission, even Atlas."

I nod and settle back into his arms, taking a second to just enjoy the quiet peace of the bedroom. I'm afraid to let it go, to get up and get back to our lives. The moment I do, this will all slip through my fingers, and I'll never have it again.

As I sigh for the third time, Gryphon shifts me in his arms, murmuring, "I've never been so sure of our ability to win this war. Whatever you're thinking about that has you sighing like that, Bonded, don't tie yourself up in knots about it. We're going to deal with these god-bonds, clear out the rest of the Resistance scum, and no one is ever going to be able to take this away from us again. This is it for us, the perfect Bonded Group and life. I'm sure of it."

The slow smile stretches over my face as I run my hand over his chest, enjoying the simple touches between us that we so often miss out on because of the demands of his job.

"It sounds like you might actually like the god-bond more than you're letting on here, Bonded," I whisper with a self-satisfied smile, the type that shows that he's taken care of every last one of my needs.

"If the god-bonds are going to keep you safe and get us all through this alive, then I'll like it a whole lot more than I was ever expecting to. You're worth every bit of that possession feeling, the helplessness, if it keeps you safe."

He lifts a hand to thread through my hair as he curses under his breath at his phone, looking down at me draped over his chest with nothing but pure male satisfaction.

He cups the side of my face and presses a gentle kiss to my lips, murmuring against me, "The one feeling that the god-bond woke up with, that stayed with it for the entire time he was in control of my body, was the overwhelming need to protect you, covet you and worship you... to destroy anything that might harm you or upset you. It's a relief to know that if I'm going to have something like that living inside of me and sharing control of my body, at least we're on the same page about that."

My heart flutters in my chest at the idea of their shared devotion, at being the catalyst within the Bonded Group, the one thing to bring each of these men to peace with the gods living within their skin.

His phone buzzes again, and he curses viciously under his breath as he grabs it. "The world won't wait for us forever, Bonded, though I might just kill Black for interrupting us like this."

As much as I feel as though I'm betraying Sage by thinking this, I agree with him wholeheartedly as he gently moves me off of his chest and gets up to walk back to his own bathroom to shower.

After a few minutes of moping quietly, Atlas ducks his head into the room and, seeing that I'm awake, saunters over to me with a relieved grin. He's careful not to wake Gabe, which is another thing that sets my anxiety off. He would normally shove at my shifter playfully or throw a pillow at him or some other show of rowdy friendship, but even he can see that Gabe needs his rest.

Atlas senses my anxiety, and after he's swooped down to brush a gentle kiss against my lips, he whispers, "He'll be fine, Sweetness. It's just the shift sapping his energy, the same way that you used to take extended naps."

I nod. I'm sure he's right, but I can't help myself either. I drag myself out of the bed to pull clothing on as quietly as I can, aware of Atlas' eyes on me as he not-so-discreetly checks me for any damage the Soothsayer may have done.

I'm more worried about whatever marks Nox's firm grip might have left, but Atlas doesn't say anything, and his face is still calm when I turn around in a pair of jeans and one of his sweaters that covers me to the knees.

I check on Gabe before we leave, pressing a hand gently

against the side of his neck to feel the steady thrumming of his heartbeat and trying to let it lessen my anxiety a little bit.

He sighs in his sleep and rolls towards me unconsciously, his body seeking me out even in his slumber. I find myself very tempted to just climb back into the bed and lie with him, but there's also a frenetic sort of energy underneath my skin; the juxtaposition of how tired I feel but how wired I really am is making me itch.

"I'll take you over to Sage's place, Bonded. We can message Gabe later and tell him to come over when he's finally up. Everything will be fine, Sweetness. Stop frowning. He wouldn't want you fussing over him like this, not when he's not awake to enjoy it."

I scoff a little and then follow him out of the door, dragging my feet a bit.

5

OLI

The door to Sage and her Bonded Group's house is opened by Wick, and he stares down at me with the sort of distrust and wariness that I'm used to seeing on the faces of everyone within the community except those close to us. I have to remind myself that just because he is one of Sage's Bonded, it doesn't mean he owes me anything, and I haven't exactly had time to make nice with him yet.

Wick growls at me, "So, Sage isn't allowed to go anywhere or speak to anyone, but you guys are allowed to come over unannounced whenever you feel like it to check in on her?"

No 'hi, how ya doin' or anything that could have passed as good manners. I have to place an arm across

Atlas' chest to stop him from launching at his throat.

I paste on a sweet smile that just about kills me. "This isn't a wellness check. This is me coming to see my best friend and see how she's coping after her personal space and boundaries were once again violated by some asshole god-bond—"

"Like the one that's living in your head?" he interrupts, crossing his arms over his chest as he continues to stare me down.

I'm surprised Atlas' teeth don't crack under the pressure as he gnashes his jaw violently, but I'm proud that he manages to hold his temper, because I don't really want to fight with this man.

I'm going to make him like me, dammit!

"Yep, just like that one, except it's on the bad side of the conflict and we're not. Team Good Guys all the way over here! Also, Sage knows I'm coming. I did text her. This wasn't *actually* unannounced."

He opens his mouth, but then Sawyer's voice calls through the house, "Just let her in, dickhead! She's the closest thing Sage has to a sister. Plus, we're all alive thanks to Oli and her Bonded Group. You're not going to get very far by pissing off North Draven's Bonded, and rumor has it, Nox has finally decided to cozy up with her. I, personally, would rather fling myself off the roof of this place than go toe-to-toe with either one of the Death

Dealers."

A goofy grin spreads over my mouth at the mention of the rest of my Bonded Group. Atlas scoffs at me, leaning down to murmur, not so quietly, "He knows my god-bond's called the Cleaver, right? He has more than just the shadows to contend with now."

The image of the bloodshed and gore from the Wasteland flashes into my mind once again, stealing my breath for a moment. I don't feel bad for what any of us did, but I also don't think I can eat anything while the memory is still so fresh. The smell still lingers in my nose, the hot, wet, sticky sensation of blood and innards, and yep, I feel like puking.

Wick finally steps aside, and I don't hesitate to gently push him out of the way, nudging past the hulk of him to make my way into the large, open area.

There's a lot of bodies living in this house.

I find Sawyer, Gray, Aro, and her younger brother, Lahn, all sitting in the living room playing video games on the large TV. Lahn is sitting in his sister's lap while she laughs along at the destruction on the screen. Both of her Bonded are shit-talking each other in a playfully vicious way, their language a toned-down version of its usual vitriol, thanks to the younger set of ears in the room, but it's playfully nasty all the same.

Atlas scoffs at them both, glancing around the room

and nodding respectfully at Felix who is pouring himself a cup of coffee bigger than my head. I make my way over to him, and he holds out the pot to me like the amazing human being that he is.

"I need something stronger than this to get me through today," Felix murmurs quietly to me as I grab the strawberry-flavored creamer and bend to rummage around in the drawers for some flavored syrups to really get me going.

"Has something happened or just the general bullshit? Gimme an idea of what we're dealing with here, buddy."

Felix watches as Wick stalks back into the living room, plonking himself down on the couch and scowling at the TV. "Things were a little bit calmer when there were only three Bonded to contend with. We're having some... teething issues."

I bite my lip to hide a smirk and gently point out to him, "Well, I have five Bonded. One of them was set on hating my guts and stirring up shit with all of the rest of them until his dying breath. We managed to make our way out of that, so I feel like you guys can get through this. He just needs to figure some shit out for himself."

Felix quirks an eyebrow at me and mutters, "If he doesn't work it out soon, I'm gonna develop Flame powers of my own and set the asshole on fire."

Atlas snickers under his breath, stealing a sip of my

ridiculously over-the-top coffee. He's good about hiding his grimace at the veritable fruit salad flavor I have going on over the rich and bitter taste of the coffee itself.

"Is he a good Bonded to Sage at least?" I murmur, and Felix raises his eyebrows at me.

"I'm not sure I could tell you if he wasn't. You'd end up tearing his soul out without asking for any extra details."

I shrug and turn towards the bedroom door as it opens. Sage shuffles out dressed in a pair of pajamas and one of Kieran's oversized Tac Training sweaters over her top. She looks a little bit like a zombie, but I rethink that description as Riley stumbles out after her, still not looking good.

I glanced back at Felix, worried, and he shrugs. "Who needs to go down to the clinic when I have enough patients in my own house to deal with?"

I put my coffee down on the bench and tuck Sage into a warm hug, hooking my chin onto her shoulder and murmuring quietly, "What can I do? You look like you need a serious blood transfusion and maybe four weeks on a tropical island away from all of this."

She sighs and melts into my hug a little more, and I catch Wick staring over at us. He doesn't seem jealous or upset, more like he's assessing the interaction and deciding for himself whether or not we're all lying about the two of us being close.

Well, fuck him, he can figure it out for himself that I'd

die for this girl.

"Do you really think that Gryphon's god-bond can keep it from happening again?" she mutters, and I nod, tucking a limp strand of her hair behind her ear affectionately.

"I absolutely believe that it can and has done that, Sage. If I wasn't sure, and if *North* wasn't sure, you'd still be in the cells, and I would be right there with you, raging about everything until we sorted it out."

She sighs and nods once more, pulling away from me and scoffing as she looks at the pink hue of my coffee. "Can you taste anything except the sugar?"

"Nope," I say, popping the P obnoxiously and picking the cup back up.

I feel a little bit awkward being in their space like this for a moment as Riley starts to pull together food for himself and his Bonded, but when Sage gets us both settled at the table and starts to quietly debrief with me about the Wasteland, I relax.

Sawyer and Gray talk Atlas into going a round in the video game with them, and I let myself just exist here for a moment with my best friend, a moment of normality for once.

Riley sits at the end of the table and eats his breakfast in silence, acting as though he's not listening in on every word that Sage and I say. Every now and then, she will shoot a look at him, as though she's checking in. After the fourth time I catch her doing this, I raise my eyebrows at her with a little wiggle, trying to lighten the mood a bit.

She gives me a sheepish grin back. "We've figured out that healing goes the best for us both when we're around each other. I think whatever that bitch did to him has destabilized our Bond. Even though we've been working really hard to sort things out, there's still some… noticeable damage."

Riley hunches in on himself, proving that he has been listening to our every word, but it's not as though we have been talking about anything private anyway.

I nod slowly and shrug with a grimace on my face as well, a mirror of hers. "That makes sense, I guess. What she did wasn't just a tactical move for the Resistance. It was an assault on your Bond, and it makes complete sense that there would be some lasting effects of that."

Sage nods slowly, and Riley sighs, setting his knife and fork down on the table. "It's my own fault for not being strong enough to fight against her. It's my fault for letting this happen."

That sounds very self-loathing to me, and I can tell it hurts Sage to hear him speak like that. But I'm also a walking pile of trauma and contradictions, so I don't have too much of a leg to stand on to argue with him about it.

I try anyway.

He's still a member of my family's Bonded Group.

Now that he doesn't have that evil woman, whose name I will not mention, around anymore, he actually seems like a decent guy. Like one who would have been devoted and the perfect Bonded to Sage from the beginning, if only this hadn't happened to him.

"You know that Gryphon can still get into my head, right? He can get into anyone's head and do all sorts of nefarious things if he chooses to. The reason he doesn't is because he is a good and decent person. He understands the responsibility of having such a Gift. He's always thought through the moral implications of using it. That bitch didn't give a shit. She was a fucking monster, and you didn't stand a chance against her. There's nothing to be ashamed of. You didn't do anything, she did."

He doesn't look as though any of this is getting through to him. I'm sure everyone's tried this tactic with him before, so instead, I take a deep breath and lay a little more of my soul out on the line than I'm comfortable with. If it helps Sage, I'm willing to do it.

"I also have no control when my god-bond takes over. A lot of things have happened, and it's taken a very long time to get to the point where I can make the distinction between what my actions are and what *its* actions are. That's still a heavy weight for me to carry, one that not even my Bonded can relieve me of, but I know where my morals lie. I know what I would be willing to do to keep my family and my community safe. That's how I sleep at night. You need to ask yourself what you are willing to do for your Bonded and what you would never do to her. Once you have those answers, and follow through with them, I promise that every day it will get a little bit easier."

Riley's eyes flick back over to Sage, but he nods at me slowly, picking up a fork again as he moves the eggs around on his plate a little more. Felix, who'd ducked off for a quick shower but had come back out part way through my sad little story, takes a seat at the table as well. He watches as Riley finishes up his breakfast and then heads in to shower too.

Once we hear the door shut and the water turn on, Felix mutters to me quietly, "You know we've been sending him to see a therapist, right? The same one North wants to force you to go see. I think you just did more for that guy with a two-minute baring of your own trauma than the therapist has done in weeks of speaking with him. Maybe that should be your major when you head back to Draven."

Sage lifts her cup up to her lips, hiding a smirk behind it. "You know, if the world doesn't end or anything."

At lunchtime, I convince Sage to come out to the dining hall with us to grab food, and when Felix agrees to tag along as well, she reluctantly grabs a jacket. She snarks at her brother when Sawyer starts barking out a food order to her without so much as looking up from the TV screen he's still happily kicking everybody's ass on.

Atlas bows out from the competition to tag along with us, and I'm relieved when I check my phone and find a message from Gabe waiting for me there. I text back to tell him to meet us at the dining hall, and the four of us slip out together for the short walk down there.

Felix and Atlas are good enough friends now that they happily walk a few steps behind us and chat with each other, so I get more privacy with my bestie than I have so far today.

I get straight to asking her the real question that's burning a hole in my head.

"So, things with Wick... How are they really going?"

She groans and rubs her hand over her forehead. "With me? Great! He's been just as kind and supportive and amazing as the rest of my Bonded. With everyone else? He has a huge chip on his shoulder, and I'm struggling to figure this out. I feel as though everybody is a second away from descending into a giant argument, and my nerves *cannot* take it."

I giggle a little, and even though Sage digs her elbow into my ribs just a bit in retaliation, she also sighs. "I know you get it, and I know that your Bonded Group has been through a hell of a lot worse than a few bruised egos, but oh my *God*, I've never had to make a schedule over who is going to be around me before. Kieran and Felix just always made as much time for me around their work schedules as they possibly could, so it never really overlapped. It was a bit of an adjustment with Riley, but again, neither of them minded making that space for him, especially because he really needed me to speed up the healing process. But Wick? He questions *everything*. Why does Kieran work so much? Why did Kieran let me go out to the Wastelands when it was so dangerous? Why didn't Felix come to it just in case I needed him? Why do we all abide by everything that North says without too much questioning? Why does Felix work so many hours, even when I need him with me? Why did no one do anything about Riley a little sooner?"

Her voice breaks on the last one, and I seriously consider turning around and going back to find Wick and thumping him. Like anyone in that Bonded Group needs more guilt than they already have. Instead of pretending that I have the answer to everything and that my own Bond was a peaceful experience, because how laughable is that, I do what I can to offer her a little support.

"Things will die down with him. It's kind of like a pecking order thing. He's trying to figure out where exactly he is on it. He probably never thought he would be sharing with such high-profile people, per se."

Sage raises her eyebrows at me. "And what exactly is

the pecking order in your Bonded Group? And how does that work out?"

I grin a little sheepishly, and I'm very careful not to look back at my Bonded or hers, even though they are probably eavesdropping on us right now.

I also choose my words *very* carefully.

"No one's in charge... except maybe me and my bond, when push comes to shove. But everybody has their own special skills or areas of knowledge, and we all naturally default to that person. North is always going to be the councilman. He's always going to have more knowledge about the families and the inner workings of those sorts of things. I would never presume to know more in those areas than him. Gryphon is the TacTeam leader. Even North, who has training in tactical response, will defer to him when it comes to missions and that sort of thing. Nox has always enjoyed more of the research side of things."

Sage nods along and glances back at Atlas. "And the other two? Because this is my problem! Kieran has a very clear job and position within my Bonded Group, as does Felix. Riley doesn't care yet about that sort of thing. He's still so lost in his own guilt and grief that he might never question his place, but Wick has just walked into a very established set of relationships and is not comfortable just gelling with everyone else. He wants his own place and his own strengths recognized."

I nod and tuck my arm into hers, pulling her in a little closer so that I can be quieter about this. "Atlas was the one who struggled. The reason that he didn't kick up too much of a fuss about it was because of his plans to run away with me. When those plans were changed, he definitely had an adjustment period. But in the end, the one thing he could agree on with everyone else was keeping me safe. He has taken it upon himself to shadow me through every mission and keep me alive, no matter what. I'm sure that once we have dealt with the Resistance, he'll find something else. There will probably be an adjustment period again, but I guess that's part of being in a Bonded Group. Everybody has to grow and change and do it together, even when it makes it so hard for everyone else."

Sage nods and sighs, and I say the one thing to her that Gryphon and North have said to me a dozen times between them, the reassurance I've needed a hundred times over. "It's not your job to police their relationships. Just because you're the Central Bonded, it doesn't make you responsible for making everyone be friends. If they're upsetting you, tell them. If they're butting in to things that aren't their business, tell them. You get to choose what your Bonded Group looks like, but it's also not your responsibility to keep everyone happy. That's way too much shit on your shoulders, Sage, and *none* of us can bear the brunt of all of these men and their egos. Not even me and my god-bond."

6

GABE

I wasn't expecting that the shift into the dragon and allowing the god-bond to take control would sap so much of my energy and leave me feeling so fucking awful. Even after a full eighteen hours of sleep, my stomach is still tender and my head feels as though it's full of sand, slowing down my brain and making me feel like death itself. If we're attacked right now, I'm going to struggle to be of any help to my Bonded, and that's not fucking good enough.

I need to pull it together.

The streets of the Sanctuary are busy with bodies, dozens of workmen carting supplies to and from the loading zones. Now that my uncle and my cousins have taken over the everyday projects, I can see progress on the streets around us, and our time away has made the changes dramatic. I wouldn't be surprised if we were able to start offering single homes to Bonded Groups in the coming weeks.

I wave and greet as many of the workers as I can as I make my way down to the dining hall. A few of my cousins give me a curious look at the state I'm in. I don't exactly want to tell any of them that I'm having indigestion problems from devouring Resistance soldiers whole. There's a few TacTeam personnel who duck away so that they don't have to meet my eye, so there's a good chance that word has already spread.

I don't care about any of that shit.

The only people I care about are the ones that I was protecting that day. As I round the corner, the dining hall coming into view, I find my Bonded standing outside of it, laughing with Sage. Her head is thrown back, and the silver glory of her hair is shining in the morning sun. It's brighter now than it's ever been before, something I know she is super self-conscious about, but it's like a beacon calling out to me. I can't help but break into a jog to get over to her as quickly as possible. The grin she's giving Sage is a sight for the weariest of eyes—stunning—but the way that her eyes light up and her entire body turns towards me as she spots me making my way over to her has my heart thumping in my chest.

It's still a miracle to me that she loves me as much as I love her, that we both see something in one another that is so unique and precious that it's worth fighting for no matter how many sore stomachs and days I might have to sleep away to get us there.

"I'm surprised you're up. I was expecting you to laze the entire day away," Atlas says with a slap on my shoulder as I walk straight past him to my Bonded.

She giggles as I lift her up into my arms, spinning her around a little even as she thumps a fist onto my chest in pretend outrage.

"We're in public. North will have a cow!" she mutters under her breath, but I kiss her all the same, answering her in our mind connection.

What do I care if everyone here knows how much I love my Bonded?

Oli melts into the kiss, into my arms, and into *me* in that same addictive way she always does. I forget about the pounding in my head and the way that my stomach is still churning, the burn of the bile up my throat that I woke up with that still hasn't quite eased away. Every last one of the physical complaints I have just disappear. I don't care how sappy it sounds, I could take on all of the Resistance single-handedly as long as I come back to my Bonded like this every time.

This invincible feeling is how Atlas must feel with his Gift.

The dragon wakes from where it's been slumbering inside my chest to make its own opinions clear to me at having her back again, everything boiling down to a single word.

Mine.

"We're just going to grab lunch for everyone," Oli says as she finally wiggles out of my arms and back onto her feet.

I scowl, a little unhappy at even the slightest of distances between us, but she tucks herself into my side and sighs happily when I sling my arm over her shoulder to keep her there.

I don't feel like sharing nicely today.

Atlas gives me a knowing look, but I must look just about as shitty as I feel because he doesn't say a word about it. He barely looks bothered by it all as he opens the dining hall's door and ushers us in.

It's busy in here today, but with the Sanctuary growing in numbers by the day, I'm not surprised to see it. Every table is occupied, most to capacity, and I'm glad to see there's a lot of laughing and general happiness in the room. It's a relief, after months of tension and unease, that families and friends are together here in safety.

It's the whole damn point of the place.

Oli is tense under my arm, enough so that I have to fight my urges to curl around her and snarl at everyone, as well as the dragon's urges within me to shift and consume them all for upsetting her like this. I'm not usually hot-tempered, but it takes three deep breaths before I feel like myself again. No one attempts to speak to us or approach us in any way. Aside from a few curious looks, the room mostly just acts as though they haven't noticed that we've walked in.

I know damn well they all know we're here, but I'll take it.

Atlas forms a human wall between the tables and our Bonded, his shoulders wide enough to mostly cover us both, and Felix does the same with Sage, who stays close to Oli's side.

"We should have called ahead and gotten something put aside for us," Sage mutters, and Oli shrugs back.

"We shouldn't have to. We should be able to come down and eat, just the same as everyone else, without having to worry about all of *this*."

I glance around again and then murmur back to them both quietly, "Nobody's really… doing much though, are they? We might be overreacting here."

Oli shoots me a look and then flicks a hand in the direction of the tables a little too aggressively, and some of the Gifted there take notice, packing away their plates and fleeing.

"They're all staring at you. You do realize that, right? I don't give a shit what they think about me, but they're all staring at the guy who can turn into a dragon and eat people. I think they're used to me and the Dravens by now, but you walking in here looking a little green around the edges has them all believing that the rumors are true."

"Which they are," Sage pipes in helpfully, glaring at one of the council members who dares to get a little too close to her.

She's being protective of Oli because we all know how much the council has rallied against my Bonded, but Oli's too busy staring down a table full of our ex-classmates from Draven, the only ones with the guts to point and whisper openly at us all.

Idiots.

I will probably regret it later when North reams me for it, but I use a finger to tip Oli's head back and press my lips to hers. "I don't give a shit about petty jealousies, Bonded. Let them gossip and whisper all they like. It still doesn't change the fact that none of them could survive without us doing all the hard work."

She hums happily under her breath, and we approach the large opening to the kitchens. It's set up like a buffet, except that the doorway is large enough that we can see into where the chef is cooking. Oli brightens as she leans forward in my arms, away from me. I would be a little more bothered about it except then I see why.

"Holy shit, you look like death, Ardern," says Kyrie as she slides a huge, hot plate of chicken wings onto the buffet and pulls a rag out of her pocket, wiping her hands as she walks around to us.

She's covered in flour and grease from the kitchens but has a big grin across her face. I can tell she has found her happy place in the Sanctuary. She always did love running the cafe, so I'm not surprised that this is where she has come to contribute here.

"I ate something that isn't agreeing with me," I say with a smirk and a wink, listening to the sounds of disgust from the tables behind us with an evil cackle.

Atlas rolls his eyes at me, but Oli laughs along with me before pulling a face. "Yeah, they're not exactly tasty. Well, their souls aren't, at least. I've never tried the rest of them before."

Kyrie blows out a breath and shakes her head as she looks up towards the ceiling. "It's going to take some getting used to listening to you lot talk so *casually* about that sort of thing. No wonder everybody around here looks like they're going to blow a fuse."

Oli looks around with a playful smirk before shrugging. "Hey, I brought the nice Bonded in with me today. If I was really planning on ruining everyone's lives, I would have brought one of the other three."

Atlas scoffs under his breath before murmuring, "You'd have brought Nox, and then we would get to see just how quickly everybody here would change their fucking tunes."

More tables start to discreetly vacate around us, and Kyrie shakes her head at our antics.

"It's definitely weird to see the two of you getting along. But I have to say, I'm glad. You guys were stressing my brother into an early grave. I also won a good amount of money off of Black for that, so I owe you a drink. Just don't tell North I was supplying booze to his underage Bonded," she says again, cackling.

Oli just grins back at her, batting her eyelashes as she snarks back with all of her trademark sass. I enjoy the sound of it all, but the smell of the wings finally hits my nostrils and makes my stomach clench and turn. I'm both hungry and sick to my stomach. I'm not sure anything I eat will actually stay down, but goddammit, if I'm not willing to give it a try.

Kyrie turns on her heel and grabs a takeout container, shoveling mounds of chicken into it before stabbing a fork into the mess and waving it in my direction. "Eat this before you pass out. I've spent enough time around TacTeam operatives to know what hangry looks like, and I'm not going to be picking you up off of this floor anytime soon. Hell, I don't think I could manage it."

Oli giggles and ducks out from underneath my arm to free it up, and I scowl at Kyrie for taking her away from me. But as the smell hits my nostrils again, I can't deny that I need it.

I clear the entire tub in under a minute.

Felix's eyebrows hit his hairline, ever the physician as he starts mumbling to me about indigestion problems and the ramifications of scarfing this down so quickly. Sage pretends to make gagging noises behind her hand.

"At least take a breath in between bites," she grumbles.

I barely listen to any of them as I stalk back over to the buffet and refill the takeout container. Oli laughs along with something that Kyrie has said and walks over to join me, as though she can't stand to be any further away from me than I want her to be, grabbing more to-go containers and filling them up for the rest of our Bonded Group and our friends.

Felix grabs bags to start packing away the containers in, but all I can think about is shoveling more food into my stomach, the sickness finally easing away. When I get to my fourth helping, I finally start slowing down a little, still eating but taking breaths in between each forkful.

Kyrie raises an eyebrow in my direction. "Do I need to go and put another flock of chickens on for you? Or are you almost full, kid? Who would have thought that eating the enemy could make you hungry instead of filling you up?"

I shrug and take the bottle of water that Oli offers me, draining it in one go before I answer. "It was probably the two-day nap I took that cleared the mountain, but really, who's counting?"

When we get back to the Benson's house, I notice the tension in the air straightaway coming from Sage's newest Bonded. I don't remember Wick growing up near us, but he was one of the Lower Tier families anyway, so it makes sense. My parents weren't particularly concerned about where people ranked in our society, but the fact of the matter is that if you weren't invited to the same parties and your kids didn't go to the same schools, there just wasn't much opportunity for mingling.

He's polite enough to Oli, though he looks at Atlas and I just a little too calculatingly for my liking, as though he is assessing our every move. He's lucky he's doing it behind Oli's back or her bond would have come out by now to shut that shit right down. I share a look with Atlas, but he only shrugs, unconcerned about doing anything about it right now. He's right though, if it's not affecting our Bonded, it's just not worth chasing. If it was affecting Sage, she would have told Oli by now, I'm sure.

Sawyer and Gray both come to the table to thank us for bringing them food before getting enough for their Bonded and the small boy sitting on the couch and heading back down there to eat. There isn't enough room for all of us at the table anyways, and they all seem very comfortable in their little bubbles.

I suppose sharing a house like this has taught them how to live in close quarters without being involved in every little thing together. I am so fucking grateful we don't have to deal with that. Oli reaches out through the mind connection to see if any of the other Bonded wants something to eat, to join us or to have her deliver to them. North and Gryphon both answer her almost immediately to say they will meet us back at the house for dinner later instead.

Nox doesn't reply.

When Oli doesn't seem too concerned about it, I guess that he did so privately with her instead of to all of us, something I assume he does more often than not. Things might be going well enough between the two of them now, but Nox has never been one to be open about where he is and what he's up to. I doubt that will ever change.

For once, Atlas doesn't seem so worried about it either.

We sit through the meal together, Atlas and I watching Oli as she watches Sage who is watching Wick and Felix bicker with one another.

It's exhausting just to see.

Riley had grabbed a plate for himself and then disappeared into one of the bedrooms, still looking like a corpse, but everyone else seems less worried about it now, so I'm sure he's not about to drop dead. We make it through the entire meal and are about to start doing dishes when Nox's voice cuts through our heads.

Don't react. Don't panic or make a scene. Excuse yourselves and slowly make your way over to North's offices.

I place my hand on Oli's back as I take her plate, putting it in the dishwasher with my own as I try not to look concerned or rushed. Atlas meets my eye with a nod, moving over to Oli as we smile and make excuses for leaving already.

He checks his phone and quietly moves Oli out of the room after she gives Sage a quick squeeze and promises to call her later.

We do all of this in a matter of minutes, but it feels like hours before I'm able to take a deep breath and shoot Atlas a look without worrying that anyone else will see it. Oli ignores us both completely, reaching out to Nox within all our hearing as she finally lets the panic she's feeling show.

What's happened? I know no one's hurt, but what is it?

North sends through a soothing feeling to her, but it's Gryphon who answers the question.

Someone has arrived at the gate.

7

OLI

The Sanctuary hasn't been a secret for months now, not since the Resistance had attacked, so it's not exactly a surprise that someone has once again come calling. The surprise, however, is that when I arrive at North's offices, instead of being greeted by my Bonded, I find all three of their bonds standing there waiting for me.

Three sets of black eyes, three blank faces, and three robotic voices. All of them are beings that I am equally obsessed with, but Atlas and Gabe react to their presence about as well as can be expected.

"Oli, get behind me," Atlas says as he tries to wrestle me back, but even though he is invincible and strong enough to move a car, I'm determined. He would never do anything that could unintentionally hurt me, so I win the fight.

"Something's clearly happened if they're all out, especially North's bond. Just let me speak to them!"

Gabe looks a lot more healthy now that he has half a chicken coop and a gallon of barbeque sauce in his belly, and he merely tilts his head to the side as he takes them in. "We were just talking to the others a moment ago, why aren't they here now?"

That's a good question.

Gryphon's bond, I really need to get used to calling it the Soothsayer, answers for all of them. "We recognize the newcomer. This is best dealt with by us."

Well, that's disturbing.

I check in with my own bond, but it has nothing but joy to give me. Joy at the sight of her beloved Bonded here and ready to make war on our behalf, ready to shed blood and destroy any Gifted dumb enough to consider being a threat to us and the life that we are building here.

"Did the vessels let you come out, or was this more of a coup?" Gabe asks carefully, and North's bond, the Crux, answers him, though his eyes stay fixed on me.

"There is no *letting*. There is a god-bond outside of the gate. It's requesting entrance into this place. It is not for the vessels to deal with."

"That sounds like a 'no' to me," says Atlas with a drop

to his tone, and I wave a dismissive hand up at them.

"My bond doesn't seem too interested though. Shall we all go down there together?"

I take a step, but the Corvus stops me, a large palm fitting over my chest. I can see Atlas' reaction to this from the corner of my eye. He hates Nox, but he trusts his bond even less. It seems a little silly to me. If anything, he should trust it more.

It was always devoted to me and eager to covet and protect me.

"You might still be tired, Bonded. Maybe the Eternal should take care of this."

I hate that word coming out of Nox's mouth. I have to remind myself that it's not him saying it. I also refuse to get huffy at the Corvus for thinking such a thing. I'm sure it comes from a good place, but I shrug.

"I feel fine. And until I need it to come out, the Eternal is happy to leave it to me. We're on very good terms, you know."

The Corvus cocks his head to one side as it looks me over. I smile, reaching out for a hug, and am delighted when it lets me. Both of the very *human* Bonded behind me make unhappy noises at all of the touching. I pull back for just a moment instead, using the opportunity to get some more information.

"Which god-bond has come to see us? Is there anything

I need to know before we go down and face it?"

"We should kill it," says the Crux, and the Soothsayer shrugs.

"It's not happy that I broke the connection and it's been forced to come crawling on its own two feet instead of using what belongs to us."

Even though the words might be a little confusing, it all snaps together in my head slowly. "It's the possession one, isn't it? The one that took over Sage. It's here because we wouldn't listen to it."

All it takes is a single nod of the Corvus' head before I'm off, stalking over to the elevator and jabbing at the button. I'm ready to run down and open the gates myself to punch this god-bond square in the jaw before I rip its soul clean out, and no one will stop me from doing so.

That asshole almost destroyed my best friend, and I'm going to kill that motherfucker.

I suppose when I think of god-bonds, I think of tall and muscular men. I think of the handsome faces that surround me and the men who are so devastatingly attractive that I never stood a chance trying to keep myself and my bond away from them. I think of the paragon of beauty and grace and desire.

I certainly do not think of middle-aged men with a receding hairline and a severe underbite.

"That's really him? *That's* the guy who infiltrated Sage's head and killed Dara, who came close to ruining my best friend's life and definitely her peace of mind? I almost feel bad for wanting to punch him," I snark.

The god-bonds don't react to my words at all, but Gabe howls with laughter, clutching at his belly dramatically. "You're struggling to comprehend that he is a god-bond because he's not hot enough?"

Atlas scowls at Gabe for a second before a shit-eating grin creeps over his face, and I have to smother the urge to throw hands at the two of them.

"I'd be more concerned if you did think they were hot," Atlas snarks back, and it's weird not having one of the other three chime in. I have to remember that they're probably in there somewhere biting their tongues and waiting for the moment that they can give me hell about this.

You won't have to wait for long. Nox's voice drifts through to me, and I startle as I glance over, but his bond is still in control. We're all standing in one of the control rooms, watching the god-bond on the large monitor, everyone just waiting for something, anything, to happen.

It's making my skin itch.

Are you okay in there? I send back.

We're all fine, don't worry. I'm interested to see what

they choose to do here. There's been a lot of talk of how powerful and incredible they are but not a whole lot of substance yet. I want to know what they will do for you.

That's a little bit sweet from him, and I duck my head. Naturally, Gabe and Atlas both notice.

"It's Nox, isn't it?" Atlas says in a wary voice. "That's definitely a Nox smile."

I choke back a laugh because part of me wouldn't believe that I had a Nox smile a few months ago, but I can already feel it on my face, so I'm not going to argue with him about it.

"He's keeping an eye on everything. I don't know how much North and Gryphon can see, but he's here to watch everything."

"Well, that's what North said, wasn't it? That Nox always got along with his. I only hope that someday I can get along with mine that well," Gabe says.

"How do you get along well with a dragon?" Atlas says as we watch the monitor together, waiting for the god-bonds to make a move. It's like a very long, very intense game of chicken. Everyone is waiting for someone to do something worth reacting to.

"It only ever talks to me when Oli is around. Even then, it's just to make the claim over her. It doesn't really have opinions like the rest."

Atlas nods slowly, thinking it over, and Gabe shrugs at

him. "What's yours like? Have you spoken to it yet?"

"Mine's pretty much the same, except it doesn't like a lot of things… like people being around Oli. In the cafeteria, it pretty much wanted to try to tear everybody to pieces."

I give him a look, but Gabe chuckles under his breath. "The dragon wants to eat them. I guess I'm expecting that sort of reaction from all of them."

Atlas nods again and then turns to me. "Sweetness, what does the terrifying and cantankerous Soul Rending god-bond say to you?"

"During the day? It's sleeping. I asked a little bit to see if it wanted to come out now and deal with this situation, but it was more than happy leaving everyone else to it. It came out when I was with Gryphon's bond and Nox, but only to share the space with me," I say, color still staining my cheeks even though everybody knew exactly what was going on and they're all perfectly aware of how I spend most of my evenings with my Bonded.

I clear my throat and continue, "It mostly lets me run the show as long as I'm not in danger. I think it's letting me get comfortable with all of the god-bonds and the changes that have happened. I think maybe once things settle down a bit, we'll have to come up with some sort of *scheduling*."

The word tastes weird in my mouth, and Gabe scoffs at me again. "So you'll have the body Monday through

Wednesday one week, and then swapsies for the next?"

I groan and slap a hand over my face. "Well, I don't know! I have *no idea* how any of this works. To be honest, I don't think the god-bonds do either. I get the idea that none of us ever survived long enough to have to worry about this sort of thing. Very few vessels matched up, I know that for sure, thanks to my bond."

Atlas leans toward the monitor, staring at it a little closer as the man there cocks his head at us. It takes a second to remember that he's not staring at us the way we're staring at him. All he can see is a camera out there as he waits for us to do something.

Atlas scowls again and murmurs quietly to us both, "What things have stayed the same? Does your bond remember anything or tell you much about that sort of thing? Or is it just from Nox's research that you know about this?"

I stop for a moment and take a breath, letting whatever information I might have squirreled away in my head without really knowing it come to the forefront. I find there's a lot more there than I originally thought. "North and Nox are always brothers. Every cycle, they come together. They've always been as loyal to each other as they have been to me. I think this has been the first cycle that Nox has… struggled with that."

I'm careful with how I word that so I don't let anything

slip. I can feel Nox in my head still, and he's not reacting to anything that I've said. Clearly, I haven't stepped over any boundaries here. "The dragon takes the longest to cycle. The Cleaver usually comes alone, and the Soothsayer… the Soothsayer has come with others a few times. We've gotten close before, close enough that it gave us hope we would make it someday. That's it. That's all I've gotten. Do you guys know anything?"

Gabe takes a breath the same way that I had, like he's trying to find the secrets hidden within himself, but he shakes his head. "The dragon doesn't give me anything. It's really not interested in anything but you."

Atlas is quiet for a moment. "My god-bond is *more* this time. I can feel it flexing in my mind and coming to terms with how much more we are. I think it's because the Bonded Group has been completed. There's just no limit to the power this time."

No limit.

As the Crux finally steps forward and shadows spill from his body, taking form around us as he prepares to go down and let the god-bond in, I hope that we're right and that there is no limit.

I get the feeling we're going to need all the help we can get.

Punching the god-bond right in the jaw is just as incredible as I thought it would be, and the sound of it dislocating is like music to my ears.

I would've swung at him again, if Atlas hadn't stopped me, planting himself between me and the god-bond. The Soothsayer had taken over his mind and forced his compliance to make sure he didn't try to swing back at me, both of them disapproving of my actions in different ways.

I might be a cocky bitch at this moment, but I feel like I could take the little weasel.

The Corvus and the Crux get him moving into one of the Tac Training Center's interrogation rooms without a word between them. Even when the Soothsayer eases up the mind control to test the god-bond, it doesn't attempt to fight them or speak to them at all. It just complies as the shadows wrap around its body and move it to where we need it to go.

The hardest part is doing all of this without the entire Sanctuary knowing what's going on.

That involves telling a *very* concerned and *very* alarmed Kieran, who then involves an *incredibly* pissed-off Vivian.

I almost see why the Tac personnel are scared of him.

"And when exactly were you planning on telling us

that all of you have these eyes now," he snaps, and I throw him one of my most shit-eating grins to deflect from the 'oh dear God' of the situation.

"It was a need-to-know basis, and until we had a handle on things you just… didn't need to know. But now that we've discovered that there are more of those things out there—"

"Hold up! Things?" he asks, raising a large palm at me that instantly sets Atlas on edge, though clearly Vivian wasn't going to do anything about it.

"So we all know that my bond is a little *extra,* and it just so happens that my entire Bonded Group also has *extra* going on with their bonds."

"What the hell does extra mean, Fallows?"

"Again, you remember that there are certain rules that have to be followed when it comes to my bond? Their bonds are all the same. I highly suggest lowering your tone around me, especially with… wait, no, they're all a bit psycho about me. Anyway, I'm more than happy to have all of the conversations in the world with you about it, except we do have one of these bonds here with us, one that is capable of hacking into people's brains and forcing them to kill people. So we should probably save the chitchat for a later date."

Vivian stares at me for a second as though I'm the dumbest human being on Earth before he curses viciously under his breath and starts barking orders into his walkie-talkie, moving operatives around while Kieran gets Sawyer on the phone to have the cameras turned off.

Gabe leans over to murmur into my ear, "North and Gryphon aren't going to be happy with this."

I shrug back. "I'm not sure what exactly I'm supposed to do about it. I only told the two people that all of us trust anyway, so they're just gonna have to get over it."

Strong words that I hope I don't regret.

When we have the god-bond sitting in the interrogation room, no one in the Sanctuary any wiser, Kieran and Vivian both insist on sitting in the viewing room to watch the interaction as well. I try to persuade them to leave, but neither of them are having it.

"I don't even want *you* in there," Kieran snaps, gesturing a hand at Gryphon's black eyes. "And I'm fairly certain that Shore would also not want you in there. If North wakes up and catches wind of any of this, he's going to go on a full shadow warpath that will scorch the goddamn earth. We can toss a coin to figure out how Nox is going to feel about it."

I don't need to.

Nox is the one who told me to go and speak to Kieran and Vivian about it in the first place, but I'm being very closed-mouth about that. It does make me worry how North is going to react to all of this, enough that the tension bleeds through the mind connection, and Nox is quick to reassure me.

He's not going to be angry at you, Oleander. Whatever happens, I will deal with it. We need the god-bonds to take care of this quietly now for us. Everything else can be sorted out. If you want to be in the room with the god-bond as well, you are more than welcome. The Corvus has already assured me that he will keep you safe, and you can always take Azrael in there with you.

As more of a reassurance to Kieran than myself, I do let the shadow pup down from behind my ear, loving on him for a moment before we step into the room with the rest of my Bonded Group.

Atlas stays close to my side as always, but the god-bond is very careful about where he's looking, never once focusing on me. I feel sort of weird about it until he finally speaks.

"I mean the Eternal no harm. If it's going to be here in the room with us, please know that and refrain from killing me before you've heard what I have to say."

So it's a respect thing, I'm sure, even if it does sort of make me feel as though I'm diseased. But with one glance, I see the look on the Crux and the Soothsayer's faces right now and that sort of excuses it, because I'm not sure how either of them makes a blank face look quite so aggressive, but damn, are they good at it.

The Corvus says, "We've already heard what you have to say. You're here because your Bonded is dead. You chose the wrong side."

The god-bond cocks its head, and even though I should probably stay out of this, I find myself compelled to ask, "So, what's your name? What do you do, other than attempt to ruin a Gifted girl's life by controlling her and framing her for a murder she had nothing to do with?"

Its eyes dart around me again before it shrugs. "My vessel's name was Gene; you can call me that."

I feel an itch of irritation, but it answers me before I can snap something back. "We don't cycle here often enough to have the same sort of legacies that you do. None of us are strong enough to cycle like you. Well, you lot and Pain."

Pain.

Not very creative and easy to figure out which god-bond that is.

"So why exactly did you pick *Pain?* What did it offer you to be on its side?"

It stares at Atlas for a moment before it answers. "It offered me nothing. Pain found me after my Bonded was already dead. Instead of just killing me as well, it decided to use me. That's what happens to the small god-bonds when the others come out to play."

He sounds miserable and jaded, but I'm not going to be

so easy to fool. This could all just be a game to him, a way to gain even a tiny bit of our trust to use against us.

I won't let him hurt us.

Gabe looks at me and then says, disbelief dripping from his words, "So you were just used by the pain god to get them in here? That's it? You really think that you could come and tell us that, and we'd just help you?"

The Crux turns to look at me, its eyes bright and unreadable, but my heart skips a beat in my chest all the same. When he looks at me, I feel the same way I had back when we'd first met in that perfectly put-together bathroom. Like he's obsessed with me. Like he's waited all eternity for us to be together again, like we're two celestial beings in orbit, just waiting to finally collide.

He speaks, his voice a powerful and commanding sound. "You've come here to die. Any god-bond is a danger to my Eternal, and I won't wait for you to become a threat before I kill you."

I get all sorts of fluttery feelings at him calling me *his* Eternal.

The god-bond turns to look at me finally before it answers with a new tone to his voice, one laced with respect and deference. "You've helped me once before. I was hoping you'd remember that and help me again. If I'm wrong and I die… Well, I guess I'll just remember that for the next life."

8

As we step out of the Tac Training Center together, I look back over my shoulder at the building with a sense of longing. I still haven't had the chance to really speak to North since we returned from the Wastelands, and other than the threesome with the Soothsayer, I've barely seen Nox as well.

I haven't even spoken to Gryphon except for the small debrief on the morning after, and it had been more of a moment to bask in each other, not exactly a check-in.

I miss my Bonded.

I know that we're so close to the end of the fighting and our time away from each other, but I can't help the ache in my chest that comes with being away from them. I also don't envy them for the conversations they're now being forced to have with Vivian about their god-bonds.

I was expecting them to be more upset at how we had been pushed to deal with things, but the moment that his void eyes had cleared, North had immediately begun a debrief with the older man. He accepts that this is the way that things are now, and there is no use in hiding this fact from him.

I doubt we're going to be burned at the stake in this lifetime.

I'm stupid enough to say this out loud to Gabe and Atlas and both of them scowl at me.

"Do you remember that? Do you actually have memories of it, or are you talking more in a hypothetical sense right now?" Gabe asks, and I shrug.

"I remember it, just sort of in a way that I also know it's not really my memories. It's something that my bond has brought with it that I am now the holder of. Does that make sense?"

"Does any of this make sense?" Atlas says with a groan, threading his fingers through mine as he directs me back through the Sanctuary towards our house.

We had left Sage's house this morning on foot, and I can tell that Atlas is frustrated at how slow we're moving, especially when a group of people spill out of the dining hall and change the direction they're walking the moment they spot us coming.

I'm not expecting much out of my own bond, so when it picks up in my chest to get my attention, I almost stumble over my own feet.

We need to go hunting, it says. I let my eyes slip shut for a moment, trusting Atlas to keep me on my feet while I speak with it.

Where and what sort of hunting? You give me a time and a place, and I'll make it happen.

My bond purrs happily in my chest at my easy acceptance of what it wants to do. I think it was expecting me to put up a fight, but we're beyond that now. The memory of what had happened in the past, of the atrocities that we had been doomed to endure time and time again, has been more than enough to convince me to switch to the offensive.

The Sanctuary is here to keep everyone safe and has done an amazing job of that so far, but the only true way to keep us and our god-bonds safe is to get rid of the threats altogether.

Our Bonded are finding out where they're hiding. We must go to them as soon as we know and take care of the situation.

I nod my head, which makes me feel kind of dumb, but Atlas and Gabe both meet my eyes when I open them back up.

"Hunting. All of us together, or are we going to let the gods take over for this?" Atlas asks, and Gabe groans as he rubs a hand over his face.

"I would like to keep the dragon under wraps for as long as I can. There's no way I want to deal with the indigestion and naps so soon after the last bout."

I wince a little, shooting him a sheepish look. "I think we should go there ourselves and be prepared for the god-bonds to take over if they need to. There's every chance that whoever we're facing might be too much for us to handle."

Atlas nods and scratches at the back of his head, glaring around at the Sanctuary as though he's expecting someone to come bursting out of the bushes towards us. He shouldn't worry so much about it. People are still running in the opposite direction at the mere sight of us, especially when we're grouped together like this.

"The problem here is that they've all been awake longer than us, right? Everyone except you and the Dravens, at least. That's why they're stronger than us. Shouldn't we be laying low until we have a better rapport with them all?"

I shake my head at him. "No, because they've Bonded. Our Bond is complete. I think that cancels that power growth out."

I shut my eyes again and check that with my bond.

It agrees wholeheartedly.

No one is stronger than us now. We can wipe them off the face of the earth and live out our lives at the pinnacle of power like the gods that we are.

Okay, that sounds a *little* bit more villainous than I would like to be dealing with this morning… When I open my eyes back up, both of my Bonded are grinning at me.

Gabe says, chuckling under his breath, "Do you think we'll ever get used to the way they speak? What are we going to do once we've gotten rid of all the threats and we just have these angry, murderous god-bonds living inside us? What are we going to use to distract them?"

We turn down the small path towards our house, which is further away from the rest of the Sanctuary and its inhabitants, and Atlas slides his palm down my back until he gets a handful of my ass. "I think we can distract them in other ways."

I scoff back at him. "So a giant orgy, twenty-four-seven, to stop them from ending the world? That doesn't sound exhausting at all."

Gabe's chuckles turn into full-blown belly laughs. "I'm willing to give it a go if you are, Bonded. I think that sort of makes us superheroes in this situation."

"Right. *So* selfless," I throw back at him, shaking my head at both of them.

Gabe and Atlas spend the afternoon finishing off Atlas' bathroom, and I spend some time organizing the mess that is my closet. It's nowhere near the top of my priority list, not with the million other things relating to god-bonds, Bonded Groups, and my own Bonded being busy and away from me for hours of the day, but it's a good distraction to keep me from going crazy over everything.

My own bond is pretty pissed off about it until I start packing a go-bag, one with enough Tac uniforms, underwear, and weapons to get me through a full week of traveling and hunting. It gets on board with that plan pretty damn quickly.

I only had two good pairs of boots, and one of them had been destroyed in the fighting at the Wasteland. I add that to my mental list of things to sort out before we head off, then I go through the clothes that I have permanently borrowed from my Bonded. I have to work out what I need to give back to them and what I need to move back into rotation.

I'm not being kind or generous at all in handing things back. Most of the sweaters have lost the scents of my Bonded because I've worn them so much myself. This isn't exactly a fashion choice I'm making.

If they don't smell like them, I don't want them.

I let Brutus down from behind my ear to play amongst the piles of clothing as he keeps me company. It's nice to have a moment to myself to get my head back together. By the time I hear the front door open and the murmuring of men returning home, I once again feel settled in my own skin.

We have a mission, a plan, something to work towards, and I'm going to harness the killing energy within me to keep my entire community and my Bonded Group safe.

That has to be enough for me.

It's certainly enough for the god within me.

When I get out to the hallway, intent on finding my Bonded and spending the evening with them all, I bump into Nox as he makes his way down to his bedroom. He has a frown on his face and a distracted look in his eyes, so I'm prepared to walk on past him with nothing more than a smile. He surprises me though, when he catches me in his arms and pulls me in close, pressing me into his chest until I'm fighting to breathe.

It's still a wondrous thing to me that he touches me like this.

"We got more information out of that god-bond. I'm just getting my research papers, and we will discuss it over dinner."

With my heart in my throat, I nod and lean forward

slowly to kiss him, giving him the opportunity to pull away if he wants to. Even now that we've Bonded, I'm aware that he may need space. I'm not going to be the type to push him even if he's the type to push me over and over and over again.

My bond hums happily in my chest when he not only meets my kiss but takes it over, pulling me in further to his embrace before he sets my feet on the ground and turns back to his room to gather what he needs.

I feel a little breathless, like my legs don't really want to work properly anymore, and I stumble back out to the kitchen, ignoring the shit-eating grin that Gabe shoots my way.

"Not a word," I snark at him, and he lifts a hand to cross a finger over his heart like the cheeky asshole that he is.

He's still covered in tile glue and dust, leaving behind a trail of debris as he moves around the kitchen. The savage look that North shoots him has me biting down a smile.

"We have time for you to go and clean up. We're not going to rush into anything here," North snaps. Gabe merely nods his head, as calm and good-natured as ever.

I might just be the best Bonded in the world, because I duck into the councilman's arms to distract him from his moody warpath. I sigh the moment that the warm, clean scent of him envelops me. I really do need to steal some more of his clothing if he's going to be working long hours away from me again.

He frames my face in both of his palms and presses our foreheads together as he murmurs quietly under his breath, "You look tired, my Bonded. Maybe we should leave this until tomorrow."

I wrap my arms around his waist and press my lips against his, enjoying the feeling of being completely wrapped up in him. "I'm fine. I just miss you, but I don't need anything."

He nods and runs his thumbs over my cheeks as though he is reacquainting himself with the softness of my skin. "Once we have a plan put together, we will take some time off, Bonded. I'll let the council deal with themselves. Then we can get to making this house our own instead of just a drop-off zone."

I'm not sure any of us can handle North diving into full nesting mode, not after hearing Gabe's story of having to rip up perfectly good tiles because they didn't quite meet North's expectation. Not that Gabe had done anything wrong, but North had snapped something about colors looking different on monitors and the wrong shade of stone being used. All of that is endlessly confusing for me but something that everyone else seems to accept without a word, so I leave it alone.

I step away from North and head over to the dining

table, giving Gryphon a quick peck on the lips as I take a seat next to him. I enjoy the way he tucks me into his side immediately, as though there is nowhere else at the table I could possibly belong but next to him.

"I picked up dinner on the way back. North convinced the chef to make fish tacos tonight."

The look of pure, unadulterated love that I beam at my Bonded has everyone cackling around me. Just to shit-stir them all a little bit more, I say, "Marry me, Bonded."

As expected, the bickering starts up immediately, all of them talking shit to North about having access to the chef and his meal plan as a form of seduction for me. It doesn't die down until Nox appears back in the kitchen with his arms full of books and papers.

"I've got it. This is everything I have collected about the gods. We can cross-reference everything that the god-bond said with this."

North stares at the papers for a moment before opening up a cupboard and pulling out a large bottle of whiskey and three cups.

It might just be a long night.

It seems as though North wants to deal with this situation just about as much as the rest of us do, which is not at all. I recognize all of the papers that Nox puts down in front of everyone from our soul-connection, all of the information already in my head if I should need it, so when he doesn't hand any of it to me, I am not bothered at all.

Atlas is very bothered on my behalf.

"Shouldn't we be giving this to *everyone* so that we can all have a look at it, including Oli and her bond?"

Nox gestures down to the empty piece of table in front of himself. "Oli and I know everything that's in it. There's no point in us staring at the pages when we can get a fresh set of eyes on it instead."

I reach under the table and squeeze Atlas' leg as a small thank-you for jumping in but also a reassurance that I don't actually need it. Nox and I haven't just found neutral ground, we've found a space for just the two of us that I might even call love. I mean, I know that *I* love him. And I know that, as much as he's capable of that feeling, he has it for me, and that's enough. It's more than I ever hoped for, more than I ever thought I would get to share with him.

"A Pain god, a Neuro god, and an Elemental god. Fucking hell, that's like the worst types of Gifted from the Resistance all over again," Gabe says with a groan, and Atlas shoots a wry grin his way.

"This is the final boss level. We've worked our way up to dealing with the biggest and baddest assholes."

I shake my head at their antics, swearing that I won't let either of them go and play video games with Sawyer ever again if this is what we have to deal with, but North is ignoring most of the chatter at the table as he stares at the list of names.

"How did you come up with this?" North asks before lifting a glass of whiskey to his lips and downing the whole lot in one go.

I didn't think the list was that serious, at least, not the type of serious that we have to drown in the bottom of a whiskey bottle.

"There are markers for the gods, clues that a person is a vessel, and I had already started compiling a list before we spoke to the gods."

North nods and glances at Atlas. "You haven't seen the list yet, have you?"

Atlas scowls back and squints in his direction before it hits me.

Athena Bassinger is on the list.

Atlas groans and shoves his face in his hands. "Is there ever going to be a time when my family isn't fucking us over?"

I desperately, *desperately* want to fuss over him, to hold him and reassure him that it's okay, that none of us blame him or think differently of him for all of these connections that he has. However, I don't think he would take it very well with the rest of the Bonded Group watching.

The fact of the matter is that he's already copped a fair amount of grief for his relation to that woman. It was always the first thing anyone brought up, though I've never questioned it before.

Nox doesn't need to be able to read my mind to know where my thoughts have gone. "Athena Bassinger is the face of the East Coast Gifted. She pretends that they're not all just Resistance supporters. Whenever something happens that requires liaising, she's the one they send."

"Her Gift is Manipulation," Atlas says, grinding the palms of his hands into his eyes as though he can wipe all of this away if he presses hard enough.

"She's a Neuro, but it's different from what Gryphon can do. It's closer to what Emmeline could do," North says very carefully, and my blood runs cold at the mention of that woman's name.

I very pointedly do not look at Nox, because North and Gryphon might be completely aware of the situation but Gabe and Atlas are not. I've already sworn to myself that I will not be the person who breaks Nox's trust in this way. I do, however, open up the mind connection to him.

I don't send him any feelings or reassurances. I just open it up so he knows that I'm with him no matter what comes from this conversation. It doesn't surprise me when he shuts down, but it's not the way that he used to. He doesn't start slinging vitriol and viciousness at everyone, but instead, he immediately becomes a blank slate.

Atlas glances around, noticing the shift in the mood, and he speaks with care. "I don't know who that is, but

Athena is not someone that I want to be dealing with without backup. If those markers are things that you think implies she has a god-bond as well, I would *definitely* not be dealing with her without the entire Bonded Group present."

The part that he fails to tack onto the end there is that we'll also need to be whole enough to deal with her, which Nox does not look like right now, even to the untrained eye. I can feel some tension beginning to build in him. I can feel the way that he's pulling himself together and preparing to face an echo of the monster from his past.

My bond does not like the way that he is acting.

My bond wants to hunt Athena down and eat her alive for causing this pain.

My bond might just not take no for an answer.

9

ATLAS

The plan is simple.

We're going back to my parents' house and tearing the place apart until we find something that proves that Nox's theory about Athena having a god-bond is correct.

The very idea of stepping foot back into that house makes me want to vomit, but I work hard at keeping all of that off of my face. I know that I have succeeded when no one questions me about it. Not even my Bonded.

If it were anything else but this, I might get a little offended that she hadn't noticed that I was losing it, but there's too much riding on all of this for petty squabbling in our Bonded Group about my ego. Too much of the danger that we have faced has been from my own bloodline, and the idea of *any* of us facing Athena is already something that turns my stomach.

I hadn't spent a huge amount of time with the woman, but I know enough about her. My mother did not like her or the power that she wields, and she'd done her best to keep me away from her. The few times she had visited my father were enough to prove to me, especially now in hindsight, that none of the Bassingers are good people. They aren't just flawed human beings, but selfish, self-serving Gifted who enjoy the power of having Top Tier Gifts and the type of wealth that people can only dream about.

I had been a spoiled little shit as a kid too, and I credit my Bonded with saving me from turning into one of those assholes. The moment I had clicked on that video on my mother's computer and found Oli chained to a torture table by Silas fucking Davies, the trajectory of my life had changed completely. One look at her and I was a changed man. One look at her and I knew that I would do whatever it takes to protect her and give her the life that she deserves, one in which she would never feel that sort of pain ever again, and certainly not at the hands of my family.

The sins of the Bassingers are plentiful and I hope that my devotion to my Bonded is enough to cancel a bit of that bad juju out.

North and Gryphon make arrangements for us to leave in the early hours of the morning. Everyone disappears to get some rest and get their things packed together before we leave. On instinct, I follow my Bonded back to her room.

I already have a go-bag packed at all times, the same as Gryphon and the Dravens, and I'm pleasantly surprised when I find one sitting in Oli's closet already. We're not supposed to be staying overnight anywhere, but it never hurts to be prepared.

She heads straight into the bathroom to brush her teeth, and when I'm busy rinsing out my mouth, she finally speaks. "We can talk about it if you want to, but we also don't have to do anything. You don't owe me an explanation just because I'm your Bonded."

My heart swells in my chest, and I take my time wiping my face so that I don't make a fool of myself. Of course she noticed, and of course she tiptoed around me and my feelings. If anyone understands trauma, it's Oleander Fallows.

"I don't want any of them touching you. I hate the idea of you walking into that house. One of those things I can do something about and the other one, I have to get over," I say in a monotone voice, but Oli just nods back to me.

"I didn't want to do it either. I'm much more interested in finding another camp and burning it to the ground, to be honest, but I guess it doesn't count as working to wipe out the Resistance if we're only doing the things we want to do.

I know that, but it doesn't make it any easier to stomach."

I let my hands tangle in her hair, tipping her head back and enjoying the way her mouth drops open instantly, ready for whatever it is I want to give her. There are dark shadows under her eyes from her night of keeping the god-bonds happy, and as much as I had joked around with her this afternoon, I'm not going to make any demands of my Bonded tonight.

I'd rather spend it with her tucked up in my arms and listening to the steady beat of her heart, knowing that everything I do, everything I sacrifice and am forced to face, even when I would rather not, is to keep that heart of hers beating. It has to be enough.

When our feet land on the street outside of the brownstone I had spent the first nineteen years of my life living in, a sense of dread fills my body. Five stories, sixteen bedrooms, enough bathrooms to drown a football team, three kitchens, an entire conference room that has heard far too many atrocities of the Resistance, and hundreds of millions of dollars' worth of cars and motorcycles parked in the underground garage. It's a classic design, impeccably maintained, and the envy of the entire street. There's a plaque on the front with my family's name on it, shining and bright where one of our dozens of staff polishes it with brass cleaner. Everything about it screams privilege and the type of wealth that cannot run dry. The dread turns to ice in my belly.

I never wanted to come back here.

It was never in my plans to see this place again, and I'm still numb at the fact that I've been forced to come. The moment I had left to find Oli, to steal her away to another country to escape everything that my parents were doing, was one of the best moments of my life. I had broken free of my name and the expectations on me. I had made my stance clear, even though my mother did everything she could to hide that fact from my father and the other elite members of the Resistance.

Now, staring up at the door, I want to vomit.

It was only days ago that we had buried my parents' Bonded Group, and I still haven't had enough time to process all of the feelings I have about that. It's too fucking confusing, and I feel a lot of shame for it all. Grief for my mother, the woman who birthed and raised me, isn't as easy as it should be because I'm also well aware that the woman was a monster. Not to me, of course, and in a lot of ways, she saved my Bonded… She's, without a doubt, the reason Oli is alive today, but these were not acts of virtue. They were things that she did for her own purposes. Self-serving, with motives I would rather not think about anymore.

I still haven't told my sister they're dead.

I don't know if North has either, or one of the others, though I secretly hope that it wasn't Nox who went down to the cells to tell Aurelia.

My feelings about her are just as confusing as my grief.

Are you alright? Oli sends through our mind connection to me as she tucks her hand into mine.

She stares up at the building with me, a vague look of disgust on her face that makes me want to kiss the hell out of her. "It's even bigger than the Dravens' mansion, and I didn't think that was possible. How the hell do people get this type of money?"

Evil and nefarious deeds.

I chuckle under my breath, but it's more of a broken sound than a joyful one. Gabe slaps a hand on my shoulder as he tries to lighten the mood. "It's exactly what I expected it to look like. Promise me there's a gold toilet in there somewhere. We should make a game to see who can find it first."

Oli scoffs under her breath. "I'm not leaving your side in there. It has nothing to do with protection. There's absolutely *no way* that I'm going to be able to find my way back out, and we all know it. My sense of direction in these sorts of houses is absolutely atrocious. I refuse to take the blame though, no one needs a house this freaking big!"

I raise our joined hands up to my lips so I can kiss the back of hers, grateful that her sass and snark is out in full force to distract me. She always has been far too good at noticing the pain and torment of others. It's something she's picked up from her own trauma. I hate that she has that ability, but I'm also grateful for it right now.

A dark cloud sweeps in under our feet and then slowly materializes until August is standing between Oli's legs, its head rubbing against her thigh as the creature stares up at her with strangely liquid eyes. Without a sound, it's clear that it's begging silently for pets, and my Bonded doesn't hesitate to shower it with love.

She giggles and scratches behind its ear, letting go of my hand briefly to let Brutus down to stand up at his brother's side. It hits me when I look down at them that I no longer feel the rage and jealousy I once did. It also hits me, though, that I can finally admit that some of what I felt *was* jealousy.

Jealousy that maybe my Bonded preferred the Dravens, that maybe these special little creatures that they assigned to watch over her might endear her to them a little more than to me.

Those feelings are gone now.

I want both of them to survive this as much as I want myself to. We all need to survive this for her. The gods have made that clear. How close we'd come to losing Nox and opening ourselves up to another lifetime of destruction, death, and pain… Well, my hands shake at the thought of it. The Cleaver has been very clear with me the few times we've spoken, and I've been sure to listen.

We *all* need to survive.

"The mission is simple—kill everyone on sight," Nox says as he pulls the gaiter up over his mouth.

North shoots him a pointed look and adds, "Let your bonds decide if we're facing a god in there or not. If we are, kill first and ask questions later. If they're Gifted, we should probably see what they have to say first."

I nod, pulling my own gaiter up over my nose, more as a way to hide my face than as protection. Oli does the same as she tucks her hand firmly back into mine. The shadow puppies begin to play at her feet, bouncing around excitedly as they prepare to charge into the building and consume whoever we come across. I feel a lot better having them here with us, knowing she has even more protection than just what I can offer her.

Gabe's hands flex at his side, and he leans in to murmur quietly to Oli, "How are you feeling? Should we leave some for you to take care of and boost your energy?"

I can't believe I didn't think of that myself.

I glance down, but Oli simply rolls her shoulders back, tilting her head to one side and then the other as she stretches out her neck. "I'm feeling okay. I think we're better off trying to take survivors with us. My bond seems to think that there's a god-bond around here somewhere. If not, we need to know where it's gone. Surely someone in there knows *something.*"

I give her a curt nod, and then we wait until Gryphon and Kieran take the lead before following them up the steps. North and Nox taking up the rear, their palms coated in black and shadow creatures everywhere. The air around us is thick with them as the Bonded Group moves as one. Time to test if it's true.

If, together, we really are unstoppable.

Gryphon's voice comes through the mind connection clearly to us all, *The staff are still in the house, and there are at least three Top Tier Gifted here as well.*

He sends through the mind patterns of the Gifted in there. Strangely, I can tell who at least one of them is. It's impossible to explain, but even the way the man is thinking is instantly recognizable to me.

I suddenly realize just how powerful and terrifying Gryphon's gift truly is.

That's one of my sister's Bonded Group. One of the men that she was sold off to, I mean, not her actual Bonded. He won't have a god-bond in him, but I suggest we kill him.

Oli glances up at me with a questioning look, and I sigh as I send through the mind connection to everyone, *he probably has information that would be helpful, so we should take him in alive. But he's also an abusive dickhead who was happy to beat the woman he recognized as his Bonded, so don't feel like getting him there in one piece is necessary. A few chunks missing would be a better option.*

From the corner of my eye, I can see Gabe's lip curl in disgust, and for the first time, it doesn't fill me with guilt or any sort of self-loathing.

I don't feel like I'm a Bassinger anymore.

I'm Atlas, one of Oleander Fallows' Bonded, a part of the Draven Bonded Group.

I'm no longer sitting on the sidelines, watching all of this go on. These people are merely a chapter in my life that I have long-since closed the door on, and none of them mean anything to me.

I'm better than any of them could ever hope to be.

Oli wasn't exaggerating—my parents' house really does make the Draven mansion look like a cozy bungalow. As we step into the foyer, I feel a ripple of disgust run through my body. It's as though this isn't just a mental thing, I'm physically repulsed by this place. We need to get this over with, fast.

The decor and furnishings loudly ensure that anyone who enters this place knows that my parents are rich assholes.

Were.

My brain still hasn't adjusted to the past tense yet.

Looking at my father's portraits everywhere leaves me feeling empty, but my mother's portraits give me that same weird mixture of guilt and grief, all of it swirling deep inside me.

We come to a halt, and Oli stands quietly until Gryphon and Nox both motion that we're clear before she points out a small collection of my school photos that are framed and displayed on one of the countertops.

She's grinning at the dumb-ass hair cut that I had in third grade, and I will never stop being grateful for the way that she can read a situation and defuse it, taking the uncomfortable and exposing trip back here and turning it into more of a sightseeing mission than something I need to feel shame over.

I roll my eyes at her when she stalks over to the photos, cracking the frames open and slipping a few of them into the front of her Tac vest to take home with us. I groan when I see which ones she's picked out, but she just shrugs and murmurs to me quietly, "I don't have any baby photos. Nox has very few as well. I think we need to keep the ones that we do have access to."

I could question why a Draven wouldn't have baby photos and why only one of the brothers is missing them, but the more time I spend in our Bonded Group, the more settled and accepting I've become.

We don't ask questions about Nox. We don't question

the things that don't quite add up, and though I started off ready to light that asshole up at the drop of a hat, things have changed, whether I want to accept it or not. I've never seen my Bonded so happy. There really isn't any denying that even with the Bonded Group complete, having Nox rejecting a real relationship with her had left a gaping hole within her, one that I couldn't do anything to fix. I'm not willing to risk her getting harmed in any way, but he does seem to have mellowed out.

Whatever happened in that soul-bond was a powerful thing.

Gryphon steps around the corner and nods his head at North before we all get the signal to make our way downstairs. I suppose the fun and frivolity couldn't last for long, and I step forward with a sigh. I know I'm being a little too fucking dramatic about this, but no one seems to give a shit, they're all just getting on with it while giving me the space to just… fucking hate this whole thing.

I slip my hand into Oli's again and move her through the building. I don't need Gryphon's mapping of the bodies in the building to know where the staff are. I also know where the Dravens really want to go in this place. Not only that, but I know I have to get us there without sounding every alarm in the building. Not that any of them would go off, thanks to Sawyer hacking into the entire system remotely from the safety of the Sanctuary, but I still think it's best to give us every element of surprise that we can.

I can tell how badly Oli has to bite her tongue as I slide the paneling in the hallway to one side to take the servant's stairs. Gabe's eyebrows hit his hairline as he steps through behind us. The Dravens don't look very surprised, obviously used to this sort of wealth themselves, but Gryphon rolls his eyes so hard that they nearly roll straight out of his head.

Fucking Bassingers, he sends through the mind connection, shooting me a grin. Oli has to slap a hand over her mouth to stop herself from giggling.

It lifts the mood a little, shifting this from the shitty experience of having to face my demons into something that we're doing together as a group, my new family coming to clean the house of my old one. The one I was born into but have chosen to no longer belong to.

Maybe I'll take Oli's last name.

Bonded Groups have always picked and chosen whether or not they've shared last names, changed them, kept them the same, or sometimes they pick something new altogether. Whatever works for each individual family, and I never put much thought into it until this moment.

Atlas Fallows sounds a hell of a lot better than Atlas Bassinger ever did.

We make our way down until we're below ground level in the vaults underneath the brownstone. The air feels different down here. Colder, thicker, more oppressive—as though it is trying to sap every last bit of energy straight out of your body.

It's also riddled with security that I'm sure had Sawyer cursing every last one of my ancestors as he had to disable it to get us here without any of the cavalry showing up. Even though my family have been killed by their own and marked as traitors, there's a huge wealth of knowledge hidden under here, enough to incriminate the entire East Coast. I'm sure there are plans in place to move it all out of here. There's no doubt in my mind that's what the Gifted are here doing.

I hold my hand up to show that we are getting closer to the end of the hallway, and Nox flicks out his hand, sending his shadows bounding ahead of us as they shrink in size until they are nothing more than a smudge, something that you can convince yourself is merely a trick of the light.

North's arms are crossed over his chest as he stands next to Nox and watches him work. The two of them may share the same Gift, but they use it very differently. Nox's shadows obey his every whim, but North's are a chaotic and consuming mess, a complete juxtaposition of who they are as men.

I hear a strangled yelp and then thudding as three bodies hit the ground.

Gryphon's eyes flash to black as he calls on his Gift.

For a moment, I think that the Soothsayer has joined us, but then he speaks, this time out loud. "They're taken care of. We can go in and get whatever we need before we take them back to the interrogation cells."

I take a deep breath, and then I do something I was never expecting to.

I turn to Nox. "If Sawyer can crack into the computers, I can get you into the database for the Resistance information. Anything and everything they have ever compiled will be in there. It's basically a wet dream of information for you. If you want it, I will give it all to you."

And that is how Nox and I find common ground in the basement of my parents' brownstone, for the sake of my Bonded, because her safety is everything to me.

10

OLI

If I didn't already think that Atlas' upbringing was exorbitant and spoiled as fuck, seeing his house seals the deal. He'd casually opened up a wall to enter a set of stairs hidden in it, weird and freaking creepy in my opinion, and then he'd led us down to the basement as though it was all nothing. I wouldn't have believed that houses like this really exist, and now I'm in a Bonded Group with *three* men brought up with this sort of wealth.

Hell, I'm sure the other two have mansions in their families too. I just don't want to think about that right now though.

We'd found one of his sister's Bonded, the last one left alive and free, and two other Gifted in here. They were attempting to hack into the computer systems and purge any information that might be incriminating to them, and to find extortion material on other high-ranking Resistance members. The moment we'd stepped around the corner to find them wrapped in shadows, their eyes glowing white as Gryphon's Gift manipulated their brains into complete compliance for us, I'd had the air knocked out of me at the sight of the archives down here.

Atlas hadn't been wrong, Nox is jizzing himself over all of this and, sure enough, he stalks past everything else in the room as he makes his way over to the large stacks of archive boxes and a huge pile of computer equipment. I can't even begin to guess what half of that stuff is, but I'm sure the power bill here alone would be enough to make a grown man weep.

North gets on the phone with Sawyer immediately, gesturing to Kieran once North has confirmed it can't be done remotely, and the Transporter *pops* out of the room to go and collect our mouthy Technokinetic.

Gabe leans down to murmur to me, "We should make bets on which one of them is going to nut themselves over this first, because my money is on Benson."

Atlas throws him a look over his shoulder. "Are you looking at the same Draven I am right now? There's no way that computers will do that much for Sawyer."

My eyes drift over to Nox and get stuck on him as he

starts tearing boxes open, leafing through the pages there and making piles as he begins to categorize them. He's methodical about it, taking photos on his phone before he touches anything. It's as though he is a fussy, old librarian making sure that none of us are going to fuck with the cataloging system.

"None of us would dare to approach him as he works. I like my head exactly where it is, and I have no intention of having it ripped off my shoulders," Gryphon drawls as I sidle up to him.

"You're reading my mind again," I say as I tuck my hand in his, but he just shrugs at me.

"I don't need to know what you're thinking. This is going to take forever, but it's best if Nox does it for himself. North might be able to help, but I've also seen Nox tear him a new asshole for doing it wrong, so it looks as though Kieran's just gonna be Transporting all day today."

I can only guess at how his second would react to that news, but it has me grinning anyway.

I glance down at the Gifted at our feet, but their faces are still blank. I don't recognize any of them, but the dirty looks Atlas keeps throwing at one of them makes it easy to figure out which one had been the abusive dick to his sister.

If killing hundreds of people wasn't already going to send me to hell, I am pretty sure my boot stomping on the fucker's hand and snapping it underneath the thick heel might be enough to get me there.

Gabe roars with laughter as Atlas smirks at me, his eyebrows raised when I shoot him a sheepish grin. I turn to North to find him staring at me like he's never seen me before. I send him a sweet, flirtatious smile as I shrug.

I would lie and say that my bond made me do it, but there's a literal lie detector in the room, so instead I say, "I'm sick of fully grown men thinking that they can hurt the women around them without consequences. My only regret here is that he's not coherent enough to know who did it to him and why."

Gryphon clamps one of his big palms on the back of my head to gently pull me towards him, smacking a big kiss on my forehead as he mutters to me, "I'll make sure he knows, Bonded. Don't worry about that. I'll make sure they all know."

Kieran pops back into the room with an armful of Sawyer, snapping at him the moment his feet touch the ground. "You really should stop being a fucking pussy about this!"

Sawyer is immune to anyone's censure, that shit just bounces straight off of the asshole. "I'm no use to anyone if I'm dead, dickhead! Setting up a remote working bug isn't even that fucking hard! It would've taken me three minutes to figure out how to do it, and then I wouldn't have had to come here! I told you guys that the Wastelands was the last time I was doing it. I'm not built for camping."

I gesture around the room at him with a snarky smile. "No one's camping here. Besides, if we had to, we could just sleep in one of the rooms upstairs. This place is practically a fucking castle. It's not like you would have been roughing it."

Atlas snaps at us both, "No one is sleeping here. We're going home."

All of the fun and games fizzle right out of me, but before I can get too far into my own head about overstepping, Nox calls out, "Black, you need to start Transporting these back to North's offices. Lock them in the safe there as you go. No, *not* that one. Use your eyes, they're clearly in piles! You need to take them in order, starting with that one. *That* one, Black! Prove to me that you have a functioning brain here."

Atlas chuckles under his breath, and I bite down on the smile trying to form on my lips. Sawyer, ever the ass, bursts out laughing as he gets himself settled in front of the computer.

Nox starts really getting into a mood about everything, and Gryphon gives my hand one last squeeze before he goes off to Kieran's rescue. He snaps at Nox to settle down before calling Atlas and Gabe over to help as well, each of them lifting as many boxes in their hands as they can. They keep them perfectly in the order that Nox needs them to be as Kieran Transports the three of them in one trip.

I feel as though I should be helping with that, but when I offer, North shakes his head at me, gesturing me over to stand with him instead. I'm secretly grateful. If Nox snapped at me like he is at the others, we'd either end up in a screaming mess of vitriol and rage... or I'd cry.

I'm leaning towards the rage, though.

It's almost a surprise to me that Gryphon's Gift keeps the prisoners under our control even as he Transports in and out of the house, but the Soothsayer's words still bounce around in my mind. *There is nothing we cannot do now that we are all Bonded. We are unstoppable together.*

Maybe the gods are right, maybe we will all survive this.

North's shadows are thick in the room, helping Nox's with the surveillance while his younger brother is focused so heavily on the piles of information, and I find August sitting at my feet as I come to stop behind Sawyer at the computer. He's dressed head to toe in Tac gear, standard procedure for coming out in the field, but I still have to contain the smirk that threatens to spread across my face at the sight of him.

He used to play football, so he's not exactly a small guy, but I've spent so many months seeing him in sweatpants in front of a computer now that I've forgotten that he's capable of this sort of thing. I still feel sorry for Aro as his smart mouth starts to run.

"You guys need to get Bassinger into some fucking therapy, because this is just the tip of the iceberg of the Resistance propaganda, and it's psychotic. The boy definitely has some demons hiding somewhere in his head."

I scowl at him, but North pops him on the back of the head before I get the chance to come to my Bonded's defense. "Worry less about what's happening in my Bonded Group and more about how you can get all of this to the Sanctuary as quickly as possible. I'm sure those three aren't the only ones who want access to all of this."

Sawyer rubs a hand over the sore spot and grumbles under his breath, "It's already being transferred. You know, you could be slightly nicer to me. I was planning on spending the day with my Bonded, not cleaning up after this bullshit."

I sidle up to him and bump his shoulder with my hip in a friendly gesture, except I do it a little too hard because of his shit-talking to my Bonded Group. "You were planning on spending the day sitting in your living room playing video games in your underwear. Don't lie. Being productive for an hour isn't going to kill you."

He gasps at me dramatically, pressing a hand against his chest, though his eyes stay glued to the computer screen in front of him. "Knock on some wood, Fallows, I'm not having you curse me right now. I'm worth my weight in gold, you know. The rest of you barely know how to open a laptop, for fuck's sake."

I know a bit more than that, and North and Nox are both well adept at technology, but I let it slide as I shift down onto my haunches to scratch August behind the ears and love on him a little. He presses his head into my shoulder, his tongue lolling out of his mouth as he enjoys the scratches I give him. When Sawyer makes the sound of disgust at my loving, I amp it up even more.

"Sage told me she saw that thing eat like a hundred people in the Wastelands, and you're sitting there telling it how much you lovey-wovey it? That's fucking creepy, Fallows. Honestly. You should tone it down a little."

I shake my head at him and talk to August as though he hasn't spoken. "Should we get the others out? Should we play with the snake for a little while and let it test out the room too? It's been such a long time."

"Draven, if you get the snake out for her, I swear on my Bond's life, I will be out of this room so fucking fast, none of you will even know which direction I left in," Sawyer says in a panicked tone, a tremble to his voice that makes me cackle like a witch.

North shoots him a glare and snaps, "Just finish it."

Then he shoots me a look, one that is much kinder than

his glare at Sawyer. "Later, Bonded. You can play with the shadows when we get home. They're needed here right now."

I want nothing more than to play with every inch of that man—it's been too damn long. My bond also wants him and the shadows, everything, and I have to bury my face in August's neck to stop them all from seeing the color as my cheeks heat. North speaks to me directly, blocking the others out as he amps me up even more.

Later, Bonded. I'll give you everything you want.

They're on the fourth trip ferrying boxes back and forth to the Sanctuary, and I'm busy looking over Sawyer's shoulder at the goldmine of information on the computer screen, when there's a crash.

Nox snaps viciously, "What the fuck are you doing, Shore?"

I look over to see that Gryphon has dropped the boxes that he was holding to take back to the Sanctuary. When I get a look at his face, I find that his eyes have shifted to black and his features have gone blank as the Soothsayer takes control of the vessel.

Everyone goes dead still for a second, and then I hear Sawyer gulp.

"What the fuck is that!?" he questions, drawing the words out too slowly as he goes stock-still, as though any little movement will trigger the god-bond into a murderous rampage in his direction.

It must be survival instinct, something so ingrained in him that he isn't aware that he even has it. Still, it's weird to see the cocky Technokinetic act in such a way. Even when he's been worried about the Dravens' shadows, he hasn't acted like this.

I dart forward, my arms out as though I'm attempting to calm a skittish animal, but the Soothsayer isn't interested.

"They've come."

North and Nox go on high alert immediately, dozens of shadows falling from both of their bodies as they send out more reconnaissance and enlarge the circle of protection around us. Kieran widens his stance and palms a gun while Sawyer leaps to his feet and ducks closer to my Bonded that's closest to him, which happens to be Atlas.

"Who are 'they' and can someone please tell me why the *fuck* Shore's eyes are black right now? I thought he was safe from this sort of bullshit!"

I'd forgotten that we haven't told everyone everything yet, not even the friends who've become our family. North and Gryphon had made the decision that this information is on a need-to-know basis. We weren't expecting Sawyer to be in the thick of it right now, maybe then he'd have been let in on that little morsel of information.

He glances up to Atlas, opening his mouth and flinging out a hand, ready to demand answers, only to make a yelping noise and jump back from him.

His eyes have turned black as well.

One by one, the god-bonds are taking over.

As the situation goes from an information deep dive to the defensive, I want to apologize to Sawyer for involving him in this, but I feel my own bond waking up inside of my chest, stretching out until it fills my limbs. In the last moment before my own eyes shift to the voids as it takes over, I hear Kieran snap, "Get your ass over here, Benson. I'll get you back to the Sanctuary while all hell breaks loose. There's nothing we can do to help the gods."

II

OLEANDER'S BOND

The Manipulation god is here.

It's not the one that I wanted to be dealing with today, but they're all marked for death at my hands. The Pain god is long overdue for a blood-soaked and violent death, but I suppose we are encroaching on the Manipulation god's space. The fact that she had cycled into the same bloodline as the Cleaver's vessel is insult enough, but the idea that she has used that bloodline to build such a long-reaching platform only makes it worse.

The Transporter *pops* out of the room, taking the mouthy Gifted with him and leaving me alone with my Bonded. I enjoy the sight of them all for a moment as I look around, each of them awake and staring back at me.

It has been too long since I looked upon them, and never have I been able to see them all together at the same time.

When the Pain god had woken the Soothsayer up, my mind was still scrambled from the attack, but now I'm thinking clearly. Seeing them all here together is everything I have always hoped it would be.

A hundred lifetimes with these men wouldn't be enough.

A thousand lifetimes with all of them together would only be the beginning of what I need from them. Even as the situation around us becomes dire, I already know that I would choose this life of ours. This never-ending cycle of birth and rebirth, death and destruction, pain and horror over and over again. I would because it would mean knowing them, knowing the devotion and love that they have given me, knowing the devotion and love that I pour back into them. I don't know what a peaceful time will look like for us, something that the girl has also questioned, but I find myself eager to figure it out with them.

The Draconis hasn't shifted beyond his eyes turning black, but the way he moves his head is telling, as is the way he pushes his nose in the air as he scents the newcomers, disgust curling his lip. He never did like anyone but me. He tolerates the Bonded Group, the few times he'd interacted with them, thanks to how long it took for him to cycle.

"They're watching us, testing us. We should take it

alive," the Corvus says, and I tilt my head at him.

"We don't need answers. We need it gone."

The Crux looks between the two of us. "It's been here longer than us, and there is every chance it's been searching out the others. It would be useful to know how many we need to find."

The Soothsayer turns to look at me again, its eyes shining brighter as it calls on its Gift. "We don't need to question it. I'll get the information out of it, and then we can kill it."

The perfect kind of compromise, one where our enemy is still dead at our feet.

I smile at the Soothsayer, happy and relieved to get my way, and then I follow the Crux as he walks back up the set of stairs, letting my power stretch out over the entire building and the street as I take stock of the souls around us.

"Stop." I speak before the feeling fully forms in me, the extra senses I have beyond those of the vessel coming alight, and the Crux doesn't hesitate to follow my command.

"What is it?" the Soothsayer asks from downstairs, and I turn back to look over to my Bonded, each of them watching me and trusting that I know best in this situation.

"Something is wrong up there. Something is here for our demise."

The Soothsayer's eyes flash into the brightest of voids, and I open up the mind connection between us all so that we can see what he can.

The Manipulation god is up there, though we don't have much information from it. The Soothsayer is stronger than any other Neuro, especially now that we've Bonded, but still, the gods can keep him out of their heads if they've been here long enough.

There are other Gifted here with it as well, and the moment I realize what she's doing, I tear their souls out, but it's already too late.

As the Flame's body hits the floor, the building is already alight, the house around her body burning. The shadow creatures move around us, searching for an exit, but the Cleaver shakes his head.

"My vessel has already said there's one way in and one way out. We need the Transporter back here."

The Soothsayer reaches out, but I already know what the answer is going to be. "There's a Shield keeping him in the Sanctuary. They knew we were coming."

I shake my head. "They've had a long time to prepare for our arrival on this earth; this is just the first of the traps they will have planned for us."

The Corvus nods as well. "They will be prepared for our every move. We need to be smarter than this."

It doesn't matter how smart we need to be in the future.

Right now, we need to get out of this building before it burns to the ground around us.

I look down at the rest of my Bonded, and they're quick to start moving. The Corvus, intent on collecting the information his vessel is so eager for, starts making a pile with the rest of the boxes so that when we're ready, we can get out of here. We can't take the computer with us, but the paper copies will at least be something.

The vessel is sure it will help, so we will trust him, trust them all to navigate this time period better than we can.

The Crux descends the staircase again, taking my hand and leading me down as the smoke begins to creep underneath the door above us.

"We need to remember that the vessels aren't all indestructible, so we need to deal with this quickly," the Soothsayer says.

The Cleaver turns his head from side to side as though preparing himself to fight. "Not all of them, but some are, and I am more than ready to face our enemies."

My net shifts over the Manipulation god, an invisible force ready to take it out. Soon. I will kill it soon, rid the earth of its evil and carve out a new way of living for us all.

I shake my head. "I don't want to be split up like that."

The Soothsayer glances over at where the Crux is now helping the Corvus with the information, both of them working seamlessly together as though they are cut from the same cloth.

The Soothsayer looks back up the staircase to where the smoke is now starting to come in thick around us, assessing every little thing before he turns back to me. The air is heating up, and we're quickly running out of time.

"Come with me, Bonded. I might not be able to reach the Transporter, but you can."

I let my eyes slip shut as I push into my Bonded's mind, following along with him as he reaches out to the Transporter. The Shield is still in place, but it's then that I find out what the power boost of the fully Bonded Group has done for me. Thousands of miles away, without ever seeing his face or knowing his name, I tear the Shield's soul out of his body.

Together, we are indestructible.

I like the Transporter.

Even if he didn't belong to the Flame and the girl didn't adore him, I would like him. As he appears in the basement with us that is quickly being filled with smoke, he seems cool, calm, and confident, on the outside.

On the inside, he's shitting himself.

It's a subconscious thing, something that any living

creature would feel when they know they're in the presence of a predator, a pack of them really, and any wrong move will be their last. I'm sure that in his years of service to the Gifted, he's had many opportunities to stare down monsters, but none quite like us.

"I will get you all out of here," he says respectfully, dipping his head in the Crux's direction as he glances over his shoulder at the Soothsayer.

The Corvus starts directing everyone to grab boxes, getting the last of the information together as we leave the building. The Cleaver compiles a small mountain, balancing the boxes precariously as he lifts them with ease. I tuck a single box under my arm, the only one they will allow me to hold. While they never doubt my abilities or my power, they're still protective of me, as though some paper might strain me.

Thousands of lives together and still they love me so purely.

We appear back in the Sanctuary in the rooms that the Crux's vessel claims as an office. The moment we set the boxes down, I place my hand back on the Transporter, smiling when he flinches.

Silly little Gifted.

"Take me back to where you first dropped us off. I have some words to share with the god-bond there."

He nods without hesitation even as his eyes race over

the other god-bonds, but none of them question me. They merely step back up to him and hold their hands out, waiting for his arm, ready to fight and face whatever may come in the hopes of building a life together.

The Transporter glances around at them, and the girl pushes me to reassure him from where she watches in the corner of my mind.

It seems petty and trite to do so, but I speak for her. "I will not let that god-bond kill or harm you in any way. I understand that you are important to our vessels, and no harm will come to you."

He doesn't look very reassured at my words but he Transports us all the same.

I do like an obedient Gifted.

If we're going to set down roots in this world and live here permanently with each other, at least we'll have these types of Gifted around us.

With an inferno of flames consuming it, the house is quickly falling apart.

The Transporter brings us to a small park across the road from the house, a few feet away from the danger. There's already a crowd of humans huddled around the area, murmuring and whispering amongst themselves. Their thoughts and opinions on the matter mean nothing, they're only here as a distraction, something to stop me from finding what we came here for.

My eyes settle on the god-bond.

Its vessel is a woman in her forties, a short, severe haircut and a slash of red lipstick across her lips. She's attractive and well put together. She looks like a rich woman with no concerns over a house burning down.

Only we can see what lies within that empty shell.

The Crux speaks. "Go back to the Sanctuary, and wait for us there. The safest place for you is far away from here."

This time, the Transporter hesitates, glancing between the Soothsayer and I. I feel irritated at the delay, but the girl whispers to me quietly.

"The vessels are safe. I won't let them die any more than I will let one of my Bonded die," I say as I turn back to the god-bond. She's waiting, watching, and preparing to speak with us across the road.

I don't wait around to see whether or not he needs any more encouragement, my eyes glued on the god-bond across the way. Even though it's watching us, it doesn't make a move to leave. I take it as a warning, a caution that it could know more about what's going on here than we do.

"Take it slowly, my Eternal," the Corvus says, but it's the Cleaver who moves first, stalking towards the woman whose vessel looks so much like his own.

They share the same coloring, the same definition in their faces, the same strong jawline. We've never been born so close together before, not to the other gods, and not even to each other. We've always been spread out and forced to search for each other.

It's not some twist of fate, though.

They designed it that way, the Crux whispers into my mind. *They wanted to own us before we found each other. They wanted things to be different in this lifetime.*

They failed, the Soothsayer sends to us as we move to follow the Cleaver over to where the Manipulation god awaits.

I slip my hand into the Draconis'. He's still wearing the skin of the vessel, not yet shifted. I can tell that he is struggling with that, itching to truly come out and play but aware of the dangers of doing so. If history has taught us anything, it's that the non-Gifted really don't like it. The Gifted even struggle to comprehend the beauty of him in full, scaled form.

Soon. If it's not needed here, we will head home and change there. We will set you free of these bindings when we can, my Bonded.

His hand flexes in mine as he sends back to me, *Mine.*

The Manipulation god does not attempt to leave or flee or even attack us as we approach. It stands at the edge of the growing crowd of people, the only person still focused on anything other than the house slowly falling apart on the street behind us. It stares at us as though it has no concerns about its impending death.

It truly doesn't seem to care.

It has to be a game or trap of some kind, the Corvus sends to us.

"How carefully you hid yourself from us," it says as it stares the Cleaver down, disgust curling at its lip.

It's been awake for a long time. It's been here long enough that there's no doubt in my mind that it has already killed its vessel and taken over fully.

"You did this," the Cleaver says. "You're the one who started the breeding plan."

It turns its head curiously, a tell of the god inside. The way we don't quite act as the Gifted and non-Gifted around us do is a glaring sign of what lies beneath the surface.

"I had hoped to catch one of you in your next lifetime. To have you and be able to get rid of you before the others awoke. We knew this was coming. Too late for that now, I suppose. Now we're simply working against the clock."

A slow smile stretches across my lips, and the Draconis flexes his fingers in my hands, yearning to shift and kill this woman. To snap her body in half with nothing but the brute force of his jaws.

"You used your chance, and you failed. That's it for you, I'm afraid," the Crux says, stepping toward her as the shadows begin to fall from his body.

The Gifted and non-Gifted around us gasp and step

away from him, some scrambling and others staring as though they can't quite look away. You know which ones have heard the Draven name, the legacy of the bloodline that my Death Dealers are born into. Those people have a knowing fear in their eyes as they stare at the wide sets of jaws that form in the shadows.

Perfection.

"You haven't been awake long enough to be able to take someone like me out of the running this quickly. I suppose we'll meet again in a few years, if one of the others doesn't trap you first. But they will, you know. We always find you. We always kill you. Some things will *always* be."

It moves to turn its back only to find a shadow waiting for it there as well. When it lifts its hand to attempt to move, the shadow grasps it by the wrist, wrapping around it like a vine. Dozens more stream out of the Corvus to wrap around the god as well, until there's no chance of it escaping.

The god turns its head and its eyes flash black, power blasting at us but not strongly enough to truly touch us. Its eyes widen, and I can see when the realization finally hits.

It's going to die here.

The Cleaver steps up once more, a hand wrapping around the god's throat as it squeezes. "You're underestimating the power of the Bond and the power of my Eternal. Though I slept in safety, others did not and I have their power now."

The god sputters, clawing at that hand as it blasts out more power but it's like kicking at a brick wall. The Cleaver is indestructible and doesn't feel a thing, the power it has now thanks to our completed bond means that there's nothing this god-bond can do to any of us now.

The shadows look hungry, eager to consume the god, and I find that though the Cleaver offers its soul to me, I do not want it. I don't want the taint of that twisted god touching me at all. It's more than just power, and I want nothing to do with it.

It's not that easy though.

It never is.

There's a satisfying *crack* sound as the Cleaver snaps the vessel's neck, which is always the weakest point on any god, and I press my eyes shut to feel as the life force of the god slips away.

It's going to enter back into the cycle. Don't let it, the Corvus whispers into my mind. *Don't let it come back for us. End it here, my Eternal.*

I reach out and take the soul.

I don't want to consume it, but if it can stop the cycle from continuing and the gods hunting us... I would do anything for my Bonded.

I take it into myself, consuming and consuming until it's gone. Nothing left to come back, nothing left to haunt us now. One less monster out there to kill us all.

12

NOX

The moment the god-bond's life force disappears into Oli, her eyes roll back into her head and she drops, passing out cold. The Crux swoops down to catch her as she falls, bringing her up into his arms and turning his head to the Soothsayer.

I watch it all from inside my own body, the one that I no longer control, but the Corvus has agreed to let me watch what's going on and listen to my input.

Neither of us are happy about Oleander passing out.

It was too much for her. She's only just waking up.

"She's been awake a lot longer than most of us," the Soothsayer murmurs, and before anyone can argue with him, there's a *pop* sound as Black reappears.

He takes one look at Oli's unconscious form in my brother's arms and curses viciously under his breath before he remembers that none of us are the men that he grew up with and knows so well right now.

"Am I just taking you back to North's offices in the Sanctuary, or should we get her to a Healer?" he asks in a formal and respectful tone, his head bowed just a little.

I don't know who he's taken lessons from on how to approach the gods but I can feel the Corvus' reaction to it. He likes the reverential treatment.

I'm sure they all do.

The Soothsayer places a hand on Oli's neck, his eyes flashing brighter for a moment. "She doesn't need a Healer. Take us back to where the information is being kept. She just needs rest and can do that there."

Black gives him a curt nod and stretches out his arm, waiting for each of us to take it to leave this place that stinks of ash and flames. I stand next to the Crux, close enough that I can smell the scent of Oleander's shampoo. As my bond rumbles happily inside my chest at her proximity, I feel a pit of dread there.

What if the god-bond's soul has done damage? What if it's given her extra power? Oli's always been so afraid of what her bond can do, so scared of getting stronger, because her power is already so close to the limit of what she can control. A thousand different fears of hers run through my mind, all of them as familiar to me as my own, thanks to our soul-bond.

I murmur quietly to my bond, *take her from the Crux. She needs us right now.*

It agrees with me, though I'm sure it will always agree if it means getting its hands on her. The moment we reappear in North's offices, it takes her from the Crux. We move over to the couch with her cradled against our chest.

She's so small.

I forget that sometimes because of her larger-than-life personality and the way that she commands every space she walks into. Her attitude is big enough for three grown men, but when she is unconscious like this, it's easy to forget all of that and see nothing but the woman left behind.

Petite, fine features. Hair so white that it's like a tumble of starlight on her head, sooty eyelashes fanning over her cheeks, plump lips that part as she sighs and turns further into my body, craving me and reaching out to me, even in her unconscious state.

It all fills me with a murderous rage.

Rage at anyone who has ever hurt her, looked at her, spoken to her, or touched what is mine. Anyone who might have thought badly of her. The soul bonding had solidified my obsession with her and though I know my own past actions with her had been poisoned by my past, now all I can see is the perfection of her, all of the ways that this woman owns me and the ways that I own her as well.

I feel a little like a hoarding dragon in the way that I want to take her back to our mansion, lock her in my room, and guard her like I had when we'd woken from the soul-bonding. Only this time, I won't let anyone in to take her away from me.

Gryphon's eyes flash and shift back to green as the Soothsayer releases him. One by one, their eyes all shift back as they take control of their bodies. Gabe groans and cracks his neck, rolling out his shoulders as though he's been holding himself too tightly this entire time. I suppose the Draconis didn't enjoy being stuck in human form, the same way my bones itch if I'm forced to keep the shadows inside of me.

I watch as Black visibly deflates at the sight of their cleared eyes. The Corvus stays with me. With Oleander in my arms, I doubt he's going to go without a fight, and I'm simply not interested in having one at the moment.

I feel as though I will be too exposed if the god leaves me right now. I would rather just enjoy the moment with my Bonded in my arms while no one will think anything of it.

"What the fuck happened back there?" Black snaps, but Gryphon is already stalking over to where I'm sitting, slipping his hand back onto Oli's neck, his eyes flashing as he checks in with her.

"She's okay, she's just asleep, the same way as when she uses her power."

North nods and blows out a long breath, scrubbing a hand across his face as he takes stock of himself and the situation. He's already shifting into 'damage-control mode', and though the situation definitely needs it, I still find myself rolling my eyes internally.

Just once, I wish he would forget about being on the council, forget about everything he's supposed to do and just relax. I wonder what it would even look like if North Draven just let himself feel whatever he needed to and took a moment for himself.

"We found the god-bond, and Oli took care of it. It'd laid the trap for us, and I wouldn't be surprised if there are more in our future."

Kieran gives him another curt nod and then looks around at each of us before his eyes settle on my bond. "Is that one going to let go anytime soon? I don't feel totally comfortable speaking about any of this with that one in the room as well. What's to stop it from getting pissed off at something I say and coming after me?"

The Corvus tilts my head in the curious way they all do. "We're always here. We're always listening. You have never had a conversation without my hearing it."

"Well, that's fucking creepy," Kieran says before turning back to North. "The General arrived this morning, and word has gotten out about the fire on the East Coast already. He's downstairs, ranting about the entire situation, so you might want to prepare yourselves for that."

"Transport me and my Bonded back to our house. I don't want her around any danger that might end in bloodshed," the Corvus says, and Kieran looks at North and Gryphon before he moves.

"Gabe and Atlas, you both should go with them to watch over her while we deal with this," North says before he looks over at my god-bond. "Once she's safe at the house, can we have Nox back? We're going to need all the help we can get and nothing handles the General quite like my brother's pissed-off attitude."

Gryphon nods his head and then smirks. "Nothing except Oli's. She's gotten pretty good at cutting the General to the core."

My god-bond nods and starts shifting her in our arms until she's more secure. "Do it. I will see her home safely before I sleep."

Black Transports us to the front doorstep of the mansion, and we all stand together as Gabe fumbles around for his keys to get us in.

Atlas stands as close to my side as he can without

touching me, his eyes on Oli. He continues staring at her sleeping form until we hear a low rustling in the bushes. He turns to cover us both as he watches to see where the sound has come from. It's nothing but the breeze, I'd feel if it were more, but my shadows dart off to double-check.

The way that Atlas covers me is telling.

Even a month ago, he would have gone toe-to-toe with my god-bond to wrestle Oli out of my arms. He would have used her safety and his impenetrable skin as excuses to get her away from us, but now he sees the value in protecting us both. I could write it off simply as his respect for the gods, and I'm sure that does play into it, but there's no denying that the Bonded Group has shifted and changed, matured in ways none of us were expecting.

The girl in my arms who I was so sure would be the catalyst for our destruction has become anything but that. She's the reason we're all pulling together, the reason we all want more for ourselves and the community. Simply by existing, she has made everything better.

The god-bond can hear every one of my thoughts, and he pulls her up further into our chest, tucking her in closer as the shadows wrap around her, forming more of a protective barrier.

When the shadow creatures come back from the bushes with nothing to report and no blood spilled, Atlas relaxes a little, though his eyes stay on the road that leads up to our house.

"Do you really think someone's going to get in here? Is there a valid argument for that or is this just Bonded behavior?" Black murmurs quietly, and Atlas shoots him a look.

He just shrugs back. "I'm not saying there's anything wrong with Bonded behavior—I have it myself. I would just like to know if I should be reaching for my gun right now to back you up."

Atlas gives him a curt nod, and his eyes narrow toward the lights down at the town center. "They had a Shield already in place just outside of the Sanctuary walls to keep you trapped in here. What's to say they haven't found a way inside? What's to say that some of the residents here aren't sleeper-cells, like the one that killed the Dravens' uncle? I mean, I trust Gryphon, and I trust his bond, but we've just found out that there are more god-bonds out there. What's to say one of them couldn't plant someone in here? The Soothsayer has only been awake for a matter of days. There is every chance that we're not safe here, and I'm not going to bet my Bonded's life on *anything* right now."

Black stares at him for a moment and then nods, palming his gun and turning his back to the door right as Gabe finally gets it open. He watches over the street as we walk in, entering last and triple-checking the locks on the doors before he holsters his weapon once more.

The glass in here is bulletproof, the best that money can buy. The entire structure of the house has been reinforced, and it's the equivalent of a bomb-proof bunker. North hadn't spared a single expense on the place. Whatever recommended rating the professionals had given him, he tripled it, just to be sure.

I know, without a doubt, that there are presidents and royalty with less protection than what my brother has in place for our Bonded Group and the little Central still sleeping in my arms.

The Corvus doesn't hesitate to walk Oleander back into her room, ignoring the conversation still happening around us. Gabe and Atlas eventually follow us down the hallway, as though drawn there by Oli subconsciously, never wanting to be too far away from her.

Even after it gets her tucked safely into her bed with Gabe and Atlas watching her like hawks, my bond is not satisfied.

It doesn't want to leave her here without one of us standing guard, and I understand the feeling well. There's something vulnerable about her at the moment, something I've never felt before. Before, when she had overexerted her power, her bond would still simmer to the surface from time to time. I could still feel it there watching over her as her body took what it needed. There's a stillness inside of

Oleander right now that chills me right down to the bone.

I don't want to leave her.

Black is waiting in the kitchen for me to return. When my bond simply stands and stares at Oleander's sleeping form, Gabe starts to get restless.

"We're not going to let anything happen to her. Atlas is indestructible, and he is going to cover her at all times. North and Gryphon are the ones who need help here."

He uses a very reasonable tone, but my god-bond doesn't react. It doesn't do anything except stare down at the small lump in the fabric that Oli makes, watching her obsessively. Her breathing is even and steady; nothing about her is saying that she needs to be watched like this.

If anything happens, she has Atlas' power to cover her, and Gabe can shift into the dragon if he needs to. It would take him less than a second to fly her back to us. I know this, the Corvus knows this, and yet, we still can't move.

"Are you going to be able to leave her or should we call North and let him know what's going on?" Atlas asks as he climbs up onto the bed with her.

He doesn't immediately move her onto his lap or fuss with her as I would. He simply presses a hand to her chest to feel her breathing for a minute and then lets her go, letting her sleep peacefully. The way that he loves and treats her is incredibly selfless, a stark comparison to the selfish way that I covet her.

It doesn't make me feel bad though. If anything, it makes me feel like I need to take more, to take everything from her until I have it all.

"I'll call North," Gabe mutters, sharing a look with Atlas, but my bond finally moves, reaching out a hand, and my palm turns black as shadows fall from it.

Mephis and Procel come down and immediately move to the bed, jumping up to flank either side of her. Atlas stares at them distrustfully, and my bond finally speaks. "They will guard her. Do not attempt to move or disrupt them. I will only be gone for as long as it takes to fix the problem."

Atlas nods, slowly shifting away from the shadows a little, but his eyes stay on her. Finally, my god-bond loosens the grip on my body, letting me take control once more, though it continues watching.

Gabe lets out a breath behind me. "What crawled up its ass? The rest all left happily."

I shake my head dismissively at him. "She's sleeping too heavily. You need to watch her, and call me the second anything changes… for better or worse."

Gabe startles and steps towards the bed. "What do you mean by that? She always does this when she uses power."

Atlas shakes his head. "This is different. Can't you feel it? She's not the only one resting."

Gabe scowls and shrugs. "That makes sense though,

doesn't it? She took out something bigger than she ever has before, of course her bond needs to sleep as well."

I shake my head. "I don't like it. Just watch her and call me. I'll go deal with these fucking idiots at the office and then I'll be back."

"You or your bond?" Atlas asks as I turn on my heel.

"Does it matter? We're one and the same," I say as I shove the door open, stalking out to where Black is waiting for me.

The relief on his face at the color of my eyes is stark. "If you'd have told me six months ago that you'd be acting like this over your Bonded—"

I fucking hate that word.

Using it like that, about her, it makes my skin crawl, so I cut him off. "We need to get this over and done with. I need to be back here."

He scowls at me as he claps a hand on my shoulder. "Do you need me to send Felix up? He's already waiting, if you need him."

I shake my head. "No one's looking at her without me there. We'll deal with this, and then when I get back, I can look her over again and make the call."

Kieran shakes his head. "It's not a good day to be the General."

It's never a good day to be the fucking General. I hate the man, even more so now than ever before, which is something I didn't think was possible. He is taking me away from Oleander right now, when she needs me the most, and that is inexcusable.

We transport into the bottom floor of North's office, the area that is open for the public to come into and wait to speak with him. It's usually fairly empty, nothing more than a glorified thoroughfare area, but we find it packed with bodies.

I'm not very surprised to find ourselves appearing in the middle of an all-out war.

The fact that North is in the center of it, vigorously brawling, is more than a little shocking, however.

If anything, I would have guessed that Gryphon would've thrown the first punch at his father, years of resentment finally bubbling to the surface, but our Neuro is the one trying to get North off of the General.

More shadows fall from my body and start cleaning up the mess around us, winding their way around the TacTeam personnel and pulling them all out of the fray. One-by-one, they line the bodies up until they are sweating and shaking in fear by the wall.

North's shadows are only exacerbating the fight, but when they come across mine, they have no choice but to calm down, secure in the fact that I'm here to help, and they can't fight against their own, no matter what the situation might be. Without the pressure of the rest of the

TacTeams around them, Gryphon manages to pry North off of his father, his hands finally wrenching away from around the General's throat. The older man makes the sweetest gurgling noises as he gasps for air.

I sidle up beside them. The black stain of my god-bond creeps up my throat, and a smirk stretches across my lips as I see the blood running freely out of his nose. It all makes me look like the demon the General is so sure that I am, and I'm more than happy to play the part.

I wish I could kill the cunt myself.

"Well, well. I didn't think it was possible for someone to goad North into that sort of attack, but I suppose if anyone could do it, it would be you."

The General stares up at me in pure loathing, and I relish it… right until he opens his fat mouth.

"With any luck, Athena has killed that little bitch bond of yours and we don't have another monster walking around this godforsaken shithole."

My temper snaps faster than North's ever has.

The General's jaw shatters under my fist just as quickly.

13

OLI

I wake to snarling, raised voices and shouting; to the chaos and rage that usually comes with bloodshed. I wake surrounded by shadows and darkness, my head pounding in my ears and my bond reaching out to our Bonded as it keens inside of me. It's called out to them all as I slept, bringing them in to help with the chasm left inside of me thanks to that god-bond's soul.

Destroying something like that, something so strong, had sapped away my power and left me an empty shell. I think I would panic about it if my bond didn't have a surefire plan to fix this terrible feeling already in motion, because sending out a siren call to my Bonded to have them come to me is the only path ahead that doesn't fill me with terror.

I need them to fill me up, to repair the damage, and restore me to my glory. I need them to turn our pleasure into shared power. I need everything from them.

Fingers clasp around my chin and turn my head, lips pressing against my own as a moan escapes me, a needy and desperate sound even to my own ears.

My bond simmers there at the surface, but I stay in control of my limbs, reaching out and wrapping my arms around Gabe's neck as I pull him into my body.

I'm already naked.

So is he.

Atlas is with us, his body hard and ready where he's pressed against my back, and another moan squeezes out from between my lips. Their hands are everywhere; their skin is hot against mine as they burn just as brightly for me as I do for them. Fingers squeeze at the soft expanse of my thighs, dipping lower to run through the slick mess between them, groans echoing through the room that I join in with as the fingers push into my dripping pussy.

I want more from them all. I want more hands on my body; I want more fingers and lips and, *my God*, I want them all to fill me up.

"We will, Bonded. We're going to give you exactly what you need."

What I need is to stop all of the talking and get to the

part where one of them is fucking me. Or both of them. All of them. I want their skin sliding on mine as they thrust into me. I want to taste their pleasure. I want to take it into myself and become nothing more than their vessel, a vessel to be used for their desires.

There's a moment when one of them moves away from me, just for a second, but the keening noise I let out has him rushing back to me, soothing words dripping from his lips like honey, warming me to my core as he reassures me.

"I'm not going anywhere, Sweetness. If you want both of us at once, then I need to grab some supplies. It's okay, I won't leave. Gabe, you need to fuck her and distract her, otherwise she's going to hurt herself rushing into shit."

I'm not though, and I'll happily take the pain to have them. I'll take it all—

The sudden thrust of a cock into my gushing pussy is enough to derail my panicked, bond-hazed thoughts. I stop thinking about abandonment, about being bereft without them, about anything except for the delicious stretch as I take Gabe's cock and the way his hands clasp at my waist and move me up and down the length of him, meeting the thrust of his hips.

It's exactly what my frantic and crazed mind wants, but after only a few thrusts, my bond kicks in, calling out to them all again as it keens for more. I want to just enjoy my Bonded, to be with each of them and savor the ways that they love me individually, but the chasm inside of me only grows bigger the longer we're separated.

I need more.

The keening sound fills the room again, my eyes squeezing shut tight as I try to get myself under control. I know they're all here and that I'll get what I want, but the pressure inside of me builds until I want to scream and claw my way out of my own skin.

Then there are hands all over me again, pushing me and moving me firmly, taking control of the situation until there's another cock pressing against my ass, teeth biting down on my shoulder, and a deep groan that comes with the anticipation of the fullness of both of my Bonded taking me together.

Gabe curses under his breath, pulling my body down so I cover him more fully, and Atlas' hand rubs over my ass as he watches Gabe's cock fill me, squeezing and spreading me as he enjoys the view. I look back over my shoulder at him just in time to see him spit on his cock as it slides inside of me, his eyes as hot as a brand.

The moment I catch my breath and the chaos eases off a little in my mind, I glance around the room to find my other three Bonded watching us, dark and greedy looks in their eyes. My skin flushes under their gazes, but my bond preens in my chest, gloating and positively relishing the way that I've snared them all with nothing but my body, my mind, and my love for them all.

My pussy clenches around Gabe's cock, my ass tightening around Atlas', and they both groan, their hips moving faster until I have to hold onto Gabe's shoulders. Gabe gives me a lazy grin, a self-satisfied one that says there's nowhere else he'd rather be right now than here with me splayed out over his chest. He uses one hand to cup my cheek and draw my lips to his for a blistering kiss, the other slipping down between our bodies to my clit. I already have an orgasm starting to build, but he draws it out of me with maddening circles, slow and in complete contrast to the pace he's setting with his hips.

When I finally come, pressing my face into his chest to muffle the obscene sounds coming out of my mouth, Gabe comes with me, pushing in even deeper at the same time as Atlas, and I feel as though I'm going to burst.

The frenetic buzz quiets for a moment, just a moment, but the second Gabe pulls out and moves me onto the bed, it doubles, triples. It fills my limbs until I want to scream.

Atlas pulls out, lifting one of my legs to turn me onto my back before he slides back into my ass, Gabe's cum dripping out of my pussy a little as he does. I don't want to lose any of it. I want to be full. My eyes close again as I lose myself to the sensations, the way he fucks me through the overstimulation until one orgasm rolls into the next one. I whine a little as the haze falls over me once more.

I'm starting to think it'll never lift.

I arch my back on the bed, my head thrashing as the pleasure rolls through me in a tidal wave. As my mouth drops open in a desperate gasp, I feel someone's fingers curl around my jaw, then they push against my tongue as though my Bonded is checking that my mouth is ready for him. I close my lips around them, sucking away to prove that I'm not only ready but craving the weight of his cock in my mouth.

I hear rustling and then I feel him shift, my eyes fluttering open to find North crouched down at my eye-level as his fingers stroke my tongue. When he meets my eyes, he nods at me as though we've come to an agreement.

"Tell me what you need, Bonded," he murmurs as though Atlas isn't fucking me, as though Gabe's cum isn't inside me right now and the rest of the Bonded Group aren't here waiting, drawn by my bond's call.

I wait until his fingers slip out of my mouth before I say, my words slurring a little with pleasure, "I need more. I need all of you."

He doesn't need me to say another word.

Atlas only stops long enough to flip me onto my hands and knees before slamming back into me while North stands again, slipping his boxer briefs off as he does. I'm reaching for him before he has the chance to step out of them, drawing him to my lips and sucking him down, moaning around him as his hips shove forward, rough in the best way.

I swallow around him, torn between wanting to shove myself further down his length and impaling myself on Atlas' cock, but they both keep pushing forward, driving into my ass and my mouth until I'm moaning like a wanton, my eyes rolling back as my screams are muffled by North's dick.

Atlas' hips finally stutter, his hands clutching at my thighs as he spreads my legs wider and pulls out to come all over my exposed pussy. He uses his fingers to push his cum in with Gabe's, making sure they're both filling me up. North drags his cock out of my mouth and waits, fisting himself as Atlas moves away, stumbling to the bathroom.

My skin is glowing, the health and vitality they're all giving me shining through, and I'm eager for more.

I know the moment North covers me that something has happened.

I don't know what it is, who has hurt my Bonded, but there's a savage energy inside of him as he moves inside of me. His hands are rough and desperate on my body, grasping at my soft curves as he takes what he needs from me, and I beg him for more.

All of the rage and anguish, the heartache and pain—I take it all from him. The pump of his hips is brutal, the pounding of his cock into my abused pussy is the sweetest form of torture. He fucks me like he's trying to kill his demons.

I would take everything from him gladly, with a smile, begging for more of this if he needs it, because even as he's taking what he needs from me, he's giving me back even more. I swear I can almost feel them healing me, pouring into my very soul, and I'm coming alive with every orgasm, every stroke, every touch of their skin against mine.

His shadows wrap around me, covering us both. When I feel the tendrils of it come out to play with my clit, pushing into my ass as though it wants to own every part of me, I come with a scream, clenching around him until North follows me over the edge.

He doesn't move away from me immediately like the others did; he stays with me for a second as though he's checking to see just how far gone I still am. There's a quietness to me now, as though some of the savage hunger has been sated, but the longer he lingers, the more it creeps back, the more it needs the rest of them inside of me.

When he leaves me, my eyes land on Nox and Gryphon, both of them watching me, both of them naked and hard. I expect it to be Gryphon who comes to me first. I expect to have to convince Nox or maybe even go to his room with him later, but he doesn't hesitate to move toward me the moment our eyes meet.

His own eyes flash black, and my bond reaches out to

him, brushing against his skin as it tries to draw the Corvus out to play. Nox holds onto control though, gritting his teeth as his fists clench at his side, the skin slowly turning black as his Gift floods him. I know it makes Atlas nervous when he does that, twitchy almost, as though they'd ever truly hurt me. So instead of letting it get that far, I smile up at Nox and his bond as though they are the sun, warming me to my core. There's no doubt how much I want them, no doubt to me and no doubt for any of them.

I move to sit up, to go to him, but a trickle of cum leaks out of me at the movement. A whimper falls from my lips, my hand snapping down to cup myself and push it back in. His eyes flash again as he watches me, and then the shadows in the room begin to move, twisting and pulling until they cover me as well, shifting my hand away and covering my pussy for me, helping me keep it all inside.

I move slowly at first, but once I'm sure the shadows have me covered, I scramble up onto my knees, reaching for him. I get a giddy thrill straight to my heart that his hands are just as desperate on my body as mine are on his. His hands span my ribs with ease, kissing me as though he wants to crawl inside me, his teeth sharp on my neck as he devours me whole.

I want it all, all of his sharpest edges, all of his pain and vicious energy. I want to take it all in and make it a part of me as well.

His hands are rough as he shoves me back onto the bed, covering me and shoving my legs open to fuck me, as dark and deviant as ever. His strokes are brutal, his hips snapping into me as I hold onto him for dear life, my head pressed against the thumping of his heart. My back arches as I come, my hair falling away from my face. One of his hands comes up to hold my chin, forcing me to meet his eyes as he comes too, so I'm staring into the depthless voids.

Nox's eyes shift back, the black bleeding out of them slowly, and I see the moment he wants to scoop me up and take me back to his room, to lock the rest of them out and guard me as though the hounds of Hell are coming after us. I see it, and then I see him decide that what I need is more important than what he wants.

I see him mentally let go of it all.

When he steps away, I find Gryphon waiting patiently, still as hard as stone, sitting next to the bed. He finally approaches and grins at me, running a hand down the length of my belly before his fingers slide over my pussy to dip inside of me and into the mess that my other Bonded have left there. My cheeks heat as I clench around him instinctively, unhappy that he might be forcing some of it out. I want it all, more. I want his cum in there too, mixing and leaving me full of them all. I'm so close, *so close*, to getting what I've always wanted.

I open my mouth, and the words that leave me are drenched with sex and need. "Give me what I want."

I don't have to ask twice.

His eyes flash black for a second as his bond chimes in, but when he grabs my ankles and yanks me down the bed, it's his clear green eyes I'm staring into. It's his grin that stretches over his lips as he fucks me, makes a mess of me, and pounds into my abused pussy with a firm hand on my chest as he holds me in place.

It's his voice that whispers pure filth to me, sends me spiraling and writhing. His voice that drives me over the edge until I'm sobbing, begging for mercy until my voice dries up.

It's his soul that takes it all in and pushes me for *more*.

When he finally comes, pushing into me, both hands on my hips to hold me in place, I feel as though I'm going to pass out all over again, the pleasure drawn out of me a vicious and delectable thing.

The moment his hips stop pumping and the ecstasy clears from his face, Gryphon pulls out to shift back onto his knees. He spreads my legs and plunges his fingers back inside of my aching pussy. I moan and writhe, overstimulated and right on the precipice of what I can take from them all, and he hooks his fingers inside of me mercilessly.

It's only when he lifts his hand to my face and pushes

his fingers into my mouth that I realize what he's doing.

"Tell me how good we taste, Bonded. Tell me how much you love the taste of your Bonded all mixed together after we fuck you raw."

I moan around his fingers, but there's no way to say what he wants me to, because the more I open my mouth, the deeper he shoves his fingers, his eyes darkening as he watches me take them.

I glance over to find Gabe sitting on the other side of the bed in his sweatpants, hair still wet from a shower, sweating and biting his fist as he stares at my lips wrapped around Gryphon's fingers as they pump in and out of my mouth.

Don't look at me like that, Ardern. I can't take any more, I send through to him, though I'm tempted, so goddamned tempted.

He grins at me again and sends back, *I think you could, but I'll save it for later, Bonded. I want your mouth wrapped around my dick like that.*

Gryphon finally gets his fill of me and he moves away, just far enough that he can grab a towel to wrap me up in, carrying me off into my bathroom to get us both clean. I could argue with him, I always have a fight in me, but my legs feel like jelly, and it's far more satisfying to just let him lug me around.

When I'm dry and back in one of his shirts, he hands

me over to Nox, and I'm surprised when he walks me back over to the bed and gets us both settled in there.

Nox never sleeps in my bed.

Before I can freak out over this change, North comes back into the bedroom, sweatpants slung low on his hips and a swagger to his walk that speaks of a deeply satisfied man. He hands me a bottle of water as his eyes trail slowly down my neck and over my chest. There's no damage done to me, nothing but the delicious burn of my muscles as I shift and turn.

There's always a deep ache inside me, a yearning for them that I'm not sure will ever truly pass, but it's quiet now that I've been so thoroughly used.

"You almost killed Kieran."

I choke a little on the water as I sit up, coughing dramatically as I thump my chest to clear it. I glance down at Nox as I sputter, "Excuse me? How? When? Oh my God—"

Gryphon smirks at me. "He means that you woke up while we were still at North's office, and we made him Transport us back here. North wasn't expecting you to already be naked and between the other two. When the door opened, you weren't exactly being quiet. The moment he heard you moan—"

"Shut up, shut up, shut up! I can never look that man in the eye again, oh my God!" I moan, shoving my face into the pillow and ignoring the evil chuckling from all of them.

When I was daydreaming of having them all here in my room together, in my bed, I was *not* imagining this side of it.

North rubs a hand over his eyes with a pained sigh. "It's not funny. I still want to go down there and murder him. Fuck it, put some pants on Nox. We're tearing his head off of his shoulders at the very least."

To my horror, Nox actually moves me away from his chest as though he's on board with this stupid plan. "Don't you dare! If you get out of this bed right now, Draven, the only murder that is going to take place is your own. Don't smirk at me. I'm dead fucking serious right now."

Nox moves back onto the bed and draws me in closer to his body, pulling me away from everyone else as he does. It's a very Draven trait, something North does all of the time, and my heart squeezes in my chest that Nox is doing it to me now too. Bearing the full brunt of the Draven brothers and their possessive, jealous, protective maelstrom of love is everything I ever needed, something I didn't realize I was missing until now.

Atlas shoots Nox a dirty look from the other side of the bed. "If you're sleeping in here, then don't be an asshole and drag Oli around everywhere. Learn to share."

Nox just stares back at him. "No."

When Atlas glares back at him, Nox smirks, his eyes and the skin of his neck slowly turning black. "If you want her, come and get her."

I tuck my face into his chest and send through the mind connection just to be sure they all hear it and understand, *I'm tired. You can fight about it once I've gotten twelve solid hours of sleep, so please stop ruining my afterglow and let me pass out.*

Atlas' eyes narrow to slits, but he does lie down finally, rolling over and shoving a pillow over his face. Gabe flings an arm over his face and falls asleep in under a minute, but Nox fusses until North climbs into the bed as well, getting Gryphon to move over. He leaves a large space between Nox and I, a small concession to keep Nox in the bed here with them instead of spiriting me away to his room like he wants to.

I feel bad about it for a moment until he sends through to me directly, *I'm not tired, Oleander. I'll watch you sleep and keep you safe.*

14

It only takes three steps outside of our house and into the Sanctuary to know that things have changed.

For one, Kieran is waiting for us, and my cheeks heat the second I see him, North's words from last night still echoing in my mind. I step in closer to Atlas' side unconsciously, enjoying that he tucks me in without a word. I have no reason to worry though, Kieran meets my eyes with a 'no bullshit' look on his face and the same nod of respect he always does. There's no sign of a smile or sarcastic comment out of him this time, and he holds his arm out for us to take for Transport.

I'm a little surprised that we're traveling like this within the Sanctuary. It seems like a waste of resources, but I take his arm without question. He takes us directly to North's offices.

Gabe and Atlas are crushing me between their hulking sizes as though they're expecting us to appear in the center of a Wasteland. I want to roll my eyes at their dramatics, but the second my feet hit the ground, my stomach roils with motion sickness and Atlas has to catch me as my knees buckle. There's cursing and then Gryphon's hands slide onto my neck, easing away the sickness. Before I get the chance to straighten and thank him, he stalks back over to the far side of the room.

For a moment, my heart sinks and I feel as though maybe I've done something wrong and pissed him off. Then I glance up and see the screens that the rest of my Bonded Group are staring at along with Vivian and Unser. There, on the three large monitors, is the footage of the Transport Zone from the Sanctuary. They're watching as groups of families leave in a mass exodus. The entire area is surrounded by the General and his TacTeams, all of them with guns in their hands as they stare out at the crowd forming to watch the people leaving, but none of them attempt to approach.

"What the fuck is going on?" Atlas asks, his arm still around my waist as we both move towards them, and North answers without turning around.

"They've decided that the Sanctuary is more dangerous

than dealing with the Resistance. They all got a taste of what Nox and I can do if pushed, and it reminded them of the Draven curse."

I don't like that at all.

"Fuck the Draven curse! They're all idiots if they think they can survive out there with everything heating up. Can't you call a meeting or something?"

Nox turns to stare at Gabe for a moment, surprised at his vehemence. When he speaks, his own words are chosen very carefully, his control over his temper impressive considering his history. "I'm not calling a meeting and telling any of those people that I will react in any other way if they wish death upon Oleander. I draw the line at that. I've had to make nice with these people for decades knowing that they are selfish cancers on the backs of this community, riding on North's coattails while he bore the brunt of the real work. I will do it no longer."

I glance between him and Gryphon before I say, very carefully because the tension is suddenly so thick in the room that I'm choking on it, "Did someone actually threaten me? Or was it more of an indirect sort of thing?"

Gryphon answers me, his face stern and unreadable. "The General threatened you while you were sleeping… twice. The first time to North and I, the second time to Nox when he arrived to try to defuse the situation."

North shakes his head, a scowl on his face and a ring

of smoke around his wrist that shows just how tenuous his grasp on his temper is. "Nox is right. I'm not going down there and telling these people not to leave. The General isn't welcome here anymore, and I think we were far too generous in giving him twenty-four hours to get out of here before we let the shadows out to hunt him down."

I swallow against the lump in my throat. I know how badly Nox and North hate the General, but I'm also aware that Gryphon has a complicated relationship with his father.

I don't need to say any of this for him to know exactly how I'm feeling about it. He reads me like an open book.

"You come first to me, Oli. The moment he opened his mouth and dared to say a word about you was the moment I cut ties with him for good. I might not wish a violent and bloody death upon him, but I've accepted that it's what's likely about to happen to him, running off half-cocked and with nothing but his ego out there. We didn't even get the chance to warn him about the god-bonds."

"Fuck warning him," Nox snarls. "He doesn't give a shit about anything other than the fact that your eyes turned a different color, and they weren't a color he wanted for his kid."

"It's not about the well-being of his child, it's about how it reflects on him. It always has been," North says, and I shift on my feet, so uncomfortable with having this conversation in these circumstances. Out in the open with Kieran, Vivian, and Unser listening in. Gryphon doesn't seem to care, and I'd hazard a guess that this isn't the first time they've heard all of this information, but I'm still prickling with discomfort.

"Does Kyrie know?" I ask, and Gryphon turns back to me with a wry smile.

"We told her. The General also showed up to where she's staying and tried to drag her out with him, but she held a loaded gun to his head to let him know exactly how she felt about leaving. She was pretty pissed off when we told her what he'd said about you. She now thinks she wasted the opportunity to finally just pull the trigger."

Jesus Christ.

"I always did like Kyrie," Atlas says as he crosses his arms and nods his head, but Vivian shoots him a look.

"What the hell are we going to do about all of these innocent people being led out of here with nothing but fear mongering? I agree that the General has to go, no man should be able to speak about Bonds like that, and certainly not about Fallows, but these people have no idea about any of that. They're all just terrified and trying to make the best call for their families."

North shrugs. "What else can we do? Some of them have been here for months and have seen the way that we run things here—they've still chosen to leave. If we take away free will, we are nothing more than the monsters in the Resistance. All we can do now is open up and let more Gifted in, those who have been on the waiting list due to the limited space. It's not an easy decision to make, but it's the only one we've got."

I'm not sure any of us are going to sleep well with that thought, but as I look up at the screen where dozens of bodies are disappearing with Transporters, there's not much else I can do.

North changes his rules for how we're all allowed to act in public *dramatically* as a response to the General's defection.

We go from trying to stay in smaller numbers and putting on a peaceful and friendly face to living however the hell we want. By nightfall the same night, word has gotten around of what had really happened in North's office between my Bonded Group and Gryphon's dad, and though no one else chooses to leave, there is a dramatic change on the streets.

They're empty now.

It makes my skin crawl.

"They're acting as though we're hunting them down," I say as I walk hand-in-hand with Gryphon to the dining hall.

Gabe and Atlas had gone to some of the newer houses to help Gabe's uncle with a problem that he had down there. North and Nox are busy working through the information that we recovered from Atlas' parents' house, so Gryphon and I had offered to pick up dinner for everyone.

When he'd moved to grab the keys for one of our ATVs, I simply shook my head and pulled on my sneakers instead, happy to spend a little extra time with him on the way. I feel like we've only seen each other in our Tac gear or naked lately. I miss just being around him, speaking to him about anything other than work or the delicious things he's doing to my body.

The problem is that we haven't spoken about his father, other than Gryphon apologizing for what he'd said, but I hated to hear that out of him. It's not his fault the General is a dick, and I'm quick to make sure he knows it.

All the guilt he feels right now is about the innocent people who just left the safety of the Sanctuary because of the fear-mongering campaign that his father started.

"They're scared. I know it. North knows it. And even though he's ready to send his shadow creatures through the entire place to wipe them all out, Nox knows it too."

He stops speaking as he looks out over the rows of eerily quiet houses in front of us before he continues, "I think they're all assuming that we're about to go rogue and turn into something worse than the Resistance. They don't understand what's really happening here. You've got to remember that they've all heard stories of the Dravens as though they were the Boogeyman. For years, they've been waiting for North and Nox to blow up someday like Nolan did."

That doesn't make me feel any better. "And what about me? Do you think they're all waiting for that from me as well with my void eyes? Because the only thing that's going to push me there is everyone acting like this."

Gryphon shrugs and hugs me closer to his side, slinging an arm around me as his hand stretches out over my bare stomach where my sweater has crept up. I feel his power heat his skin where it touches mine, and the ache across my shoulders eases off. I hadn't complained to him about it, the result of being twisted up into fifty different positions by each of them, and he chuckles under his breath at the color that stains my cheeks.

"Thanks," I murmur quietly, and instead of acknowledging that, he gives me something far more powerful.

"Know that if any of them ever attempt to call you anything, it'll be the last words they say, Bonded. I'm done playing around with this, and if they think that they're going to find a stake to burn you on, they've got another thing coming."

A memory flickers in my mind, one of my bond's, at that exact fate happening to me, and Gryphon nods his head as the shiver runs through me. "I remember it as well. The Soothsayer was there. It saw the whole thing. If I shut my eyes, I can see it as clearly as if it was my own memory. *Never* again, Bonded."

The dining hall is full of people, though it's quieter than any other time I've been here. Gryphon greets the Tac operatives who are standing watch at the door. Each of them nod respectfully back to him, then me, without a word, completely obedient to their leader. I sigh in relief.

Any of the operatives who are still here that have questioned us in the past have been put on leave, effective immediately. I told you that we're not messing around here, Gryphon sends through to me, and I nod back.

I move to the buffet-like station and begin filling up containers for each of my Bonded. It's a surprise to me when I realize I know exactly what each of them will eat, little bits of information I seem to have picked up without really trying, and when I hand Gryphon his, he smirks at me.

"I thought this was a North Draven trait? If you start taking on his personality as well, I'm out."

I laugh at him and grab a bag to start stashing away the food. "Liar. You love me too much to give up on me so quickly, and North is *definitely* not your least favorite

Bond."

He laughs at me and grabs the back of my neck to smack a kiss on my lips. "You've got it all wrong, Bonded. I don't play favorites unless we're talking about you."

"Can you two keep that gross shit out of my kitchen, please? I don't need to see it. I already know what's happening, and that's disgusting enough," Kyrie drawls as she places another tray of roast beef on the buffet.

I move away from Gryphon's arms to start filling up more containers with the fresh meat, knowing that Atlas and Gabe will devour a full container between the two of them alone.

"I'm pretty sure this isn't your kitchen, Kyrie. Plus, I've seen enough of you sucking face with my operatives for a lifetime, so you don't have a leg to stand on here."

She shrugs and sends me a grin. "Alex is pretty hot though, am I right?"

I shrug back. "I have no idea who that is."

I see Gryphon's shit-eating grin from the corner of my eye, the pure male satisfaction at the complete honesty of my words. His reaction is so instant, it's as though I've started talking dirty to him here in the middle of the room.

Kyrie sighs as though we're killing her. "Of course you don't. You're in the 'Bonded Group bubble' where you don't give a fuck about what anyone else looks like. Again, it's disgusting!"

I can't argue with her there. I haven't looked at any person, male or female, in months and had their looks factor into any part of my stance on them. I couldn't even tell you if there was someone attractive in the room right now. Except that Gryphon is here, and of course, he is one of the five hottest men that ever walked the earth.

I'm dumb enough to say this to Kyrie, and she makes a gagging noise as Gryphon smirks smugly back at her. His arms cross over his chest as he turns to beam down at me for a second before he looks back at her.

The smile slides off of Kyrie's face for a second. "Did Mom call you? She tried to call me, but I was too busy ignoring everything from the General to pick up."

I try not to flinch, knowing how much Gryphon adores his mom. The thought of him being separated from her again, and my part in it, kills me.

He just shrugs back at her. "She did. I think we are no longer on speaking terms."

My eyebrows shoot up my forehead, and I'm sure I look like an idiot right now. "You didn't tell me that."

He shakes his head at me, his eyes soft. "I knew that you'd blame yourself, and there's no need for it. She was very concerned about the god-bonds, and that's not anyone's fault. I'm not going to be upset or ashamed about any of it either. My bond is what brought me to you, so I will be happy and grateful for it for the rest of my existence.

Nothing about any of this bullshit is going to change that."

Some of the fight leaves me, but I still just want to curl up in a ball and cry for having any part in this.

Kyrie shakes her head and taps one of the large serving spoons on the tray in frustration. "This is why I don't want to find my Central. I can't imagine just *blindly* following some man away from my kids and my family and friends just because his ego gets in the way of things. It's disgusting."

Gryphon shrugs again and then holds out his arms, beckoning towards her until she darts around the table to hug him back. I can't think of anything to say to her. There isn't much that any of my Bonded could ask of me that I wouldn't do, but I suppose that's got more to do with trust than anything else.

I trust them all.

I trust them to make decisions for our entire group and not to act irrationally or in a selfish way without fully considering how it will affect the rest of us. I know it's something that North struggles with a lot, thinking through every one of his moves, all day, a thousand times over until he's sure that it's the best one for us all. Though it's taken me a long time to see it, I know that Gryphon holds his temper more often than not. Atlas gave up everything to be with us. I know that while it ended up being the best decision for him overall, it still was something huge to undertake at such a young age. Especially without ever having the promise of a good life or a good Bonded Group. Still, he had faith and was a good person despite everything.

Nox died for our Bonded Group.

He died for North and for us all to have the chance at a good, long life. He had no idea that my bond could bring him back like that. I will *never* take that sacrifice for granted.

"Give me a call if they try to contact you or if you need anything, Kyrie. Promise me. You're too secretive about things these days. I don't like it."

She scoffs and pats him on the back, pulling away to nudge him with her elbow. "I'm secretive about things because I don't need my brother sticking his nose into my business just for the sake of it. You do the same; please call me if they get their heads out of their asses or if something happens."

My blood chills at the thought of something happening, but Gryphon simply nods and reaches out to grab the bags of food that I've put together. "Prepare yourself, Kyrie. I already know that this mass exodus from the Sanctuary is bound to hit the Resistance's radar, and I have no doubt that there are going to be casualties. Before I told Mom that I was done with them, I made my peace with her too. If they don't come back… that has to be enough for me."

She clears her throat and nods, heading back to the

kitchen after a quick detour to hug me too.

I follow Gryphon out the door without another look at any of the dining hall occupants. We walk in silence, and it's not until their mansion comes into view for us both that I find the words to speak, my mind a whirling mess. "Do you really think something's gonna happen to them?"

Gryphon sighs and nods, squeezing my hand a little. "It's not a matter of if, it's a matter of *when*. My dad is the leader of some of the most wanted TacTeam operatives, and the Resistance will attack them the moment they find a weakness. I just hope my parents are strong enough to make it through, not that they deserve it after what they said about you."

I shake my head. "I don't wish them dead just because they don't like me. That really would make me a monster."

He smirks at me again, lifting our linked hands to kiss the back of my hand sweetly. "That's all right, the rest of us will be the monster for you. Fuck, I thought Nox was going to tear the General apart with his bare hands. Who would have thought that he would love you so hard once you got under his skin, Bonded."

I blush and duck my face into his chest, happy when the contact is met with quiet, satisfied noises. That he loves the contact just as much as I do fills me with a deep satisfaction.

"I don't deserve him or his love, but I'll do my best to

take care of it."

He shakes his head back at me. "Nobody deserves it more than you, Bonded. We are the ones who aren't worthy."

15

GRYPHON

We start taking in new members of the community the very next day.

North has a waiting list ten miles long ready to start calling people to bring them in, and we mindfully inform them about what had happened to free up this space for them.

None of them cared.

Every single person we contact about coming into the Sanctuary is nothing but grateful and desperate to come. I think we could tell them that they have to face the shadow creatures to enter and they'd do it with a smile. The problem with the Gifted who'd left with my father is that they haven't lived through the worst of what the Resistance is doing out there. They took refuge somewhere safe and forgot what it was we were running from.

I only hope that life on the outside isn't treating them too badly.

Scared people could do stupid things, and I have no doubt that the tales of what the Dravens can do have only been exaggerated and twisted over the years. Especially as they've gone from a powerful family of Top Tier Gifted to the stuff of urban legends and nightmares of biblical proportions.

They've even grown since I heard them as a child. I remember seeing North for the first time as a kid and thinking to myself, 'well, he doesn't look *that* scary'. Although, other people don't have the luxury of an entire lifetime of friendship to fall back on.

I get it, but it doesn't make any of this any easier. Watching my oldest and closest friends, the ones I share my Bonded with and have built an entire career and life around, struggle with the guilt of their actions sets my teeth on edge.

I wish I could go back to that moment and punch my father in the face as well.

"How many more families do you think we can fit? Did Gabe give you an updated timeline for the housing?" North mutters as he looks over the list again, and I shrug.

"The earliest ETA for the houses to start opening up on

the southern block is next week. They're already pushing themselves hard to get it done by then, any faster and it won't be safe for the workers."

North lets out a breath and nods his head. "They're already doing more work than we ever thought was possible, and a hundred houses will be ready. Two hundred more families will be able to squeeze in if we can allocate them correctly."

I move some of the papers and point out the demographic lists he's had made. "If anything, we need to start thinking about expanding the school. All of these families have young children in them, they've got the priority here."

North nods and starts shuffling through his plans until he pulls out a blueprint of the school with extensions. "It's on my list. I will speak to Gabe about it and keep going from there. He's talked about it before, and we can figure out how best to put it into place."

I nod and glance back over at Nox who's created a small fortress of boxes and information in the far corner of North's office, shadow creatures slumbering in open archive boxes and on cushions around him. If it were possible to take photos of the nightmare creatures, I would take one and send it to Oli, knowing that she'd treasure it more than she'd ever admit. Since I can't, I concentrate and send her the mental picture instead. A smile breaks over my face when I feel her joy at the image, the way that it overtakes her and rushes into me, making my chest tighten up.

She loves those damn creatures and the vicious man they come from more than I ever thought possible.

"How many of the newcomers do you think are able to be trained as operatives?" I murmur quietly, and North shuffles papers again before pulling one out. I swear he has information about everything on his desk, every option and opportunity to be explored and discussed and picked apart before he makes any moves.

He's too good of a man to be a councilman, they don't deserve him. They never have.

"I have already told the Transporters to send this list to the Tac Training Center for interviews. I was going to head down there in an hour or so to start the process, but Rockelle and Hannity have already requested a meeting with me to discuss what's been going on."

I shake my head at him. "You shouldn't be dealing with any of that bullshit. Just tell them you've got bigger things going on."

North takes his coffee cup and knocks back as much of the caffeinated liquid as he can in one go, looking as though it's been months since he slept. I'm going to have to threaten him with Oli soon to get him back into a sleeping pattern.

He's doing everything he can to not stress her out. If I

threaten to tell her how badly he's taking care of himself at the moment, he'll get back in line, I'm sure of it.

"I think I'm going to dissolve the council."

I startle, my head snapping around to look at North as my mouth tumbles open comically. Not much surprises me these days but that sure does.

"How are you going to do that? *Why* are you going to do that?"

North glances back over at Nox, but he is so far in his own world that we could be talking about just about anything without him noticing. "The how part of that is easy. There's only three sitting members left other than myself, and two of them are here already. The council is an outdated structure, something that was put into place by those who were abusing power anyway. We've said it for years, the categorizing of people by what their Gifts can do is disgusting. No one should have precedence over others just because of something they have no control over. Did you know that every single family that followed the General out of here was a Top Tier family? All of the Lower Tier families stayed. They're the only ones who understood what would happen to them if they left here. They've always been left to fend for themselves. I'm not just saying this because of their loyalty to us at this moment. I've been thinking about it for years. My father even discussed it with William, and I suppose my uncle is the reason I have hated this position so vehemently from the get-go. No one should be able to be born into this position of power."

I didn't know any of that, the inner thoughts of North Draven often don't see the light of day, and I've never gone snooping through his brain without his permission. None of it is surprising when I really think about it, though. All of it lines up with the character that I know he has.

I scratch at the back of my neck for a moment and think over his words, about the actual logistics of all of it. "So we're going to turn this into a democracy and have people vote? What do we do if they vote an idiot in? I'm not following some brainless civilian anywhere. Rockelle has been bad enough."

North shrugs. "I still own the Sanctuary, and I'm not going to give up control of it to just anyone, but I suppose it's something we can work toward. I think that the old council needs to be replaced with a new one, one where people have been voted into positions of power and only serve for a term or two. You're right though, there needs to be one of us on this damn thing. Otherwise, it's going to go to shit. I'm not having anything come back to hurt Oleander just because we want to be fair and nice to people."

North flicks out a hand dismissively, meeting my eye for a moment before looking back over at Nox. "Obviously, I would never do anything that might harm her in any way, but there is no mistaking that we need a change in the community, and we need it now."

I nod and tilt my head to the side, feeling very 'godlike' as I do so. "Setting up voting and a whole new council is going to be a nightmare. You should probably wait until we've dealt with the gods before getting into that."

North's eyes flash to black for a moment but when he speaks, it's his own voice that comes out. "Everything can wait until they're dealt with, but we need to think about what our lives are going to look like afterwards. Otherwise… what's the point of it all? My Bonded needs a better life, a better world. I'm going to make that for her, no matter the cost."

The Tac Training Center is writhing with bodies when I arrive.

Vivian and Unser are already here, directing people in and out of groups and taking forms with Gifts and background information as quickly as they're being filled out. Kieran and Rockelle are both already on the mats, testing skills and Gifts. I'm surprised to see that the groups are moving through the tests reasonably quickly. There are a lot more men and women who can hold their own in the sparring circles than I ever thought there would be, something that instantly fills me with relief.

We need all of the help we can get here.

I walk over to Vivian first. When he sees me coming, he shakes a clipboard at me. "You need to call the Dravens down here. We need all hands on deck, because we're drowning."

I take the clipboard and look over to watch the skills test of the man standing in front of Vivian. He's a Flame, elementals are one of the more common Gifts, but the part that has Vivian's eyes gleaming at him in such a manic way is his profession.

He's been a martial arts teacher for the last fifteen years; a black belt.

He could be a huge asset to get more people trained. I hope he's as good as the paper in front of me says he is.

"North and Nox are both out of commission for the day. We'll just have to make do."

Unser side-eyes me and waves his hand around at the doors. I glance over my shoulder to see that they're open again, more bodies streaming in. "I'm not sure we can simply 'make do'. We're not going to get through everybody today. At this rate, we'll have to start turning them away."

I definitely don't want to do that. "I have someone who can help faster than anyone else, and I have backup."

I reach out to Oli who has been spending the morning

resting, at North's insistence, under Atlas' watchful eye. He was so happy to have North's trust in the matter, and I know how happy it made my Bonded that we were all able to pull together during this time of unrest.

Can you pull on your training gear and come down to the Tac Training Center? We are overloaded with new recruits, and I need a set of eyes I trust down here.

She sends through a flash of pure joy, and I have to stop myself from smiling back at it. *Atlas as well? Or just me? He can always go and help Gabe if you just need it to be me.*

I don't have to think twice. *Bring Bassinger. We're trying to weed people out who aren't going to be useful for Tac missions. Those who aren't will be given other work on the construction sites. I'm going to use the Soothsayer to process faster. We've discussed it before, and it's much quicker than I am. It'll also be a good way to see who's uncomfortable around the gods.*

Atlas, who is listening in now that Oli let him into the mind connection, chips in, *Everyone should be uncomfortable around the gods, that's just smart.*

I get what he's saying, and that's the real question here. *We're looking for those who can't handle them or who feel a negative reaction towards them. Any sort of hatred or distrust. Fear is natural and won't be held against them.*

They both agree. I can feel them getting things together

quickly, the perfect operatives, even though they've never really been recruited.

I look up to see Vivian raising his eyebrows at me as he takes more pages from people, directing them over to Kieran. "Anything you want to share with the class there, Shore?"

I nod my head. "My Bonded and Bassinger are on their way down to help."

Vivian just shakes his head at me. "I don't feel like that's going to be much help here. Fallows will end up pushing someone into a sparring match with her attitude, and Bassinger will only egg her on. You know I love that kid, but she's got a mouth on her at the best of times. All hell breaks loose the second her eyes change color. Then we'll be dealing with a stampede situation."

I smile at him, and then my own eyes shift to black. "I'm three steps ahead of you there."

"Fuck me, that's still as creepy as ever," Vivian grumbles as Unser flinches back from me.

The Soothsayer fills my mind, taking control of my limbs, and I can feel as the emotions and personality melt away from my facial expressions. The Soothsayer reaches out to take the clipboard and Vivian gives it to him quickly, damn near shoving it in his direction, as though he's afraid to touch it.

It starts to hand the pages back to him with nothing

more than a yes or no, its mind moving faster than mine ever could.

Vivian and Unser scramble to set up a system to collect them, and I have to speak directly to the Soothsayer inside my mind to change the way that it speaks, not wanting it to piss anyone off right now. The last thing I want my Bonded walking into is an all-out brawl with hundreds of people using various Gifts. We'd win that fight, but how many would we lose in the process? It's just not worth it to me.

It agrees for her safety alone.

The moment the doors open and Oli walks in, the Soothsayer drops the paperwork and marches straight towards her, the terrified crowd parting like the sea as everyone gets a good look at the void eyes.

Oli lets out a little squeak of joyful surprise, grinning and throwing herself at the Soothsayer. I would say that she was putting on an act just to rub everyone's faces in the fact that we are her Bonded and she loves the gods within us as much as she loves us, but the joy is oozing out of her very pores.

She is thrilled to see him, the same way she is thrilled to see me. "What can I help you with, my Bonded?" she asks, and the Soothsayer rumbles back at her happily, pleased at being acknowledged by his eternal purpose, his love, his reason for existing.

I reach out to her through the mind connection, *We will*

send recruits over to you and Bassinger. Then you can set up a sparring match for them. It's working through the lists faster than anyone else can at this point. I will get Vivian and Unser moving people into the construction area if they don't check out.

She nods and reaches her hands up to cup the Soothsayer's face, drawing him down to her lips for a kiss.

Anything for you, my Bonded.

She has the gods wrapped around her fingers as tightly as the Eternal within her does. I can feel the pleasure and satisfaction thrumming through the god at such treatment. She is the perfect vessel for them to worship along with their god-bond.

I lose track of the time as I wade through the scores of people who come through the doors, moving them off into the direction that the Soothsayer sends them. At one point, I look over to find Oli staring at the mat that she has people sparring on. Kieran murmurs to her, pointing things out to her as he accepts her help seamlessly. Atlas watches over her as much as he watches the mats, stepping closer to her side the moment anybody approaches our Bonded, but everyone in the room treats her with respect.

Out of close to a hundred and fifty applicants, two-thirds of them are accepted to start training here in the center. Of the third that we move to the construction process, only one has a bad reaction to seeing my void eyes. His fear borders on an angry reaction, something the man can't control, but it isn't smart to be around us.

I reach out to North to let him know the Gifted's name and family so that we can do more research into him. We need to see whether or not we should remove him from the Sanctuary and find some other safe lodgings for them. All in all, it feels as though we have won something today.

When the Soothsayer finally lets me go, slipping back into the dark recesses of my mind, Vivian comes forward, holding a cup of coffee out to me.

"That thing isn't very friendly, is it?" he observes, sipping at his own cup as he looks out over the sparring mats.

Kieran has gotten into the ring with the black belt, and it's highly amusing watching them scuffle. The Gifted isn't very scrappy. He has a lot of perfected techniques that could be an absolute asset out in the field, but Kieran is more of a combination fighter, intent on doing whatever it takes to win the sparring match. It's an interesting match.

"It doesn't really have any feelings towards anything except Oli."

Vivian nods for a second and then shrugs. "If it's ready to burn the whole world down just to keep her safe, then it's a good thing we have it on our side. Maybe we can channel it a bit to keep the community safe as well."

"That's the plan. Who knows if we can make it happen."

I go back over to my Bonded, and Atlas slaps me on the back in a friendly gesture as I move past him. His eyes are narrowed on the group of men standing together murmuring amongst each other. They're not talking about anything of note, but Atlas is on high alert anyway, as he always is with our Bonded around, and I'm not going to blame him for that.

"You're back! How did it go?" Oli asks, leaning into my side as she watches two of the women fight.

Both of them have a little more than basic training, which is a great starting point, one that will get them on missions quickly under the right training regime.

"Everyone who came has been processed. Honestly, everything that happened might just turn out to be for the best."

She sighs and nods, calling out directions to one of the women as her feet shift a little dangerously, and I smile down at her. "Who would've thought that the girl who hated the treadmill would be correcting other people's stances?"

She scoffs at me and groans a little under her breath. "I still hate the treadmill, and you were an asshole to me. The real reason I'm here today is because Vivian was a true gentleman."

Black looks over at her like she's crazy, and Rockelle jabs a thumb over his shoulder. "*That* Vivian? Because that

Vivian's a way bigger asshole than Shore has ever been, that's for sure."

Oli props a fist on her hip as she pulls herself into her own fighting stance. "You better not be talking smack about Vivian right now, Rockelle. I will piss in your Cheerios so fucking fast."

He makes a face at her, glancing at me as though he's expecting me to jump in and save him, but only an idiot would speak badly about Vivian in front of Oli.

"We've almost gotten through the entire crowd. I didn't even think that was possible this morning," Kieran murmurs to me, and I nod back.

"Any standouts?"

"The black belt, but we already knew that, and maybe a handful of others. We should be able to replace those we lost fairly easily. How are North and Nox doing?"

I don't want to say much, but I never have to with Kieran. "Busy, both of them. I'll be dragging them out of the office later, I'm sure."

He gives me a curt nod before he starts barking out orders to rotate the people on the sparring mats once more, moving the last group in.

Oli bumps me with her hip, careful about how much affection she's showing me now that we're in business mode while still grabbing my attention. "You're going to make sure they come back tonight, right? They're not going to be sleeping up there again, are they?"

I nod my head. "Even if I have to physically drag both of them down, we will all be at the house tonight, Bonded. I promise."

Her shoulders deflate a little in relief, and just to make sure I keep that promise to her, I send the image through to North and Nox.

Your Bonded wants you home tonight. No excuses.

Neither of them question me.

16

OLI

I wake to a hand stroking my belly and a hot, hard body pinned against my back. I grind my ass into the thick, hard cock that's pressed against me, a low moan creeping out of my mouth. I don't need to open my eyes to see who's here with me.

I can smell their cologne, and I'd know by the feel of their hands on my body alone, but the low tone of their voices mixing together proves that the Draven brothers have finally come back to me.

I don't need my bond to tell me, I know exactly how much I needed this, how much I needed them.

Lips press against my own, a dark demand for more. More of me, more of this shared pleasure, more and more until there's nothing left between us that isn't shared. North's hand runs down my spine, slowly stroking and teasing the soft arches of my skin. I'm almost purring into the kiss, my body becoming liquid between theirs. We're all naked, not a stitch of clothing anywhere, and I'm squirming at the heat coming from them.

I'm scorched and lusting for more.

They work in tandem to reposition us, moving me onto my knees as Nox kisses me, his tongue stroking mine until my legs are shaking. The memories of that tongue against my clit fill my mind and stoke the fire within me until I think I'm about to implode. North's fingers make their way down my spine again, except this time when they make it to my ass, they keep going, curving around until he finds the wet mess between my thighs, his fingers plunging inside me. He groans appreciatively when my pussy clenches around him as though I'm trying to keep him buried there.

"Open wide, Oleander," Nox murmurs against my lips, placing a hand on the back of my neck as he moves back. I don't know if he means my mouth for his cock or my legs for North's, so I do both, flushing with pride when they both make rumbling noises of praise at me.

I want that praise. I want to be their good girl. I want them to love every fucking second of this the way I do too.

He pushes me down onto my hands so that I'm on all fours, but I go more than willingly, my mouth still open as he guides the thick length of his cock between my lips, his fist wrapped around the base of himself as his eyes flash to black. The shadows in the room deepen, darken, and take on a new life as his Gift fills his body.

It's just him here though.

All of our bonds sleep as we come together finally after too many nights apart.

North waits until Nox's hips slowly pump down my throat before his fingers slip out of me. He replaces them with his cock in a single, hard thrust, his hands tight on my hips as he holds me still for them both.

I forgot that I'd fallen asleep in Nox's bed, but I know for sure that North hadn't been in here then. I'd curled up in Nox's sheets, buried my face in his pillow, and just let myself wallow in his scent while I waited for him to get home. Gryphon had promised they'd both be here, but I guess I hadn't expected them to both be in here at the same time.

I didn't expect to have both of their dicks pumping inside of me at the same time either.

It was different before, their bonds had been out, and mine had demanded every little thing that it craved from them. This is definitely not that. This is both of them needing *me*. This is the three of us finding pleasure in each other, taking what we want, an elaborate dance of movement and lust and worship.

I never want it to end.

More shadows spill into the room, falling away from North and wrapping around me, stroking and caressing until I'm writhing between them. When I moan around Nox, stars exploding behind my eyelids until I think I'm going to pass out, my arms begin to wobble. Before I can panic about falling flat on my face, the shadows wrap around my limbs, lifting the weight from them until I'm suspended, laid out for my Bonded's viewing pleasure, to take and use however they see fit.

North's fingers bite into my hips as he moves, dragging me back to meet his thrusts and then pushing me forward onto Nox's cock with each stroke. The shadows around him grow and morph, curling around me until darkness consumes us, binding us together, filling us all and branding us forever.

We're Death Dealers, all three of us, and we belong to the darkness within.

When I come again, this time unable to move thanks to the shadows around me, a strangled scream bursts out of my throat around Nox's cock, and the rhythmic pulsing of my pussy around North's dick sends him tumbling over the edge with me. He pounds his release into me, his hips snapping against my ass as he lets out a roar, and my pussy gushes at the praise of his rapture.

Nox watches me come, drinks it all in, and only when

North pulls away does he move, his hand coming up to stroke my cheek. It's a soft and gentle caress, a small moment between the two of us before the burning lust fills his eyes again.

His fingers move to curl around my throat and he squeezes a little, just enough that he can feel the rough slide of his cock as he pumps his hips, forcing me to take the whole length of him. His eyes darken even more as he watches me take him, gulping him down so greedily when he comes with a groan. Who knew that the dark voids could become such bottomless pits of pleasure? That's a wondrous discovery that is burned into my soul, something I will remember in this lifetime and the next.

I need a hundred more lifetimes with these Bonds of mine.

I stretch my body out in the shower and let the hot water run over all of the sore spots I still have. Every inch of me is satisfied and happy as I get my head around the fact that I have to get dressed and go about my day in the Sanctuary today.

I'd rather spend the day in bed, but there's just too much to do.

Instead, I'll be doing whatever I can to help my Bonded

with the lives that we are building here. For a moment, I almost forget about the god-bonds and the Resistance, about how many people are out there hunting us down and wishing us dead. For a moment, I forget that I'm anyone other than Oleander Fallows, the luckiest woman alive with five Bonded men who only want to love me and worship me.

That's all I ever want to be now, the version of myself that couldn't possibly be happier with my life.

Nox is busy at the sink brushing his teeth, a towel wrapped around his waist. He'd started off in the shower with me, carefully and lovingly cleaning us both up, but I still had to wash out my hair and his mind had already wandered to the boxes of information waiting for him back at North's offices. I'm not upset or jealous by this at all. I know how important his research work is to him and how important it is to all of us.

The god-bond we have hidden in the cells underneath the Tac Training Center has given us a few clues on where we should be looking. Nox is determined to hunt more of them down, determined to wipe them all out before they become a problem for us.

North had gone to his own bathroom to shower, his eyes dark as he told me that I was too much of a temptation to him, a temptation to stay in bed all day and do nothing but revel in each other. As soon as the words leave his lips, it's all I want to do. Someday, maybe.

Where is everyone? Gryphon sends through to us, but the moment he opens up the mind connection, he knows the answer to the question without a word.

We all sound off anyway.

I'm at North's offices with my uncle, going over building plans. Atlas is here too.

North and Oli are at the house with me, we haven't left yet, Nox replies.

Why? What's happened? North sends through.

Everybody needs to come to North's offices now. Oli needs to be driven down in one of the ATVs, both of you need to come with her.

On high alert, I shut the water off and grab a towel, stepping out of the shower as I meet Nox's eyes in the mirror, my heart already starting to thump in my chest.

What is it? What's happened?

The gods have made their next move. I'm sure it's a trap, but we need to be ready to move out.

Nox grabs a shirt and pulls it over his head, his shadows falling down from his body and slowly forming into Mephis and Procel at his feet. I let Azrael down as well as I quickly towel off.

What's happened? North asks again, and I hear his footsteps down the hallway as he works his way back to Nox and me. I duck into my closet to change into my Tac gear.

The General is dead. His second brought my mother back right before he bled out, and we've let her through and put her in the cells for now. I'm sending Kyrie down to see her, but the Resistance took out an entire town. We need to mobilize and go look for survivors.

My heart leaps into my throat right as North makes it to me in the closet, his eyes guarded as he looks me over. I shove my feet into my shoes and straighten, swallowing roughly around the lump in my throat. There's a million things I want to say to Gryphon, but all of them sound wrong.

How many casualties are there that we know of? North questions instead, happy to keep things firmly on the business at hand instead of the very human side of things.

We're facing somewhere in the ballpark of a hundred and seventy. My mother had two children with her that she'd managed to find and bring back with the Transporter as well.

A hundred and seventy people are dead because they let the General talk them out of the Sanctuary. A hundred and seventy people that he had sacrificed because he couldn't face the thought of his son having void eyes and being the same kind of monster as the Dravens that he so desperately loathed.

All of those men, women, and children are gone, and

for nothing. A waste of life on such a horrific scale.

We're on our way now, Nox sends through, and as he steps closer to North, they share a look, and I follow them out to the garage without a word.

There's nothing I can say anyway.

I open my mind connection up to Gryphon. Regardless, nothing comes down the line to me, nothing at all. He has emptied out and become a blank slate, the same way Nox had, and I refuse to push him on this. I mean, I would never push any of them on something like this, but we also have a job to do. We need to be looking for survivors and maybe finding another god-bond to deal with.

There's no time to unpack any of this for him.

North drives the ATV, and I sit jammed between him and Nox, half on each of their laps. Nox had originally pulled me into his lap, but North had dragged me across his as well, both of them wanting to keep me close and protect me as much as they could. The shadows run alongside the ATV as we drive through the quiet streets. Whether people are still too afraid to move around freely or if Gryphon has put a stay-at-home order in place, I have no idea, but it's helpful not to have to explain ourselves or make nice on the way down there.

When we arrive at the base of the building, I want to throw up, but I put on a brave face as we make our way into the elevator together.

As the doors shut behind us, North murmurs to his brother, "Don't be an asshole about this."

I glance up at Nox as his lip curls and he shrugs. "I'm not going to apologize for not feeling bad about that dickhead being dead."

"I'm not asking you to. I'm just saying Gryphon can't help feeling a certain way about his father being dead. Don't be a dick about it."

"I'm never a dick."

That's the biggest lie I've ever heard in my life.

I'm not brave or stupid enough to call him out on it though. North isn't so kind, scoffing under his breath as he pulls the ATV up alongside the council offices and helps me off of the vehicle. August falls away from his body in an easy motion, as though North hasn't even really thought about letting him out, but merely being in my presence is enough to have him wanting the shadowy sentry out for my protection.

I let Azrael down from behind my ear again, having let him ride along with me here, and I lean down to give them both a quick pat. I would love on them a whole lot more, but I don't want to waste any time right now. Instead, we walk into North's offices together, finding chaos and bedlam waiting there for us.

Dozens of Tac operatives are already dressed and ready to move out, standing around and murmuring to each other quietly as Gryphon, Vivian, and Unser stand over one of the planning boards together, moving pieces around and making a plan as we get closer to them.

The door to the locker room opens as Gabe and Atlas both step out wearing the Tac gear and speaking quietly amongst themselves, somber looks on their faces. Atlas has a determined set to his jaw, understanding shining in his eyes at the confusing grief in the air having just gone through something similar himself.

He's careful not to look at Gryphon, and so is Gabe, both of them respecting his space at the moment.

I have no idea what to do in this situation myself.

I think it came more naturally to me with Atlas because I understood exactly what he was feeling.

Gryphon is a different pile of trauma.

He hadn't cut ties with his father, not really. My own involvement in the exodus of the Sanctuary makes it hard for me to figure out what I'm supposed to be doing here, how *exactly* I'm supposed to react and treat everyone. I might not have been the reason that there's a god-bond inside of my Bonded, or the reason that it woke up, but I'm still the one his father chose to throw his hatred at.

I'm the reason Gryphon decided not to fight him on his plans to leave.

There's also a part of me that is sure that the god-bonds have had something to do with this. I'm *definitely* the reason for that, and they've been watching the Sanctuary so closely, biding their time and waiting to try and draw us out.

This is where they're going to make their move.

North squeezes my hand one last time before he stalks over to Gryphon and the others, clapping a palm on Gryphon's shoulder for a moment before he joins the planning, just a small acknowledgement of what has happened, and that's all that my Bonded seems to need from him.

I understand that he is in a position of power and he won't necessarily want anything from me, but I still feel awkward not acknowledging it.

Stop panicking, Oleander, Nox sends to me. I dart my eyes over to him.

He's checking that his weapons are secured to his uniform correctly. Checking, double-checking, and triple-checking the way that Gryphon always has, the way he taught me to as well.

Now isn't the time for it. Gryphon has been trained to work through this sort of thing. We've lost a lot of people in our lives before and been forced to continue working. Don't count him out so quickly.

My eyebrows furrow. *I'm not counting him out. I just don't think it's fair. I didn't want to move for a week after my parents died, and no one else has been given that opportunity. None of us! Everyone has just had to… keep on working. I don't want that for any of you. You had to go to your uncle's funeral with a brave face just so the rest of the community could watch and gawk at it. It sets my teeth on edge.*

I want to scream as tears prick at the back of my eyes, but I duck down to fuss with the shadow creatures, swallowing roughly as I get myself back under control.

Gryphon's voice echoes in my mind, *it's something I will think about later, Bonded, when I see my sister and go down to see my mom. Right now, all I'm thinking about is the potential for survivors. Don't worry about me. I'm more worried about you right now.*

You should be worried about me, I send back, *because when I get there, I am going to tear the souls out of every single living creature in that place that has ever wished harm upon our community or my Bonded. I'm going to commit acts of crime on such a scale that it will rock everyone to the core. You should probably prepare your men for that, and this isn't even my bond speaking.*

A hand slowly wraps around the top of my arm and draws me up until I'm standing with my side pressed against Nox's as he sends through the mind connection, *Burn it all to the ground, Oleander. Burn it, and let's be done with it.*

17

I had thought that the horrific level of destruction at the Wasteland was the worst thing that I would ever have to face. I thought that walking into camps that had been turned into a field of blood and death would be the most chilling and horrifying thing I would see. That facing Silas Davies, enraged psychosis in his eyes as he stared at me like I was nothing more than an outlet for his rage and insane purpose, would be the bravest thing I could ever do.

As my feet touch the ground, Gryphon's hand slips away from my neck as the sickness eases, and I open my eyes to find myself in the worst type of hell.

Entire families are lying on the ground dead, mothers' arms around small children, fathers covering as much of their family's bodies as they can, all of them in piles, all of them gone.

I think this street had once been a normal suburb, a cookie-cutter neighborhood that would be such a beautiful place for kids to grow up and thrive in. We're somewhere out in the middle of the country where no one thinks to go, somewhere the General would have assumed was so far out of reach to the Resistance and their cause. I suppose he'd put some thought into it, made a plan assuming that he was right, and come out here hoping for a better life for all of these people.

I assume all of this because to assume anything else would add even more pain and grief to this situation, and it's already overflowing with that.

What I guess was once grass all around us is now nothing but scorched earth from the Elementals they must have faced, and blood is covering every surface my eyes touch. My stomach doesn't just drop, it bottoms out with rage and grief at all of this destruction, and for what? *Nothing*.

Nothing but to draw us into a trap, to get our attention, to cause us to stumble.

All of these people were cannon fodder to the Resistance and the gods that live within them. These lives all meant nothing to them.

I try not to look at any of the faces as we begin to move

through the rubble of the area. I'm aware that we've been living amongst these people for months now; there's a very real chance I will know some of them. I guess the best way to not fall into any sort of grief right now is to avoid it altogether.

Unfortunately, Gabe and Atlas don't do the same, cursing under their breaths as they recognize the faces around us.

I almost look when I hear the sharp intake of breath at my side, but then Gabe says, "Don't, Bonded. It's bad enough that it's in my head now, I don't need it in yours as well. Let me carry this for us both."

I swallow and nod, trying to forget the smell that lingers in the air, trying not to let *any* of this imprint on me the way that I already know it's going to. There's no avoiding it, no avoiding the way that every single time the Resistance hits our community, it chips away at us and our strength, our resolve and our sanity, eroding us until we're nothing but shells of ourselves.

I only hope that in the time between these attacks, we'll be able to build ourselves back up enough so that doesn't happen. It feels as though I've spent the last six months doing nothing but fighting. I feel drained at the prospect of any more time doing this, losing people senselessly and watching as those who are innocent of wrongdoing pay the ultimate price for those who just want power.

All of it is gut-wrenching and heartbreaking.

This is the worst sort of hell to be stuck in, and yet here we are again. I swallow back the bile that just won't leave my throat, and I keep my eyes on North's back as we move together. One of Gryphon's TacTeams fans around us as they move through the street in their search for survivors. I feel terrible that they have to roll the bodies over and press their fingers against necks to check for signs that maybe a Healer will be able to repair the damage.

I cast out my net of power; it's a much more reliable way to find survivors and my own way of helping out.

I want to vomit at the vast, gaping chasm of emptiness in the field.

"They're all dead," I murmur, my voice breaking, and North nods his head without turning around to look at me, his eyes carefully watching the area around us.

"I already guessed they would be, Bonded. I'm sorry I didn't prepare you well enough for that."

I shake my head. "I guessed it too. It's just... I already knew that's what was going to happen, but it's different being here, seeing it. There's no Resistance here either. There's no one left for me to hold accountable for this."

North nods his head again, reaching his hand out as the shadows play around us, sniffing the bodies. "Can your bond tell us anything? Who was here or if it can guess at which god may have done this?"

I scowl a little as I think about it, reaching out to my bond and finding it just as pissed off as I am. "It doesn't know. It can guess, but there are a lot of options, especially if they have help from other Gifted."

He sighs and turns back to me, carefully taking off one of his gloves before he cups my face, rubbing a thumb over my cheekbone and murmuring to me quietly, "None of this is our fault. I know that doesn't help, but hold on to it until we get home. I'm sorry you had to come here."

I shake my head a little and look out over the line of trees just outside of the suburb. The cold hasn't reached here yet. The leaves are still changing color, and there is an eerie quiet to the world around us. As I stare out over it all, I see a playground there, and my heart breaks in my chest.

I can imagine the children moving here and being so excited to find one. The Sanctuary only had one small play area at the school, something that we had discussed making a priority. North and Gabe had already started planning a large park for the children to play in, something we wanted to move up the list, but it's so difficult when we know how many people are waiting to be let in once housing becomes available.

Everything is a constant battle, a give and take. Do one thing and neglect another; it's an impossible weight for my Bonded to carry.

North steps away from me and with his ungloved hand,

he presses his palm to the neck of one of the men on the ground, his eyes flashing to black. I scowl for a moment before I remember that this is one of his gifts, a variation of the death touch. Yes, he can take life away, but he can also see the cause of someone's death, a trait I haven't seen come in handy until now.

"There was the Pain god. That's what came here and did this. At least we know what we're facing," he says.

Gryphon and Nox come stalking back over to us from where they had ventured a little further out, making their way through the lines of bodies.

"Kieran's caught the trail, he knows where they've Transported to. It could be a stop-off point to get to where we're going."

"It could also be a trap," Nox says, but Gryphon just shrugs.

"I'm confident that we can get out of any trap that they set for us, aren't you?"

Nox scowls, and his eyes dart down to mine for a moment. "I don't want to make any dumb decisions here just because we're pissed off at what they've done. There's no use in getting ourselves killed."

I let my eyes slip shut as I reach out to my bond, but the answer is already waiting for me there. "Let's go hunting, my Bonded."

Adrenaline fills my body as Kieran strides towards us,

a look of disgust on his face as he avoids the victims on the ground. "You're going to kill them, right? This isn't going to be a recon thing? You're going there, and you're going to gut every last one of the motherfuckers who did this? Promise me, Fallows."

North bristles at him speaking to me like this, but I nod my head. "Every last one of them."

"Good. I'll stick around and make sure you're okay. We're not going to get split up by any Shields this time."

Kieran shoves the gaiter from his neck up over his face, and Gryphon sidles up next to me, wedging me between himself and North as we grasp his second-in-command. "It doesn't matter who they stick between us, Oli's got it covered. Just try to stay out of the way if her bond comes out. I doubt it's going to be in a very forgiving mood."

"None of them are," Kieran snaps as his eyes flash to white, and then we *pop* out of the area without another snarky word.

The moment we appear, a body slams into mine and takes me to the ground. My stomach roils and my bond presses against my skin, but the smell of Atlas' soap and clean sweat, so familiar, stops me from spiraling completely out of control.

Gunfire sounds around us, explosions and hell breaking loose. I hear a grunt and then a roar. The crunching sounds of Gabe's bones breaking as he shifts, the god-bond taking over and the Draconis coming to our rescue. As the shadow of his huge body blocks the sun, more shadows fall over us all as North and Nox both jump into protection mode. The Draconis' jaws open and a roar comes out as it shoots flames up into the sky, the sound so loud my head begins to pound.

I feel so disoriented, so unprepared for what we've just stepped into, that it takes me a minute to figure out some vital details.

We're in a Wasteland.

One that used to be a Resistance camp, if the charred remains of the tents around us are any indication, and we're not the first TacTeam to arrive.

I don't remember any conversations about operatives being moved anywhere except for our attempt at a rescue mission, so my guess is that these are the remnants of the General's teams, that they too had caught the trail of the god-bond's Transporter and followed it here to get vengeance for the civilians that were taken out.

I don't know how good of a job they're doing so far, considering the heavy gunfire and Gifts being slung around everywhere. When a car is suddenly hurled through the air towards us, Atlas scrambles to his feet to catch it, to stop it from crushing the rest of our Bonded Group.

He grunts as he takes the full brunt of it, his legs moving underneath him even as his hands slip against the black, steel casing. For a moment, I think he's going to tip over—the weight knocking him off-center—and it's going to be goodbye for us all, but then his heels dig in and he regains his balance. He sets it down in front of us as a barrier, his hand slapping the hind leg of the Draconis as he steps back over to me and reaches out a hand to help me back to my feet.

"That was a fucking good catch," Gryphon mutters under his breath as he brushes himself off, reaching down to grab his gun from where he'd dropped it.

Nox and North have both already had their god-bonds take over, their eyes shifting as their shadows move out and begin to work. Though my own bond is here with me, it hasn't fully taken over yet. I think the prospect of watching me rip the souls out of people myself, of not letting it take over and using every ounce of our power, is too tempting for it. It's used to having to protect me from such things, my mind struggling with the morality and consequences of our Gift, but I can't deny how ready I am to be done with all of this.

I'm tired of all of the senseless death around me.

I take stock of the Wasteland area, trying to gather clues before I let myself get swept up. The tents are all destroyed, mostly charred, but some of them are also frozen solid, as though the Elementals have been battling it out here, fighting over which is more deadly. The layout doesn't look familiar to me, though. With how badly destroyed the area is, I'm not sure I would recognize it anyway. Since there aren't any tents left standing, there aren't going to be any prisoners to be able to take home.

The air around us is still suffocatingly hot, so we're probably hundreds of miles away from home, and the sun still hangs heavy in the sky above us. We're surrounded by woodland, which the Resistance loves, lots of coverage so only aerial searchers can find them.

Bodies flash around us on the battlefield, movement everywhere that makes it difficult to tell who's the enemy and who are the operatives on our side.

Gryphon's eyes flash to black as he lets his Gift kick in, taking over with his mind ability and making things easier to distinguish. I feel as though my head is spinning on my shoulders, too much is happening at once. The chaos of bodies around us and the crush of the heat against us as the Elementals wage war makes me panic. I feel as though I'm standing in the Wasteland again, waiting for Silas Davies to show up. I had thought I was coping a little bit better than that situation, but my throat closes and a cold sweat breaks out over my entire body.

Azrael lands silently at my feet, pressing against my

legs as he tries to distract me from where my mind has gone. I glance down to find August trotting towards us with blood and other unnameable liquids oozing from his jaws. As he approaches me, he grows even bigger until he can press his head against my belly above his brother as they calm the storm brewing in my head.

Perfect, precious puppies.

The fighting around us isn't just loud, it's vicious. At one point, I hear the sound of laughter, sickening as it mixes with the screaming. No one ever talks about the things you hear in a battle zone, no one ever talks about that or the smells of burning flesh, of gunpowder, of hot, sticky blood around us, of things that are so much worse than that... things I don't have words for.

There's no real glory in any of this.

I have to remind myself that this isn't forever, this is a job we have to do to clear everything out. We need to leave this place, to mark it down as history that we will do our best never to repeat. I feel as though we're waging a losing battle, because there's always going to be evil in this world. It just shows up with a different name, a different banner to march under, and a different person it serves, but it's always the same. Always happy to take innocent lives while furthering a pointless fight.

It all just pisses me off.

The god within me is filled with just as much rage.

"What's the plan?" Kieran asks.

Gryphon glances at the Dravens for a moment before he replies, "Don't die, stay close, and try not to get in anyone's way."

I shake my head at them both. "We're getting this over with. No more games."

I let my power out, casting a wide net as I feel where the Shields are in place to keep people trapped in the Wasteland. I feel them all—the Flames, the Transporters, the other Elementals, the Shifters, and the Neuros. Dozens of Gifted who have been convinced by the gods that the Resistance is the right way to go. All of them are helping to kill innocent people who just want to live peacefully. All of them think that they are better than everyone else, forgetting that in the end, people like Silas Davies really only care about themselves.

To think that all of this might have started with the god-bonds setting elaborate, decades-old traps for us. Just because they're jealous that we have each other.

It only makes it more satisfying when I pull my power all at once, yanking out hundreds of souls at one time, taking them into myself and consuming them. My skin glows with the power that it gives me, burning brighter as I funnel it through to my Bonded.

Gryphon gasps and clutches his chest as he feels the full extent of what I'm giving him. Kieran grabs his arm to steady him, and I cast the net out wider until I can feel all of the Shields as well, yanking their souls out to do the same. The edges of the Wasteland come down and reveal the thick woods around us.

I cast the net out wider again and again, yanking souls out until there is no one and nothing left here but the TacTeam members we followed out. It's not until my Gift hits the closest town, thirty miles away, that I accept that the god-bond has disappeared again, finding another Transporter to take it away from here. It's playing the never-ending game of 'cat and mouse' that makes my teeth clench.

North and Nox both let their bonds settle back into their minds, and the look they give me at the sparkle of my eyes and power they feel sliding down their limbs has my chest pounding. North looks worried about me, but Nox has nothing but pride shining there, pride in me and what I can do. Pride in the hard work that sometimes feels like too much, but I did it anyway.

Pride that he found me; that I'm his and he is mine.

18

NORTH

When our feet touch the Sanctuary ground, I wait until Gryphon has eased the sickness in Oli before I take her hand and lead her away from the group for a moment.

My eyes roam over every inch of her that I can see to check for wounds, but she was guarded closely while we were there, and there isn't a scratch or bruise to be found. Her eyes are bright as she looks me over the same way, a soft smile on her face, and I move to wipe a smear off of her cheek. It's just a small spatter of blood, but I don't want her to see and get upset when she returns home. I want nothing more than to fix every last one of these problems so I never have to see that anguish on her face ever again.

"How are you feeling? Tell me the truth, Bonded," I say.

Her smile turns into a grin and she bounces on her heels. "I should probably feel bad about how good I feel, shouldn't I? They were just regular souls, so I feel as though I've just slept for a month straight, and I'm ready for more. More hunting, I mean. I only wish we'd found that god-bond.

I nod my head, stripping my helmet and gloves off before throwing them on the ground, careless for once in my life because nothing matters to me except this perfect girl standing in front of me.

"I can't go back up to the house with you just yet. There's something I need to do first, but I need you to go up there and be safe."

Her eyebrows furrow for a moment, but she nods her head, leaning forward to press her hands against my chest as the others begin to murmur behind us. I want to tell her before I do it, but I don't want to start another argument with any of them either.

Instead, I lean forward to press our foreheads together and then send through just to her, *I'm going down to speak to the god-bond. I'm going to offer it something to get more information out of it, and when I'm done with that, I'm going to have a meeting with the rest of the council. I need you to know that I'm getting rid of it. I'm done with that. Our people are done with that.*

Her eyes widen, but she doesn't pull away from me, instead leaning in even further, like she's trying to crawl under my skin. It makes me want to scream, not at her, but at everything else for keeping us apart. All I want to do is lift her into my arms and carry her back up to my office, lay her out on my desk, and eat her out for days. Worship her in the ways that only I can.

I'm a selfish and terrible man, but I want to lock the door and have her all to myself for as long as she will let me.

If that's what you think is best. Just promise me that no one is going to try and stab you in the middle of the night for suggesting such a thing. That will definitely make my bond cranky.

I smile at her. *As if anyone could get past all of us. As if anyone would try, Bonded.*

She shrugs and then leans up on her tippy-toes to kiss me, a simple press of our lips together. But the moment she touches me, my control snaps. My arms band around her waist as I deepen the kiss, ignoring the groans behind me.

"We're out in the open! You're the one who calls the rest of us out for that," Atlas snaps, and I find myself acting completely out of character when I do nothing more than lift a finger up to him, flipping him off.

I enjoy the giggle that Oli lets out at my expense.

When she breaks away from me, breathing hard and her eyes twinkling, I glance over to find Kieran standing with his back to us both, his fingers in his ears as though he's trying to completely remove himself from this situation.

The savage look on Gryphon's face explains why, but Nox is staring at Oli with the sort of hunger that he only just allows himself to show around her, and it tempts me to abandon my plans and just drag her upstairs instead.

She gives me a coy smile, patting my chest for a minute. "We have time, Bonded. We have a whole lifetime ahead of us. Go and do what you need to do. I will wait for you back home."

She's the perfect Bonded for me and for everyone else, there's no question of that.

I wasn't expecting the cells underneath the Tac Training Center to fill up so quickly with people that we can't process because of their relationship to my Bonded Group.

As I walk down the long hallway, still covered in the blood and gore of the Wasteland, I peer into each of the cells at the people that are our biggest issues to work through at the moment.

Gryphon's mom is in one of them.

Aurelia is in another, and Jericho is rooming next to

her.

They stare back at me with varying levels of distrust as I walk past them, their eyes tracing over the filthy Tac uniform I'm wearing, a clear indicator of where I've been today and the lives I've taken. Gryphon's mom stands from the bed and walks over to the glass, pressing her hand against it as she stares at me with distrust written all over her.

I would rather not have this confrontation with her right now, but I know how much she means to Gryphon and Kyrie. The fact that she had brought Oli's parents' ashes home without question for her son, even when the General had tried to refuse, also makes my steps slow a little. I bite my tongue and step forward to speak with her.

"Are there any other survivors? Anyone at all?"

I shake my head, the corners of my mouth turned down in disgust, but I try not to let it show, another concession. I shouldn't have to hide the repulsion I have for this woman, but I do it for Gryphon.

"Why did you go? You could have stayed here, just refused to leave the house. He would still be here raging about it, and the rest of those people would be here too."

It's not fair of me to say. The entire catastrophe that has taken place isn't exactly her fault, but some of the blame can be laid at her feet. With no one else left to share that burden, it's placed all on her.

She sighs, looking thirty years older than she had only a week ago. "No, he wouldn't. He wouldn't listen to me about this. He never did. I can have all the regrets in the world about what happened, but he never would listen."

Her eyes fill up with tears, and I have a sinking feeling in my chest. I've seen Bonds lose their Central before. I've seen it a lot, unfortunately. They turn into an empty shell. You can see that the person left behind has had everything good sucked out of them. All their past joy is forgotten and every future opportunity is torn away as well. There's no hope for that light to return, no chance of ever feeling anything positive ever again.

It's not like this.

This is the regular kind of grief, the grief that says you've lost someone very important to you. Someone you shared a life with and had children with. This is not like losing a piece of your soul, something so vital to you that without it, your life is rendered meaningless.

This is *not* how Gabe's mother reacted when his father died.

Trying not to arouse her suspicions, I get out my phone and send a quick message to Nox, something I don't usually have to do anymore thanks to the mind connection. I don't want to force Oli to keep secrets from her Bonded though, and I don't want Gryphon involved just yet.

I'll rely on technology for now.

"Is there anything that I can do? Anything except sitting here in this cell and rotting?"

I give her a cold look and shake my head. "There really isn't. Everyone that could be spared went out to the Wasteland to fight, but it was too late. You'll just have to wait here until we can decide what we're going to do with you."

Her eyebrows dip down low at that, confusion clear on her face. "What are you going to do with me? It doesn't make any sense to leave me in here. I was a victim of the Resistance out there, you know."

I shrug back at her apathetically. "You'll stay here until a decision is made. I can't exactly let you out now that we all know what you think of my Bonded and the rest of the Draven Bonded Group, now can I? We can't very well let someone who was part of the defection freely roam the streets. If harm came to my Bonded… Well then, you might finally see the monster I can be."

Her jaw drops open a little as she glances around, but I continue, "Gryphon went home with our Bonded to break the news of the General's death and what we found in the Wasteland to Kyrie. He deserves to get some rest after everything that's happened. He doesn't have time to come down here and coddle someone who left him."

She closes her mouth and opens it again, no sound coming out.

I lean forward and lower my voice, my rage clear in my tone. "You did more than just leave your children. Every time the General snapped his fingers because he was so angry or jealous about something that his son was doing, instead of feeling proud of him, you left. You told Gryphon and Kyrie you were doing it to get him away from them, to give them a break, but you never even tried to stick around. Your son is far more understanding than I will ever be. Loyalty means everything, and you have plenty of it—just for the wrong person. Now you really can rot here for all I care."

I turn on my heel, and she slaps her hand against the glass to get my attention. "You're never going to pick someone else over your Bonded, Draven. You can't judge me when you haven't been put in that position yourself."

I turn to look back at her, shaking my head, aware that Aurelia and Jericho are watching this entire exchange and finding that I just do not care anymore. I really have lost the ability to put up with people's bullshit. Something inside me has snapped, and it won't ever go back together.

"I will never have to make that decision because I will never let it come down to a choice between my Bonded or my child. I will sacrifice *everything else* instead. I will never, ever do that to my children, and I already know my Bonded feels the same way because she's a good person... The very best. I will never put myself before them. All you're proving is your weak character. I hope you rot down here, but know that if you do get out, you should stay very far away from me, because it was not at my request. I will let my shadows consume you the moment they see you."

I stalk back down the hallway, ignoring the challenge in Jericho's eyes as I do, the way that he leans against the wall separating him from his Bonded.

I hate the whole lot of them.

Sometimes I wish that we could fill this entire space up with gasoline and light a match just to be done with it all. Some things aren't that easy.

I find the god-bond sitting at the small table, his palms flat against the wood as he watches me enter the space. He doesn't try to speak to me or comment on the little display he's just watched. He just stares until finally, with a sigh, I reach out to the Crux, offering him my body in exchange for the information that I require.

THE CRUX

The god-bond looks too healthy sitting in the seat across from me as I take over my vessel. It looks too well-fed, too taken care of here, too pampered, considering the threat that it is to my Eternal.

I raise this complaint with my vessel, but it gives me the paltry excuses of the human folk, things like 'the Geneva Convention' and 'acts of war' and 'setting a good foundation of expectations' and 'making us different from our enemy'.

I do not care for any of that.

I especially do not care about the mistreatment of those who would harm us. They deserve death, blood-soaked and gory. They deserve pain and torture before my Eternal eats their souls and turns them into nothing more than a life source for us, something to increase our power and our hold on this earth.

They deserve the worst that we've got.

"I thought you had been here for longer? You're not very good at hiding how you feel yet, or hiding the robot nature."

I incline my head at it. "We're not here to discuss me. You have information that I want. You can either give it to me without blood and pain or we can make this very fun for me and very unpleasant for you."

He stares at me for a moment, looking me up and down. "Why do you and the Corvus always look the same? Why are you always born into the same family, untouchable to the rest of us? The Draven bloodline has protected you all for generations. Even when the others tried to stop you from coming, you still found a way."

They were behind the manipulation of the Bonded Groups, the pairing of Gifted to people who were not right for them in an attempt to stop us from cycling.

All it did was make us stronger.

The vessels that we were born into now are more powerful than they ever have been before. I brought the shadow creatures to my vessel, but they are not the only weapon in our arsenal now. I know that the Corvus has even more abilities lurking within him. I don't know how my brother managed to win over his vessel so quickly, but he has access to it all without there ever being a fight.

The truth of the matter is that my vessel doesn't want me taking over, so I have not learned yet how to act in the way that the Gifted do in this time. I haven't had the opportunity to mimic them. Instead, I have nothing but the long and shifting sands of time under my belt, the old and tired soul who desperately hopes that this is it. That this is the last time I will be here. That this will be the one perfect lifetime that I will get to have with my Eternal before we all go to rest together in whatever comes next, finally finished cycling.

"Are you going to answer my questions or not?"

The god-bond in front of me sighs and shakes his head, muttering under his breath, "You haven't even asked any yet. Do you know how to make friends, or is that too hard for you in this lifetime as well?"

"I don't need friends. I have a Bonded Group and the Eternal. That is all I need. Tell me which gods are awake, which gods are here. Tell me who has already woken and died. Tell me everything you know in this lifetime."

He sighs again, splaying his hand out on the table and staring down at the scars there as though there are a hundred stories behind them, a whole life that he has lived here on this earth this time along with his vessel.

I care for none of it.

"When I woke, there were six of us. Now there are only four."

My eyes narrow at it. "Including yourself."

He nods. "They killed my Bonded, and your group took out another. They were hunting for you from the beginning. They knew you were due back, but none of them guessed that you'd all arrive together. They made a mistake."

Of course they did, but I cannot blame them.

The Draconis was not due to wake again for another hundred years or so, his cycling taking much longer than anyone else's. The fact that he has awakened in the first place is a miracle of its own.

"That's why they took the Eternal and didn't just kill it. They wanted to see how far they could push things, what they could force it to do. They really didn't think the rest of you would find it before they had taken their fill."

The room around me explodes into darkness, the

shadows forming so suddenly and completely around us both that the god-bond is choking on them. The black smoke curls around him, smothering him, engulfing everything until there is nothing but perfect night around him, the sort of darkness that is terrifying in its completeness.

"Which one? Which one took it and did that to it? They are all marked for death, but I need to know which one."

It makes a gurgling sound as the words squeeze out. "Pain. Pain has always been the ringleader. It's always pulled the strings and done everything it could. It doesn't just wield pain. It *is* pain. It cares for nothing but suffering for all of us. It doesn't want its Bonded. It wants everything to burn, over and over and over again. While the rest of us search for completeness, it wants nothing but destruction. The last cycle, it killed its own Bonded, and if its Bonded comes back again in this lifetime, I'm sure it will do the same. It wants nothing. Madness like that needs to be dealt with swiftly, or it will swallow the rest of us whole."

My vessel agrees completely, eager to be done with all of this.

"Tell me how you did it," the god-bond says as the shadows leak away, slowly drying up as they filter back into my body.

He's shaking like a leaf, his teeth chattering together. Even in this state, he begs me for what he truly needs. "How did you all wake up together? How did you keep the Eternal safe? How? I just want my Bonded. I just want what you have."

I shake my head slowly. "You'll never have what I have. When we are done with the rest of them, the Eternal will kill you and consume you too. You'll never cycle again."

I stand to leave and he stands with me, his hands flying out from his sides. One of the Gifted watching from their own cell startles at the sight of it. "I'm trying to help you! There's no use in killing me."

"You said it yourself... You're tired. You want this to be over with. We're going to make sure that that happens. This time, we'll make sure it's permanent. You should be thanking us. The time of the gods warring on this earth is over. There will be nothing but peace for my Eternal."

He shouts again, trying to get my attention to beg for his life, to stop me, a hundred other things, but I let go of control of my vessel as we exit the cell, creeping back into the dark recesses within his mind as I plan.

I plan to deal with everything to give the Eternal a better life. The life that it deserves, where it knows nothing but joy and pleasure, a life that they both deserve.

The Eternal and the perfect vessel it lives within.

Both of them mine.

Chapter Nineteen

Oli

The soft, luxurious fabric of my dress itches as though it were made out of some disgustingly inferior fabric, though I am very aware that North picked this out for me, so there is every chance that it is cashmere or some other luxury fiber handmade by artisans. It doesn't matter though because, as far as I'm concerned, it's made out of barbed wire.

"Stop fussing," Sage murmurs at me as she lifts the curler from my hair, and I shoot her a sheepish smile.

"I can't help it. I hate this. Can't we just… call in sick or something? I'm sure Felix could write us a doctor's note."

She grins at me and shakes her head lovingly. "I'm the only one allowed to use my Bonded for nefarious purposes like that, Fallows. You and Sawyer need to get in line."

I press a palm against my chest as though I am deeply insulted by her words, gasping dramatically. "And here I was sharing North Draven's power and prestige openly with you. I'll be rethinking that in the future, so you better not set any more buildings on fire."

She cackles and pulls out another section of my hair, winding it around the curling wand for me carefully.

I hate curling my hair or touching it in any way, shape, or form, especially since it has gotten even brighter. When North had informed us all of the town meeting he was calling, he'd made it clear that we all needed to show up in our *finest* attire with our *best* attitudes to show a united and confident front.

He'd argued with Nox about it for days.

I wouldn't be surprised if Nox showed up in nothing but a garbage bag and a cloak made of shadow creatures just to really ram home his opinion on such things. He vehemently hates them all and hates that North is going to be dealing with them on our behalf.

I care little for it all.

Just the thought of their eyes as they look up at me with a mixture of fear and loathing grates on me, but I know that it's not my fault. I was born the way I was, and at least I'm doing something good with my Gift.

"I still think that North should just send out a decree about what he's doing and let people just deal with it the same way that kings used to. It makes no sense to me that we are going to grovel for them right now," Sawyer says as he steps into the room, buttoning up the dress shirt that Aro's forced him into wearing.

He had every intention of showing up in an old band

tee and sweatpants as an act of rebellion, but his Bonded has him firmly wrapped around her finger. A single word from her had him scrambling for his Sunday best.

I roll my eyes at him. "We're trying to make sure that the community doesn't think that we're vicious dictators who think of them as nothing but pawns in a war. I'm pretty sure that sending out decrees would kind of set us back."

He shrugs with a grin, ducking his head so that he can look into the mirror and fuss with his hair. "North owns this place. I know it, you know it, everyone knows it. And to be honest, he could tell me that he's building a giant statue of himself and putting a throne at the bottom of it for him to sit on, and I'd still lick his boots every day. The alternative is to go back out there into the world and hope that I can face the Resistance, and now *god-bonds,* by myself. There's no way. I know exactly what those people did to my Bonded and her family. I know what they did to Gray's family. I know what they did to you. That's enough for me. I'm more than happy to stay here with my sister and my Bonded Group and know that we're safe because of people like North Draven. Even if he does turn out to be an evil asshole, it'll be worth it for me."

My bond does not like Sawyer calling North an evil asshole, but I can appreciate what he's saying.

He always did have a special way with words.

There's a bang on the bathroom door and then Gray's

voice calls out, "The three of you really need to get a move on. We're going to be late at this rate, and I'm pretty sure North will throw a fit if his Bonded isn't there on time."

Sage winces and shoots me a look, fussing with my hair one last time before finally declaring herself done.

"He's not wrong, you know. North really will lose his shit if you're late, and I'd rather not have that be my fault," she mumbles under her breath, and I shrug.

"Perks of being my bestie. I will absolutely deflect North away from any anger he might have at you."

She rolls her eyes at me and bounces my hair one last time, smiling at the results, but I look anywhere but the mirror in front of me. I don't need to see it. If she says it's perfect, then it's good enough for me.

I shove my feet into the small pair of kitten heels that North had dropped off with the dress and fuss with the back of them until they're comfortable, groaning under my breath as I pick at the dress again, trying to get comfy. It's simple and black, elegant without being fussy, and while it covers me from collarbone to knee, it's still a very glamorous cut. It's exactly the sort of dress that I would expect North Draven to pick out for me. It gives just enough hints that says he thinks I am beautiful without sharing his Bonded with anyone, even the rest of the Bonded Group.

When I mention this to Sage, she giggles and nods her head. "That sounds exactly like any Bonded man, Oli."

We open the door to find Gray and Aro waiting for Sawyer, their arms crossed as they both stare him down as though he's a petulant puppy refusing to do as he's told.

It's incredibly funny; even more so when he ducks his head and mumbles an apology for his bratty behavior.

"I never thought I would see the day," Sage mutters to me, and I cackle along with her, giving Aro a quick hug as I pass her by.

She only sticks around for as long as it takes her to reassure herself that Sawyer is getting ready and wearing the appropriate attire before she's off and running around after her younger brother. Lahn has no interest in wearing dress pants and a nice shirt. I'm surprised when Wick is the one who convinces the boy to slow down and get dressed with nothing more but a few kind words and the promise of a few rounds of Mario Kart when they get home.

He's incredibly kind and patient with the boy, helpful to Aro, and very respectful of her as they work as a team to get the boy dressed. I watch, a little shocked for a moment, before I turn to Sage, finding my bestie staring with literal heart eyes at her newest Bonded.

I bite down on a smile, and when she notices me, she nudges me with her shoulder. "I can't help it. I've been so worried about finding him a place in our Bonded Group that it didn't even occur to me that he would figure one out by himself."

"Has he? Figured it out, I mean," I say quietly, and she nods.

"It's still pretty rough around here. Lahn had a nightmare about the Resistance a few nights ago. He was screaming, and we all woke up in a panic. Aro couldn't get him to calm down, and Wick was so quick to jump into helping her. He sat with him for most of the night, and he helped Felix to check him over once Lahn was calm enough. He didn't even hesitate for a second, and it just proved to me and to the rest of the Bonded Group that he really is a good person. It's just a big adjustment period for us all."

I've had a few of those myself, so I can't help but nod back, slipping my arm into hers as we both watch the little boy dance around Wick on his tippy-toes, chatting away about high scores and the color of the car that he wants to win in one of the games.

Wick smiles back down at him, chatting away nicely and pointing things out to him that his sister needs, getting his shoes and socks on and finishing off the basic care tasks to get the little boy to the town meeting.

The difference in the way that Gray and Sawyer both regard Wick is like night and day. When we'd last been here, there had been nothing but derision and snark thrown in his direction, but now there is a thankful air around them, kindness and respect as they help their Bonded with her brother. I'm grateful that Sage might finally catch a break.

We head out to the ATVs together, Atlas and Gabe waiting at the door for us all. They were both happy to give me space while I got my hair done, especially since they know how much I hate the experience. When they see me, I duck my head to hide my grin from them.

Who would have thought such a simple dress would ignite both of them like that?

"The entire town is about to get an eyeful of you guys if you don't get your shit together," Sawyer snarks, choosing his words very carefully as he directs the small boy into one of the ATVs.

Trust Sawyer to figure out how to make dirty innuendos on the sly around small ears. Aro just shakes her head at him, buckling Lahn in and handing him one of the small, handheld consoles that he loves so much.

"Just until we get there and the meeting starts, and *only* because you did such a good job getting ready, then it's off and you have to be quiet and respectful while we listen to Mr. Draven speak, okay? He does a lot for us in our community. You need to be a good member of this town that keeps us safe."

Lahn listens intently to her and then nods his head, taking the game from her and switching it on without another word. He always seems so good and well-mannered to me, but I've heard from Sage that he definitely has spirit and some trauma that has kept his sister up a lot at night.

I can't imagine how difficult the burden of raising her younger sibling is. The way that she does it with such devotion, love, and respect for him is a huge credit to both her and her Bonded Group. I only hope that things will settle down in the world soon so that we can get to know the little boy a little bit more and help him make friends in the Sanctuary.

With the way things are at the moment, Aro doesn't even want to send him to the school in case he gets targeted for being so close to our Bonded Groups. It was something else I felt a small sprinkling of guilt about until Sage pointed out that it was as much about her own Bonded Group as it is about ours.

Kieran and Felix are notable players, as well as Sawyer, thanks to his job doing security.

Not everything is about me and my void eyes.

That was a quiet dose of reality I very much needed. As we approach the dining hall, the only structure big enough to house the entire population of the Sanctuary, if everyone stands, I remind myself of that again.

Not everything is about me.

But this meeting just might be.

It doesn't matter how prepared we are for the situation. There are always hiccups, the first of which is Nox's complete meltdown about where everyone is going to stand. I can see how much it grates on Atlas until he realizes what exactly is going on here.

Nox is concerned, of course, that someone is going to try to attack North as he's speaking. It would be a stupid idea, but it's also a very real possibility now that we know about the god-bonds and their ability to mess with things even inside the safety of the Sanctuary walls.

He also knows that I am the bigger target here.

So Nox finds himself split between who he is going to protect himself, the only person he truly trusts to do the job properly. I think we're going to have to watch the Draven brothers fight it out over canceling the meeting, except then I witness a minor miracle.

"I'll stand with North. I can project my Gift onto him the entire time, and if you guys all stand closely enough, I can project it over Oli as well, that way you can stand with her but know that I have North covered, as well as our Bonded," Atlas says in a very firm and confident voice.

I watch as the cogs turn in Nox's brain. He doesn't answer him right away, but it's also not a disrespectful thing, he's figuring out whether or not this situation feels safe enough for him. Whether or not he feels as though his brother is going to be guarded enough. I can tell that North is having to physically restrain himself from getting involved, but we leave it to Nox for a moment until finally, he turns to me, three shadows falling from his body as Mephis, Procel, and Rahab appear.

"Stand right here with me, Oleander," he says, pointing. I do as he says, ignoring the shortness of his tone.

It's all the answer that Atlas needs as he steps up beside North and gives him a nod. Gryphon flanks my other side and talks to Gabe quietly as they figure out exactly where best to position themselves. If anything happens, Gabe will need the room to shift into a dragon if the Draconis takes over.

Gryphon has a good point of view from where he's standing, able to not only reach out with his mind to see where everyone is but also to check for any discrepancies within the crowd.

As I prepare myself just in case we require Soul-Rending today, though I sincerely hope that isn't going to be the case, Nox's fingers wrap around my wrist like a bracelet, holding me as though he thinks I'm going to attempt to run away from him. Or maybe he thinks I'll run head-first towards any danger that might appear. I'm not sure, but I don't attempt to pull away or move from him even as the room begins to fill up around us.

I hate the feeling of all of their eyes on me.

I never did enjoy being the center of attention like this, and my sarcastic nature wants to kick in, to deflect away from the situation. Unfortunately, I promised North I'd be on my best behavior.

Something I kind of regret now.

Sage's Bonded Group comes to stand at the front with us where Kieran can watch over his Bonded as much as he watches over the room, and Sawyer's Bonded Group comes in shortly after, having waited outside until their parents had arrived. The Bensons stand close to their children, looking well-dressed and confident as they throw their support behind us as well. Vivian, Unser, and Adella shepherd in their own children as they join us.

North had taken a very calculated risk when he called the meeting, and he and the others had spent quite a lot of time making sure that security was in place, knowing we were all going to be in one spot for however long this takes.

I don't feel as concerned about it.

Not with my Gift cast out like a net over the entire building and knowing that Gryphon is doing the same, our eyes both glowing black with the use of our power. I'm sure it's making some people here uncomfortable, but I'd rather be sure we're all safe.

Nox's fingers tighten around my wrist, and I glance up at him, but his eyes are fixed on the end of the room as more people fill the space.

What is it? I send to him, and he doesn't react as he answers me.

I recognize some of the newcomers from Draven. I don't like them, and North should have warned me.

I nod and flex my fingers but there's nothing I can do to fix that situation, something for the brothers to work out amongst themselves. Instead, I stand there with my void eyes surrounded by my beloved Bonded Group as the entire town watches us. I stand there with my back straight in the beautiful dress North had picked for me, my white, ghostly hair curled to perfection, makeup on, kitten heels, and red lips stretched into a smile as though I'm not a monster in disguise.

I stand there and hope that they all believe me, because it's true.

Then North starts the meeting, carefully stepping up to the microphone as he smooths a hand down his tie and buttoned jacket. Atlas shadows him the whole way with his own void eyes as he calls on his Gift to ensure that our Bonded Group is safe.

"Thank you for joining us here tonight. I know that this is unexpected, but there have been a lot of changes here in the Sanctuary over the last few days that we need to discuss. I am happy to be the one to go over it all with you and keep you up to date. Please save all questions until the end."

The meeting with the entire town goes about as well as we were expecting.

Half of the room can't believe that North would want to give up control of the place, and the other half feel as though they're being thrown out to sea without a life raft, though we do everything we can to reassure them that this isn't the case.

"The council cannot continue. It is an outdated form of control, and as a community, we have moved past it. Ranking everybody's Gifts into Top Tier and Lower Tier is a sign of elitism, and it only serves those in power," North says, and I hear the ripple of disgruntled voices at the front of the group.

I'm quick to look over at them, using the haunting sight of my void eyes on each of them as a deterrent for the grumbling, and it works swiftly.

I see members of the now-defunct council swallow roughly and shift uncomfortably on their feet. Unhappy as they might be with no longer being at the top of the food chain, they aren't willing to take me on to get their status back.

"It's been a breeding ground for Resistance recruiters, and we all know it. Look around. There are only four families from the council here in the Sanctuary, only four families could make it through the vetting process. It's unacceptable. We can't continue that way. We know this already; only a madman would continue trying the same thing over and over again and expect a different result."

I feel my bond's pleasure inside of my chest, and I'm careful not to let the smile show on my face. We were those 'mad men', of course. The bonds chose to live over and over and over again until this time, finally, we all live together, but there's no need to be fussy over the way that North is wording things right now.

We're here to show our support of him and his decisions, to show a united Bonded Group, along with our friends, as we attempt to make things better.

"You really think this is going to work as a democracy?" someone calls out. Although North had asked for the questions to be held off until he finished, he's happy to answer.

"I think that's exactly what we need. I think that a voice needs to be given to members of many different Bonded Groups, from all upbringings and experiences. Then we can come together to make decisions that serve us all, not just those who have always held power."

"That's easy for you to say, Draven," someone else calls out, and I tug a little at the net I've cast out to figure out exactly who it was. Unsurprisingly, it's a family member of one of the councilmen; a son who had hoped to someday hold the chair his father currently sits on. North is a lot more kind than I feel when he addresses the kid.

"I have made it very clear to every member of the council over the years and every person who has come into this town that they are more than welcome to question my stances on things, but to question my integrity over something like this comes with only one answer. You show me where you have funneled all of your resources, your wealth, your privilege, the things that you were given by birth and not just worked for yourself; you show me that you have funneled them into something that is purely for your community, without any payment or expectations. Then you can speak to me on such issues. I built this town for my community. I have fed this town. I have provided utilities and supplies, and I have done it all without ever asking for a single thing in return. I did so with my father's money, my grandfather's money, and my great-grandfather's money. I did so with the seat on the council that was given to me by birth and by blood. I did so without ever expecting so much as a 'thank you', which is a good thing, because most people haven't thought to thank me for a damn thing."

He takes a breath and looks down at me for a second before looking back up, using a single moment to square away his own feelings before continuing. "My father started this town with my uncle. My father, who you're all so terrified of for a single moment of extreme anger and emotion that he had no control over. Every last one of you villainized him for a single moment of his life that wasn't his best. Let me make one thing very clear to you all now—my mother deserved the death she got."

The entire room goes silent.

I refuse to look around at anyone or make a face that might give away how I feel about what North is saying. Nox's fingers are cold around my wrist, but he's not surprised by this admission.

North must have warned him that it was coming.

"I will not speak on this issue any further. I won't tolerate any gossip about it either. My mother transgressed on such a level that I feel nothing towards her death but gratitude to my father for doing what was right, even at the cost of his own life. I have borne the brunt of the hatred and distrust for my family name because of an act of real love from a father, and I did so because it's no one else's business. My father died with a clear conscience, and I have always intended to live up to his legacy. Dissolving the council and setting up a new one does so."

No one dares to speak, no one moves, and no one in

this room dares to question the honesty or integrity of North Draven again.

20

OLI

L ife enters a weird, new normal for us all.

Gabe and Atlas spend their days helping build houses and working on the new extensions for the school that are under way. North and Nox occupy themselves organizing an election for the new council. They go through the logistics of setting something like that up and how they can best use their resources to ensure that the Top Tier families don't attempt to corrupt the voting process. I think it would be incredibly bold of them to attempt it. When I say this out loud, everybody stares at me like I'm either dumb or naive.

"Men in power will always choose to stay in power, Bonded. You should remember that," North drawls as he sips his whiskey at the dinner table, pages of information still spread out in front of him even as he eats.

I smile coyly back at him. "I don't need to. I have a Bonded Group for that. I get to dance around and think the best of everyone at all times. Isn't that great?"

Gryphon scoffs at me and takes one of the rolls from my plate, ignoring the daggers that North shoots at him, but I bat my eyelashes until he serves me a spoonful of potatoes in exchange. I wasn't expecting to love them as much as I do, but the chef has always been insanely talented at figuring out exactly what carbs I need on any given day.

"You don't think the best of *anyone* at *any* time, not even your Bonded, so don't try that bullshit here, Oli." I flick a pea in his direction, but he's not exactly wrong.

Gryphon spends his days down at the Tac Training Center, working with the new recruits to get them as trained as we possibly can before our next conflict crops up. There's no doubt in any of our minds that it's only a matter of days, not weeks, before we're hit again. The Resistance have always tried to throw everything they can at us without taking a break, and the news of the deaths has already quieted down. I feel as though we're in the calm before the storm.

I spend my days bouncing between the three groups, trying to help but mostly being a distraction to them all.

More often than not, I find myself pressed up against a hard surface somewhere. My Bonded are just as insatiable for me as my bond is for them. I might also enjoy their presence a little more than I'm willing to admit, which is a whole lot.

I spend more time with Gryphon than I do the rest, though it isn't favoritism. I'm keenly aware that he's just lost his father. His mother, from whom he is estranged, is still sitting in the cells underneath the Tac Training Center. She's not exactly a prisoner, but she's not trusted enough to walk the streets of the Sanctuary.

I tried to reassure them all that I'm fine with her being out and about. I don't think she's going to attempt to hurt me, and I doubt she could even if she tried, but her words are still very clear in my Bonded's minds. Gryphon was the first person to shut down that idea.

It's only after I go to visit him at the Tac Training Center and he squirrels me away into the small office that he finally reveals what has been eating away at him all this time.

He sits me on his desk in front of him and takes a moment to lay his head across my lap, enjoying my fingers as I scratch his scalp after I pull the hair tie out, threading my fingers through it as I work. I'm intent on just being here for him and offering him whatever comfort I can. Physical, mental, emotional; I'm here for it all.

"My parents weren't really Bonds," he mutters against my thigh, and my fingers falter for a moment before I get back to scratching.

"They did the blood tests?"

He shakes his head. "My father refused. I got Sawyer to pull them and rerun them. He's only doing them on my request because the database is so big. It'll take him years to rerun everything, but there was something that I just couldn't let go of that the god said… North too. So I asked him to rerun them. My mom also requested that we don't do it. She told me she knew exactly how she felt about my father, and she didn't need a blood test to tell her they were Bonds. I guess she was wrong."

I scowl a little as my eyes wander over the large map of the entire country he has hanging over his desk. Small flags mark the Resistance camps. It looks a lot like the one that Atlas' mom had sent to us before she died, only there are a lot of older camps and Wastelands on it that have already been shut down.

I'd questioned him about it the first time he brought me up here. He'd sent me a sheepish grin, which was so foreign on his face that I almost wish I'd taken a photo of it.

"It's proof that we're actually getting something done around here. Proof that we're making a difference. That even though more Resistance camps and Wastelands keep popping up, we are still getting rid of some. It might not seem like a lot, but to the people trapped inside of them, it's huge. I have to remind myself that every life saved might be a single number on our data sheet, but to that one person? It's their entire life. Remembering the small things in this big mess is what gets me through the night when everything becomes just a bit too much."

I don't like him speaking like that.

It sends a small tingle of fear into my belly, but I understand what he means. Sometimes I lie awake at night, the sound of their breathing all around me, and yet, even in the safety of their arms, I can't go back to sleep.

I know exactly what he's talking about.

"Do you really think she doesn't know? Or that she's just convinced herself that she does? I can't imagine not knowing."

Gryphon shakes his head again, rolling his forehead against the soft flesh of my thigh as he groans at the firm tension of my fingers as I scratch.

"You know what this feels like because you have felt a true Bond between us. How else are they getting everyone into the wrong Bonded Groups? Unless they really have been manipulating people's minds... Except that none of these people know what a Bonded Group really feels like. They get butterflies at the idea that someone belongs to them, and they think that's it, that's enough. They haven't felt what it's like to look at someone and have their entire world shifted on its axis so that that person is the center of it. They don't know what it feels like to look out and see your heart living and breathing outside of your own body. They don't understand what I felt when I saw you."

My throat closes, and I bend at the waist until I'm hugging him, awkwardly laying myself over his back that's draped over my legs. We're a messy pile of limbs, but it's perfect and exactly what I need at this moment. It's what he needs too.

"Well, that means that you weren't a product of a Bonded Group. North and Nox weren't either, or Atlas. I guess that leaves me and Gabe."

It's never occurred to me that I could rerun my parents blood, but I suppose there's a way that I could. Do I need that information? Do I want to have it? Will it change the way I think of them? Has it changed the way that Gryphon thinks of his?

I'm not sure, and I don't want to ask anything of my Bonded right now, not at the moment anyway.

Instead, I revel in the way that he's enjoying my touch, in the pleasure of us being here quietly together. Honestly, for now, it's enough.

The prospect of my parents not being Bonded weighs heavily on me. It's not until a few days later, when I am holding pieces of drywall in place for Gabe to fix them, that I finally find a way to speak to him about it—a way for the words to come out of me and not sound broken and desolate or just plain wrong.

"Do you ever wonder if your parents were Bonded or if they were also part of the Resistance scheme?"

We're alone in the house.

Atlas just left on one of the ATVs to go and pick up more grout and boxes of nails for us, leaving with a kiss for me and a slap on the shoulder for Gabe as he got to work. He's flourishing now that he has picked up the basics of building under Gabe's tutelage. The first time that Gabe had declared some of his work as perfect, I saw Atlas beam with pride.

It occurs to me that he's never had to really work for anything before.

Being a Bassinger on the East Coast had made his entire life very easy, and I'm reminded of when he'd first started training with Gryphon and I. Gryphon had declared his form and technique lacking, thanks to overpaid trainers who wanted nothing more than his parents' money and prestige. They didn't really give a shit about whether or not Atlas truly knew how to defend himself.

I remember *exactly* what it looked like the first time

that Gryphon had also declared his form perfect. Atlas gets serious pride from working hard at something and doing it right, and doing construction with someone that I now see is absolutely his best friend is no different.

Gabe tacks the drywall into place and then shoots me a wry grin. "I've done my best to make sure that you never have to meet my mother, and I don't really want that to change. I don't need Sawyer to rerun the bloods to know that my mom was definitely Bonded to my dad at least. You don't break the way that she did without there being a Bond in place. She's not really here anymore."

I have accidentally stepped on my Bonded's trauma, one that he has always been so careful about keeping hidden from everyone. When I wince, he chuckles under his breath at me, bending down to give me a quick peck on the lips as he moves to the next piece of drywall to tack down.

"Don't worry about it, Bonded. It's not something I feel ashamed of anymore. It's more like frustration that she's just chosen to tap out. Gryphon has assured me that this isn't a choice for her, that her mind is absolutely broken, but it still feels like a choice to me, no matter how hard I try to see it any other way. Meeting you helped a little, because I know how badly I would take anything happening to you, but she's still my mom, you know? It still feels like a rejection."

Even feeling that way, he's taken care of his mom with all the understanding in the world. No matter how he felt internally, he's cared for her, and that speaks volumes about the character of my Bonded.

I nod and bend to help him lift up the next sheet, doing exactly as he asks, carefully and with consideration. I know that this is the one area of his life where Gabe is a perfectionist, the one area that he holds himself and everyone else to a very high standard. I don't want to be the person to mess his work up for him.

"Do you think we'll feel differently when we have kids?" I ask quietly, shifting my weight on my feet as he straightens up with wide eyes.

I realize what I've said, and my cheeks turn red as I fumble to explain myself. "I mean, *if* that happens, I guess. I just—I'm trying to figure this out and how it relates to me and my parents, because I'm thinking about running their blood as well, and, *shit*, I've really put my foot in it—"

Gabe cuts me off. "This is the first time you've ever brought up kids in our entire relationship, Bonded. I'm allowed to be surprised for a second. I'd started assuming that you didn't ever want them because anytime anybody talks about anything to do with the future, you space out and try to figure out how you're going to fill your days up. That kinda makes it sound like you're not planning on another generation around here."

My blush deepens and I shrug. "That's a valid response to things, Gabe. What *are* we going to do with our days if Gryphon isn't having to train people all day? If Nox and North aren't doing tactical planning and research and we're not having to house people running away from conflict… What are we going to do?"

Gabe carefully sets down his tools and then takes the drywall off of me, putting it down at our feet as well. Then he frames my face with his hands, gently leaning down to me. I'm sure we look like an absolute mess covered in dust and debris from the building site, but neither of us care as my breath catches in my throat and he stares me dead in the eye.

"I think what we'll do is spend a few years doing absolutely *nothing* except spending time with each other without any obligations. Then we might travel, see the world, and do all of the things that we're supposed to do. Then I think that nothing sounds better to me than a million kids."

A laugh sputters out of me. "I don't think I can have a million kids, thank you very much, Gabriel Ardern!"

He kisses me, sweet and pure, as though he's pouring that beautiful happy sunshine of his into me, and it warms me to the core. "I think you'll love every second of it, Bonded. I think we'll have one and you'll see how much the entire Bonded Group loves that child, how much we all will love and nurture and cherish a child born here with us, and you'll want even more. I *also* think that North is going to lock you in a tower the moment you say that you want kids to demand that you pass on the Draven name first. I can already imagine him and Nox battling it out over this since technically either of them can father a Draven child."

I think I forget how to breathe at the very idea of any of that, but then as I think about each one of them having a child, I feel the exact same way.

That's an entire side to our Bonded Group I've never thought of before, something that I never assumed we would have peace for long enough to really consider. I'm absolutely not going to bring a child into the world as it currently is. With god-bonds chasing us and the Resistance having a target on our backs, it's not fair and it's not right, but the whole point of us getting rid of them is to live in peace. To live and love and do everything that Gabe has just described, everything we could ever want with each other.

"A Draven baby," I murmur, and Gabe grins at me, pure sunshine and happiness.

"I don't care who goes first, Bonded. I know that I'll be able to convince you to have just one more with me."

I shake my head at him again, picking up the drywall and getting it back into place, happy for the distraction to calm my racing heart.

We work quietly for a moment before I find myself having a whole new mental crisis. "What if I *do* only want one? What if the thought of more than one is terrifying to me and that's it?"

Gabe shrugs. "Then just have one. Like I said, it's going to end up a Draven, we all know it. To be honest, Bonded, if that's what you want too, then that's okay with me. I'm more than happy playing football with our kid no matter what last name it has or what color hair. Though to be honest, I think white would be pretty cute."

I blush again and mumble under my breath, "My hair was originally black, you know, as black as the Dravens', so there's a pretty good chance it's going to be black, no matter what."

Gabe shrugs again, picking up his hammer. "It doesn't bother me either way, and I already know it doesn't bother anyone else either... except for maybe North. Have fun having this conversation with him someday."

I hope that day is *very* far away.

If Atlas notices the change in the mood between Gabe and I when he returns from collecting supplies, he doesn't comment on it. Instead, he just joins in with the good-natured bantering and the flirting that happens whenever the three of us are on site together.

I've fallen into a sort-of menage relationship with them both. One where I'm equally excited to see both of them together as I am to see them by themselves. There's never an expectation of being with either of them alone anymore because they find it easy enough to share me between them, and the only thing stopping us from taking advantage of the empty building is the fact that it is a school for young children, and I refuse to be inappropriate in such a way.

Atlas rallies hard to convince me otherwise.

"I can't stand up in front of an entire community at a meeting, acting like I'm so pious and good, if I've been railed by the two of you in one of their kids' classrooms. It's just wrong!"

Gabe roars with laughter, but Atlas only waves a hand out in front of himself as though none of this is a big deal. "It's not their classroom yet. It's not as though we're going to be sweeping crayons onto the floor. If you're that fussy about it, I'm sure that between the two of us, we can hold you up. You wouldn't even have to get your knees dirty, Bonded."

Gabe smiles lasciviously at me, getting a palmful of my ass as he squeezes and pulls me in close to his chest, smelling like clean sweat and dust. There's a small smudge on his nose and it is way too endearing to me. "I'm happy to get my knees dirty for you, Bonded, if that's what you'd like."

My entire body runs hot at his words, my nipples hardening underneath my shirt as I groan at them, and both of my hands fist in his shirt as I try to tell my body to push him away. "Don't make this any harder for me than it already is. I really can't look anyone in the face if this happens here. Let's just head home and do it in a nice comfortable bed or a shower…hallway…kitchen counter—"

"Fuck it, the front doorstep," Atlas cuts in, pressing up against my back, and he kisses down my neck.

I melt into a puddle between the two of them. I really can't take much more of this.

"Please," I say, my voice ending in a moan, and Gabe finally has the strength to step away from me, grabbing my hand and tugging me along behind him, leaving Atlas standing alone in the room with the hard outline of his cock clear in his taut jeans.

"Home and bed, right now," Gabe says with a laugh, pulling me through the building until he can deposit me back onto the ATV, tucking the seat belt around me as he climbs into the trunk, leaving the driver's seat for Atlas.

They take turns on who gets to drive and who has to sit in the back. We'd learned long ago that having me sit in the front, half on each of their laps, is not a good idea. Especially when we arrive at building sites to find Gabe's uncle and cousins standing around waiting for us.

The amount of awkward situations we've nearly gotten ourselves into is embarrassing, to say the least.

Atlas drives like a maniac on purpose, I'm sure, just to make me laugh. As we pass people on the streets, he throws them all his usual haughty look, even as Gabe calls out and waves to everyone he knows, as always, the golden child of the Bonded Group.

I try to look friendly enough without waving at anyone. I have limits of how far I'm willing to go to be nice to these people, and I'm happy when we finally pull up to the house. I'm not good at playing nice like that, not at all.

Atlas parks the ATV in the garage, and he's careful about making sure that it's locked up, putting the keys in the lockbox and shutting the door behind us. He's doing all of the responsible shit that he should be doing thanks to the lecture that we'd gotten from North and Gryphon about such things.

Gabe never worries about it too much, doing all the tasks as required but without the look of intense concentration that Atlas has. He's not worried about impressing or proving himself to anyone, I suppose. He's happy just being Gabe, the youngest Bond of the group who was mostly raised by the other members in his teenage years. He relied on them as 'older brother' figures as much as other members in the Bonded Group. He has nothing to prove, and the confidence he has is a testament to that.

I think Atlas is close to realizing that he *also* has nothing to prove to anyone anymore. Every hoop that was presented to him, he jumped through beautifully, no matter how high or whether or not they were on fire. I am incredibly proud of everything that he's achieved.

"Why are you getting teary, Sweetness?" he murmurs quietly as we move into the house. "That's not the mood I was hoping you'd be in when we got here."

I shake my head at him, threading a hand into the small patch of curls that have started growing at the base of his neck now that he's not so concerned about keeping his hair short. I tug him towards me as I capture his lips with my own.

He goes along with this more than happily, taking the kiss over the moment that our lips meet. I enjoy the heady taste of his lust against my tongue. There's no urgency in either of us as his hands move down my sides until they reach my hips, yanking me forward to feel exactly how hard he has been since we first started this back at the school.

It's the perfect ending to a long day of hard work... Part of my mind is wandering toward the shower, thinking about getting ourselves clean before I run my tongue over every inch of them both. There's also a frenetic energy that needs to be sated first, energy that needs to be fulfilled.

"Find me a bed, Bonded," I break away from his lips to murmur.

A slow, easy grin stretches over his lips as he cups my ass with one hand, lifting me up until my legs wind their way around his waist.

Gabe chuckles under his breath as he puts a hand over his shoulder and grabs a fistful of his shirt, pulling it off in one easy motion as he drops it on the floor carelessly. I know at least one man who's going to end up very angry at him for such messiness, but Atlas' lips are very distracting as he kisses his way down my neck, completely disregarding the layer of dust that covers us all.

I find myself ignoring it as well, my hands tangling in his hair and yanking at the small length of it as I pull his lips back to mine. It's slow and easy, and it's everything I want right now. Fun, carefree, and without any sort of obligation. There's no bonds battling it out inside of us or making demands, there's no giant void of energy that we're trying to fill. There's nothing but me and two of my Bonded wanting to be with each other, and that in itself is perfect. Gabe leads the way towards my bedroom, swinging open the door and making his way over to the bed, taking his shoes off as he goes.

Atlas refuses to put me down, not even onto the bed for a moment, while he gets us both naked. Instead, we become a confused pile of limbs, interconnected as we try to shimmy out of our own clothes while still kissing. I get pretty close to getting my pants off when there is a tickle at the side of my throat that doesn't feel like hands. I assume for a moment that Gabe has decided that watching is no longer enough and that he wants to join when Atlas curses and turns us both.

There, at our feet, is Azrael. He's slowly growing bigger and bigger and *bigger* as he takes over the room.

My brows furrow as I watch all of this. It's completely out of character for my little shadow puppy, but then his puppy form distorts until it's almost as if he's trying to shape himself into a man.

My heart begins to thump in my chest.

I have no idea what is going on, and then suddenly, through the shadow puppy walks Nox, shifting from one space in the Sanctuary to another.

Atlas grumbles under his breath and opens his mouth, ready to tear Nox a new one, but the look on his face tells me something else has happened, something terrible, and the first thing that he's done is come to me the fastest way he possibly can, faster even than the Transporters could get him here.

"What is it?" I whisper. "What's happened?"

Atlas' grip on me relaxes a little, and I slide down the front of him, completely unbothered by my nakedness, and Nox's eyes never leave my face.

"One of the Transporter Zones for the new Sanctuary residents was hit. They've taken Kieran."

21

GABE

The moment we arrive at North's offices, I feel a grim hope start in my chest. The largest number of TacTeam operatives that I've ever seen are here, all of them dressed and ready to move out as they stand in neat lines the way that they've been trained to.

Vivian and Unser look over the crowd with stern and discerning eyes, but I've known them for long enough to know that they're happy with what they are seeing. A lot of work in a very short amount of time might just pay off here.

Nox opens the door to the office, shepherding Oli in front of him as he covers her with his body protectively. Atlas doesn't even flinch at the sight of it, something that has taken a very long time for us to work our way to. The two of them have finally found a middle ground, all that truly matters to either of them is our Bonded.

The way it should have been all along.

The moment we step into the office a gasping sound breaks out of Oli, and she steps around Nox as she flings herself in Sage's direction.

I almost don't recognize the girl that I grew up with and have known for my entire life.

The Sage back then, the one that Oli had first met and befriended, was a broken shadow of herself. A girl who had been manipulated by the Resistance into losing one of her Bonds, rejected by our community, and was everyone's punching bag for something she had no control over. The girl who befriended Oli because she saw something in my Bonded that everyone else missed, a good heart. Now we're here, one of her Bonded kidnapped, and the rest of her Bonded Group is in a mess over it.

Everyone except Sage herself.

She catches Oli and holds her shoulders. "I need you to help me bring him back, Oli. I need you to help me find him."

I'm happy her words come out strong, like she's full of fight, brimming with strength and power. I feel weirdly proud of her in this moment.

She's not going to let this break her.

"Of course. I'm going to hunt him down, drag him home to you, and then I'm going to set my bond on anyone and everyone involved in taking him in the first place. I'll eat all of their souls for you. Someone get me some matches, I'm ready to light something on fire! I can't believe they would go after him like this."

A grin stretches over my lips, pride swelling in my chest as the Draconis wakes inside of me. It likes the way she's talking. It likes the promise of bloodshed and vengeance.

Sage scoffs under her breath. "You don't need matches, *I'm* coming with you."

"We all are," Felix says, stepping forward with a bulletproof vest already covering him.

I scowl at him for a second, but as his eyes flick over us, he shrugs. "I'm not going to risk anything happening to him, getting him home. The rest of our Transporters aren't as strong as he is, and anything could happen on the jump. It's just not worth it. Sage is already going to be using so much energy in fighting, and I'm not going to let her risk herself. I'm going."

He sounds so strong and sure about it as he bends down to grab one of the Tac helmets at his feet. He always did run headfirst at things. Even being a Healer, he had never really been too concerned about what could happen to him out there. He'd been on the football team our entire way through middle school, high school, and then college.

He'd always been just as physically active as the rest of us, even knowing that his path in life was going to lead to hospitals and not the field.

It's working in our favor, though.

No other Healer is so quick to sign up to travel like this.

"We're all going. We'll all be there to bring him back." Wick steps up, his hand slowly sliding down Sage's arm until his fingers thread through hers carefully, as though he's waiting for her to pull away.

She doesn't.

She's definitely taking strength from him right now, and I look around to find that even Riley looks determined.

I don't want to voice my concerns about him coming with us on the mission, considering the state he's been in. If North and Gryphon have made the call to let him go, then who am I to question that?

Instead, I step forward and look at the giant screen in front of us showing the map of the Transport zone. It was highly populated just a few hours ago, making it a safer jumping point. The Resistance historically haven't wanted to hit major cities unless they're sure that they can take the area.

It looks as though a bomb has flattened an entire suburb.

A whole block of apartments is now nothing but rubble, even more senseless destruction underneath their belts.

I glance up to meet North's eyes, and he nods at me as though we've come to an agreement, then Atlas as well. He's slowly checking in with each of us before we head off on our mission.

"Our god-bond target did this. It has Resistance with it, but our main concern is that it's one of the god-bonds trying to lure us out."

"It succeeded," Oli snaps, and North only nods his head at her.

"We always knew that they'd come after our friends first. Unfortunately, they found a crack in our security and exploited it. We knew that there's always the chance for something like this, but time is not on our side here. We need to go in, find him, and kill everyone we can."

North chooses his words carefully.

Normally, he tries to sugarcoat things—'take people out', 'deal with them'—and all the other words that the council have used to make the missions feel less like acts of war.

This time, there's no need for it.

This time everyone is clear on what we're doing.

They've taken one of our own, and we won't stop until we get him back.

I'm expecting Oli's bond to kick up a fuss about whichever Transporter is chosen to move us. The moment that everybody starts heading off towards their Transporters of choice, Nox grabs her by the elbow, spinning her his way as his eyes and the skin of his arms and his neck slowly turn black.

I can see North hesitate, his worry palpable, but Nox cuts him such a savage look that his mouth snaps shut and he accepts that this isn't something he can fight his brother on.

Instead, he grabs the Transporter we've been assigned and snaps, "Hurry up, we need to beat them there."

Atlas and I move swiftly to him as well, grabbing his arm. We move into space, everything melting around us before suddenly becoming clear again with that tell-tale *pop* noise.

We find the smoke beginning to form slowly, morphing up into the solid form of a person, but it's as interesting to watch them shift through it here as it was having Nox appear in the bedroom. The two of them suddenly appear in the shadows as they arrive. One second, there's nothing, and the next, my Bonded is here with us. The anxious energy that had begun to build up in me eases off the moment I can see her again.

Gryphon takes half a step towards Oli, then his eyebrows shoot up his forehead as she smiles at him with a slight shake of her head.

"I don't feel sick," she says quietly in a pleased voice, the surprise and wonder evident in her tone.

There's a Shield in place, so the chance of a surprise attack right now is low, but North and Nox move into military mode the moment that Oli steps away from them and into Atlas' orbit.

Sage and the rest of her Bonded Group arrive shortly after, moving over to us as Sage mumbles quietly to Oli, "I hate Transporting with anyone who isn't Kieran. It feels gross."

Oli nods, quietly slipping her hand into her best friend's as she offers her what little comfort she can.

The entire situation is manageable right now, but it's teetering on the edge of becoming worse.

Gryphon murmurs to Sage, "Can you feel anything? Can you feel if he's nearby, or anything from him at all?"

She scowls a little as she closes her eyes, but she shakes her head pretty quickly. "He's blocking me out. Whatever's going on is probably not pleasant, but it's not strong enough now to leak through the way it would if he's in too much pain."

Oli sighs with a nod. "That makes sense, but at least it's survivable. Is it strange that I already know exactly how much pain that is? Never mind. He's going to be okay. I promise you, Sage."

Gryphon frowns at the mention of the torture that Oli had endured, and I understand that completely sick feeling sinking into my gut at the very idea of it. Before I can spiral too much about the torture she'd endured, Gryphon starts directing everyone.

The teams are made up of a fifty-fifty split, half of them being Tac operatives and half being the newcomers we've had to train. That way, when he starts using hand signals, at least half of each team understands what he's saying and can direct the rest.

The shield that's in place is strong, but not strong enough to give us a clear vision of what's happening outside of it. We already know that it's going to be bad from the surveillance footage that we had, and Nox sends one of his shadow creatures out to get eyes on the situation before we let the shield down.

He curses under his breath for a moment and then sends through the mind connection, *Prepare yourselves. It's so much worse than what we were expecting.*

I watch everyone square their shoulders. Oli squeezes Sage's hand right before she drops it, widening her stance and rolling her shoulders back as she prepares herself for whatever is to come. I swallow roughly for a moment, and then I reach out to the Draconis, making sure that it is not only awake but prepared to shift the second that I might need it.

It isn't just ready, it's hungry.

Hungry to do everything that it can for our Bonded to prove itself to her, to let her know that even though it had the longest cycles between lives, it loves her just as much as any of the rest.

The moment the shield drops, I shift without fully processing what's happening, the god-bond taking over and shredding through my Tac gear as though it's nothing but tissue paper.

Atlas curses and moves Oli into his arms to get her away from me, but I'm grateful he does when a bullet whirrs past him and buries itself in my scales. It must be a reasonably low caliber because it doesn't quite penetrate my skin, but I feel it all the same.

My bond lets out a roar. I hear the chatter of everyone around us, but the Draconis doesn't care for any of it. All it cares for is my Bonded and eating every last one of the Resistance until we're sure that she is going to be safe.

There's a rumble all around us as we begin to move, and I have to prompt it not to step on any of our own people. I remind it that they are just as invested in keeping our Bonded alive as anyone outside of our Bonded Group can be. It's not particularly happy about making such concessions, but it does tiptoe around them until it has enough room for our wings to take flight.

I get the same rush as we take to the air as I did the

very first time I'd shifted into a small bird when I was a teenager, the same shot of adrenaline to the blood. It's addictive in the best way.

The Draconis looks around the area, hunting for our prey. Curiously, the buildings here aren't burning. Every other fight we've gone into has been full of ash and fire and smoke that burns my lungs for days afterwards, the taste of it sticking in the back of my throat.

It's not until we do our first pass over the city block that I see it. The god-bond is an Elemental, but it's not using fire, if it even has access to it.

There's an entire suburb here that's been frozen solid. Watch out for ice, I send through the mind connection to everyone, and the Draconis is very unhappy with this.

I reach out to it and it sends back a small snippet of memory, something that it can't explain in words but can show me through images. A god-bond sent icicles that were sharpened to a point flying through the air. They skewered the Draconis that was already injured and unable to access its fire. Then there was a long, slow arc through the air until it came crashing down to the ground, a slow and painful death at the hands of a god who murdered our Bonded.

A vengeful god who wants nothing more than everyone to suffer, the madness of living so many lives alone having eaten away at it until there was nothing but chaos and destruction left.

The Draconis doesn't want to kill the god.

It wants to find it, snap every bone in its body, disable its power, and then deliver it to the Eternal to feast on. It wants to destroy it in such a way that it will never exist again, and with the painful memory of the impact of those icicles fresh in my mind, I can't agree with it more.

Let's hunt.

I leave the Draconis to hunt as it knows best, instead shifting my consciousness to keep track of where Oli and the rest of the Bonded Group are. I do it just to reassure myself that she's safe at all times, because honestly, letting the god-bond take over makes me feel a little bit useless. I watch, though Atlas and Nox stay with her at all times. They make a surprisingly adept team at protecting her while she moves through the rubble with Sage and her Bonded Group as they work together to find Kieran.

He's in there somewhere, trapped by the god-bond as bait for the rest of us.

Gryphon and North take up the mantle of finding it, using the path that the Draconis is taking as a guide for where to look. I find myself surprised for a moment that Nox isn't also insisting on proactively looking for it as well, until it occurs to me that he doesn't have to; the Draconis fills in the blanks here for me.

The gods have always gone after the Eternal first.

They enjoy nothing more than breaking our spirits. If he stays with her, the god-bond will simply come to him. This way, he's able to keep an eye on our most treasured Bonded and have front row seats to whatever it is that the god-bond is planning.

I watch as the Draconis takes out legions of the Resistance, all of them staring up at us in horror as we fly over and breathe pure fire on them.

I already knew that the entire Resistance would know about the Draconis by now, but hearing about a lizard the size of a bus that can fly and breathe fire and seeing it in action are clearly two very different things.

I feel like Oli's bond now, a savage satisfaction at seeing the awe and horror on their faces. They deserve every second of their fear, and they deserve the fiery death I'm going to give them too.

I feel nothing as they burn.

I don't feel any sort of guilt or sadness, but I also feel no joy either. I feel nothing but hollow at these brutal acts of war, perpetuated and manipulated by the madness of those who continue to return as we do.

It's not until I have a vast section of the Resistance cornered and burning that they finally set a plan against me in motion, sending bullets and some sort of projectile that looks like a fucking harpoon through the air. They've clearly been tailor-made just for me, the design an echo of those from the past.

The Draconis moves into a rolling spiral to get away from it, dodging everything that they shoot at us and moving faster than ever before. They were prepared for the creature they had faced in the past, but not this one. Not the one that has the power of my Bonded thrumming through my blood as I cut through the air with ease.

A bullet finally skims the soft underside of my belly, but as quickly as I feel the burn, it heals. The power my Bonded sends pushes into me, healing me as she takes souls from the Resistance that make their way through the rubble towards them. All of it is making me feel as though I am as indestructible as the Cleaver as well.

Bullets begin to rain down on those on the ground as they change tactics, moving towards the Eternal once more, and I'm taken by surprise as Sage's Bonded Group joins the fight.

I'm expecting a wall of flames or something to be moved telekinetically, thanks to Riley. I'm not expecting huge balls of fire to rain down on the troops as Sage and Wick work together with Riley, sending burning debris everywhere as the ground lights up around them. I watch as Riley lifts a bus and Wick sets it on fire, his eyes flashing white as he calls on his Flame ability.

He might not be as strong as Sage, but he's smart enough to know how to best use his Gift, teaming up with Riley as they throw vehicle after vehicle. I watch as the gas tanks light up and the vehicles explode as they hit the ground, bolts and pieces of metal acting as shrapnel as they tear through the crowd. The Shield kicks into place around them as the next spray of bullets come out, and the Draconis shifts paths once more to send out another spray of liquid fire, flames exploding through the smoke as the screams of the injured begin to fill the air.

Those who have hurt my Bonded do not deserve a quick or clean death. I told her they would die screaming, and scream they shall.

I agree wholeheartedly with my bond.

As we circle around once more, I spot exactly what we're looking for, directing the Draconis until it spots it as well. A freshly laid patch of ice, one that wasn't there on our last pass, and a sign that the god is still working here.

With nothing more said between us, the Draconis swoops down, ready to prove his devotion to our Bonded and the god within her.

22

OLI

I have traveled enough of the country to know some of the major cities, but I don't recognize where we've chased the god-bond to. There's no major markers or touristy spots that give it away, just lines and lines of apartment buildings that now have ice damage to the side of them, sections of them blown to pieces and, of course, the two apartments that have been completely demolished by the fighting.

We'd landed directly in front of one of the piles of rubble—the only spot there wasn't already Resistance fighters camped out and waiting for us—though that in itself shows that it's a trap. I'm not sure if walking into a trap is better or worse if you know exactly what it is, but all I can do now is cling to the hope that we're stronger than these people, strong enough to handle whatever they throw at us.

Strong enough to go home safely at the end of this all with Kieran in tow and Sage's Bonded Group back together.

I realize now that the reckless streak in me, the one that has me running off after my friends without a thought for my own safety, has calmed a little. Not that I wouldn't still run headfirst after them if they were in danger, only now, I would ask my Bonded to tag along too. I need to have them with me now the same way that I need air.

Knowing that Silas Davies is dead and no longer out there, ready to strap me to a table and carve me into pieces, bolsters my courage a whole damn lot. It's probably stupid and naive of me, but I feel as though I can face the god-bonds far easier than I could ever face that maniac.

I don't have trauma when it comes to them.

Sure, my own god-bond does. All of them do, thanks to a hundred deaths in a hundred lifetimes, but me? I still get the sweats and the shakes thinking about that goddamn table and the box of weapons that was used against me over and over again until my bond had to come out and play. All of the tactics used by a madman against a child, all of the ways he broke me.

I can admit that now that I'm a little older and I've

seen a little more of life, both through my eyes and through Nox's. I was a *child,* and he was a fully grown *man,* playing his little games and torturing me in the most creative ways. His sick mind would come up with a hundred different ways to carve a body up, only to have a Healer put me back together so he could start again.

If that pain couldn't break me then whatever Gift this god-bond has can't either.

I'm not even sure the Pain god can touch me with its power anymore now that we're all awake and the Soothsayer has reinforced our minds. We're not just stronger because of the power boost. I'm stronger because I have my Bonded with me. I'm stronger because I know that every last one of my moves is backed up by them, all of them are here to work with me to get us out of here alive and whole. We're going to get through this together and be ready to take on whatever else might appear in our future.

Otherwise, what's the point?

The moment that Gabe shifts into the Draconis and the dragon hops off into the air, I feel a moment of panic at his disappearance that is only eased by Gabe's voice in my mind as he reassures me that he's going to keep us safe, that everything here is going to be okay. I'm more worried about what's going to happen to him up there than anything else, as though the distance between us is an unbridgeable gap when really, I know that we're going to be fine. Everything *has* to be fine.

I wouldn't have come out here unless I was sure that it was going to be fine.

Liar. You chased after Kyrie to a Resistance camp that terrified you purely because she's Gryphon's sister. The reckless, self-destructive tendencies in you are strong, Nox sends to my mind connection, and I startle for a second.

Are you reading my mind right now? Because I can only handle that happening with one person. To have you in there as well is terrifying.

He shakes his head at me, moving us away as North and Gryphon start mobilizing teams on the ground, pushing out and beginning to head towards the Resistance battalions waiting for us on the next street. They're trying to draw us away from the rubble here. I don't need anyone to tell me why when I get an eyeful of Sage as she stares at the piles of rock as though her life depends on it.

Kieran is somewhere in that rubble, alive and breathing, for now.

Everything is fine, I'm sure, but he's trapped under there, and we have no way to know if he's bleeding out or something right now.

Gryphon is quick to confirm it before I'm even able to cast out my own Gift. *He can breathe just fine, but he's unconscious and at the very least, his arm and both his legs are broken.*

I look over at Sage and give her a thumbs up, pointing at the pile for a second, and she's quick to dart over to it. She scrambles a little on the rocks as she begins moving them away, as though she's going to lift them all by herself to get to her Bonded.

It's cute but highly impractical, and time isn't exactly on our side here.

"I brought someone with me who is kind of an expert at this," I say to her loudly enough that if anyone's around, it would give away our position, but the thick streams of smoke around us slowly forming into creatures are more than enough to do that.

Atlas carefully guides me over to the pile, making sure I stick close to him, and then, as though it's *nothing*, he begins to move giant chunks of building away from the pile.

He literally picks up an entire wall and moves it away as if it's nothing but a pillow.

I have to remind myself of the seriousness of this situation so I don't swoon. I hear the screeching of the Draconis in the air as though it's miles away, then the heat of his fire as he spits it out a few streets over. It feels hotter than the sun, even from this distance, and I lift a hand to shield my face from it.

"Do you think he's gonna be okay?" Sage asks me as she watches Atlas, and I nod my head, rubbing her arm.

"Of course. He's going to be perfectly safe and very grouchy while he gets completely healed up. I'm sure he will also hate every single second of you fussing over him and all of the shit that Gryphon and North are going to give him for scaring them like this. Everything is going to be fine."

Everything is definitely not fine.

As the bullets and harpoons, *freakin' harpoons*, start to arc through the sky towards one of my beloved Bonded, my chest tightens and my eyes shift as I call on my power.

I throw out my Gift as though it's a net, finding as many of the Resistance as I possibly can and tearing their souls out. All of that energy and power that I take, I funnel through to Gabe. I feel as it seeps into his body, strengthening him and healing any small wounds he may have already. I feel him take it into himself, and the next stream of fire he breathes covers twice the distance of his last, burning hotter and devastating our enemy with ease.

It's magnificent to watch.

While I work, Wick and Riley start talking amongst themselves. I can't pay attention to their words while I rip souls out. I have to focus to get the right people, but the next thing I know, they join in with the fighting while Atlas and Sage dig for Kieran.

I'm surprised to find them working together.

Riley uses his Gift to lift objects as Wick sets them on

fire, and then they're flying through the sky, landing on the Resistance and crushing them as though they are nothing.

When there's shouting and more gunfire to the left, Sage slides across the rubble towards us, reaching out her hands, and a wall of flames bursts out of her. It slams into the building next to us, the entire front wall catching fire as dozens of soldiers stream out. Whether they were lying in wait to attack us, or simply waiting for a safe moment to retreat because they were too scared of the shadow creatures to face us, it doesn't matter now. As they descend from the staircase, yelling as their uniforms catch fire, I tear their souls out and let their power fill my veins.

North and Gryphon push their TacTeams further out, trying to draw the god-bond to them. My instincts tell me to funnel all of the extra power to my Bonded, but I try to remember what I'm going to be facing here soon. Instead, I keep some of the power that I get from the souls for myself.

I don't like doing it.

It feels selfish to me, but I also don't think I can afford to take a three-day nap this time. I can't leave us exposed like that.

Atlas continues to move the rubble away, glancing over his shoulder every so often at me. It's as though he's sure I'm going to disappear the second he steps too far away. Nox sidles a little closer to me, his shadows casting out more and more, dozens of them covering the area.

As another hail of bullets fly through the air, Atlas straightens for a moment, pushing his hands out in front of him. The bullets all stop mid-air, hitting the barrier that he has been working so hard on perfecting, and they roll away.

We haven't just managed to become a Bonded Group that gets along well, we've become a cohesive unit that can face our worst enemies and have each other's backs, to protect our family and make it through this in one piece.

I've never been sure of our ability to do so before, but now, I think maybe we can do this. I think we can make it through the fight with the god-bond and create a better world for ourselves.

I think we're going to survive this.

There's a loud screech overhead again as the Draconis closes in on another section of the Resistance, this time above where North and Gryphon are pushing the teams further.

I can feel all of this happening through the net that I've cast out. I can feel what everyone is thinking, where they are, what they're doing. I can feel everything around me, so I feel when the god-bond makes its next move.

There is a strange absence in my net, an empty pull that has no explanation, no reason for being there. And yet, there it is. I feel it the same time I feel the Draconis turn and circle back.

Panic flares in my chest, but my bond speaks to me. *Trust our Bonded. All of them. They know what to do here. They have lived every life with us, and they will not throw away a chance at being together. Not this one.*

I swallow roughly and glance at Nox, to his eyes that are glowing black. When he turns back to me, I can see that the Corvus has taken over in preparation of what's to come.

Atlas continues to move the boulders, but his speed picks up. He's less careful about what he's doing, and it takes me a second to realize the Cleaver has taken over as well.

Sage scowls at him for a moment until she catches a glimpse of his black eyes, then she gulps and turns back to me.

"It's alright. He's just getting ready for the god-bond. He's going to find Kieran first, and we're going to get you guys out of here. I promise, Sage. Everything's going to be okay."

As sure as I feel about my words, I'm glad that Gryphon isn't here to hear them, just in case there's a lie in them, one I refuse to face myself. We have to find Kieran before the god-bond gets here.

We have to get him out.

North and Gryphon move towards us, leaving their

TacTeams where they are as they continue to work through the Resistance. They have a bunch of Elementals in their numbers, and they've figured out that the quickest way to fight this Ice god is with fire. They melt away the giant shards it sends flying towards us so that we get hit with nothing but a gentle splash of water.

Just when I feel as though I'm going to scream with anxious energy, Sage gasps and a sob rips out of her throat as she calls out for Felix. The Cleaver turns with Kieran's broken body in his arms, his legs pointing in the wrong directions and blood all over his face as it pours out of his mouth. His breath is uneven and choppy, with a terrifying rattling sound coming from his chest.

I have no idea how he's still breathing in that state.

Sage moves towards him, but Felix barks out an order. "Stop! If you heal him like this, you might do more damage. Just wait there, Bonded. I'll do what I need to do first."

She falters and comes to a halt, but I can tell how much it's breaking her to do so. Wick and Riley both stay steady and sure as they work together against the hordes of Resistance that surround us. I give myself one more minute with my bestie before I turn my attention back to the gods; one more minute to observe as Felix patches Kieran up enough to make the jump. I watch as Sage and Felix find a Transporter to take them back to the Sanctuary. I also watch as Wick and Riley make the choice to stay here and continue fighting, to do what they can for us and our community.

My respect for the two of them skyrockets as they both kiss Sage goodbye and tell her not to worry, that they will come home once everything here is over with. They might not be my favorite of her Bonded Group, but I can now firmly say that they have my respect.

The moment that minute is over, my eyes shift to black and my bond takes over, ready to deal with this god-bond once and for all.

THE ETERNAL

The Draconis has not only found the god-bond but it's working towards capturing it and bringing it directly to me. An act of love and devotion that cannot be ignored.

Instead of waiting for it, as I'm sure it would like me to do, I move towards the Corvus. I'm ready for him to Shadow Shift us directly to where the god-bond is lying in wait. I'm ready to use my power and consume the soul, to take it into myself and ensure that we will never face this god again.

Pillars of ice are appearing around us as our enemy prepares to make its final move, trapping us here and attempting to use its strengths to take us out.

Little does it know, we are beyond such things now.

As I move towards the Corvus, ready to take his arm and shift with him, I feel the earth begin to move under my feet in an unnatural way. With an ear-splitting rumbling sound, a cavernous hole opens up around us. I stumble, my feet slipping on the loose rocks, and the Cleaver lunges towards me to cover me with his body as the earth gives way to a sinkhole, both of us tumbling into it as though we're ants under the feet of giants.

Instead of landing terribly and breaking my body into a million different pieces, I feel nothing as the Cleaver rolls us both so that I'm on top of him. He takes the brunt of the fall with no reaction other than the tightening of his arms around me as we hit the bottom of the hole.

It ignites my temper.

I cast my web further, throwing it out wide and pulling out the souls of everyone around me that does not belong to the small community we have built. Every living being within the destruction zone is gone in the blink of an eye, all of their power churning through me as we prepare to face down not one, but two god-bonds, both of them working together.

"An Elemental," the Cleaver says to me as we stand back up, trapped in a hole at least ten feet deep.

"Two Elementals," I reply, and the Soothsayer speaks

into our minds.

The Draconis is taking care of the Ice. We will bring you the other one, Eternal.

I have no doubt that they will do just that, but I also don't particularly want to be buried alive here. It's a death that I have unfortunately faced before, and it's not one that I'm particularly inclined to re-live. I hear a screech overhead as the Draconis weighs in on the matter as well, the roaring of his flame breath blocking out all other sounds as he decimates our enemy.

The Cleaver pulls me onto his back as he finds footholds in the earth around us, climbing out of the pit with ease, as though ascending a ladder. As we reach the top, the Corvus is waiting for us, his arms ready to lift me out. The shadows are thick around us as he prepares for whatever's next.

The ground begins to shake again.

I funnel my power into the Draconis and the Crux, carefully reserving some for myself, knowing that I will be consuming two gods' souls. And though I came out stronger on the other side of the last feast—disgusting as it was—it might not be enough this time.

We might have to send one of them back into the cycle.

The Corvus turns to look at me, a scowl on his face. "That will not be happening. We can give you whatever you need to be taken care of. I refuse to spend the rest of my life looking over my shoulder for one of these things to come back and find us."

I smile at him as though he has declared his love for me, and he has—in his own special way—and reach my hand out to clasp his hands.

The Draconis lets out another screeching sound and for a moment, I worry that he has been attacked or harmed, but then I see him circling again. A long stream of fire sprays out of his mouth, destroying everything around him until there's nothing, dead or alive, left for him to target other than the god-bond he hunts.

I step over to the Corvus once more. "We should join him."

He shakes his head. "He will join the others when he's ready. He's having fun playing with his food at the moment."

A smile stretches across my lips as the Cleaver and I each take his arm, the shadows engulfing us completely as he shifts through the air in an instant. It's completely different than how the Transporters do it. There's no sickening motion, no feeling that what we're doing is unnatural, and my stomach does not churn horrifically.

Instead, I'm enveloped by his shadows for a brief moment, safe and beloved there, only for them to part and be somewhere else entirely. I find myself standing shoulder-to-shoulder with the Crux and the Soothsayer once more as they face down the Elemental. My Bonded has it captured and wrapped in shadows.

This one is young.

Young enough that I'm sure the vessel is still alive, not yet killed off, as the god still requires sleep to recover from the cycling. It might even be younger than the vessels of my Bonded, but its eyes are black all the same. There's a tugging in my chest as my vessel wants to speak to me.

I know her, the girl says. *I know exactly who that is. She's been so close to us before.*

It doesn't matter though. It's something for the girl to discuss with the vessels at a later point. What does it matter to us if it has appeared before? All that matters is that it's dead now.

It just doesn't know it yet.

"You don't deserve to be together," it starts to say, but I have no interest in listening to these things anymore.

Why should I lower myself to listen to the tirade of madness that their broken minds have conjured? Instead of staying true to the one thing that matters, their Bonded, they threw it all away, because they're weak and pathetic.

They are nothing to me.

I reach a hand out to anchor myself as my Gift flows out of me and into the god-bond's being, wrapping firmly around their soul. The moment I have them trapped, I yank my power back into myself, taking the soul with it. It's easier than the last one, this god having only been awake for a short amount of time. Still, I'm thankful for the extra reserve of power I have as I wrestle with it, pulling and pulling and *pulling* until finally, it comes loose.

The vessel's body drops as I take the soul into myself, dead and gone before it hits the ground.

I take a deep breath before I consume it, disgust rippling through my body at the thought of it being inside of me, but the power-kick it gives me rocks me on my feet. It's like being struck by lightning, an almighty explosion trapped within my skin as volts of energy race up and down my limbs, burning everything it touches as I force the power to obey me, kneel for me, become a part of me.

Another one gone.

Another one finally set free, no longer cycling, but gone from this world forever. One more god that we never have to worry about killing us again.

The shadows ease away from the vessel. There is a quiet moment as we stare at the body of a teenage girl before a screech cuts through the air once more. The Draconis flies overhead, and we're forced to scatter like ants as a body falls from the sky, landing with a thud at our feet. A pile of blood and bones pokes through skin, and a wheezing, rattling breath is somehow still coming out of the bloodied mess. It is the most gruesome gift.

My favorite kind.

The Draconis lands close by, blood dripping from its teeth as it snuffs and snorts happily, satisfied that it has brought me a god-bond to consume but utterly frustrated that it can't do more to right these wrongs. I reach out a hand to my Bonded, pressing against the scales of its neck for a moment as the sparks still play under the skin of my palm.

This soul is a lot harder to get out.

The vessel is older, already long dead, and the god-bond is strong after years of hiding out and developing. It takes a moment, but the Soothsayer floods my mind, sending me more of his power as he opens up my mind to the others, letting them help with this burden.

I'm careful not to take too much from them, careful not to open us up to the risk of too many of us being weakened, but I do take what they offer. I use it to pull the god-bond's soul out with one hard *yank*, watching as the body twitches violently before finally it stops breathing. This time when I consume the soul, I pass out from the waves of power that flood me, everything going dark around me as I feel the lifeforce flood my body.

The Crux catches me as darkness envelops me.

23

OLI

I wake up *wrong*.

I know exactly what it is even before I come to properly, the out-of-body feeling that's slowly becoming familiar to me. It's the sensation of knowing that I am not in my own *vessel* anymore, but I'm still safe, nestled happily within one of my Bonded. I'm comfortable and loved and *home*.

I hate how much I love it.

It's an invasion of privacy, at the very least, and a violation at worst. I feel guilty even though I have no idea how I keep doing it or how I would stop doing it. It's not like I've ever thought to myself 'Hey, this nap would be a great time to go mind-hopping', for God's sake!

The only upside is that I instantly know whose mind

I'm in. Gabe was perfectly happy for me to be here last time; I doubt much has changed since then. At least I know that I'm not going to trip over any nightmares in here, ones that Nox in particular would hate me having to see and experience alongside him.

I hear the familiar sound of the rumbling and know right away that it's the sound of the Draconis sleeping, tucked away safely somewhere.

I sit down once again, not really understanding what exactly it is I'm sitting on or what anything around me is as I wait for my Bonded to appear.

It doesn't take long.

"Everything okay?" he asks as he sits down next to me, and I smile up at him.

"Of course. I don't know why I'm here, but I'm happy to be."

"Something in me obviously called out to you. I'm sorry, Bonded." He sighs, rubbing his head on my knees as he all but collapses on top of me.

We're both going through the energy drain that comes with our god-bonds' abilities, him still trying to adjust to the Draconis and its eating patterns while I am going through the aftermath of consuming not one but *two* god-bond souls.

I still don't want to think about it.

The very idea of it still fills me with a sense of dread,

my stomach roiling as though I'm allergic to it. I feel as though I've been tainted in some way, as silly as that sounds. It doesn't matter how it makes me feel though, all that matters is that the god-bonds can't come back now.

They can never come back.

So whatever it does to me, it's worth it.

"I don't think we should wake up," Gabe says under his breath, startling a laugh out of me.

"I'm not sure the rest of the Bonded Group would agree with that idea, Bonded," I say in a stern voice, a grin still flitting across my face jokingly, but he grimaces a little back.

"I'm not so sure about that. Not at the moment, anyway."

The smile slowly slides off of my face, and I glance around, but I still can't really see anything about the area we're in. "What do you mean? What happened?"

He licks his lip and then forces a smile on his face, but it doesn't reach his eyes. "It doesn't matter right now, Bonded. We can deal with it when we wake up. Our Bonded Group is safe; don't worry about that."

The Bonded Group.

He just says that and nothing else. There's a million other things that it could be, all of them sparking panic that floods my brain until I feel as though I'm going to vomit.

"I saw them get Kieran out of the rubble. I saw Felix

Heal him enough for the Transporter to take them home, and he was okay," I say, the words falling out of me in a stream.

Gabe fits his hands across my face, drawing my head down to his as he murmurs, "Kieran is alive. Sage, Felix, Wick, and Riley are all alive. They made it back. I shouldn't have said anything, Bonded. Just rest now."

My heart rate slows a little but not enough to distract me from everything that he isn't saying. There's a huffing noise again and he stands, pulling me to my feet. "Come see the Draconis with me. Let me distract you with my bond for a little bit. You know he'll want some belly rubs if you're in here."

I don't want to be distracted. I want to know what's going on, but I follow him anyway, feeling selfish for my ability to stay ignorant while my Bonded is so conflicted.

"We're asleep anyway, Oli. There's nothing you can do. Just come and say hello to my bond, and enjoy the last few moments before we return and face it together."

I take a deep breath and turn in his mind, following him into the deep, dark recesses until I find the beast waiting there. It's crouched down as though it's in a small space, but that doesn't make much sense to me.

Nothing here does.

The moment it spots me, its eyes glue themselves to me, drinking me in hungrily. If I wasn't so sure about him,

I would assume I was about to be eaten. The all-consuming need the Draconis has for its Bonded is certainly not something to take lightly. It craves me in this form and every other.

"Do you think the Draconis can only shift into a dragon? Or do you think it's just its favorite form?" I query as I lean down to drape myself over the beast, stroking its scales and enjoying the oddly velvety feel of them.

It rumbles happily, slowly moving its head side to side as it gets comfortable with my weight. I would move and find a better angle but the moment I try, it rumbles again, unhappy to lose contact with it in any way.

Gabe watches us both, enjoying the interaction without having to be a part of it. "It's just its favorite form, the one that comes most naturally to it, and I suppose it's the one that does the most damage. I can still shift to anything that I want if I take the reins, but my bond always chooses that one."

I nod slowly, reaching out to scratch behind the Draconis' ear, and again, the rumbling happiness vibrates against my belly. I take a deep breath and shut my eyes, letting myself soak in the moment as I feel my body get heavy the way it always does right before I wake up.

"I love you, Bonded," Gabe says to me suddenly, his eyes tight and worried as he watches me.

I slip my eyes open for long enough to reply, "I love

you, too. Whatever happened… that's not going to change."

The smile he gives me this time is sincere. "I'm not worried about that. I'm worried about them breaking you. I'm worried about you losing something important."

If my life has taught me anything, it's that as long as it's not one of my Bonded, I'll survive. It might hurt a whole lot, but most things do.

I'll survive it.

Gabe looks at me again and sighs, turning his head to look upwards. It's the last image in my mind as I drift off to sleep, leaving the safety of his mind and returning once more to my own body, waking up to discover exactly what he was trying to protect me from, if only for a moment.

I wake up in my own bed back at the Sanctuary, nestled up against Gabe's bare chest, his breathing slow and even as he sleeps.

I stare down at him for a moment, and he must feel my eyes on him because, with a quiet groan, his own eyes flutter open. He looks at me the same way he does every day when we wake up together, that same soft wonder that he hasn't just found me… he's got me. We're here together, and the simple pleasure of being with each other is *everything* to us both, the only thing that matters in the entire world.

Then whatever it is that's happened filters back into his mind, and I see him slowly shut down as those shadows darken his eyes. Slowly, the joy and wonder disappears, and it's replaced with the exact emotion I don't want to see there.

Grief.

"What's happened, Gabe? Tell me." My voice comes out as a rasp.

He swallows and opens his mouth and then shuts it again, swallowing once more. My heart begins to beat like crazy in my chest, and he carefully brings an arm around my waist to hold me against his body, fitting us together as though he can hold my mind together the same way.

"The god we left behind, the one in the cells? It got out while we were gone."

My heart thumps wildly, and though he can feel it against his own chest, I'm sure, Gabe continues ripping the Band-Aid off in one swipe.

"He used his Gift to do it, waiting until everyone was being fed down there. He killed the operative who went down there. He got Xander to shoot himself so that on tape, it looks like a suicide, but we know better. When the operative didn't go back up... Vivian went looking for him. He checked the cameras, but he could only see Xander's feet. We don't know what he was thinking, going by himself."

My heart leaps into my throat.

Gabe swallows again, his voice coming out all wrong. "The god-bond killed Vivian. The moment he entered the basement, he took him over and killed him, then it killed itself."

My eyes fill with tears, my mind blanking out, the low buzz of white noise taking over. Gabe just keeps on talking, passing along all of the heartbreaking, devastating details to me.

"Sawyer found the bodies when he was doing a security scan of all of the areas. When he rechecked the security cameras, he found the god-bond muttering to itself in another language. When we arrived back, Nox translated it—it was an old dialect of Latin, some remnant of his time on Earth before. He figured out that we were *consuming* god-bonds. Their souls, I mean."

He says 'we', but we both know he means me.

I can't find the words to say that to him though. I can't find anything in my jumbled mess of a brain.

"His Bond was already killed and returned to the cycle. He didn't want it returning, only to be lost without him, and so he killed himself to be put back in the cycle as well. He just took Vivian and Xander out with him when he went."

As per usual, the gods don't give a fuck about anyone but themselves and their own agendas.

The tears start streaming down my cheeks, and Gabe curses under his breath, wiping at them as he murmurs, "Unser was the one who went down there after them, before Sawyer could sound the alarm. He already knew Vivian was dead because of Adella's reaction. He thought it was a heart attack or something, but when he got down there and saw it all… he went off. He's a Trigger, you know, so he took out half of the training center. The cells were left standing, thanks to all of the work that Atlas and North had done to make sure that they could contain Aurelia. We didn't lose any more operatives in the explosion, thank God, but everything is a mess. I Transported back here, and when I saw what had happened, I stayed awake long enough to make sure that there was nothing else I could do to help. The rest of the Bonded Group are down there now, figuring it out."

"Figuring what out? How can you 'figure out' something like this?" I croak, and Gabe shrugs, a miserable look on his face.

"I know. I know there's no way around it. I know that there's nothing that any of us can say or do. What we're figuring out is where to go from here. How to best support Adella, and Vivian's kids and Unser. How to continue the training that needs to happen without a training center, because no matter who dies around here, we have to keep going."

"That's not fair... he deserves more than that."

Gabe nods. "I know. We all know it, but what else can we do? This isn't just a job for us, you know, this is life. None of us like it. None of us want to live it, but here we are." He lets out a long breath again and presses the palms of his hands against his eyes. "Everyone blames themselves. North and Gryphon blame themselves for not letting the god-bonds kill it in the first place. Nox is furious that we didn't know it could still use its power even with the upgrades to the room. We're all feeling more than a little deflated about this one."

I feel completely different from what he's describing. It's not deflation or even grief. It's almost an out-of-body experience, the numbness that comes with too much loss culminating in losing someone who was very important to me.

I realize now how much I didn't know about Vivian. I'm sure my Bonded Group knew more about him, having spent years with the older man. I only spent a handful of months with him learning how to trust my Bonded Group, learning how to defend myself, and learning how to grow a backbone in the shortest amount of time possible.

He had faith in me when no one else did.

He saw something in me and liked it enough to watch over me and stop people from giving me shit around him. He pushed me harder than anyone else, formed me into the person that I am right now, though I'm sure he would never say so.

"How many kids did he have?"

It seems like such a paltry question to be asking now, something that I should have asked ages ago instead.

"Their Bonded Group have three. They never really cared about paternity, but two of them were biologically his. Two girls and a boy. They're all only a little bit younger than us. Adella made them both wait years before having kids until they were out of active duty and into a permanent position. She didn't want to raise the kids completely by herself."

A sob wrenches out of my throat. "Well, I guess she's going to now, isn't she?

Gabe shakes his head. "She has Unser; that's something. Trust me, I know."

I stare at him for a moment and see the glossiness to his eyes as he processes all of this right here along with me. The loss of someone he respected as well.

I nod my head, swallowing roughly. "So what are we going to do about Vivian? What can *I* do right now to help? I can't just… sit here."

"I think Adella wants to bury him here. She has no intention of leaving, and she knows how much this place meant to him. As for our next move, I'm sure North has something up his sleeve. We all know this goes back to the

Pain god. Three out of four are gone now. We only have one left."

I nod my head again, and then I press my forehead against his for a second, murmuring under my breath, "Gene better hope he doesn't wake up again in my lifetime. I will never forget this. I will hunt him and the rest of his Bonded Group down until my last day. I swear to God, I'll eat his soul without a fucking word of complaint."

24

ATLAS

The hole in the side of the Tac Training Center is still letting out a long stream of black smoke when we arrive home.

Gabe only stays conscious long enough to find out what's happened here and if Oli is safe to sleep back at the house before he takes our Bonded home, preparing himself for the conversation he's going to have to have with her when she wakes up.

I don't envy him.

I'm not afraid of having hard conversations with my Bonded. If it came down to it, I could have this one, but there's something still raw inside of me at my parents' loss. They were people who didn't deserve to live after all of the sins that they had committed, but losing a good man, someone who Oli had known such affection for, is particularly confusing for me.

I worry for a second because I have no idea how Gabe is going to break this news to her. He's not exactly the most serious of us all, but Gryphon claps me on the shoulder and shrugs. "He's surprisingly good at this shit. You forget that he's lost as much as the rest of us have. He's just better at hiding it."

North sees them both to the house before he comes back to deal with the fallout. I move straight into the recovery mission along with the rest of them, ignoring how much my bones ache inside my body, as I'm sure they are as well.

I've never felt so drained by using my power before.

Usually, being Indestructible also means that I don't feel any pain but even in this, my Bonded has changed me. I'm willing to take it, and any more pain that comes with having her around, without a word. I will never tell her about this, because I know Oli, and she would absolutely feel guilty about it.

We find Felix inside the small bit of the Tac Training Center that's still standing, doing his best to help the survivors of Unser's explosion. No one was killed by it, thank God. The only casualties of the day are Vivian, an operative called Xander, and that piece of shit god-bond.

He deserved so much worse.

Unser is in a pretty bad state himself after Triggering and, grimacing, North is forced to call Adella down to help heal him. She'd been back at the house, breaking the news to their kids and waiting to get the all-clear from North and Gryphon to come and see her Bonded.

I've only met her a handful of times, but she's the no-nonsense sort of woman you would expect two leading TacTeam operatives to be Bonded to. When she arrives, she has a stern set to her face that tells us that she's putting on a very brave facade to get her through everything that's happening to her today.

There's no question in my mind that the three of them truly were a Bonded Group. Her hands shake as she presses them into Unser's chest, her power flowing slowly through her and into him.

With a groan, his eyes finally flutter open. He looks confused for a second before reality crashes back in and he realizes he wasn't dreaming, that his best friend and a member of his Bonded Group was murdered in cold blood in the safety of our own town, in our own building.

He stares up into his Bonded's eyes for a moment, their shared pain reflected in their gaze before finally he reaches a hand out to cup her cheek. I glance away, knowing that we're all intruding on a very private and painful moment.

"I should have stayed with him," he mumbles, and she

shakes her head.

"We're not playing the blame game here. No one is, because if we start pointing fingers, they win. I'm not letting every second of his life go to waste. We fought hard for this, and he deserves better." Her voice breaks.

I have to clear my throat and step away from them both so that I don't do something mortifying like burst into tears here in public over a man I barely knew. Seeing their pain so clearly reflected is heartbreaking, to say the least, and the weird mix of guilt still bubbling around in me rears its head again.

Vivian deserved better.

Gryphon steps forward to help Unser up, slinging his arm over his shoulders as he helps him out of the rubble. Felix watches his unsteady gait for a moment before standing again, stepping over to where North and I are waiting as he mutters quietly under his breath, "Everyone here is stable, I've checked them all. I need to get back to Kieran."

North frowns and nods. "He's going to be alright though, isn't he?"

Felix sighs, scratching the back of his head. "There were a lot of breaks. Sage and I are working together to get him healed up, but it's going to be a few days at least. You're going to have to work without him until then."

North nods and waves a hand. "He's alive, that's all

that matters. We can cover him for as long as he needs. Rockelle can step into the second position for now, and we'll try holding off any more missions until Black is back. Go. Go back to your Bonded and the rest of them, and we'll clean up this mess."

He nods and moves away, but as he does, Wick comes to stand with North, nodding respectfully at him. "There's nothing else that I can do at the house. Felix and Sage have a handle on the healing process. What can I do here?"

My opinion of Sage's Bonded has changed a lot in the last few days.

I know that he already convinced Oli, and he wouldn't have gotten into the Sanctuary if he hadn't passed Gryphon's rigorous vetting process, but just because he's not evil doesn't mean that he isn't an asshole.

I'm relieved to find that he's stepping up, the same way I did.

He's finding a place not only in his Bonded Group but in the community itself. It's not an easy thing to do, especially when you have a chip on your shoulder. Wick certainly had one of those, but he's made a choice, and his choice is Sage.

No matter what.

I can't argue with that, and neither can anyone else. Choosing your Bonded above all else is the right thing to do, and it'll make him friends here faster than anything else he could try.

That same respect is reflected in North's eyes as he takes him in. "We're going to have to Transport the prisoners out of the cells and get them locked up in the old cells underneath the council offices with a Shield in place. It's not ideal, but it's all we can do until we have made the repairs. You can help the rest of us with that."

Wick nods without another word and rolls up his sleeves, figuratively and literally. Even with the horrific death weighing on our shoulders, it feels like a step forward, one that I know will break my Bonded's heart.

Coming together after the loss of a great man.

Moving the prisoners is easy work when you have Gryphon's ability to shut down minds to do so. Seeing my sister is not my favorite thing, but I help ensure that the holding cells at North's old offices will hold her before we move them all.

She still looks so thin, but there is a lightness about her now that I was not expecting, and it takes me a second to realize what's going on with her.

She's relieved.

My parents are gone. Peter and the rest of her cursed Bonded Group are all dead. It's only her and Jericho left now. If they're ever able to convince North and the rest of the council, or whoever ends up making these decisions in the future, to let her and Jericho go, they will never have to worry about being hunted by our family ever again.

They're free now.

Trapped by their so-called enemies and yet, they're free. It makes my very confusing grief over my parents amplify all over again. I suppose when everything with the god-bonds is over and done with, I'll have to help come up with a plan on what to do with them. At the moment, we're all just waiting. Waiting in case we need them, waiting to see if there's a use for them, waiting to decide what their fate is for the roles that they have played in the deaths of so many.

"You can go back up to the house and keep an eye on Gabe and Oli if you want to," Gryphon says as his eyes flash to white.

Aurelia and Jericho's faces blank out as he takes over their minds and directs their bodies as though they are nothing but puppets.

I look around for a second and then shake my head. "I'm of more use here. I'll help clear the rubble and debris, get the place into a safe enough position to rebuild. We both know Gabe is going to be down here the second he's awake, ready to see what can be patched and what has to be demolished."

Gryphon shoots me a look for a second, his eyebrows falling low over his glowing eyes. "I thought you'd be eager to get back to Oli."

I take a deep breath and then shrug. "She's in good hands. There's no point getting bent out of shape and watching over her as she sleeps when she already has more than enough of that going on. Nox is heading back up there with his research, right? She doesn't need three of us sitting around with her, not when all she's doing is resting."

If anything, this just seems to shock him even more, but he accepts my words, nodding and getting back to transferring the prisoners. His mother presses her hands against the glass, staring at him with the sort of motherly longing that mine had perfected as well. Gryphon deflects it as though she is nothing more than a stranger to him. He shuts her mind down as easily as he did my sister's before marching her out of the building as well. The Transporters are already waiting there for them, moving all four of them at once.

I already know that Gryphon's power has grown enough that he can keep them cut off even without close proximity, but he probably doesn't want to freak everyone out by doing so, not unless it's truly needed, so he goes along with them.

I get to work helping Gabe's uncle clear the debris, listening to his instructions and doing the same work as ten men in half the time. At some point, they realize that they're only hindering me with their attempts to help me directly, so the group of workers all step back, watching as

I move entire sections of the walls and ceiling myself.

It's good to feel useful in such a way. The storm in my mind keeps raging, but I lose myself in the manual labor until I forget about anything but clearing rubble.

It's the least I can do.

In the days after Vivian's death, the change in the Sanctuary is stark. It's probably not as noticeable to the inhabitants themselves, but to me and the rest of the Bonded Group, it's as though we have been transported somewhere completely different, an alternate reality.

Long gone are the suspicious looks and whispers from the members of the community. The looks of fear and the obvious way that they used to cross the road without a word if we were coming, as if they thought they were being subtle, has vanished.

Gone is the division that was once so keenly felt, even if it was quietly done.

I question North about it a few days in, and it takes him a moment to answer. "Vivian Bentley was a highly respected member of our community, not just by the council or the TacTeams, but by the Lower Tier families as well. He gave a lot of money to charities. He helped food drives, and he and his Bonded Group were responsible for getting a lot of the families that are here to safety. During the riots in the seventies, he was a young Tac operative, and he made a name for himself then. There isn't a single person here who isn't mourning his death, who isn't ready to see those responsible brought to justice. There's a good reason that he was chosen to run Tac Training back at Draven, and it had nothing to do with nepotism. He was a good man, one who did not deserve the death that he got."

North looks away from me as he says this, staring down at the paperwork that has already been put together for the rebuild of the Tac Training Center.

The moment that Gabe had woken up and come down, he worked with his uncle and North on the plans. The rebuild is taking precedence over everything else due to the serious nature of keeping the people in the Sanctuary safe. Without a training center, we can't have more operatives joining the ranks, and without more operatives, we'll quickly lose our task forces. The only thing more important than this place is the dining hall, and that's only because the chef needs a decent place to cook.

I take the plans from North that Gabe had sent me out here for before clapping him on the shoulder, a small show of respect for the grief that he so obviously feels for the man who taught him so much and was a very important figure in his life. He nods back at me, thanking me in his own quiet way before turning back to the other sheets of paper and leaving me to find my way out without another word.

Only a few months ago, that would have pissed me off, but now I see it for exactly what it is. Now isn't the time to talk needlessly, to offer me pretty words when he's feeling so wretched about the world. Right now is the time to get on with things, to work through it or to make things better, no matter the cost.

I get on one of the ATVs downstairs and slowly make my way over to the remains of the Tac Training Center. There's already a large monument of flowers slowly appearing. I've never really noticed anyone leaving anything, and yet there are hundreds of bouquets and wreaths, all of them picked from back gardens or quiet hikes. All of them have cards, offerings of condolences, and provide small bursts of color against the harsh gray concrete.

They are an offering of sympathy and grief for a man who meant so much.

I find my Bonded standing in the rubble, her fists on her hips as she stares around at the mess left behind. Her eyes are red and her cheeks are scrubbed raw from how often she has wiped away tears. It breaks my heart and makes me want to plant my fist in someone's face and break it for daring to hurt her like this. Except the man who did this is already dead, taking his own life so that he can return again someday. I'm not pissed about that, just about the lives he took with him.

He better hope it's not in this lifetime of ours.

I watch as the other members of the community work around us and all gravitate to my Bonded like she's drawing them in. They never actually approach her however. They leave a small circle around her as though there is a barrier in their way.

I've never noticed it before.

I've always spent too much of my time glaring at people and trying to keep them as far away from her as I possibly can, for her safety, but also because I covet her. I want all of her time and attention. I covet the very sight of her, to the point that it makes me angry that anyone else gets to be in her presence. Now, in this moment of the entire community mourning Vivian and trying to piece itself back together, I see it for what it is.

They're terrified of her, of course, but some of that terror is definitely laced with respect.

They all know what she can do, and it's only natural that they're scared of that, but they also understand that their safety hinges on her ability.

In a way, it always has.

The Dravens have been working tirelessly for years. They've poured billions of dollars into this town, all of them working towards having a safe community and peace, towards finding a way to deal with the Resistance, but in the end, the shadows can only do so much. They are not all-consuming. They aren't able to stop people dead in their tracks from hundreds and hundreds of miles away.

They can't do what Oleander can.

I meet the eye of one of the builders, and he startles for a moment before he inclines his head at me respectfully, stepping up towards me as he begins to point out more areas that need work. He's respectful enough, but he also knows a hell of a lot more than me. When I listen to him attentively and begin to move as directed, I can feel not only his relief but his approval.

I feel for a moment as if I've suddenly woken up inside Gabe's body, because this is how they all treat him. Suddenly, it all makes sense to me. He always works with everyone in the community, regardless of what they whisper about him behind his back. He ignores it all, taking the high road, and just gets on with things.

It's never occurred to me to act in the same way or to build relationships the way that he has, but as other builders and TacTeam personnel begin to approach me and speak to me quietly about various different things, I find myself leaning into it.

North has spent so much of his time making the Sanctuary a place of safety for all, so much of his resources and money and time has gone into it. I know Oli has no intention of leaving, even once we've dealt with the god-bonds.

This place is home to her now.

If we're going to continue to live here with these people, then I can't just lock myself in the mansion with her forever, as tempting as that may be. I might not be able to achieve Gabe's level of friendliness, but I can certainly try and cultivate some form of relationships and goodwill with these people.

This might be what growing up feels like.

As badly as I don't want to admit it, so many of my formative years were spent with my mind being twisted by Resistance propaganda and my parents' expectations for me. Then my later teenage years were spent planning an escape for my Bonded and I. Now, I suppose, is the time to find and explore a new normal.

We just have to find the god-bond and kill it first.

It's the last one left that we know of, and then I suppose we'll spend the rest of our days waiting for more to wake up, watching carefully for any signs while we build a life and live it to the fullest. We will learn how to be the best versions of ourselves, for our Bonded and for everyone else.

My eyes drift back to Oli. The pull of her magnetic beauty, both inside and out, is so alluring to me that I find myself once again growing angry that other people are in her presence.

Except then I see what she's doing.

As she fusses with the flowers on the ground, the small memorial for Vivian that has started, I calm myself down once more. We're working on our next move and we've almost got it planned out. Just a few more days of waiting for the next move, of repairing what we can and helping everyone around us.

A few days of giving what we can in the hope that it is enough, that we can build something that will survive all of this death and destruction with us.

25

OLI

The physical changes to the Sanctuary after the explosion that took out the Tac Training Center are a glaring reminder of the loss within the community.

I can't walk down to North's offices without passing through the town center, which has now been turned into our makeshift training area. When we first moved here, I couldn't help but gently poke fun at North's intense need for aesthetic perfection for the areas that he's in control of, and the town center is no different.

With perfectly cobbled pathways and a large fountain in the center of a landscaped area, it's the perfect place for members of the community to sit and eat lunch or meet up with friends. It's something that I've always hoped to do but never quite felt comfortable enough to, thanks to all of the eyes that are constantly on me. It's idyllic, the center point of the entire town, and it faces both the dining hall and North's offices, with a small road that leads to the Tac Training Center. It has always felt like the heart of the Sanctuary. The very first day that Kieran Transported us in, it was here that I got my very first view of the town. It was a beautiful introduction. Now it's covered in training mats and bodies, people flooding the areas as they work through their stances and wait for their turn in the sparring ring.

I stand and look over the lines and lines of Tac personnel with a critical eye. With this many bodies, you would think that there would be some dissent or disorganization, but as a testament to how the entire Sanctuary has pulled together since Vivian's death, there is none of that.

More surprising than anything else, there have been lots of new recruits. Dozens of people from Top Tier families have finally come forward to offer their services, adding a huge arsenal of Gifts to our skill set, and I can see the respect in North, Gryphon, and even Nox at the families' apparent change of heart.

I haven't been brave enough yet to ask Gryphon if there's an ulterior motive in play.

I'm sure there has to be one, but instead, I focus on what this means for whatever comes next with the god-bond. The god-bond who wields Pain and has reportedly gone insane because of the years of rebirth. The one who killed Nox while targeting North, happily taking out his brother instead.

I get the feeling we will need all the power we can get our hands on.

I watch Gryphon as he scrutinizes the recruits. It's one of my favorite things to do, to guess how he's feeling about their progress before he opens his mouth. I like to see if I can read him as well as the rest of them can read me. It's surprising to me how quickly I have come to know my Bonded as well as I know myself.

The reactions these days hardly ever surprise me. Even when I'm caught off guard by something, I have such security now in our relationships, both individually and as a whole. I know exactly where I stand with all of them, and there's nothing quite so incredible as all of us working together as a cohesive unit.

I wait until I'm sure that Gryphon is too busy to notice whether I'm here or not before I head back up to North's office, leaving him behind with a quick, cordial nod of my head. I see the dark look in his eyes as he watches me walk off. I know that he is far happier with PDA than North is, but it still feels entirely inappropriate to engage in such things in front of his TacTeam. Especially only meters away from where the flowers for Vivian's monument still stand, growing little by little every day as the community continues to mourn him. I get choked up if I stare at them for too long, and I duck my head as I step into the building.

There's a few operatives in there, a couple of them getting changed in the locker room, but each of them smiles and nods at me respectfully as I move towards the elevator without a word.

It kills me a little inside to know that it took Vivian's death to bring people together like this. When the doors open to North's office, I find him sitting behind a table, working through the plans for the council vote. There is a coffee cup the size of my head sitting next to him, already half-empty, and the vicious muttering under his breath lets me know exactly how well this is all going.

"I don't for the life of me understand how there are so many ways to cheat at voting. The corruption in this world is baffling."

I smile and shake my head at him. "You always told me I was naive for thinking people could be good. Sounds like you're confused."

He places his pen back down on the desk and then leans back, his hands rising above his head as he stretches, and I enjoy the sight for a moment. The long lines of him, even covered in his suit like this, are a welcome sight.

His voice is a seductive drawl to me. "I'm well aware that men will always be corrupt. It just pisses me off that it becomes my problem to deal with."

I blow out a breath and move to the window to look out at the lines of Tac personnel as they're put through their paces on the sparring mats. I watch as a son of one of the Top Tier families uses his Telekinetic power to throw someone away from himself, marveling at his ability to do so.

My bond is quiet in my chest, happy to sleep and build up energy for what's to come, and I leave it be. It has always known best about these things, even when it didn't know how to communicate that to me.

North's old assistant, Penelope, is the perfect example of that.

The hatred and utter loathing it had for her, even before it knew why, was something that we should have never ignored.

To think that we had a fledgling god-bond in his inner circle for so long sends a chill through my body now, as facing the Elemental had only days ago. I'd watched the entire fight through my bond's eyes. Seeing Penelope there with her arms stretched out wide, her eyes glowing, black voids, all of it had set my temper off all over again.

I've been very good about not rubbing North's face in it, but probably only because of Vivian's death.

"Are you really that worried about corruption now, considering the way everyone's acting?"

He can hear the resentment in my voice, so he steps up

behind me to sling an arm around my waist, moving me closer into his body as he watches the sparring with me. "It wasn't just Vivian, Bonded. It was the council dissolving as well. You know? A lot of those men and women down there felt as though they couldn't join TacTeams because of their family legacy. If they ran off on a mission and died, who would take up their council seats? What would happen to their families? There's a lot of responsibility on all of them, one that I understand keenly. Dissolving the council and making it a popular vote has changed a lot of things for some of these kids."

I scowl for a moment out the window, but I know there's no point in arguing with North. He wouldn't lie to me anyway. It serves no purpose.

I grumble under my breath, "So now they're just free to go off on missions and die without having to think about what their parents will think of it? That also sounds pretty crazy."

He chuckles and dips down to press a kiss to my shoulder. "I don't think any of them believe that they would die on a mission, Bonded. Especially when they haven't been out there before. There's a recklessness when they first join that takes a few missions to shake out of them. I have no doubt that some of them are using this as a campaign platform. They're planning on going out on a few missions, and then they'll run for the next council seat using their experience as a party platform. I have no doubt that a lot of them have ulterior motives, but there are a handful that Gryphon has found who are genuine. Plus, the strengths that they all bring are useful, no matter what has led them to this point. Quite frankly, we can't afford to be picky right now."

I sigh and lean back in his arms, letting my head drop back against his chest and enjoying a quiet moment with him.

One of our last.

I'm surprised, but not completely shocked, when the next part of our plan comes together thanks to the work of Sawyer and Nox.

Both Sawyer and Sage have made comments to me about their work together, and I was surprised when Sawyer was so nonchalant and calm about it. He's only really gotten snappy about the lack of organization on the Bassingers' part when it came to their digital records.

"Considering how fucking perfectly they've archived all of their paper shit, they really did not give a fuck about labeling files or setting up any sort of indexing matrices. Honestly, I feel like showing up at your house and punching Atlas in his smug, rich-boy face in the hopes that his dickhead ancestors feel it. But I also like my soul where it is, so that's probably not the best idea," Sawyer had snarked at me when I showed up at their house to check in on Kieran and have lunch with Sage.

Unfortunately, even with Felix's full attention and his Bonded's healing abilities, Kieran is on a slow track to recovery. Every bone in his body had been smashed to pieces, and that's not exactly something that's a quick fix. The stress it's put Sage under makes me feel bloodthirsty all over again.

The only upside to this is the fact that Wick has stepped up to the plate for his Bonded Group and the community in a big way, filling in with Gryphon in the Tac Training sessions beautifully, without complaint or any need for praise. I can see why he was such a great candidate for the TacTeams when he studied at Draven. There's no mistaking that he is a leader in his own right. Even with the cloud hanging over their house that comes with Kieran's injuries, I can tell how united and settled Sage's Bonded Group has become.

It's an immense relief for me, even while I am concerned about Kieran. Vivian's death has brought up old traumas I was hoping to leave in unmarked boxes tucked away in the back of my mind, never to be opened again, and yet here we are.

Nox and Sawyer aren't exactly the most obvious duo

to pair together on missions, however all of the work that the two of them were doing has paid off. Going through the Bassingers' files, both digital and the hardcopies that Nox managed to categorize and get home safely, has been a full-time job for them both.

Between that, and the memories that the Corvus has been filtering through to Nox, a plan becomes very clear to him. The problem is that he hates the plan with a vehemence that has him searching for something, anything, else for weeks.

Nothing else comes up.

Once he accepts that it's our only option, he's forced to broach it with North and I. He does so before the rest of our Bonded Group, and that in itself sends warning bells into my mind.

"Under no circumstances will my Bonded be used as bait. Find a new plan," North says in his most savage and firm tone, one that I have never heard in our Bonded Group's direction, let alone his brother's, but Nox doesn't react to it, he simply crosses his arms and raises his chin in defiance.

It's a fighting stance that I know so well, and I start to mentally prepare for the fallout of this conversation. I already know it's going to be horrendous.

"You're making it sound as though I'm going to drug her and string her up somewhere, nothing more than cannon fodder. That's not what I'm talking about. The information that the Bassingers had been collecting concurs with what the Corvus has said. The Pain god uses its power as a trap to separate us; it always does. That's exactly what it's going to do, North. It will drive a wedge between us once it has lured us into a trap. As soon as it gets Oleander alone, it will kill her."

North shakes his head at him. "It can't. We're stronger than it now. There are also six of us and one of it. There is no chance that it will get the better of us."

He doesn't sound cocky, merely confident, stating the facts that the god-bonds have said to us over and over again, but I still feel the same pit of unease in my gut.

We're going to be stronger than the Pain god-bond, thanks to our Bonding, but are we going to make it out alive? We currently have a success rate of zero in hundreds of lives, so I don't find myself feeling very optimistic about it, even knowing the difference of this lifetime from the last. I feel stronger than I ever have been before, but who knows if it's enough?

Who knows if it will ever be enough?

Nox keeps his eyes on North, staring a hole right into his brother as he does whatever he needs to do to win this argument. "The Pain god will use that against us. It will use our confidence against us. We both know it, because that's exactly what we would do. As much as we all might want to think differently, it's smart. Smart enough to have survived this long and to start an entire movement amongst the Gifted community to hide within and build resources against us. It has manipulated the strongest of our community, over and over and *over*. If we let our egos into this conversation, it will win again."

North shakes his head, and then his eyes catch mine and he shakes it all over again. "The risk is too great. Find another plan. Send me… or you. Send any of the rest of us, I don't care. Not Oleander."

My bond prickles inside my chest at the very thought of that, but I understand the hypocrisy there. The moment Nox suggested I be used as bait, I was happy to throw myself headfirst into the danger that is sending such a chill through North's blood, the evidence so clear on his face.

"It won't come after one of us, and you know it. It always takes the Eternal first. The only way it can *beat us* is by taking the Eternal first. Hundreds of lifetimes— it always goes for her. Why do you think it hunted her parents the moment it heard of her ability? Why do you think that it wanted to carve her into pieces? It wasn't just Silas Davies, you know. He was just the idiot that lost her, in the Pain god's eyes. Whether you like it or not, brother, it has always come down to Oleander. Even now, we can't deny that… no matter how badly we want to."

North shakes his head again, pressing his hands against

the table as he searches through the paperwork like a 'Plan B' might suddenly spring out of the words there, but all that stares back at him is the black ink.

There is no arguing with Nox about these things, and we both know it. He's the researcher. He always has been happiest losing himself in books and data, building a path for us once he's sure he has checked every angle. If he says that using me as bait is the only way, I don't actually need to hear anything else.

I trust it.

I also trust him, not just because he's my Bonded, but because I've seen the heart of him. I've seen every moment of his life, every second to this point. There's no doubt in my mind that he wouldn't even be suggesting this to North if there was another way, and he certainly wouldn't be suggesting it if he didn't think that we could win. He would still be tucked away in that little library of archives, searching for a loophole.

If he doesn't believe that we need that, then that's enough for me.

"I can do it, North," I say confidently. He shakes his head again, turning away from us both, but I force my voice out even stronger.

I push away from the table and circle around to North, forcing him to meet my eye. "I want to do it—and I'm going to—with your blessing or not. My bond and I are sick of this cycle, sick of death and the way that it just seems to follow us no matter what we do. My bond is tired. It wants us all to be safe and together. It wants the future that we just keep promising will someday be here. Instead of promising it, it wants us to work towards it, and I agree. If Nox has a plan that he believes will work, that's enough for me."

North turns back to me, and I see the stark fear in his eyes, the terror that we've gotten to this point, and that no matter how brave or how in control he might have been up to now, everything is spiraling slowly out of his grasp. Now that we're facing the end, I see it all. I take it in, and it only strengthens my conviction. I give him a nod and then one to Nox.

"Let's get this over with."

North stares down at me for a moment longer, and then he looks back up at Nox, a snarl curling his lip for a moment before he gets it back under control. "Fine. Tell me the plan, the whole thing. We're not leaving this room until I'm positive there's no holes in it. If anything happens to my Bonded out there, I'll let the shadows consume *everything* until we're all in Hell. It's the least we'll deserve."

26

The city is dark around me.

There are cars weaving past me with honking horns and people shouting, disorienting me quickly as it's been months since I've been around vehicles like that. The Sanctuary only has ATVs, and when we Transport elsewhere, it's mostly been to Wastelands or places affected by the gods, nothing like the real world.

It smells like every city I've ever been to, smoke and hot garbage filling my lungs as I pull my sleeve over my hand and press it to my nose. It's been years since I've been somewhere like this, but you never really forget the smell.

A light above me flickers off and on, off and on, and

there's so much light pollution that I can't see the stars. You wouldn't even know that there were millions of them shining down right now.

I instantly feel homesick, but there's work to do. I could put a vulnerable look on my face of uncertainty or worry in some way, but I'm not going to play into the trap that much. When I hear the telltale sign, the *pop* of a Transporter arriving with the Pain god wearing a senator's body, I stare back at them unflinchingly with my own blue eyes.

I don't want to give them the satisfaction of dealing with the Eternal right now.

"You really think you can outsmart me like this?" it asks, clicking its tongue as it steps towards me.

The voice grates on me.

For many months, I sat in North's office and listened to this god play games with him, pretending to be a human scared of the Gifted and laying more and more roadblocks for us to deal with. All of the time it had stolen from North as it wove its web, distractions leading us all away from what was really going on.

The Pain god is smart, but I refuse to let it be smarter than us.

I tilt my head in the same way that all the gods do, almost mockingly, and the Pain god smiles again, more teeth than emotion.

"Arrogance always was your strong suit," it says, drawing out the vowel sounds as though it's chewing on them. Its voice sounds more and more demonic as the conversation continues.

The Transporter, an older man in his late fifties, watches the two of us warily but with clear eyes. What I wouldn't give to have Gryphon here to tell me exactly what that man is thinking, what he's been promised, or what righteous mission he thinks he's on when really, he's nothing more than a pawn in a game far bigger than he could ever imagine.

The Pain god pitches its tone low for a moment, mimicking real concern that it has no grasp of. It helps that its vessel is an older woman, homely-looking and unassuming, but I know better. "You should come with me, little human. I can try and help get that god out of you, if you'd like. It's like a parasite, you know. We all are. You really should let me get it out of you before it takes the vessel. You know they do that, right? We *all* take the vessels at some point."

I stare back at it, unblinking and unflinching. Eventually, she nods slowly at me. "Well then, let's not waste time talking. If we're going to play our final game, then let's play."

The Transporter holds his arm out to her and when she takes it, they disappear together, reappearing right next to me before he clamps a hand on my shoulder and takes me with them.

I take a deep, calming breath.

Everything is going to be okay.

We're following the plan that Nox has put together, and I am not in danger. I say it over and over and over in my head, even as the Transporting seems to take three times as long as it ever has to travel with Kieran. Whether that is his strength or merely that my perception of time is messed up from the tense situation, I don't know. All that matters is that when we finally appear and I see our surroundings, I want to put my fist through the Pain god's face.

I refuse to give it the satisfaction.

Instead, I open my mind to my Bonded to make sure they know exactly where I am, following the steps of our plan perfectly. I empty myself of all emotion, everything I feel about where I am, everything that nags at me. Bile creeps up my throat, the motion sickness from the trip here still kicking my ass, but emotionally I let myself have nothing. The tears that desperately want to flow prick at the backs of my eyes, but I will not let it win this way.

The bridge isn't even that high.

"I'm not sure how they ever convinced anyone that your family died of natural causes and not your little Gifted temper tantrum," it says as it looks over the side of the bridge.

I refuse to blink, because I am so afraid that even shutting my eyes for a millisecond will cause me to have a flashback of the night my parents died, the car hitting the side of our SUV and plunging us off of the bridge. My power had ripped out of my body to decimate everything around us, killing everyone. *Everyone*, not just our enemies in the car that had been hunting us, but my parents and the family that ran the small dairy farm just a few miles up the road.

It was blamed on a gas leak, a mysterious accident that occurred at the exact same time as the car accident here, like some horrible twist of fate.

The first souls I ever tore out, the ones that weighed most heavily on my shoulders.

"Are you sure you don't want me to get the god out of you? Are you sure you want to keep it? Choosing the side that killed your parents seems awfully short-sighted."

My bond recoils in my chest, rolling there as though it is slowly pulling itself up into a fighting position. It's deceptively slow and languid in its movements, when I know that it could lash out faster than the speed of light if required. I feel the way that it reacts to every word that comes out of the Pain god's mouth, the way it tastes them for itself, chews on them, finds them wanting, and spits them out.

The way it sees everything that Pain is doing for

exactly what it is, a lie to attempt to trap me. I wonder if it's ever worked before? If this, too, is a part of the trap that it lays? I wonder whether it is feeling cocky about all of this because there is a long history behind it.

If it knows how ridiculous all of this seems to me when it's wearing the face of this woman.

Nightmares, to me, look like Silas Davies.

They look like a man in his prime, handsome to those who are blind to the evil within, the cruel set of his mouth and the way that his eyes pick me apart. He didn't need a god-bond living inside him to be dangerous, deadly, cruel, and wicked.

That was all the man.

"How exactly would you get the god-bond out?" I ask in a low voice as though I'm trying to keep this a secret between the two of us.

I doubt I'm fooling anyone, but I suppose this is the game of cat and mouse that we're now playing. The Pain god tilts its head, looking me over slowly before reaching out a hand and letting it hover above my temple.

"I know the Eternal has probably told you that it's stronger than me because all of its Bonded are here too, but that's a lie. Power is not something that you share. It's something you *take*. These gods that live within you and your Bonded Group, they live in a fairy tale, a twisted version of the truth that they desperately want to believe, but it cannot be. You don't have power unless you take it from someone."

A cold breath of wind rustles the leaves in the trees that line the riverbank. The night air around us seems to drop ten degrees as the god keeps talking, rambling on about its opinions of the way the world should be. It's all nothing but a ploy to win my compliance.

Again, I can't help but wonder if it's ever worked before.

"You know that it's true. Your god-bond exists to take the life force from those around it. You cannot deny the truth in my words when that is how it derives its power. I will get it out of you, whether you submit to me or not. One way or another, I will get it out."

I nod and lean away from her as if I'm afraid of her touch, as though I'm afraid that the pain will come dripping from her fingers the moment it touches my skin. I can feel the way that she's pushing at me with her Gift, the way she's poking and prodding and trying to find a hole in my barriers to wield that dark power against me. I came here prepared for all of that. I came here not only with my own mental securities, but those of my Bonded as well.

I didn't come here alone, even if the Pain god thinks I did.

"Your devotion to them is disgusting, you know. A thousand lifetimes and not once have they ever protected you. A thousand lives, and you always ended up dead. You're more powerful than all of them put together. If you sacrificed them, you could become as I am."

I look over at it as I digest its arrogance. "It must have been so frustrating for you to be born into that body. I'm sure you've had more than your fair share of obstacles, thanks to it."

It shrugs at me and nonchalantly tilts its head. "A Gifted born to a lower Tier family. It was easy to kill my vessel and the family it was born into, to hide myself amongst the humans. It's far easier to do such things when you remember exactly who you are from the moment you are born into the vessel. I've had a lot of years to plan what this would look like, lifetimes to prepare for your cycle. I don't want to kill your Bonded Group. I want something else entirely."

I make a big show of swallowing as though terrified, my eyes darting back to the river rushing underneath the bridge to convince the Pain god I'm telling the truth, and it steps up alongside me once more.

"There is no power without taking it from someone. A thousand lifetimes, and I have killed a thousand gods, but I have finally unlocked it. I have finally unlocked how to take that power into myself. Taking from your Bonded Group will give me everything I need to build the world that I want."

A shiver runs down my spine, because I already know that the world it wants to see is one of pain and blood and madness. The same world that the Resistance has been fighting for because they were fighting on her behalf.

"I don't want to fight the god within you. I want to take its power and become it. I want to consume it."

I know that things are not going to stay so civil between the Pain god and I for very long. The more I try to keep the god-bond talking, the more that it snares me in its trap. And the more that it pushes me closer and closer to the edge of the bridge, the more that it draws my eyes down to the water rushing beneath us.

The more that it gets me where it wants me.

I don't know how it intends on doing what it claims it can do, and the Pain god reads my disbelief with ease, a cruel smile curving over its lips as it bares its teeth at me like a true predator playing with its prey.

"Silas Davies figured it out, you know," it continues on, and I shudder unconsciously at the mention of his name.

"He figured it out thanks to you, of course, because consuming people is your gift, after all. I know that you all seem to think it was a misstep of mine to let him play with you for so long, to let him play his little games, only to have you disappear out of his grasp as if you were smoke. It was never about killing you or the thing that lives inside of you. It was about *harnessing* you. Of course, he thought that I wanted mass destruction, for you to kill as many Gifted and humans as possible. He was a crazed being, one after my own heart, but we can't ever really befriend the Gifted. The wolf cannot befriend the sheep, but I suppose we can use the most creative of them to our benefit."

Creative.

I suppose that's a word you could use for Silas Davies. I also have to acknowledge that spending time with him trained me pretty well to have this conversation. There's nothing but madness spewing out of the Pain god's mouth right now, nothing but the sort of maniacal insanity of a nihilistic dictator.

There's no doubt in my mind that this is exactly where the Resistance started, from a group of Gifted worshiping the wrong god. One who had promised them power and convinced them all that they deserved certain liberties, when really all it wanted was cannon fodder for a war of its own design.

"We can't spend all night talking about such things, little girl. You're not going to find a flaw in my plans, and I'm not going to convince you to join my side, am I?"

The wind rustles in the trees on the far side of the bridge again, this time louder, and it's an ominous sound that echoes through the night.

I shake my head. "I think we both know that I'm not going to give you my bond. I also think you know that you couldn't get it out of me even if you tried. You haven't been able to push your way inside of my head in the ten minutes we've been talking, so I doubt you're ever going to be able to. All of your convincing has been for nothing. I'll stick with real power. The Eternal will win this."

I watch as the senator's face contorts, twisting and turning as the disgust and madness bleeds into the woman's features. I almost feel glad that the god killed the vessel a long time ago, that there hasn't been some poor Gifted trapped inside there with it all this time. It's a fate worse than death, I'm sure.

"The Eternal would certainly like to think that, wouldn't you?" it spits out, its voice changing, darkening, deepening, and its eyes bleed to black.

My bond stretches in my chest again in retaliation, preparing and readying itself to finish what evil has been started here. We're both ready to take back the life that we want to have with our Bonded, the one we all deserve.

The Pain god raises a hand, centering its power on me, only this time, I feel the full blast of it as it pulses out of the god-bond's body. It hits mine as though it's a physical wave, crashing over me and flooding me with sensation. I do feel the pain but not in the way that the Pain god intends, because my bond is shutting it out of my mind, taking it from me as it took Silas Davies' pain. It's protecting me now as it protected me before, taking it all even as my body begins to shut down.

Protecting me now as it always has.

As my vision begins to blur, my eyes slowly begin to flutter shut. For a second, I feel myself panic.

What if it doesn't work?

What if everything that we planned was all for nothing? What if we die here, and my last moment with my Bonded was back at the Sanctuary, back where Nox was the only one confident of this plan. He was the only one pushing it, while the others were furious at us both for this. What if all of this is for nothing and we're going to be forced to cycle again?

As my vision goes black and pushes me into darkness, those words echo in my mind, the last thing I think as the Eternal takes over… What if we fail?

What if *I* fail?

27

NOX

Convincing North to let Oleander walk into the Pain god's trap with nothing more than our shadow creatures at her side is only the very first of my hurdles.

Convincing the rest of the Bonded Group is almost impossible. Even after Oleander said she was going whether they liked it or not, it came to blows, Gryphon almost taking my head off and Atlas only being stopped by North's intervention.

I have to come to terms with the vicious, loathing looks that I'm going to receive from each of them throughout this.

It doesn't matter though.

None of that matters, so long as the plan succeeds.

For the very first time, my brother insists that Oleander takes his shadow creature with her. She tucks August behind her other ear after he shrinks down to the size of a penny, invisible to the world and everyone in it other than the three of us.

North has never trusted his bond or the creatures with her like this.

He's never allowed them to spend time with her, especially at such a distance. He's never trusted that side of himself, and certainly not with someone as beloved as his Bonded. Those fears inside of him haven't just changed, they've evaporated altogether.

There is no doubt in either of our minds that she's safest with our eyes on her, and if our eyes cannot be there, then our shadow creatures are the next best thing. I would trust Azrael with her no matter what, but there's also something reassuring about August being with them too.

I've seen what North's most vicious creature is capable of.

Standing at the edge of the Wasteland that I'm sure we're about to be pulled into, my eyes voided out and the hard glares of the Bonded Group on me, I watch the moment the Pain god transports Oleander to the bridge.

I almost second-guess my own plan.

Not because I don't believe that Oleander is strong enough to go through with our plan at the site of her parents' death, but because the memory of that car ride lives within me just as it lives within her, and a vicious, *violent* reaction bubbles out of me.

North side-eyes me for a moment, his own eyes black as he watches through his shadow creature, but when the others begin to question what's going on, he's the one to answer.

"The god-bond is trying to get a rise out of her. It's trying to find a weakness in Oli to get through to the Eternal—"

"And it's not going to work," I cut him off. Even if he reads the pure truth in my tone, Gryphon certainly doesn't believe me.

"What is the point of a Bonded Group like ours if we're going to just split up the moment one of these things snaps its fingers at us? This is fucking stupid," he mutters under his breath, checking out his weapons again.

It's a tic that he usually does when we arrive on a mission to calm himself down, and yet here it is, cropping up as he tries to keep a handle on his emotions. It's not usually this hard for him, but I suppose this is the first time we've had to do something like this. We haven't been separated from Oleander since she chased Kyrie to that Resistance camp and got herself sliced to pieces. The echoes of her pain back then still reverberate in my mind, and my bond seethes in my chest at the reminder.

We won't let it come to that this time.

"Tell me again why you think this is going to work." North mutters under his breath, and I take a long, calming breath of my own.

He's not questioning me. He's trying to stay calm. If I keep telling myself that, maybe I won't lose my shit at them.

It's almost fucking impossible not to.

"They weren't testing Oli at the camps because they wanted to use her as a bomb. The Infinite Weapon program was a smokescreen, a way to convince the underlings to do their work for them."

The records are very clear about what the god-bonds were really doing during the experiments. The patterns are there, and it hadn't taken long for me and Benson to figure out that we were looking for a very particular type of experiment within the archives. They weren't just looking at how to shift souls from bodies, but how to mix some bloodlines for certain types of Gifts.

The Pain god knew that whatever vessel it was moved into, it would gain access to that power, the same way that while the Shadows are an indicator of the god-bonds, it isn't the only thing that we can do. The Draven line gave me the god-bonds, but my mother's gift of the Madness had given me the Dread that terrifies all of those who hear my name. North's mother had passed on the Death Touch to him.

The gods have access to these things now, a growing arsenal of weapons, and if the Pain god is able to take over the body of another Top Tier Gifted, it could kill the soul within and take control of the vessel. It could slowly start to collect whatever powers it desired, and it might just start with Oleander and work its way through our Bonded Group. Shapeshifting into a dragon with the shadow creatures at its beck and call, the Neuro ability to hack into anyone's brain, and the ability to inflict gruesome, bloody deaths by tearing bodies to pieces, all wrapped up in one crazed god-bond.

I can't imagine anything worse.

If we allow that to happen, we might as well say goodbye to the human race, because the Pain god will just consume and kill and maim over and over and over again until there is nothing left. This goes beyond just wanting to give our god-bonds the life that they have been yearning for or living a life with our own Bonded Group in peace. As selfishly as I want those things, this is about whether or not the world is going to be taken over by, quite frankly, the root of all evil.

"What they really want is to be able to shift vessels. They want to live forever, and none of them give a shit about who they live within. They don't care about lifetimes or sleeping or any of that. All they care about is power—"

"But none of them have a Gift to manipulate souls within a vessel,"Atlas finishes off for me, a scowl on his face as he rubs a hand across his chin.

He's been surprisingly quiet about the entire mission, keeping to himself and taking Oleander at her word when she said that she trusted me and wanted to do this. He hasn't spoken to me or looked at me. He hasn't questioned me in any way, and he hasn't started a fight either, which is definitely a change.

I have no doubt that if anything happens to her, hc will be the first person to kill me.

It won't matter if the Pain god comes looking, I will already be a corpse if he has anything to do with it. It really would be a test of whether or not the Cleaver can take on the shadow creatures, though I suppose that if Oleander and I are wrong and something does happen to her, I won't fight back.

I don't think even the guilt I've had on my brother's behalf will be enough to keep me around if something does truly happen to her. I've always felt an obligation to stay here for him, even in my darkest days after he'd found me and killed my mother for what she'd done to me.

"This is fucking stupid," Gryphon says again, his eyes flashing to white as he lets his Gift kick in.

He scans the area, almost as though he's developing new techniques to settle himself, and I choose not to say anything about it, not to him or to the rest of them. I keep my eyes on Oleander, and when the Pain god finally strikes, pushing everything it can at her until I know her bond is forced to take it all, I square my shoulders and prepare myself.

I glance over at my brother. "They're coming."

North nods, a scowl on his face as he watches the same scene that I do, Oleander's body slumping down to the ground as the Pain god and the Transporter take her once more, Transporting into the Wasteland before us.

"I want this over with," he says, and I nod slowly, lifting a hand as the shadows fall away from my body and begin to fan out.

The TacTeam personnel all lined up behind us in neat rows stay calm as the shadows overtake the area. The original personnel have seen it all before, and the new recruits were warned about how tonight will go. There's an air of trust that has never been there before, a preparedness that was hard won.

Tonight.

Everything will be finished tonight, their death or ours.

We feel the moment that the Pain god appears in the Wasteland, moving Oleander's unconscious body into the impenetrable area they've built specifically to keep us out.

The walls of the Wasteland are strong, the strongest Shields that we have come across; which is exactly how

I knew that this is where they would end up. Hundreds of Gifted have been brought here to work together to make the entire area impenetrable.

When the scouts came across it, we knew right away that it would be endgame for the Resistance. We spent a lot of time trying to infiltrate it but failed again and again.

Except that was part of our plan as well.

The god-bond doesn't realize the strength that we have taken from our Bonded, the unprecedented growth in our abilities, or the fact that the Draven family has taken in the powers of the gods over hundreds of generations. Instead of their manipulations of the Bonded Groups affecting us in a way that would weaken us, it has only made us stronger. It has only made the arsenal of weapons that we have at our disposal even more formidable.

It's given us a way in.

"We need to go now," North says under his breath, and I nod, glancing over at each of them for a moment just to be sure that they're all as ready as I am.

Gryphon gives one last command to the Tac unit at our backs, and then each of them grabs my arm. The Shield can protect against Transporters that aren't welcome within the Wastelands, but they can't protect from something that's already in there.

The Transporter just let us in.

We'd been standing outside the Shield wall, unable

to move or advance any further. We hadn't been trying to hide, and they hadn't attempted to engage with us either. They've been so secure in their protections that they haven't even attempted to mobilize against us. They just ignored us entirely.

One moment, we're looking at that Shield wall, and the next moment, we're stepping through the shadows. I'd spent a lot of time honing this skill, sharpening it, perfecting it, and making sure that it's not the slow process of the shadow growing anymore.

I made sure that we wouldn't give them enough time to prepare themselves for the death that is coming their way. The moment we appear, the alarm goes off, but it's too late for them.

We're not here for anything but death.

The Crux takes over North's body before the Pain god even realizes that we have Shadow Shifted in.

It is so confident in its ability to keep us out, never dreaming that we'd find a loophole through its plan of Shielding us from our Bonded. It would have worked; it *has* worked a hundred times before.

Thanks to the breeding experiments that the Resistance had been conducting and the mixing of my mother's blood, my incidental Gift was something that the Corvus had never had before.

Shadow Shifting.

Simply by having Azrael tag along with Oleander meant there was nothing they could do to keep us apart, nothing they could do to stop me from arriving here. When we'd soul-bonded and forged an unbreakable connection, I knew that I'd never again let anything come between us, and that was all thanks to the Pain god.

I'm going to make sure it dies a horrific death, regretting that fact.

It used a lot of its power knocking Oleander out, more power than it should have been willing to, leaving it vulnerable to attack.

A vicious roar tears through the air as Gabe shifts, his body snapping and crunching as the Draconis takes over. The Crux moves towards Oleander, blind to everything else that is happening around us as it sees her unconscious form lying there, its devotion to her as blind as my brother's. The Soothsayer takes control of Gryphon and moves with him, getting a hand over her throat as it pours power into her.

The Corvus pushes at my mind as it attempts to take over, but I push back, letting the streams of shadows fall away from my body and pushing them to devour their Transporter whole. I'm eager to remove any potential threats before the Pain god has the chance to get out of here.

I watch the way that its mouth twists scornfully, the hatred there a sickening thing as my shadows turn their heads towards her. How it ever managed to pass as a simple, non-Gifted woman is beyond me, because all I can see in those depthless void eyes is the sort of murderous madness that isn't so easily disguised. A smirk stretches over my own lips as I see the realization set in, the tension filling its body as its power washes over me without breaking into my mind at all. It's desperate, and it now knows it's used its trump card too soon.

It knows that we don't want to simply kill it.

Doing such a stupid, rash thing would just send it back into the cycle; and I'm not spending the rest of my life waiting for this evil to return. If we cycle again, if this keeps on happening to us over and over, I'm not going to risk this coming after Oleander again. Not this version of her or the ones to come. Never again.

I watch as it scrambles away from us, throwing out its power as though it has a chance of getting through to any of us, but it can't. The one and only time Gryphon used his Gift to knock Oli out, he told us it was like she pulled the power from him.

I'm sure the Pain god is hating every second of my poison girl's power right now, every inch of it perfection.

The Draconis roars again, and this time, it takes off, leaving us behind as it senses something out there that none of the rest of us can see. A burst of fire lights up the night sky moments later as he wipes out the threat before it can even get close to Oleander. I push my shadow creatures even further, letting them free to start taking out the Resistance.

I watch as Atlas follows the line of the dragon's body in the sky, torn between moving to Oleander and watching to see what is coming for us next. The Cleaver hasn't taken over yet, it's still the man in there making the choices, and as he glances back over in Oli's direction, he curses under his breath.

I glance back to find a gun in the Pain god's hands.

Atlas shakes his head at it, pushing his power into the barrier around it, but it's not as simple as keeping us protected from the bullet.

It's not aiming at us.

One of my shadows jumps up to grab it by the hand, another wrapping around its body to stop it from killing itself. It starts cursing and shouting as it squirms, fighting uselessly against the shadows, and I enjoy the sight of it all over again. I let one of the dark tendrils wrap around its mouth before I snap its arm, breaking the bone in a single movement.

The sound is like music to my ears.

The Draconis roars again, and Atlas curses under his breath.

"What the hell is going on up there?" he murmurs as he walks towards the opening to the tent, lifting it slightly and then jolting back.

"We have a lot more than the Pain god to deal with," he says quietly, and the Soothsayer finishes healing Oli, standing up behind Atlas to glance out for a second.

"Tell me you've got her back, Crux. We can't stay in here for much longer," Atlas says, his tongue only tripping over the god-bond's name a little.

There's no answer, but the Crux stands smoothly, Oli looking so small and fragile in his arms. The Corvus pounds at the edges of my mind, demanding to be let out, but I hold onto control desperately. I need to see her wake up first. I need to know this wasn't a mistake.

Her eyes stay closed, but her chest is moving steadily, her breathing even, as though she's just enjoying a good night's rest.

My eyes drift back to the Pain god, the loathing and disgust dripping from its gaze as it stares back at me.

I don't really care about what this god-bond thinks.

The Soothsayer steps over to where the Crux is now cradling Oli against its chest, rocking her gently as their skin glows. He's letting her feed from his power, seeping it into her through touch to fill her inner well and revive her.

I'm ready to take over the moment she needs it.

The Crux is clearly unhappy with what is going on, the skin on his hands turning black as he taps into his own well of power. He's on the edge of losing control and taking down the entire Wasteland with his own Gifted rampage.

The Resistance have no idea what they've unleashed.

I stare at the Pain god, watching the madness writhe underneath its skin. "You should've known when she brought me back that it was all over for you."

It snarls at me, too rabid to play these mind games, and yet it keeps on trying. "You say that like she hasn't brought you back before. Always the same, always simpering after the rest of you like some pathetic little bitch in heat. You could be so much *more*."

I shrug, the picture of calm even as dread pools in my gut due to Oleander's unconscious state. "Why would I want to be more if I don't have her?"

It spits on the ground between us. "*Disgusting.*"

"And yet, one of us is going to die today and the other is going to walk out of here, perfectly safe and with a complete Bonded Group. A long life ahead of us all. Tell me again how weak we are," I say with a taunting tone, and Bassinger shoots a grin over his shoulder at me before it slides off of his face again, almost as though he's just realized who he's in on the joke with.

I don't particularly care about that. I care about the

details and how I can use them here to really extend the suffering of this god-bond.

I want it screaming.

"How many times have you killed your Bonded?" I say, lifting up a knife from the table in front of us.

It looks a little too much like the table on which Oleander had been subjected to torture for my liking, the echoes of her memories are as clear in my mind now as they have ever been. Her screams and the blood and the terror are waiting there for me the moment I shut my eyes.

I could hate this god for killing me, for being the one to spark the soul-bond that I share with my Bonded, but there's a part of me that will always be grateful for my death.

I wouldn't have found Oleander in the darkness of my mind without it.

No, I hate this god-bond for what it built. I hate it for the movement that it began purely to kill the rest of us. The Resistance has harmed so many, but ultimately, I will revel in this god-bond's death because of what it did to Oleander. For Silas Davies, the death of her parents, the nightmares she still has lurking in the back of her mind, and for her years of loneliness and suffering.

For that, I will see this god-bond destroyed so permanently that it can never come back.

There's a gasp behind me, and for the first time, I take

my eyes fully off of the god-bond as my entire body turns towards Oleander. It always has, even when I fought it off so desperately.

She is awake, she is mine, and she is *hungry*.

She devours the god-bond's soul before her eyes even flutter open, tearing it out as though it's nothing more than a small, fragile being, ridding our world once more of this vengeful god. Only this time, it's for good.

The Pain god is no more.

28

OLI

Everything is burning.

The smoke and ash in my nose burns all the way down my throat, and my skin is hot and tight like it's melting straight off of my bones. My chest feels as though I've swallowed hot coals, and everything is burning.

Everything is burning.

"Open your eyes, Bonded. You're really starting to freak us out here," Gryphon murmurs, and there are hands against my throat.

I want to open my eyes, but they feel sealed shut, as though maybe my skin really is melting and it's melted right off of my face. What if it slipped away so that I couldn't open my eyes even if I tried?

"Don't be so dramatic. I can see your face right now, and it's as beautiful as ever. Just open your eyes, Bonded. I need to see them, just to be sure."

"If you can hear her, then she's clearly fine," Nox drawls, and though North snaps back at him, the hands slowly stroking my hair stay gentle and soft.

"Will you ever take anything seriously? How are you not fucking terrified?"

I hear footsteps, and then more hands are on me, these ones on my wrist as though Nox is taking my pulse. They already know that I'm alive, clearly.

"Just because devotion looks like two different things doesn't mean they're any different. You covet her power and want to protect her so much that she never has to use it. I enjoy watching her eat god-bonds alive."

Gryphon scoffs at them both, leaning forward to press our foreheads together as we have on the battlefield before. His breath fans over my skin, and even with how much pain is coursing through my body, I can still feel the sensation and enjoy it.

It must not be so bad.

"Open your eyes, Bonded," he murmurs again, and this time, I finally find the strength to let them flutter open.

Everything hurts.

I can't say it out loud; my mouth won't work. My throat is too dry to even consider speaking, but Gryphon nods, rubbing our noses together as he does.

"I know. I'll get you home, Bonded, the second the Draconis and the Cleaver are finished hacking everyone to pieces out there."

My eyes flare open a little wider, the closest I can get to startling in my current state, and a lazy grin slides over Gryphon's face. "You dealt with the god-bond, and its grand plan of murdering us all and consuming our Gifts has thoroughly gone to shit. It had the last of the big Resistance camps here, bursting full of soldiers ready to back it up and start a new blood-soaked revolution. I don't think any of them were truly prepared to face the Draconis and the Cleaver. They're both making a real mess."

I blink again and swallow, wincing at the dryness of my mouth, but Gryphon only nods again, reading every last one of my questions and concerns about his words. "The Draconis went out there first, and the Cleaver eventually followed. We have the shadows out there helping as well, but we're getting ready to move you home. You did what you needed to do."

I don't remember doing it.

Not the ripping the soul out part, and certainly not the consuming it, which I guess is a blessing in disguise considering how much I hate it. I feel as though my entire body has been flayed open, so there's no doubt that I consumed the soul. Being knocked out never felt like this.

I feel as though there's nothing good left inside of me.

There's a screeching noise, and North curses under his breath, his hands soft as they stroke my hair one last time before he gets up and checks the flaps of the tent again.

Nox stays with me, but his eyes flash, so I know that he's checking in with his shadows as he keeps an eye on what's happening out there.

Gryphon helps me sit up, his fingers stroking over my neck as he checks in with me again. "We had to take out the Shields ourselves to let the rest of our personnel in, but I'm pretty sure Gabe just ate them. Quick, effective—"

"Disgusting," Nox interrupts with a scrunch of his nose. "He's going to be a mess once we get him home after all of this."

I want to shrug, because I'm *also* going to be a mess. No matter how much power I had saved for this moment, it had still come close to taking me out, I think. I can feel that they're sharing power with me, but still... it's not enough.

Gryphon scowls at me, pressing a hand on my forehead, and his eyes flash to black again. "Don't say stuff like that. You were nowhere near death's door. If you were, one of us would have chased after you by now to pull you back. Do you need Felix? I will go and pry him from Kieran's side if you feel that it's necessary, or should I let the Soothsayer back out instead?"

I do love the Soothsayer dearly, but right now, feeling

as exposed and in pain as I do, I just want the comfort of my Bonded. All of them together with me in a giant bed, naked bodies driving into mine as we share power. I want soft stroking hands, quiet murmurs, and no one leaving to go and do a million important things because nothing is more important than that for a little while.

Gryphon's eyes flash again and he nods slightly. "The moment I can get that dragon back here, we'll go home and do exactly that."

Nox, whose eyes have been slowly drifting between the two of us, takes a moment to point out the obvious. "We can't just leave the Tac operatives here to be slaughtered without us. The Draconis and the Cleaver are doing well out there, but we're nowhere near ready to leave yet. It would be going quicker if we were willing to go out there and help, but… we needed you awake first."

Gryphon curses under his breath again, pulling away from me as he points to the doorway. "Then you'd better get your shadows to work a bit faster, because she needs to go home and heal up from all of this. I am done denying my Bonded what she wants and needs because of Resistance bullshit. That part of my life is over with now."

Nox rolls his eyes back and snaps, "Until the next god-bond wakes up and we have to hunt it down. This is only over for now, but we'll be hunting again until there are none of them left."

It sounds a bit like a dream. No more Resistance, no more gods, no more anything getting in the way of our lives. That sounds like literal heaven, so my brain has trouble processing if it is even a remote possibility.

As they argue, I keep my eyes on North while he watches the area outside of the tent flap, his body tense and his eyes voided out as he directs the shadows around us. My hands shake a little as I try to rationalize the emptiness inside of me, but there's no denying the weakness that I'm filled with. It isn't just tearing out the soul of the god that has done this, letting it into my mind to knock me out for our plan has also taken its toll.

I'm facing the prospect of a long recovery back at the Sanctuary, and I find myself frustrated before that even starts. I don't want to have to lie around in bed. I don't want to have to miss out on anything else, and I certainly don't want to worry my Bonded the way that I know they will.

I cast out my net of power.

They all feel it and the bickering stops, their eyes all shifting to me. I feel the Cleaver and the Draconis where they're working. I feel all of the Resistance who are still alive and fighting, as well as our own TacTeam personnel, who are outnumbered in a big way. None of my Bonded had pointed this out to me yet, secure in the fact that the Cleaver and the Draconis are a thousand times more powerful than any of those Resistance grunts, but Nox wasn't wrong.

We'll be here for hours if it's just the two of them fighting.

I already know that the others joining in isn't a possibility. None of them are going to let their god-bonds take over and do what needs to be done, not with how weak I'm feeling.

I turn my head to face North, meeting his eyes, and I find myself asking him the same moral question that I have asked him before, the one that nags at me the most.

"There's no saving them, is there?"

He stares back at me without having to ask for clarification, and he slowly shakes his head. "I've been doing this a long time, Bonded. Once they take in the Resistance propaganda, they're poisoned by it. We've poured resources into trying to rehabilitate, but so far we have only had three separate cases of people being able to get away from the Resistance, and the fact of the matter is... none of them chose the Resistance in the first place."

My eyebrows creep up my forehead, and a lopsided smile stretches across his face. "Atlas, Aurelia, and Jericho. All three of them were born into the Resistance; all three of them saw no other options. The moment they were given some, they walked away. These people chose to be here. These people are beyond saving."

I nod my head slightly and then for what I hope is the last time it will ever be required, I pull the souls out of hundreds of Resistance soldiers all at once, pulling their power into me and filling my energy reserves back up.

I take it into myself, and I let it restore me. The light and the energy buzzes down my limbs, filling my lungs like a gasp, my blood coursing through my body as my heart races.

It fills me up so quickly that I begin to push the power out to my Bonded as well, but each of them stops me.

"We don't need it, Bonded. Take it for yourself," Gryphon murmurs to me quietly, and I let my eyes drift shut as the power settles within me.

There is a whooshing sound of wings beating against the air and then a thump as a body lands. The doorway of the tent comes open, and North is forced backwards as the Draconis' head pushes through, filling up the space with the sheer size of him.

I smile and reach out a hand to pat his velvety soft nose, my skin coming away with blood from his battles, and Nox makes a sound of disgust in the back of his throat.

I ignore it and instead murmur to my beloved Bonded, "Thank you. I'm feeling a lot better now. You can let Gabe come back, if you want to. It might be easier to get him home if he's a bit smaller."

It snorts and snuffles under its breath as though it is

unhappy at the idea, but with a simple shake of its head, it slowly retreats. Then we hear the telltale snapping and crunching sounds of Gabe shifting back.

There's footsteps around us and North meets my eye for a moment longer, nodding before he steps back out to start directing the Tac personnel, surveying the hundreds of dead bodies left behind.

Gabe stumbles into the tent, naked, sweaty,

and blood-soaked. His skin has turned an ashy-green color as his stomach protests the feasting of his god-bond.

Gryphon takes one look at him, shrugging off his jacket to hand over, and says, "Try not to vomit in here. If you're going to puke, head back out."

Gabe shrugs the jacket on, checking that it covers him all the way down to the knees before he clamps a hand across his mouth and mumbles from behind it, "Half of the Tac personnel are women, and I thought Oli would lose it if I was out there naked. I'll try and keep it down."

Instantly, I want to fuss after him, but he shakes his head at me. "It's getting easier. Don't worry about me, Bonded. Let's just get you home safely."

There's more sounds of boots outside crunching as though someone is running, and then the flap of the tent opens again, revealing Atlas. He looks as though he's about to pass out from fear until he sees me, relief sweeping over his features as he stumbles towards me.

"You took way too long to wake up that time, Bonded. Let's not do that again."

I shake my head at them all, reaching my arms up so that Atlas can help me to my feet, and then I get one around him and the other around Gabe, holding them both close to me. My bond tugs in my chest, chiming in on how it feels about all of this, and I let my eyes slip shut to hear it out.

They did well. Take us home to rest, girl, my bond whispers to me. *You fought bravely. They all did. Rest so we can wake up in the new world, a world built just for us that no one can take away this time.*

I wake up naked from the waist up, lying on North's bare chest, and I have a déjà vu moment, one where my heart stops and I think that maybe the last few months have been a dream.

The last time I woke up like this, his arms banded around me and my legs wrapped around his waist even in sleep, I found myself in his office back at the Draven mansion with the councilors in the room with us. North was snarling viciously that they dared to question him while I was hurt in such a way. I was taking the power that I needed directly from him, that healing energy seeping through his skin and into mine.

468

It was an exhausting and terrifying moment for me. I didn't remember how I had gotten there or what could possibly have transpired between when my bond had taken over and when I was woke up that would make North hold me in such a way. I remember the intimate way his hands cradled my thighs protectively, every inch of him curved towards me as though he was sheltering me.

I desperately wanted it.

I was so sure that it was some cruel trick to break me open just a little more, to dangle something I wanted over my head just to rip it away again. I feel that same echo now. I remember the Pain god's death and the destruction of the Resistance camp. If those moments were just a dream... I think I'll break right open.

"You're awake, Bonded," North murmurs quietly in my ear, and I nod, but I keep my eyes shut, leaning further into him to press my nose against his neck.

His skin burns against mine, and his hands pull me in closer until I struggle to breathe under the pressure, but it is so perfect that I would happily suffocate here.

"That's a little bit dramatic. Ease up, North," Gryphon drawls, and I finally open an eye to look around the room at them.

We're home, in the Sanctuary, in the kitchen of our perfect house, for some reason, but it is just my Bonded Group. I find them all in some state of undress as they peel their Tac uniforms away from themselves. They inhale the food that's in front of us as though they're starving to death. The only one not doing so is Gabe, who looks as though he is trying not to vomit all over himself.

I scowl at him, but Gryphon shrugs at me. "He won't go to bed. We got a gallon of antacid into him, but he said he's not going to bed until you are, so he's just going to have to wait until North is ready to give you up."

North cuts in, "Which is never. The power transfer is still happening, so he can either give up and go to bed, or he can wait."

The scowl stays on my face, but I lean forward to press my nose back into North's neck, sighing happily under my breath as I soak in not only his power but his calmness, his soothing energy, and the way that he is completely calm and confident.

A phone rings, and when I wince and bury myself a little closer, North snaps, "Turn it off. We already told them they can wait until Oleander is feeling better."

Footsteps approach and then Nox drawls, "Give it to me. I'll answer it."

I almost feel sorry for whoever is on the other end of the line, but I'm wiped out. This feels different to the Wasteland though, a different sort of tired. I feel like a nap will fix this, just a regular one.

"Are you hungry, my Bonded? I have plain food if

your stomach isn't feeling up to much, or there's a salmon risotto if you want some comfort food instead."

I'm hungry but definitely not for that, so instead of answering, I wriggle in his arms a little, pressing myself into him and lengthening my spine, almost purring when his hands trace down my back exactly how I hoped they would.

"You know the best way to power up, right?" I murmur to him quietly under my breath, and his answering chuckle sends goosebumps bursting over my skin.

"I would never say no to my Bonded. I'll never have to now, either," North says with a low drawl, his hands cupping my ass as he stands up, taking me with him as easily. "Whatever my Bonded wants."

As he walks me down the hallway, the chorus of voices behind us is loud as the rest of our Bonded Group finishes eating, getting ready to follow us to bed. There's no rush in any of them, no urgency, and it finally hits me that this moment is real.

We did it.

The god-bonds are gone, the Resistance is dealt with for now, and there's no one left to chase after us. Sure, there's probably some left that we'll need to deal with, and our Bonded Group is always going to attract negative attention, but we achieved the impossible; and now, we're free.

I press my face back into North's shoulder, rubbing myself against him instinctively as he kicks open the door to my bedroom and nudges it shut behind him. I'm sure if there were a lock on it, he'd be barricading us in right now, and I want to laugh at his possessive nature but instead, I press a kiss against his lips.

He hums appreciatively under his breath, deepening it the moment he can as his hands peel away my clothes. He maps out all of the little bumps and bruises on my skin, most of them from my own clumsy nature, and I shudder as his lips touch them all.

I shouldn't be distracted so easily. I should ask more questions, hear more about what is going on in the Sanctuary. I should ask about Kieran and Sage; did Felix get him healed up? How are Adella and Unser doing—

"I will put you over my knee and have you screaming if you can't switch that brain off yourself, Bonded. Everyone is fine. Everything is *fine*. The only thing we have left to worry about now is how many times I can make you come tonight before I have to share you, so focus on *me*."

He punctuates this demand with two fingers plunging straight into my pussy, so I have zero options except to give him my full attention.

I hope his obsession with me never ends.

29

I wake up before the rest of my Bonded, before the sun has even risen in the sky. I have blackout curtains on the tall windows in my room, but there's an early morning *feel* to the air—when you wake up and know that the entire world is still sleeping, that you're having your own small moment in the day without anyone else.

I lie there for a moment, naked and with random aches and pains running through my body, but the hollow emptiness isn't inside me anymore. My Bonded have fixed what consuming the god-bond's soul had broken within me, and now it's just me in here.

Me and my bond, of course.

I watch North's chest as he breathes deeply in his sleep,

completely unaware that I'm awake and eyeballing him this hard, and I slowly look around at each of my Bonded.

Gryphon is on the other side of me with an arm flung over his eyes, looking like a god at rest, even though he'd actually spent a good part of last night worshiping me. I'm pretty sure the pinching in my lower back is from the way that he'd bent me in half, and I'm sure he'll wake up with another dozen ways he'll want to fuck my brains out.

Gabe is on the far side of him, still clutching at his belly even in his sleep. My heart aches in my chest at the sight of him, at the lines of discomfort still etched into his face. Even sharing all my power with him wouldn't fix that sort of stomachache, and I get the feeling that if there are more battles like that in our future, we're going to have to take out stock in antacids for my beloved Shifter.

I feel vicious about the Pain god again.

Atlas is on the far side of North, and he's sleeping soundly on his stomach, his head buried in one of my pillows as he surrounds himself in my scent, as I like to surround myself in all of theirs. He needed a lot from me last night. The moment that the Cleaver had left him, a panicked energy filled him that could only be eased by my presence. He's going to be my shadow again for the next few weeks. I already know it.

Nox slept in his own room.

His boundaries are still important to him, and even

though I would rather have them all in here with me every night, I can definitely respect that he needs his space. I know he finds being vulnerable and sleeping in a room with all of these people too difficult. I don't just accept it, I'll fight for him to have that space.

I might just need to find my way into his bed tonight.

I very carefully slide my way out of the bed, wriggling downwards and out so that I don't wake any of them. After I find a pair of Gryphon's running shorts and one of Atlas' hoodies to throw on, I head quietly down the hallway and into the kitchen for a glass of water.

There's something I want to do this morning, something big and important that is also a little too… exposing. Taking a minute to do it by myself is just what I need, like the real, final battle. I'm also not an idiot, so I let Azrael down from behind my ear and then I grab August from behind the other one. I'm still a little in awe that North finally trusts his shadow creature enough to give him to me.

I give them both loves and scratches behind their ears, murmuring affectionately to them both quietly before I duck back into my closet to grab the box I need. Then I slip out of the house without another word.

I can imagine the look of horror on North's face at me wandering around before dawn by myself, but I also know that I am completely safe. The god-bonds are all taken care of, I have a bond that rips the souls out of my enemies, and

I have two shadow creatures following my every move. Anyone else at this point would be overkill.

I'd gone on a few quiet hikes with Atlas in the weeks leading up to the battles with the god-bonds. I never discussed with him exactly what I was looking for and he never asked, probably assuming that I was just enjoying the space and quiet away from everyone. That's true enough, but I was also looking for a resting place.

When Gryphon gave me back my parents' ashes, I originally intended to scatter them right away, but part of me couldn't bear the thought of what would happen if we had to leave the Sanctuary behind. There was every chance that the god-bonds would take it from us, and I already had to leave my parents behind once before.

I didn't want to have to do it again.

I know that this is my home, the place I will always come back to. It's something built for our community but also for me, an act of love and devotion from North and the rest of my Bonded Group. I reach the small ledge at the top of the incline that looks out over our house and down into the valley where the town lies, and I find the first budding wildflowers there, just a small sprinkling of color as the sun begins to rise and the light hits them in the most beautiful orange burst.

I sit down on the rock and open up the box, pulling out each of the small containers of ashes, and even though

I know that my parents are long gone at this point, I kiss each one before I put it down on the rock next to me.

August sits at my side, pressing against my back, but Azrael sniffs each of the containers, his void eyes staring up at me as if they know what is going on, and when he ducks forward to lick at my cheek, I realize that I'm crying.

The person responsible for my parents' deaths is gone.

The permanent sort of gone, I know that my bond will never have to deal with it again. I suppose I could pretend that they are happy tears, but really, they're just the first tears I have let myself cry for my parents without feeling any guilt attached to them at all.

They're gone now, and there's nothing I can do about it. Nothing except to scatter their ashes here so they're all together for eternity.

It feels weird to just open up the containers and dump them out over the wildflowers, but that's exactly what I do. I watch as the wind picks up a little and the ashes dance in the air in front of me.

I observe it all with my shadow puppies and then, finally, I let it out. I let myself cry all of the tears that I've ever wanted to for my parents. I cry because I'll never get to hug my mom again or any of my dads. I cry because they loved me and they had no idea of what was living inside their daughter, of the legacy that I was continuing.

I cry because they'll never meet my Bonded.

My mom would have loved them. I'm not so sure what my dads would have thought though. Not in the beginning anyway, but I'm sure that my Bonded would have slowly won them over. They would have been proud of me. I think that's maybe the hardest part, the part where I feel as though I have worked so hard to get to this point, and yet it still hasn't brought them back.

Some things can't be fixed.

Some things are permanent because life isn't a fairy tale, no matter how wonderful it may seem sometimes. I'm still going to argue with my Bonded. I'm still going to feel sad and lost. I'm still going to need space and time to grieve, but that doesn't mean I'm not incredibly proud of what we've done.

Footsteps crunch behind me, but neither of the shadow creatures react. I don't need the familiar tugging of my bond in my chest to know that one of my Bonded has followed me out here. I make an educated guess on which one it is, and I'm proven right when Nox slowly eases himself down to sit next to me, snapping his fingers at Azrael to have him move spots.

He doesn't say a word to me.

He doesn't comment on the open containers sitting in the box in front of us or the white powder that still is coating some of the flowers. He doesn't mention that the sunrise before us is beautiful or that my cheeks are stained with tears. He just sits and is still in the moment with me, offering me support without ever uttering a word.

I reach over and take his hand, threading our fingers together and squeezing gently, sitting there until I can muster up the energy to head back home and be the Bonded that everybody wants me to be, the Bonded they deserve to have. The Bonded that comes most naturally to me when grief isn't quite so heavy in my heart.

The one that needs to figure out what our future is going to look like now, once and for all.

When we eventually get back to the house, it feels surreal to stand in the kitchen and make breakfast together as though our lives haven't completely changed. I move to the fridge to grab the ingredients to make an omelet, something simple that I've done a million times before and shouldn't fuck up too badly, but Nox places a firm hand on my back to direct me towards the table instead as he takes over breakfast preparation.

By the time he slides a plate of food towards me, all of the rest of our Bonded Group have joined us, still half-dressed and weary-looking. It's clear they're half asleep as they serve themselves from the giant pile of food that Nox has whipped together for everyone.

Gabe still looks green at the mere smell of the eggs, so instead of eating, he buries his nose in my neck, huffing quietly under his breath as though the rest of us are doing something disgusting by eating while he is feeling so shitty. I leave him tucked there as I dig in.

Atlas flanks my other side, pouring me a large cup of coffee and adding all sorts of fun flavors for me, while North and Gryphon discuss work quietly amongst themselves. They both have their phones in their hands as they check in with TacTeams and other personnel, seamlessly getting back to business as usual while I'm sitting here like my whole world has been tilted on its axis.

They're all acting as though this morning is just like every other morning that we've been at the house together, as though nothing has really changed, when we know that in reality, it has.

"What are we gonna do today, Bonded?" Atlas murmurs quietly to me as he kisses my cheek and hands over the giant cup of coffee.

I take a sip and enjoy the peppermint and mocha undertones to it, sighing as I bat my eyelashes at him. "I want to go see Sage and check in on Kieran... Then I guess we'll help Gabe build things. Is there anything else we need to be doing?"

North shoots me a heated look and shakes his head. "There's nothing you *need* to be doing anymore, Bonded.

Anything else that comes up, we will deal with. Your job now is to be happy. That's it."

I nod slightly and look down at my plate of eggs, getting a few spoonfuls in as I think his words through. "And what if I don't know how to be happy? What if it's not that simple?"

North shares a look with Gryphon for a moment before his eyes flick over to Nox. The brothers seem to have a language of their own, they always have, but I'm not used to it being used against me like this, not in such a kind and loving way.

Nox says, a little too gently, "Then you need to figure that out, Oleander. That's your job from now on, figuring out exactly what you want to do. Something that will make you happy."

Gabe groans under his breath, rubbing his face on my shoulder before he pulls away from me and huffs, "You're going to send her spiraling off the deep end again talking like that, you know. She's only just stopped freaking out about how she's going to fill up her days."

I use my training from my time with the Resistance to keep my mind very carefully blank, putting up a wall the way that Nox taught me so that Gryphon doesn't hear anything in my head, and then I send through to Gabe, *If you dare to tell any of them what we talked about back at the school, indigestion from the Draconis will be the very last thing on your mind, Ardern.*

The lazy grin he shoots back at me is so self-satisfied and not at all discreet. He might as well put a sign on his forehead to let them all know exactly what's going on in my head.

"What are you guys going to be doing?" I ask, trying to change the topic, and Nox shrugs as he finishes his cup of coffee in one go, gulping it back as though he had a rough night's sleep in his room by himself.

I'm going to sleep in there with him tonight, no matter what else happens today, to see if I can ease away some of that tension that is building in his limbs.

"There's a vote happening for the council. Once we have that established, we'll be able to take some time off. We don't all have to be here all the time."

I nod and then I smile back at him. "Maybe I should get back to my schoolwork. Maybe that'll help me figure out how I'm going to spend the rest of my days now that we're not running after god-bonds."

Atlas reaches under the table to squeeze my leg, nodding his head before he smirks at me. "It might be easier to pass your classes now that you don't have a professor failing you for absolutely no reason."

I groan under my breath, not wanting to listen to the two of them go at each other's throats this morning, but Nox just sends him a haughty look back. "It'll be far easier for her to pass all of the classes considering she now knows enough to teach them if she wants to."

I forgot about that, one of the least acknowledged perks of our soul-bonding.

It feels as though a weight has been lifted from my shoulders, and everybody gets back to their breakfasts, talking quietly among themselves. It just reinforces that this is our life now, happy and whole and together, working as a team to figure out exactly what it is that we're after. Exactly what it is that's best for us and for everyone else, because no matter if we have dealt with the Resistance, North is still a very notable member of the community, someone who will have to make decisions for the rest of his life. People's lives depend on his experience and knowledge, after all, but that doesn't feel as suffocating as it did when I first arrived here.

Now it feels hopeful, something to be proud of, something for us all. My phone chimes in my pocket, and I pull it out to find a message from Sage asking me what the hell had happened at the Wasteland and if we're all okay.

I message her back to tell her that I'm going to come find her and hang out today, that I'm going to check up on Kieran and the rest of their Bonded Group, and then I put the phone back in my pocket with a sigh, enjoying the sounds of my Bonded all here together. The way that they bicker with one another over small things and discuss big plans for the community. How they organize their time together and share their ambitions with one another, and the way that they're a family, just as vibrant and amazing and loving as the one whose ashes I scattered this morning.

It might be completely different, but in a lot of ways, it's exactly the same. I found my home. I've fought for it, I've bled for it, and now I get to enjoy it.

My Bonded and I deserve it.

Epilogue

OLI

The only thing better than waking up on a yacht moored offshore a tropical island is being woken up by your Bonded's tongue burying itself deep inside your pussy.

I should know.

Every inch of my body aches, love bites cover my inner thighs and my chest, and my legs feel as though they might never stop shaking, but this is what my life looks like now.

It's fucking incredible.

"Look at this perfect Bonded pussy, all red and swollen from being used. Do you need a break, Bonded? I'm not going to give you one. I've waited too long to spend my days fucking this pussy whenever the hell I want to."

My eyes roll into the back of my head as my thighs

clamp around Gryphon's ears, his words spoken directly against my clit so that I'm practically weeping for him to finish me off. You'd think that having sex with my Bonded so much would get old, that maybe we'd all get over each other or need some time away, but I still go to bed every night naked and sandwiched between two of them, and every morning, I wake up to at least one of them demanding my time.

It turns out I had nothing to worry about.

After two years of living in peace, we finally decided the Sanctuary was running well enough that we could go on a nice, long holiday. North was sick of being interrupted all day long and the hours that he was still being forced to work even after the new council had been elected, so getting away for a while was really our only option.

Gryphon continued to run the TacTeams, mobilizing and coordinating the cleanups to get rid of the last of the Resistance. I'm sure we'll be doing that for many years to come, thanks to how far that poison had spread, but I'll take that over the constant attacks any day of the week.

Nox went back to teaching the moment the new university had been built. I'm pretty sure he just missed telling students how dumb they were and scaring them with his creatures, but he loved putting together the new units for Gifted 101 now that we're written into history.

He wants me to teach a class on god-bonds, but I don't

think I'm the right choice to mold future minds at all.

Gabe took over his father's position at their family's construction company and used it to continue expanding the Sanctuary. It's now eight times bigger than when we'd first moved in, and he's the busiest of my Bonded after North, but he's also the most fulfilled in his work. I never see him without a grin on his face, and nothing makes me happier.

Atlas is where the biggest change can be seen in my Bonded Group. After he came home to me with a change on his birth certificate proudly proclaiming that he's a Fallows now too, he spent a lot of time trying to figure out what the hell he wanted to do with his life now that protecting me wasn't going to be a full-time job. I was totally expecting him to continue to work with Gabe and help build the Sanctuary but instead, he works with Gryphon, teaching the TacTeams about the Resistance and their propaganda.

It turns out that being born a Bassinger means he knows quite a lot about how brainwashing works and how these people act. There's even been some talk about him teaching classes at the new university, teaching how to spot sympathizers and de-escalation.

I'm unbelievably proud of them all.

I decided to go back to my classes and graduate. Sage came too, both of us studying insanely long hours for degrees we're not really sure what we're going to do with. I suppose that's a normal part of being a college student too, right?

I'm just happy to be with my Bonded for now.

My bond is sure that this is the last time that the god-bonds inside of us will be here, their purpose now fulfilled thanks to our completed Bonded Group, but I'm not so sure about that. Either way, I'm happy to spend this lifetime with my Bonded and the gods within us, each of them perfect and mine.

Especially when Gryphon pulls away, lifting himself up to cover my body with his, whispering wicked words directly into my ear and into my soul as he fucks me so hard and deep that I feel like I'm never going to be able to walk straight again.

It's heaven, and it's mine. They all are.

Each and every one of my Bonded men.

SIGN UP FOR MY NEWSLETTER TO HEAR ABOUT UPCOMING RELEASES

Also by J Bree

The Bonds That Tie Series

Broken Bonds
Savage Bonds
Blood Bonds
Forced Bonds
Tragic Bonds
Unbroken Bonds

The Mortal Fates Series

Novellas
The Scepter
The Sword
The Helm

The Trilogy
The Crown of Oaths and Curses
The Throne of Blood and Honor

The Mounts Bay Saga

The Butcher Duet
The Butcher of the Bay: Part I
The Butcher of the Bay: Part II

Hannaford Prep
Just Drop Out: Hannaford Prep Year One
Make Your Move: Hannaford Prep Year Two
Play the Game: Hannaford Prep Year Three
To the End: Hannaford Prep Year Four
Make My Move: Alternate POV of Year Two

The Queen Crow Trilogy
All Hail
The Ruthless
Queen Crow

The Unseen MC
Angel Unseen

About J Bree

J Bree is a dreamer, writer, mother, and cat-wrangler. The order of priorities changes daily.

She lives on the coast of Western Australia in a city where it rains too much. She spends her days dreaming about all of her book boyfriends, listening to her partner moan about how the lawns are looking, and being a snack bitch to her three kids.

Visit her website at http://www.jbreeauthor.com to sign up for the newsletter or find her on social media through the links below.

f   ⓞ   ♪